WHERE LEGENDS WALK

ISBN 978-1-7333938-8-1 (paperback)

Edited by Jacob Jones-Goldstein and Nicholas Leamy
Cover and Interior by Jennifer Marang
OPP logo by Steve Myers

Published by
Oddity Prodigy Productions, LLC
302 Arbour Drive
Newark, DE 19713

www.oddityprodigy.com

WHERE LEGENDS WALK

A SUPERHERO ANTHOLOGY

Edited by
Jacob Jones-Goldstein
and Nicholas Leamy

DEDICATION

For Keith Giffen,
Who made us laugh, made us cry, made us think, and taught us how
to deal with editors.

SPECIAL THANKS TO OUR BACKERS

We would like to give special thanks to our Kickstarter backers! You got this project off the ground and without you we would be nowhere.

Elizabeth Alban

Matt Alexander

Colin Anderson

Mary Anderson

Donald Bell

eSpec Books

Bernard Brick

Michael A. Burstein

Ian Chung

Brigham Daniel Morrison

Mickey Davis

Chris DeAngelis

Brian Dellinger

Nancy Dellinger

Jude Deluca

Joel Dowling

Shannon Dunn

Colleen Feeney

Zachary Fissel

Violet Geary

Brian Gibson

David Glinski

Rev. Stephen Goldstein

Sharon Lee Harte

Darrin Hunt

Rosemarie Ison-Edgington

Jeffrey Jenkins

Mary Jo Rabe

Kimberly A. Johnson

Norman Johnson

Jeremiah Jones-Goldstein

Rachel Kane

Andrew Leslie

Kody Looper

Jean Martinez

John McNish

Kent Messner

Devon Miller-Duggan

Krystal Mitchell

Ian Mondrick

Johnathan Morgan

Becky Muth

Kyle N. Nielsen

Ryan Noble

Stephen Padbury

Steven Pope

Laura Pyer

Nick Roby

B.S.H. Garcia

Madalyn Simpson

Craig Smitherman

Jessika Stieffenhofer

Nicholas Stember

Ann Stolinsky

Randy Stubbs

Thomas Super

Raymond Urbanski

Aaron Van Treeck

Kenneth Vierck

Ron Wenger

Craig White

Marcy Wiesemen

Caryn Wojtowicz

Karen

T.C.

CHRONICLES OF HEROISM

A BETTER WAY by Kareem Miskel 17

PIRATE QUEEN OF THE BAYOU by Liam Espinoza-Zemlicka 29

STANDING WAVE by Kelli Fitzpatrick 39

THE FADING STORM by Fred Phillips 55

THE BALLAD OF CORNMAN by Colin Anderson..........................71

TO FLY OR NOT TO FLY by Grigory Lukin 79

CLAP BACK by Jon Resnick 87

FIVE GOLD RINGS by Nicholas Samuel Stember 103

VILLAIN EMERITUS by Ross Tuohy..113

RATCATCHER VERSUS THE SPRING HEELED FIEND
by David Turnbull 121

GOOD INTENTIONS by Nicholas Leamy....................................135

FEAR OF REPRISAL: BLOOD WILL HAVE BLOOD
by Michael Joseph Tharnish Roby 147

WHAT THE GARGOYLE KNEW by Brian Gibson 161

UNCLE SAM'S ANGELS by Eric Remington................................175

ILLEGALS by Jon Negroni..183

TOO INVINCIBLE by Michael Penncavage 197

CIVIC GUARDIAN by John Haas...211

BEST FRIENDS by Jay T. Levy 219

ROOFTOP INTERVIEWS WITH THE MAN OF MIGHT
by Steve Gillies 225

SAVING THE WORLD by Katie Kent.......................................241

MEMORIES OF A DEMON by Daniel Medrano 247

CAPTAIN POWER by Zacheriah Tucker....................................257

INMATE_382A4L by Andrew Leslie 271

WALK THROUGH FIRE by Marlaina Cockcroft.............................281

DARKLIGHT by Scott Kinkade 293

ALTER EGO by Owen Townend 303

X-TREME GENES NEPTUNALIA SPECIAL #1:
"WATERED DOWN" (JULY 1997) by Jude Deluca........................313

BITTER PILL by C.N. Wheaton 327

THE REAL LIFE ADVENTURES OF AWESOME GIRL
by Gregg Chamberlain 335

HEART OF THE STORM by J. Patrick Conlon..............................343

THE CULT OF THE BLACK HOLE by David Boyce.......................355

FLASHBACK by Violet E. Geary 373

VILLAINY IS FOR LOSERS by Paul Popiel 385

NOBODY by Kay Hanifen 401

WHEN WE COULD STILL FLY by Paulie Wenger......................407

THE KNIGHT OF ENDLESS AUGUSTS by Eric Dellinger 417

ONE TIME, ONE NIGHT by Jacob Jones-Goldstein 437

CONTENT WARNING

This anthology contains content that may be difficult for some audiences. Stories contain some strong language, depictions of bullying, depictions of transphobia, and violence. Reader discretion is advised.

FOREWORD
by J.M. DeMatteis

Faster than a speeding bullet! More powerful than a locomotive!

I must have been four or five years old when I first laid eyes on the last son of Krypton.

Look! Up in the sky! It's a bird! It's a plane!

There he was, in glorious black and white on my TV screen, standing against a cosmic backdrop of planets and stars, arms akimbo, cape blowing in the breeze. Every inch a hero. No, not just a hero: a superhero.

It's Superman!

I don't think I'd discovered comic books at that age, but I'd already been mesmerized by the Sunday comics sections of the *New York Daily News*. (It's as if there's a chemical in the brain, unique to those of us who love comics, and the first time we see that magical combination of words and pictures, the chemical drops, floods our consciousness, and we're hooked on this glorious art form for life.) I'm sure it wasn't long before I realized that the guy on television, so perfectly portrayed by George Reeves, also existed in comic books.

Superman. Batman. Wonder Woman. Green Lantern. The Justice League. Then, later, the Marvel heroes: Spider-Man, the Fantastic Four, Thor, and the rest. I loved them. Hell, I loved *all* comic books—from Casper and Sad Sack to Archie Andrews and Richie Rich—but the superheroes were something special and they touched my young soul in a unique and profound way.

And still do.
But *why?*

I've asked myself that question many times over the years. There are some who dismiss superhero stories as childish power fantasies, a way for readers to imagine themselves as something they're not, to project their psyches into the bodies of these spandex-wearing, overmuscled guardians of humanity and, for a moment at least, smash through their personal struggles, their psychological wounds and traumas, with a simple punch. There's truth in that—a little power fantasy goes a long way—but I think there's something more at work here, something deeper.

Years ago, when I was in India visiting the Tomb-Shrine of the spiritual master Avatar Meher Baba, I had a dream, more like a vision, during which I was shown my true height and power, as both an individual on this earth and a spiritual being in this universe. I quickly realized this extraordinary experience wasn't unique to me; that we're all more powerful than we've dreamed; that every man and woman has, within them, a divinity, a cosmic heritage, as tall and broad as Creation. A heritage that's masked, suffocated, by our belief that we're small, limited, and alone. In essence, we're all, each and every one of us, Superman, but we're trapped in the false belief that we're weak, bumbling Clark Kent—and our life's work is to throw away the glasses, put on the super-suit, and become the inner hero we've been all along. These colorful characters embody our highest selves. Represent our decency, our compassion, our ability to transcend our imagined limitations and do genuine good in the world. They remind us that, in the end, we are the superheroes.

I believe we've collectively conjured the superhero pantheon into existence because we need them, birthing them from the universal unconscious to remind us of who we truly are. And I believe that the energy *behind* these symbols of our highest selves has existed as long as humankind; that we, as a race, have continually dreamed these beings into form in different times, different cultures, under a thousand different names. And we will continue to do it as long as they're needed. (Of course, there's always the possibility that *they've* dreamed *us*, but that's another essay for another time.)

Have I reached too far, gone too deep down the philosophical rabbit hole? Then how's this? Superhero stories, at their best, are *fun*. Everything is colorful, larger than life, on a grand scale: big emotions, big actions, big risks, big stakes. Most important: they're fueled by a seemingly-unlimited ocean of pure imagination.

The book you're holding in your hands has emerged from the depths of that ocean of imagination. Within it, you'll find tales written by people who adore superheroes and the strange worlds they inhabit, and who invite you to journey with them through those worlds. And if, along the way, you encounter the hidden truth of your own soul?

All the better.

J.M. DeMatteis 9/25

A Better Way
by Kareem Miskel

"I'm standing outside Gordon-Jones Penitentiary, better known by its nickname: Power Prison. Here, dozens of superhuman inmates serve sentences great and small for crimes involving their fantastic powers. But that population decreased by one mere minutes ago as Deitrich Sanders was pronounced dead. Mr. Sanders – better known by the moniker Wrath – attained powerful electrical abilities in an experimental attempt to cure a debilitating condition known as Withering Syndrome. The experiment mutated his body and projected him into a world of crime and terror. His illegal exploits would pit him against federal authorities and such superheroes as Spirit Guardian, the Astromancer, and Brightstar. But no hero would run afoul of Wrath's violent career more than Paragon."

"The two superhumans engaged one another in more than fifty battles in the last twelve years. The final of which took place eighteen months ago in Kenosha, Wisconsin, where Wrath's actions tragically ended one hundred sixty-seven lives and injured hundreds of people. Under the Grafton Act, which was ratified into law six weeks prior, all superhuman felonies are now classified as federal crimes, and all Class A or Class X superhuman felonies are capital. Wrath will be the first super criminal executed under the statute despite strenuous objections from Paragon himself, who held firm that..."

Click. The television winked off, replacing the news report with a black screen. Leon stared at the TV, his expression bitter and grave. Francis slid next to him on the couch and slipped his fingers into his hand. "Every report is like this," Leon murmured. "No talk about his glowing military service. Not a word about the wells he dug, the shelters he built, or all the charity projects he spearheaded. He was a murderer. That's it."

"But, baby, he was a murderer. A mass murderer. You can't really be surprised that..."

"That *wasn't his fault!*" Leon sprang to his feet. "Those experiments damaged his mind. When we could get the power drained from him, he was fine."

"I know, but it would always come back. No matter what they tried, it always came back."

"But that wasn't his fault!" he repeated.

"No, it wasn't, but it wasn't the fault of his victims either."

"But that wasn't Deitrich. That was…"

"…Wrath. I know. But, baby, while the world waited for a working solution, he killed more than a thousand people and irreparably damaged thousands more."

"So, we just execute the mentally ill? All the people it's not convenient to help? Where does it end?"

"I don't know, Leon. All I know is that most people aren't like you. They can't shrug off falling rubble or recover from getting hit with a million gigawatts after a few days. We can't quip and ignore bullets and missiles. People are scared."

"I know," he whispered, struggling to keep tears of rage and pain from escaping his brown eyes.

"Even he knew in the end. When he told you to stop defending him. He accepted it."

"That makes it worse. It's like he didn't matter to anyone. Even himself."

"He mattered." Francis stood and rubbed Leon's arms. Those arms that lifted so many from danger and despair. He rubbed Leon's shoulders, shoulders that bore the weight of all the Earth. "But maybe I'm selfish. Because to me, you matter more."

"Francis…"

"He got so close, Leon. More than once. To the world out there, you're indestructible, but I know better. I saw the Lichtenburg marks before they disappeared. I see the cuts and wounds before they close. I see the burns and bruises before they heal. I'm a doctor. And I know more about your physiology than anyone alive. You might not know how close you've come over the years…"

"I do," Leon insisted. "Trust me, I know. Better than you do."

Francis turned him around so their brown eyes could meet. "You have all these contingencies for what happens if you go bad. Spirit Guardian's blade, alerts to the Astromancers and the Star Wardens. Barrels of stellarium you've given to the U.S. military. Dozens of people who you've begged to kill or imprison you if your power is turned upon the people of this world. Is it really so surprising that another good man came to the same decision?"

Leon's lips curved upward in a weak smile. He slipped his hands around Francis's waist and kissed his forehead. "You'd have made one hell of a lawyer, you know that?"

"I'll leave the courtroom speeches to you, counselor."

Before their lips could touch, Leon's head snapped to the side, his eyes focused on the distance.

"What is it?" Francis asked.

"An explosion. In Chicago, I think."

"Go."

Bands of light rippled over Leon's body. The bands turned a black man into a black man, the color of coal or onyx. Brown eyes became shimmering brass. Black hair became snow white. Comfortable home clothes were replaced with his heroic vestments – a bold getup of white, red, and gleaming gold. His body stretched and expanded, turning a tall man with a casual gym body into a god among mortals. A champion. The first among heroes. The Paragon.

He was gone a second later, in a flash of blinding speed that scattered papers and sent a gust of air sweeping through the house.

The Loop was a war zone. Police and rescue workers did their best, but they were outclassed. A massive lizard man, seven foot two if he was an inch, rampaged his way past the Thompson Center. The chatter of automatic weaponry filled the air, but the bullets were like raindrops on his scaled, yellow hide. A dismissive slap overturned an armored SWAT vehicle and sent it tumbling a hundred yards down West Randolph. "Where is he?!" the creature demanded in a roar that would bellow through the city for miles.

A rocket whistled through the air, hitting him center mass. The explosion sent a blast of air and thunder blossoming across the beast's chest.

The lizard man was little more than annoyed. He sprang forward, the claws of his bare feet cracking pavement as he landed before the SWAT officer who fired the rocket. The man set his jaw in horrified defiance, ready to meet his fate, but it was not his time.

"Snarl!"

The sound of his name turned the creature's head. "At last!"

Paragon surveyed the destruction. "All this to get my attention? I'd be flattered if it weren't so brutal."

"Your pets all live," he growled. "And they will continue to, if you hand over Caston Arahn."

"The Despot? That's what this is about? I thought you were done serving that monster."

"Leaving his employ doesn't mean I will abandon him to the tender mercies of the human race. Give him to me, and I will depart this backwater world."

"He's not here."

"You lie! His ship, the Glorious Victory, sought me out and told me everything. You fought him in this pitiful solar system. Where else would you take him?"

"I didn't take him anyplace. He tried to open a portal into Dark Sector to increase his powers. I randomized the coordinates and damaged the gate, but I don't know where it sent him."

"Liar!"

Snarl was easily a head taller and a shoulder wider. Paragon was the faster of the two, but that didn't mean the creature was slow. And he had a longer reach. The hero could easily match his strength, but a landed blow from either of them could have sent the other smashing through train tracks, office buildings, and skyscrapers. Exactly what Paragon wanted to avoid.

He rolled away from Snarl's first strike and ducked beneath the next. Attack after attack caught air as Paragon dodged and evaded.

The beast's assault increased in speed and intensity. The hero started to block and deflect, catching blows on his forearm.

Finally, a right cross came in. The hero took hold of Snarl's wrist and tossed him to the ground, plowing up concrete with his landing.

"Listen to me," Paragon said. "I know you're trying to help your friend, but Caston isn't here. I haven't seen him since our battle on Mars. He could be anywhere in the…"

The tail.

He always forgot about the tail.

As long as Snarl's legs and every bit as strong.

It came around and clocked him in the jaw. The world flashed white.

Two city blocks passed by in a second. Stone and glass shattered as he crashed through one wall and out of another. He hit the street and rolled to a stop in frantic traffic.

Snarl marched toward him. "I won't tolerate any more of your lies. I'll beat the information out of you if I have to."

"This just in! Chicago is under attack once more from a menace with superhuman powers, a reptilian alien named Snarl. Sources say the creature landed near Millennium

Park an hour ago, demanding the release of the would-be alien conqueror known as Despot.

"Paragon is currently fighting to subdue the creature, but it seems a match for the Champion's Champion. One can't help but wonder, what will become of the Windy City if he fails."

"As you can see, Paragon seems to be fighting defensively and trying to reason with his opponent. I can tell you now, that's not the right tac here."

"Really, Mike? It seems to me he's trying his best to make sure the fight doesn't do much damage. If you look here, he's clearly trying to herd Snarl toward Lake Michigan. I think he wants to get him to the water or one of the Michigan islands as he's done in the past."

"If he ended it quickly, there would be less damage. Look, I get that he don't want to knock down any buildings or anything, but this ain't like our days in the ring. Nobody's looking for a show. One champ to another, I'm sayin' he needs to start takin' the chumps down quick and stop playin' around."

"Another super menace! And one that Paragon has fought before. This guy came down eight years ago with that Despot fella, trying to conquer the Earth. If Paragon and the Vanguard had taken them out then, we wouldn't be here now. This is why the Grafton Act is so important. This is why we have to start killing these men. Do what these bleeding-heart superheroes won't!"

"But do you really want superheroes acting as executioners? I agree with the Grafton Act. Let the heroes apprehend these criminals and bring them to justice. But justice must always be dispensed by we, the people."

Blow after blow echoed through the city. The streets quaked with the percussion of their battle. Glass cracked. Trees fell. Terrified people fled for some semblance of safety. All the while, Snarl lived up to his name, baring razor teeth as he growled his demands.

Paragon caught a downward blow on his forearm, the ground fracturing beneath his feet as he pressed against it. "You need to listen," he said. "Things have changed since you were here last. If you're not careful…" *What? He'll die? Do you really want to threaten your enemies with death?*

Before the litigating mind of Leon Adams could put together his case, Snarl came in for another attack. He lunged forward, clamping his fingers around Paragon's neck in a vice grip.

The hero grabbed his attacker's wrists and soared back, taking control of their flight. He landed and kicked Snarl away in a backward roll.

Paragon was moving before the alien menace could recover, unleashing a barrage of blows at superhuman speed.

Gut.

Ribs.

Left jaw.

Right jaw.

Temple.

Until, finally, a kick to the stomach sent the lizard man flying back.

Not through a wall or into another building. Just far enough to give them breathing room.

"Stand down."

Snarl wiped a streak of brown blood from his mouth and spat orange mucus onto the sidewalk. "Never. Not while Caston rots in one of your barbaric human prisons."

"Barbaric?" Paragon scoffed. "He should be so lucky. Your friend has personally murdered thousands of innocent people. He has commanded armies to kill a thousand times more than that. All without remorse. Without mercy. I can think of nobody better deserving of permanent incarceration, but he's not here. Now, once again. Stand down. Before I have to make you."

The alien's face split into a smile, revealing a row of teeth that could crush stone and puncture steel. "You've been fighting too long, Paragon. You've started to believe your own legend."

"I've beaten you before, Snarl. Several times."

"But how many of these soft humans will suffer before you do? How many will die from the debris of our conflict? Do you really want to lose so many precious lives for your authority? Your pride? Is that what a true paragon would do? Can you truly be worthy of the title your people gave you if you fail to protect them?"

Paragon stared for a moment. "You don't understand," he said. "You never did. This name, this title I carry. It wasn't a gift or a whim. I've had to earn it. Time after time, day after day. By helping a lot of good people and defeating a lot of bad ones. I'm asking you – begging you – please don't make me earn it today." Silence allowed the words to hang between them for a few breaths before Paragon added.

"There's too much at stake."

Snarl eyed him for a few seconds. "Caston…"

"Isn't here," Paragon insisted. "And I wouldn't turn him over if he was. But I might be able to help you find him."

The alien's eyes narrowed. "Why?"

He shrugged. "Because it's always best to know where a monster like the Despot is. Because you may not be a good man, but you're leagues better than him. Maybe you can be a mitigating influence. Show him a better way."

"You can't believe that."

"I have to." Paragon sighed and approached. "Take me to your ship. I'll provide directions and coordinates to Olympus Mons. Maybe the Victory's sensors can trace the residual tachyon wave."

Snarl glared at him. "I accept your terms. Prepare for transport."

It was more like Stargate than Star Trek. A circular door of shimmering silver opening before them. A rush of movement as they were whisked through space. Paragon hated teleportation of every kind. It wasn't painful, but it was disorienting. *At least this one doesn't itch,* he thought as they moved through the opening.

The ship was right out of science fiction. Glass consoles, floating holograms, buttons, and switches with high-tech names only a scientist could understand. All it was missing was a werewolf copilot, a hyper-logical first mate, and a snarky rogue of a captain. "All right," Paragon said. "Let's get this over with so you can get the hell away from my planet and I can get back to arguing geopolitics with my husband."

"I'm afraid your rebuttals will have to wait indefinitely."

A cable of red light whipped from the ceiling and seized Paragon by the wrist. Before he could mount any sort of struggle, another lashed out and caught his other one. They spread apart, stretching his arms in a Y pattern.

"What is this, Snarl?"

The alien grinned. "This is the future, Paragon. With Caston lost in the great universe, the Glorious Victory is mine to command. I will go to the worlds he ruled, riding her as my flagship. With the great Paragon as my slave, I will prove to be more than his successor. I will be his superior! Then, I will show the cosmos a true despot. One with no opposition."

"No opposition? You really think the Astromancers and the Star Wardens are just going to let you keep Ahran's old territories now that they've been liberated?"

"With you as my hostage? They'll be held at bay long enough for me to reinforce my authority. Build my power base."

"That's a solid plan, Snarl, it really is. There's just one problem." Paragon opened his hands, sending a pulse of white energy blasting from his palms. The ceiling ruptured as the twin bolts hit home.

The red cables dissipated instantly, freeing Paragon to surge forward and deck Snarl square in the face.

The would-be despot flew back and crashed into the wall.

"I didn't know you could project energy," Snarl said in a that's-not-fair tone.

Paragon hovered inches from the ground, pacing back and forth. "There's a lot you don't know about me," he said. "Did you actually think I bought that story? That the ship told you everything, but you still thought I had Caston on Earth? That's what we humans would call a plot hole."

"Then why did you let me bring you up here?"

"Because hoping is what a hero does. We hope that things can be better. That people can be better. That our worst suspicions can be proven wrong."

"Then your heroes are fools."

Snarl lunged forward.

Paragon held his ground. He blocked the attack and responded with one of his own.

This time, the wall didn't stop Snarl's momentum. He crashed through it, sending an explosion of panels and circuitry into the next room.

"But there's another reason I let you bring me up here," Paragon said, floating toward him. "You see, every time we've fought, you've always been able to hide behind innocent people. But your illustrious predecessor was even more vain than you. He could have had a crew of hundreds on this ship, but it had to be all his. He automated everything but the highest command functions. That puts us fifty thousand miles from my people."

It was Paragon's turn to grin. "Think about it, Snarl. An aspiring conqueror. A pissed off Paragon. And nary a servant, hostage, prisoner, or bystander in sight. Just the two of us," the hero's hero, the champion's champion, cracked his knuckles. "And a hundred thousand cubic meters for me to beat your ass in."

"One hundred thirty-seven injuries. Millions in property damage. But thankfully, no fatalities."

"Ken, the people of Chicago are resilient. The news is rife with stories of people coming together to help each other both during the battle and after. But one must ask,

what happens next?"

"The attacker, a reptilian alien named Snarl, is in federal custody. With so many violent crimes under his belt, will he be executed under the Grafton Act?"

"I want to hear from Paragon on this."

"Paragon's always tried to stay out of political matters. He tends to remain quiet on these things."

"Well, he defended Wrath with all that 'sanctity of life' crap. Why's he being all tight-lipped now?"

"Maybe he just doesn't have anything to say."

"Or maybe he knows we're tired of his bleeding-heart philosophy and want permanent solutions."

"Kill 'em all, I say! Get out the guillotine! Do it on national television and broadcast that shit into space. Let everyone know what happens when you mess with Earth!"

Francis turned off the TV. "My God. It's like Wrath's execution has them out for blood."

"Yeah," Leon said with a somber nod.

"They'll cool down."

Leon leaned back on the couch. "Will they?" he wondered. "Maybe I am naïve. I knew Snarl was a snake, and I still let him bite me."

"You were ready for him."

"And next time I might not be."

"Listen to me," Francis took his hand. "You can't be cynical."

"I'm not trying to be cynical. I'm trying to be realistic."

"Realistic? Isn't Snarl some sort of alien royalty? Doesn't he have powerful ties in the Crab Nebula or something?"

Leon chuckled. "Something like that."

"Well, we've got his ship now. We'll be joining the rest of the universe in space before you know it. We can't get up there with royal blood on our hands or following death threats we've broadcast into the cosmos."

"A couple days ago, you were saying something different."

"A couple days ago, I was being stupid and afraid. Fortunately, I've got someone to show me a better way. And the rest of the world does too."

"Prisoner 98298-7232. On your feet."

Snarl glared, his crimson eyes blazing with hatred.

"On your feet," the guard repeated. "You've got a visitor."

"A visitor?"

"Yeah. Someone actually wants to see your ugly yellow face."

Snarl almost grumbled out one of the many threats and dark promises he'd issued since his arrival, but decided against it. The shock collar they had on him could be most unpleasant. On top of that, he was rather curious about this visitor. Who on Earth would want to see him?

He stood to his full, proud height and staggered for a moment. The technology that suppressed his titanic strength often left him disoriented when he moved too quickly.

Snarl was becoming accustomed to the routine. The clasping of his hands and feet in metal restraints. The asinine instructions. The armed detail as they led him through their paltry detention center. It was all becoming familiar.

They brought him to another cell, this one split in two by a force field.

On the other side of the field was a man. Brown skinned with a dome of short, black hair. He seemed tall for a member of his feeble species. Strongly built as well. Hardier than his guards, Snarl thought. The man was dressed in soft, gray clothing and carried some sort of luggage.

"Good morning, Lord Snarl. My name is Leon Adams. I'm your lawyer."

Snarl narrowed his eyes. "Lawyer?"

"Attorney. Solicitor. I'll represent you in court."

"You humans mean to judge me?"

"While you're on our planet? Yes. Now, you've been charged with several crimes. Assault, resisting arrest, destruction of property, both public and private. But the terrorism and attempted murder are the most concerning."

"And why do these concern you so?"

"With your abilities, they're considered capital offenses."

"Capital," he repeated. "You mean the humans will execute me for them?"

"Yes."

Snarl scoffed. "They're welcome to try."
The human – Leon Adams – met his gaze. "Not while I'm here."

Pirate Queen of the Bayou
by Liam Espinoza-Zemlicka

The only difference between a row of flashbulbs and a firing squad is that when the firing squad is done, they don't reload for another go at you. Lydia's father had told her that when he accompanied her to her first red carpet premier, speaking in his capacity as a former actor and a veteran of the Great War. Up until six months ago, Lydia had taken it as gospel and laughed to herself every time she walked down a red carpet half blind and spent the first reel blinking stars out of her eyes. Now, after six months of putting away hoods and dodging bullets in back alleys, Lydia had come to a startling and irrefutable conclusion.

Her father was full of shit.

Bullets ripped through the mast that the production team had spent so long putting together, getting just the right shading on the timber to make a convincing pirate ship on camera. When the producers showed up on Monday, they were going to throw the mother of all tantrums. Hopefully, Lydia would live to see it. She threw herself into a cartwheel as the mast tumbled, crashing through the painted backdrop. She landed behind a collection of barrels filled with weights to keep them in place.

"Flashbulbs," she said, "I left flashbulbs for this."

"What was that?" Called a voice from the direction of the gunfire.

"I wasn't talking to you," Lydia snapped at the gunman. Only too late did she realize her mistake.

"She's over there."

Damnit.

Not that the day had started off particularly well, but it had devolved into this debacle in record time. Some wunderkind in the production office had gotten a bright idea for a rope swing stunt and had pushed it through planning in a frankly unsafe amount of time. The stunt team was worried; hell, Lydia was worried. Even though her face was too valuable to the studio to risk anything really dangerous, she knew this could end more than a few careers if it went wrong. So she had gotten up early on a Sunday and driven all the way to the backlot to double-check the rigging and run through a few maneuvers when who should she spy, but cheap thugs in cheaper suits strongarming a delicate young lady into a dark corner. The rest of it was Lydia's fault. She had put on the mask and made a big show of herself, trying to scare them into letting the girl go.

A drum of Tommy Gun ammo later, and they had all corralled into the Pirate King of the Bayou set, which meant Lydia had nowhere to run. The soundstage had two exits, and there were gunmen at both of them. Up by the faux helm, one of the goons struggled to keep hold of the young hostage. Her hands were bound, but when the goon tried to place a gag on her, she snapped her teeth at him. Lydia let herself smirk at the lady's audacity before the crushing weight of her impending doom set in again. She could hear them reloading, and there was precious little cover left on deck.

"Boss," a different goon shouted. "Someone else followed us."

The reloading stopped. Lydia peeked out from her hiding spot. Two goons, built like wrestlers wearing ratty fedoras, carried a man between them. He was blond and square-jawed, with a nasty swollen eye and a camera on a strap hanging around his neck.

"Damnit, Nick," Lydia said to herself, quieter this time.

The goon that Lydia had decided was probably in charge, on account of his spiffier suit and the fact that he was the only one not openly carrying a heater, stepped up to Nick. He patted him down, plucking the press pass out of the breast pocket of his blazer.

"Ah, Mister Nicholas Horne," the goon said in an impeccable New England accent. "I so enjoy your column." He raised his arms theatrically. "I concede we are in your domain, but I see no stars. So tell me…" He reached out and gripped Nick by the sides of his face. "What is Hollywood's premier gossip writer doing shadowing me?"

Nick tried to smile, bless him, but having his face squeezed warped his lips, and he ended up looking like a trout. Lydia brushed her fingers against the lariat on her hip. Nick complicated things. She could jump out and try to put the eyes back on her, but that ran the risk of getting them all shot. Much as she hated it, her best option was to use Nick's distraction to sneak away before they remembered she'd given away her position. She lay flat on her stomach and began army crawling, using the barrels and shadows as cover as she made her way to the edge of the deck.

"Would you believe I mistook you for movie stars?"

The head goon looked around at his men — the best looking of the lot still fell pretty heavily on the rugged side of ruggedly handsome.

"I would not."

Nick scowled, still looking like a fish.

"That's my friend you've got. So why don't you tell me what you're doing with her?"

Damn it, that's where I know her from. The hostage was Mary Ellen Becker, one of the script girls that Nick went to for gossip. Now she could guess what the goons wanted with her. Nobody paid attention to the Script Girls, but Script Girls paid attention to everything. One of Lydia's coworkers must be in deep with these lowlifes, and poor Mary Ellen overheard something she was not meant to. That meant Lydia knew what the stakes were. This was not a kidnapping; they would see what she knew and then fit her for a pair of cement shoes — Nick, too, the chivalrous idiot.

One of the goons punched Nick in the stomach, making him double over. Another socked him right in the nose, drawing blood and snot. The strap slid up over his head, and the camera hit the deck with an expensive-sounding *thud*. A smile crept along Lydia's masked face. She had a plan. It was not a good plan. There were Bela Lugosi B-pictures that had tighter plots than she had come up with, but if she was careful, she might make it work. First though, she would need one of the goons' heaters.

The head goon slipped on a pair of leather gloves.

"This town is becoming tiresome. Back home, when somebody owes you money, they tell no one, and they always have a summer home they can sell to you. Out here, everyone hears everything, and you *Show Folk* don't have the material capital to make good on your debts."

"That's rich coming from some two-bit mafioso."

If he kept flapping his gums like that, Nick was going to get himself killed — but he was also keeping the goon's attention. That was one thing Lydia could say about Nick: he made a good distraction. She crept along the barrels, moving silently from cover position to cover position.

Her costume, unitard, boots, gloves, and mask, were all deep night sky blues that in the dark faded into the shadows. That, combined with the pointed ears of her domino mask, had been meant to evoke the image of a black cat, an ill omen crossing a criminal's path. But the red carpet training had kicked in as she faded into the shadows that first night and she smiled, leaving just her dazzling teeth and bright green eyes hovering against the darkness for witnesses to see. The papers ran with it, and the name stuck.

She kept her mouth shut this time. If the set had been hot with all the lights up, Lydia would have been out of luck, but with all the shadows, even the goons still actively looking for her, did not spot her. She did a mental count as she went. Three up by the helm, and the two goons by the exits had left their positions to bring Nick to their boss.

"Please," the head goon said, patting Nick's cheek with his gloved hand. "Do not mistake me for the urban trash who run illegal alcohol and gambling dens. I am a man of breeding. My lineage goes back to Plymouth Rock and…"

Lydia tuned him out as she vaulted over the edge of the ship and dangled off the side, hanging over the padded mats she and the stunt guys fell onto when the Royal Navy shoved them over the side. The goon kept rambling as she shimmied, hand over hand, to the helm. *This guy was insufferable, like those cowboy actors who started to really think they were tough guys. Snobby crooks. What was the world coming to?*

One of the goons—she was pretty sure it was the one who had first fired on her—had strayed from the pack. He leaned against the railing at the edge of the deck and tucked his pistol into the back of his waistband. *Good way to lose a few pounds in a hurry,* Lydia thought, smirking to herself. The goon struck a match and lit up a cigarette. Smoke wafted up into the catwalks with the lights. Lydia hung by her fingers, face to face with the gun and the man's backside.

Muscles bulged, and she grit her teeth as she held herself up with one arm and reached for the gun with the other. She got her fingers around the handle and slid it out of the waistband. There was a rhythm to this. Do it too quick or too slow and they noticed. She had learned that from a teen pickpocket who liked to hang out around the back of the Inkwell Club waiting for drunk partiers to stumble out and lose their billfolds. *It was always good to try to learn something from the youths.*

She got the pistol out, and the goon kept puffing his cig. Time for phase two of her incredibly shaky plan. Given how sparse her costume was, one of the first things she had decided to add after a few nights of daring-do was a leather pouch that hung against her hip. It was just big enough for the gun. It was a complicated maneuver one handed and hanging off this ship, but she had done harder stunts on *The Crimson Cavalier*. Once the heater was safely secured, she put her other arm back on the railing.

The big goon let out a sigh, dropped his cig, and turned around, resting his folded arms against the railing. Lydia hoped her mask hid just how much her eyes bugged out. The goon looked down, meeting her gaze. He blinked. She blinked. He opened his mouth to shout.

Lydia leaped up, not very far, just high enough to get a grip on his hair. She got a good fistful and then let gravity do the rest, yanking the man's head hard against the railing. She had smacked her head on that same railing when an overzealous co-star had missed his mark. The makeup team had a hell of a time covering the bruise, but she had recovered.

Still using gravity as her aid, Lydia pulled the goon over the railing and dropped him onto the padded mat below. Faint wheezing confirmed he was still alive. A commotion by the helm confirmed the encounter had not gone unnoticed.

"Here, kitty, kitty," crooned the head goon. It made Lydia's skin crawl every time she heard it. The worst part was just how uncreative it was. Every two-bit thug out there thought they had the one clever cat pun.

"Cat," came Nick's voice. She could not see him, but there was a wet sputter to his words that made Lydia think he was talking through bloody teeth. "They got guns, stay clear."

Helpful as ever. They would be closing in on her soon. There was no chance of shooting her way out. Even if she was willing to go in blasting like that nut in the cloak operating out of San Francisco, there was no way she could plug them all before she went down. She was good, but nobody was that good.

Footfalls approached the edge of the deck where she hung. She could slink back into the shadows, try to flank them, but the longer she took, the more risk they would just shoot Mary Ellen and Nick and torch the place. She doubted this debt collector would be too precious about disrupting the production.

"Somebody find the damned light switch," the head goon shouted.

Lydia flicked her eyes upward. Heavy stage lights hung like the Sword of Damocles over everyone's heads. She had witnessed many arguments between overzealous producers and unbothered grips patiently explaining that lighting took as long as it took or else somebody on set was going to get squished.

Lydia let go of the railing and dropped onto the mat, rolling away from the downed goon. She whipped out the pistol and lined up her shot. She had made a point of memorizing where those lights hung just in case a producer won one of those arguments someday. She squeezed off a shot, and the bullet sparked up in the rafters. She imagined all eyes on deck going to the ceiling as they registered what had happened.

Seconds later, a 200-pound light smashed through the deck of the ship. The goons that had been coming for her dove to the side. One of them smacked into the mast, knocking himself out cold. The other went right over the railing. Lydia ran at him before he had a chance to get his bearings. She hit him with a spin kick that let her springboard off of him and get a grip on the railing again. This time, she did not hang there waiting; she vaulted over the edge and went into a tuck and roll on the deck.

Another goon came at her. In the commotion, they had forgotten they were armed, and they just wanted to rush her. Still on the ground, she sprang into a handstand, kicking the goon with both heels and flipping into the air. She grabbed hold of a low-hanging rope, praying this one was attached to something up in the rigging. It let out a length of slack before suddenly going taut. Lydia arced through the air, landing on the yardarm. It wobbled slightly, having been built to look good on camera, not stand up to the stress of real swashbuckling. Now at least she knew the rope stunt would work.

"Cat," Nick yelled, a big blood flecked smile on his bruised face.

"Ah, the crime-fighting burlesque act," The head goon said, clapping his hands slowly. "That was quite a show. I must say, this is all turning into quite a complicated endeavor. But I can kill three as easily as two."

"Well, that's plainly untrue," Lydia said. "Especially with so many of your goons out of the picture."

The head goon's smile faltered for a moment. He looked around. Of his original five, only two were left, and even they looked confused as to how their numbers had dropped so rapidly. The three Lydia had laid out were staying on the ground for the time being. Unfortunately, the two that were still up and running both had heaters. The head goon drew a pistol from an underarm holster hidden beneath his coat and leveled it at Mary Ellen's head.

"I make my money reading bad gamblers, Miss…Cat. And I like my odds here. Three on three, but I have guns."

Lydia drew the stolen gun and aimed it at the head goon. Nick blanched, his eyes locked on her and widened in a clear expression of: *Have you lost your feline mind?* The head goon did not falter. Instead, a thin smile spread over his lips.

"The Cheshire Cat does not kill. Even the cowardly and superstitious criminal element of this God forsaken city have pieced that together. You may claw, you may maim, you may even cripple, but you never kill. So, what have I to fear from an altruist with a gun?"

Lydia cracked her phoniest smile. She made a show of lowering the gun very slowly. The head goon, apparently impatient with her theatrics made a *get on with it* gesture with his own gun, pulling the barrel away from Mary Ellen's head.

With a speed that a camera might not catch, Lydia whipped her pistol back up, took aim, and fired. The bullet smashed through the flashbulb on Nick's busted camera. Lydia shut her eyes, but even through her eyelids the blinding flash was visible. She leapt off the yardarm as everyone clamped their eyes shut, blinking away the stars from the flashbulb. There would only be seconds before they regained their composure.

Lydia landed beside the head goon and drove her fist into his face. He flew back a good three feet before landing flat on his back. The two remaining muscleheads that had come with him blinked the last stars out of their eyes and looked at their downed boss. Lydia flashed a grin that showed off the sharpness of her canines. Maybe that was risking exposing herself. More than one film reviewer had brought up that sharp smile of hers, but it was as effective on the criminal element as it was on the moviegoing public.

"Okay, boys, time to decide if the paycheck is worth going through me to drag his sorry keister out of here."

The two goons exchanged a glance. They holstered their guns and backed toward the little ramp that led off the back side of the ship façade. One of them threw Nick a little wave.

"Love your column, Mister Horne, sorry about the nose."

Nick scowled, rubbing his nose, but nodded at the goon.

"It happens." He took a hankie out of his coat and dabbed away some of the blood. He must have figured he looked clean enough because he tried to give Lydia a charming smile that was ruined by his blood-flecked teeth. "Thanks for the save, Cat."

Lydia scooped the broken camera off the floor and handed it back to Nick.

"Thanks for the distraction. Sorry about the camera."

Nick looked it over with a hopeful grimace and then set the strap back around his neck. Lydia turned her attention to Mary Ellen, who had dropped into a crouch with her arms wrapped around her knees. Lydia knelt in front of her.

"Let me guess, you found out somebody owed him money and he needed that to be a secret."

"Carl Peters."

"The Kid?" Lydia thought about little Carl Peters, the studio's perennial scamp who had played her kid brother twice.

"He hit the race track on his eighteenth birthday last month and uh…it didn't go well. The bookie there came around while he was on set. I was making notes behind one of the big columns on the *Little Rome* set and heard everything. Carl didn't see me, but the bookie must have. Next thing I know, I'm getting dragged all over the studio."

"Well, you're safe now." She looked over her shoulder at the bookie laid out on the deck. Once he was in custody, Mary Ellen would be safe…and she had a very cinematic idea of how to give him over to the cops.

Sergeant Kapowski liked the studio beat. There was never any real danger, and he got to see movie stars all day. Most of the time, when he heard a scream, he got to assume it was someone on a set and keep walking. This morning, though, it had just kept going and going. He walked into the studio, following the impressive set of lungs to one of the sound stages where the brains at the studio had built the harbor of a little colonial Spanish town. The dock was lined with three steel gibbets, those little one-person cages the Royal Navy used to lock pirates in to make an example of them.

Standing under one of the gibbets was one of the most gorgeous women Kapowski had ever seen, flowing red hair and a body like an Olympic diver. She had her hands up to her cheeks and was screaming her head off, looking up at one of the gibbets. There was a man inside, small, with a bloody nose and a strip of black tape over his mouth.

"Whoa, whoa, Miss…Holy smokes, Lydia Tanner? Oh, cripes, I am a big fan."

The woman stopped screaming and met his eyes.

"I just…I came to run lines for the shoot tomorrow, and I found…this man."

Kapowski did his best to look tough in front of the movie star. He sauntered up to the cage. The man's leg stuck out the bottom, and there was a piece of paper taped to his patent leather shoe.

Nick Horne from the Daily Globe is in the commissary, he's got the skinny on this guy for attempted murder-CC

Kapowski lifted the brim of his hat and whistled. Getting to meet Lydia Tanner face to face and what looked like a big-time arrest, the only thing that could have made this night better was if he had gotten to meet the Cheshire Cat herself in person.

Standing Wave
by Kelli Fitzpatrick

I feel the pulse of the star even stronger than the funeral drum that reverberates over the rocky plain. The surface of Kraylik is so close to its sun — a tiny, desolate world raked by radiation. Only the recycling monks and the dead venture here.

And me.

The priestess Ganalsa raises her hand to the sky that is dominated by the blue glow of the white dwarf sun, Astoria. "We return the bodies of our kind to their source," she calls. Behind her, a dozen monks murmur accord, long silver robes covering black climo-suits. "We send them to become starstuff once more."

I stand at Ganalsa's side, ready for her to call on me for my role in today's ritual. My gold and brown suit glitters in the harsh light. Everyone else needs a polarized helmet, needs air, but I don't, so my coily black hair shifts freely over my shoulders. The dead lay in a stacked pyramid of ice prisms, thirty-some clear crystal cocoons holding citizens who chose as their last act to recycle their flesh as fuel for a slowly dying sun. A symbolic act. It won't change the star's lifespan. Not on a scale that would matter to us. But it does complete a circle — a cycle? — of energy transfer, and that is something. An acknowledgement that we are part of physical processes greater than the boundaries of ourselves.

Isn't that what you always told me? *Find the edge of yourself. Find where something else begins.*

The priestess turns to me. "Cora Vasco. Star Singer. Honored guest. We invite you to send these souls on their way."

This is the seventy-eighth time I have participated in the recycling ritual. I was honored to serve my planet in this way even before I got my powers, back when I was a young, broke shuttle pilot ferrying bodies of the deceased from the bio-glow cities and mushroom caves on Maddock, Astoria's dark outer planet.

The sky there never brightens above dim grey, so the society lives underground to take advantage of geothermal energy. It was a rough job that paid very little, but I looked through the manifest every trip, learned all the names of the dead, listened to their final life expressions—songs or stories or memory-paintings they had recorded toward the end—on the three-week long haul in that little skiff. I wanted to be a witness, to see their souls laid bare the way their naked bodies lie inside the sheaths of ice, stripped of everything except final glorious intention.

I'm still honored to serve. But it's different now. I don't need the shuttle. I don't need a climo-suit. Since I got my powers four years ago, I can fly unaided through the cold vacuum of space. My body compensates by repurposing the energy that lands on my dark skin—the light, the radiation from the star—to cancel out whatever environmental factors might do me harm. I don't have to think about it or actively will it. It's like breathing, like a heartbeat that will keep running in the background as long as there's ambient energy to tap. I can immerse myself in the interior of a star—my suit optimizes the energy conversion, but I would survive without it. I can even dive to the deepest, blackest depths of the ice-sea on Nadev, Maddock's ocean moon, if I sun-bathe beforehand. Ever since the accident, there is no place in this star system I cannot venture, at least for a time. I've never tried to go beyond it. I don't know if my powers extend to other stars.

Some part of me wishes you were here today, that you could share in this regal formality. I think you would appreciate the symbology, the ceremony, the self-aware marking of significance in a particular moment, almost like decorating time. But you're not on Kraylik or Maddock. You're on the *Mirrorless*. And you're never coming back.

Ganalsa motions to me again. The monks are waiting. Slowly, with a precision-edged reverence that emanates from deep in my bones, I grasp the transport cable tied around the crystals, rise above the planet's surface, and lift the ice coffins up toward me, a glass pyramid of finality. Their faces inside look ghostly in the blue light, beautiful, transfixed, eyes open, staring at the stars. Once free of the planet's gravity, I push them toward their destination.

As I approach Astoria, the vibrations inside its sphere become clearer to me, and a chilling fact runs through my core: there is something very wrong with the star. A very large wave is building inside.

You were such an unlikely friend. Pavlina Yeshona, daughter of Maddock's resource manager, the closest thing to aristocracy our subterranean civilization had. Assigned to my transport shift as a municipal duty because a high-ranking councilwoman's body was aboard. Your father was too busy to pay his respects, so he sent you in his place, but you didn't understand politics yet. You didn't know to hide your true self.

You sat on a jump seat in the tiny cockpit beside me, my palms immersed in the orange biogel on the console that connected my nervous system with the navigation controls, and you grilled me with questions about the ship, its cargo, the flight path. How far it could go, how fast, why it looked so dirty and run-down. Why had I stayed in the job for years, this sad freight run with its silent passengers, its unending funerary pall? "It lets me think," I said, but the truth is I didn't think much on those weeks-long journeys. It was more like sinking down into ambient feeling, sort of like the gel, being suspended in knowledge that there was an end, to the passengers and, by extension, to me. And an end meant a plot, a story. An end meant a chance to make meaning.

"But you're so young," you said. "Your end is far off."

We were the same age. And I have never been young, I think. Too much to do. Too much to take care of. Still, you made me feel young that day.

We arrived at Kraylik with the councilwoman's body and the priestess came aboard to perform a special blessing for her. The perks of power, I suppose. Special treatment even after you're gone.

I loaded the others into the bay of my ship, the ones I had previously dropped off to go through the soul purification process by the monks. That process involved a daily regimen of poetry readings, light painting, and instructions written for descendants regarding disbursement of assets into areas of society most needful. It is this last bit that forms the heart of the recycling temple. Give back. Render everything down and send it out to where it can do the most good.

I hauled the bodies to the hot ball of Astoria, as close as my vessel's heat shield would allow. You watched from the tiny observation deck that was more like a loft of windows, the space barely tall enough to sit upright, your face pressed against the tinted glass. When I jettisoned the bodies into the sun, the ice sublimated, their flesh and bones atomizing.

When I joined you in the loft, I said, "I wish I could go with them." You looked at me in horror. "Not to die. I mean get close to the sun. To experience it."

"We could." You pulled a device out of your handbag, a small hollow glassy sphere, iridescent like a soap bubble. "It's for emergencies, but I can activate it whenever I want."

We floated outside my ship, inside the bubble that expanded to contain us, a cutting-edge piece of technology meant to shield you from nearly any harm. We used it to sunbathe. The blue-white surface swirled below. I was a mere mortal then, no powers. I can't believe how much I trusted you. I pretended to pop the bubble as a joke, but I knew it was indestructible. Your father would never send you out here with anything less. "What do you think your end will be?" you asked.

I didn't know then, and still don't. It doesn't matter anymore. I've lost the meaning in my story.

Approaching the blue-white disc of Astoria feels like entering a hole in spacetime, the black void torn open to whatever blazing reality lies beyond. The star may be in its final stages, but it's still diamond-bright this close. I push the ice coffins in front of me, and they refract the light into a rainbow of color. They are protected by a thick thermal shield spray, so they can get all the way into the sun before sublimating.

The closer I am to the sun, the better I can sense the waves inside. There's no mistaking it now: there's a wave building deep in Astoria's core, much more powerful than normal. That could pose a serious threat. I will execute my duty, then investigate.

As a white dwarf, Astoria is a dead star. It is the core of a star that has already gone through its main life cycle, expanded into a red giant, and consumed any planets that used to be in this system, then lost its outer layers so it is just a dense plasma core. After its red giant phase, new planets formed around Astoria. Our civilization evolved in the wake of that destruction, in the very final stages of our sun's life. I've always found that a bit tragic, but beautiful. We're here at the end to witness the final dying light. Shouldn't someone see it?

I get to view it like no one else. It's a strange superpower, the ability to sense and control the vibrations inside stars. These vibrations are pressure waves, like sound waves, that propagate through the star's medium. All stars have them. They are usually generated by the motion of convection as material is heated near the core and rises, then cools and sinks, like a massive pot of boiling water. White dwarfs don't typically have convection because they are not burning. No nuclear fusion happens there anymore, they are just cooling down via radiation, like a hot stone cooling in the night air. But they can enter a temperature range of instability that creates these waves. That's where Astoria is now.

When the vibrations reach the surface of the star, they cause the surface to oscillate, with patches bulging inward and outward in beautiful standing waves. These stellar vibration patterns can't be seen with the unaided eye. Astronomers on Maddock have installed spectrographic equipment on Kraylik to observe Astoria's patterns. They can tell which parts of the star's surface are moving toward or away based on the way the light is red-shifted or blue-shifted. I can tell all that information in a microsecond, even with my eyes closed. I feel it. I know it.

When I tell people I hear starsong, they wonder why they can't hear it. The frequency of these waves is too low for others' ears, even if the sound could travel through space, which it can't. But I can hear the waves all the same, a kind of music that plays inside me always. The closer I am to a star, the louder and clearer its song. Astoria, with its thousands of "modes" — ways of vibrating, like musical notes — has been the symphony of my life for the last four years, but I can hear the others, the faraway stars in the night sky, as faint notes, as if in a half-remembered dream. You'd think it would be mostly noise, with so many different bodies singing at once, and some of it is, but there's a distinct harmonizing that rises above and seems to get more complex over time — or am I just getting better at recognizing it?

I have always been fascinated by the sun. On Maddock, where I grew up, the sun looks like an eerie, dim speck, like a glow-slug crawling across the dome of the sky. I used to pester my uncle as he worked on the heating pipes underground, asking him how far away the sun was, could we not take a ladder to the surface and reach up and touch it? He humored me, handed me his stepstool, and said to bring him back a chunk of it to use as a night-light. He died several years before I got my powers, but I thought of him the first time I touched sun-stuff. Bring me back a piece, kiddo. I wish he could see me now.

I reach the surface of the star and pause to take in its harsh blue light, then start to push into it. Astoria is small, not much bigger than Maddock. It is incredibly dense and hot. The thermal shield spray has nearly burned off the prisms — they will start to melt soon. These citizens did not go through all of this trouble to have their bodies become dust in orbit. I must get them into the interior of the star, where their matter will add to the radiative energy coming off Astoria.

To me, being inside a star feels like the pressure of being at the bottom of a deep pool, sometimes a sensation of closeness and safety, sometimes intensely uncomfortable, but I am used to dealing with difficult situations. Your father gave you a good early life. My parents died in a cave-in when I was three. My uncle was the closest I had to a guardian, but how much can you give a kid when you're working sixteen-hour days?

Down into the star's bulk I sink. Before I release the bodies, I add a ritual step of my own. I manipulate the frequency of some of Astoria's stellar vibrations to match the resonance frequency of the ice.

I make the prisms sing before they are consumed.

When I activate my wave transformation powers in this way, it feels like a point tensing in my core, like a set of strings attached to me being pulled outwards as I connect to the waves and reshape them. I don't understand why I can do this at distance. The wave doesn't need to be touching me for me to manipulate it. I don't even need to be inside the star, though it seems like the effect diminishes exponentially the further away I am.

Once the bodies have been converted to light and heat, it's just me and Astoria. We know each other well. I have dived into her depths many times, sometimes as part of the recycling ritual, sometimes for fun or escape. The song in here is loud, as always, but now a single wave is overpowering all the others. The phases of the thousands of waves moving through Astoria are aligning. That increases their amplitude. If a wave that size reaches the surface, the brightness of Astoria could increase ten or even twenty percent over a period of hours. Such a burst would be catastrophic for Kraylik—everyone there might be killed. It would be harrowing for Maddock as well. All the equipment there is tuned for low sunlight. A sudden spike might burn everything out, send us back to the Stone Age. From the way it's building, I estimate I've got an hour before it reaches the surface.

I plunge deeper. Something is making those waves align.

Down and down, into greater and greater pressure. I have never gone this deep.

Near the center, I find it: a piece of tech, black, an octahedron about half the size of me, emanating complex waves. A forced resonator. Someone is manipulating Astoria's stellar vibrations by singing back to them.

I got my powers the day you nearly launched yourself into the sun.

We edged closer and closer to Astoria on our bubble-protected sun-walks. You convinced your father to give you a "backup" bubble so you and I could float separately, and we chased each other around the outside of my ship, or twirled like skydivers, hands clasped through the soap-like film.

"Let's do it," you said. The stars whirled behind your hair in carousel fashion.

"Do what?" I said.

"Go inside Astoria. You said you wanted to."

"Enter the sun? Are you *crazy*?"

"These bubbles are indestructible. Don't you want to know what it's like?"

You knew the answer to that. You've always known me better than I know myself. But before I could respond, you let go of me and plunged backward toward the sun.

I didn't know if I could catch up to you in my bubble, so I boarded my ship, collapsed my bubble, and sank my hands into the biogel. I flew after you, listening to you laugh through the comm. We were sun-diving, falling right into the blaze. I caught up just as something split the space in front of us. A glittering flash, followed by a dark shadow.

I didn't know what was happening, but I knew I didn't want to lose you. I darted the ship ahead, so it was between you and the unknown threat. The left wing clipped the edge of that bright tear in space.

Searing pain arced through my body, like being stretched and reformed. I don't remember much of the following hours. I learned later that my nervous system, fully entwined with the ship's systems, got zapped by the flash. I blacked out, and the ship entered free-fall. You pulled me from the fried vessel and summoned help. The doctors on Maddock couldn't explain it: I had no damage from the mysterious flash, or from being that close to the sun, or from the vacuum of space. I was fine. When I awoke, I heard music: ringing, pulsing, resonating notes. I asked where it was coming from, but no one knew what I was talking about.

"You idiot," you said to me through a tear-stained smile. "What were you thinking? The world will forgive a manager's reckless daughter, but not a reckless shuttle pilot."

Maybe you understood politics more than I gave you credit for.

This dark device in Astoria's core—I recognize it. It's the shadow that came out of the flash that day. Did it come here from somewhere else? Another star system?

That would mean it's been hiding here for four years. Maybe working its way through the dense plasma to the sun's center. Or maybe biding its time, waiting for the right moment to activate.

The device is sending out pressure waves. Now that I'm this close, fully steeped in the patterns, I can tell that the vibrations it's sending out are causing the constructive interference: this object is driving the crescendo, the mega-wave.

An hour. That's not enough time to learn how the device works, then attempt to shut it down. I'm handy with a shuttle engine, but I'm not a technologist, certainly not for advanced alien tech, if that's what this is. I could try to destroy the device, but that might have unwanted consequences. My best shot is to try to cancel out its effects, to remove the immediate threat to Kraylik and Maddock, then figure out a more permanent solution.

I spread my arms to maximize my perception, then concentrate all my attention on Astoria's inner wave patterns and isolate the interference from the device. Then I make adjustments to the waves—destructive interference. The mega-wave begins to subside. But because the device is still actively intervening, so must I, indefinitely, to keep this threat at bay. This level of intervention takes effort and concentration. I can't do it forever.

As I'm floating here holding back oblivion for my species, I recall the other times I've tried to use my powers to help my society. Even though planets have internal waves too—called seismic waves—my powers don't work on planets or moons. But my strength, flight, and imperviousness to heat and pressure seem to follow me everywhere. I tried to convince the resource managers on Maddock to let me help the work crews in the deepest mines, but they said they can't allow an outside influence to disrupt the fragile social order. Outside influence? I told them I grew up there, that I wanted to give back so other children wouldn't have to grow up without a guardian. They politely but firmly declined, and then asked if I would be willing to increase Astoria's brightness enough to allow industrial agriculture on Maddock's surface. I told them that would render Kraylik uninhabitable, but they didn't care. I politely but firmly declined.

So I spend most of my time on Kraylik, on its plains or at the temple, with its reflection towers and cairn gardens, or traveling the solar system. I spend time in Astoria, practicing my powers on small waves, making tiny adjustments that will have no consequences to the system. The blue and white ice moon of Nadev and the copper belt of shiny-flecked tumbling asteroids are my favorite outer destinations. I never got the chance to take you there. I suspect you would have seen the same beauty in those stark landscapes that I see. I wonder if there are caves on the planets around Haveshii Prime. Will your great-grandchildren play there? Sometimes I try to picture what a day is like for you aboard your transiting vessel. Do you miss the musty smell of the moss tunnels, the hazy glow of Maddock's surface? Would I?

Inside me, in the same way I hear starsong, I hear a voice. "I don't know what you're doing, but I was here first," it says. The voice is deep like Astoria's pulses, ancient-sounding.

I am startled, but I continue counteracting the device. I "speak" back in my mind. "Who are you?"

"If you're mining carbon or opening a lightspace gateway, you'll have to go someplace else."

"I live here," I say, and realize that statement has never been truer than when I'm inside Astoria. "This is my solar system."

"Impossible." The voice sounds vexed. "I selected this system because white dwarfs have no planets, no life. They have already expanded and destroyed all other bodies in their orbit."

"My people evolved after that destruction."

The voice groans, something like recognition and annoyance. "How extremely rare and unlucky for you. Your species is of no consequence. I've spent hundreds of thousands of years jumping through lightspace to make each star sing as I need it to for my final composition. I won't have it ruined for beings whose entire civilization will rise and fall in a fraction of that time."

I shudder at the scale of this conversation. Stars, lightspace, ancient aliens—how did I come to walk in this land of incomprehensibly large and long-lived things?

"You must stop your device," I say, much more confidently than I feel.

"I'm sorry. I need that star to complete my piece."

"And I can't let you destroy my home." I turn my powers on the device, focusing the waves on its location so it will receive what I hope is damaging compressive force. It will take a few minutes for this effect to reach its peak, but the voice clocks what I'm doing.

"Stop! You'll wreck it! This is my last chance to make something worthwhile."

Something twinges in me. I should not feel sympathy for a person trying to kill me, but I know that desperate yearning. "Shut it off and we'll talk," I say. I imagine this is the kind of ultimatum leveraged by those with sanctioned authority. I'll leverage whatever I have to to save Kraylik.

The device shuts off. Relieved, I relax my grip on the waves and they begin to ebb. "My name is Cora Vasco of Astoria." I have never introduced myself in this way, but it feels right.

"Mhazhev Zee. Tell me, Cora Vasco of Astoria, what technology are you using to wave-carve? I have traveled many systems and never encountered another civilization that could do this."

"I'm using myself. I have this ability." I leave out how I got it.

A trilling noise. "Remarkable. But I must have Astoria sing true."

"Zee, if you are so long-lived, why not choose a different star?"

"As I said, this is my last chance. I am dying. This symphony is my final gift to the universe."

The background music I've been hearing in the stars. My mind reels that I've been listening not just to random oscillations in balls of plasma, but to someone's intentionally-composed masterpiece. I have spent most of my life helping others die well. The choice seems clear. "Zee…what if we could make Astoria harmonize in a different way? A more complex chord than a burst?"

"My device cannot do that. Not in a white dwarf."

"I believe I can."

"Show me."

I calculate the options. Something that will harmonize with Zee's melody, but with less power than a burst. Once I've identified a chord, I take my time, connect to each wave, adjust frequency, phase, amplitude, initiate new waves, cancel out others, but keep the amplitude low. I am encouraging Astoria to sing a new combination of notes, but in a way that won't break anything with the volume.

As the chord coalescences, I hear fast chattering noises from Zee. I am incredibly curious about Zee's physiology, but I don't ask. They are clearly having a moment. "Yes, Cora Vasco of Astoria! That is even better than my original concept!"

"Now…will you leave Astoria alone?"

"Yes," Zee says. "But I request one thing further."

What do you say to a dying alien? "Go on."

"There's a flaw in my symphony. A star I visited long ago has since degraded. The device in that star is no longer responding. I am near my end. I do not have enough life left in me to correct it. Let me transport you to fix it."

I have always done what was needed, for myself and those around me. This time, when space splits open in front of me, I am not afraid.

I knew something would pull the two of us apart eventually. I just didn't realize how far. Maddock held out against the doomsday-ists for decades, but eventually the cry for planned species survival won out, and the council engaged Maddock's construction cave crews in fabricating the pieces of a massive generation ship, the *Mirrorless,* capable of traversing the vast distance to the next nearest star, Haveshii Prime, and starting a colony on one of its planets. But those who embarked on the voyage would not see the destination. The journey would take generations. The opportunity being offered was the adventure of a life in space, to be a link in a chain.

The night before launch, you and I met in the cavern beside the dark pool, our secret space. The green glow from the luminescent mushrooms on the ceiling reflected off the still water, broken by the occasional rock you tossed, making ripples dance to a far shore hidden in darkness.

I couldn't join you on the *Mirrorless.* Only dignitaries and manager-class were allowed to buy tickets. I would never have been able to afford one anyway. Gaining powers did not grant me an increased monthly stipend. I'm grateful you saved my dignity by not trying to convince me there was a way.

"It seems like dying," I said. "As soon as you set foot on the *Mirrorless,* your fate is sealed. Your life will end on that ship. It's a death sentence in space."

You shrugged, fiddled with a small stone. "*Life* is a death sentence in space. Your only choice is which parts of space you'll see and who you'll see it with."

I felt like there were mushrooms growing in my throat, expanding up around my vocal cords, choking my words. "Don't you like seeing it with *me?*"

You hugged me, and we sat in the mushroom glow for a long time.

The trip through lightspace feels like a second and an eternity. Baking light. Disorienting color. Impossible velocity. And then I am floating in a starry void.

"Listen," Zee says.

I do. My mouth falls open in marvel. The galactic symphony, the one I've been hearing for years, sounds so much clearer, so in-tune and in-sync with itself.

"This is my listening spot," Zee says. "It's where I designed the music to sound the best from, given the travel time of the light from each star. Except, there's one that's not right—"

"That one. Near the cluster of seven."

"Yes! Its period is—"

"Too long." The star is a Cepheid variable star. Its entire surface is pulsating in and out in the fundamental mode, as if it is breathing. But it's pulsing too slowly for it to be in sync with the symphony. "You want it sped up."

"Yes."

"I've never adjusted a Cepheid," I say. "I've never adjusted any star except Astoria, and never this far away." The star is one of the nearer stars in the collection that is singing in harmony, but orders of magnitude farther than I've ever tried to use my powers.

"You've proven to me that your perception and control are remarkable," Zee says. "I believe you are capable."

There is another concern. "What about life in *that* system? I don't want to harm others there by messing with their sun."

"My trip there long ago recorded no planets, and it is vanishingly unlikely for life to evolve around such a variable energy source. Its light and heat output more than double at its peak. I calculate less than a 0.0003 percent chance that life could ever develop there."

"Then I will try."

I focus my attention on the Cepheid, and its single note steps into the foreground like a soloist stepping forward onstage. I try to sense the wave inside. It's so far away. I draw on my energy reserve from soaking up sunglow inside Astoria and burn through it to boost my sensitivity and signal. Then I carefully intervene in the Cepheid's wave, just enough to increase its frequency slightly. Its period changes from almost three days to just under two.

"Too far!" Zee exclaims. "Now it's pulsing too quickly!"

I'm almost out of energy. What if I fail? Will Zee leave me here in the dead of space?

Find the edge of yourself. Find where something else begins.

I try again. This time, I calibrate my intervention to the smallest increment I can manage. A touch that's barely there, a brush against moss, a drip in a cave pool. Then, I wait patiently for the star's breath to adjust.

Zee makes a noise like exuberant coughing. "You've done it! It's in balance! Listen!"

I do. I pull my attention back to take in the entire spherical space around me, and let out a sigh of wonder. Complex, transcendent alien music. The harmonics are superb. Perfectly balanced. Intricate layered rhythms, and what sounds like songs within a song, all adding onto each other. I change my attention so that I'm focusing on a small number of them — and fresh nuance emerges. It will take years to appreciate fully. "This symphony was composed for people like us, who can listen to stars, wasn't it Zee?"

"Of course. But I did not expect to find such a worthy audience and collaborator outside my kind. Cora Vasco of Astoria, Wave-Carver — Thank you."

"I will remember this," I say. "I will remember you." I hold so many inside me. I have space for one more.

When I land on Kraylik's surface, Ganalsa is waiting for me. A group of monks walk the plain in a staggered line, holding up sanctification rocks that have been cursed with the reading of the misdeeds of the dead, to be purified in the light of the star, and then sent back to Maddock with reparation payments from their estate accounts.

"The souls you entrusted to me have completed their cycle," I report.

"Good." The priestess's eyes search my face. "You found something else in the heart of Astoria."

"An instrument." I explain the device, Zee, the song. We discuss the implications. "I'm definitely calling it *wave-carving* from now on."

Ganalsa sways thoughtfully, watching the procession. "Sounds like you helped this being navigate their last act."

"I did my best."

"Should we expect you at the next recycling ceremony?"

"I'll be here," I say. "I'm always here."

"If someday you're not, I need you to know that we'll manage." She smiles at me.

This is the first time anyone has told me it's okay to leave. To walk away from a long-standing commitment. I know from my trip to Zee's listening spot that my powers function outside this solar system. I can connect to other stars and manipulate them. It also showed me that my powers are much more precise and far-reaching than I imagined. Zee deactivated the device they had planted inside Astoria, but they told me how to use it to enter and exit lightspace. If I master traveling through lightspace on my own, I could visit other stars, see other systems, explore the limits of what I can do. Maybe even visit you on your ship.

Ganalsa joins the monks' procession and I lie down on the stone, watching the stars, listening to a cosmic serenade I helped create. Are there others out there hearing it? Is it possible there are more superpowered beings like me? Zee is the first alien my people have encountered. Who else populates this vast spinning galaxy?

I understand now why you boarded the generation ship. I think I will always return to Kraylik, but for now, I stand and fly sunward, waving goodbye to the priestess and the monks.

I have a device to master.

Author's Note: Special thanks to Dr. Steven Kawaler for introducing me to the basics of asteroseismology and informing me of the white dwarf stars that undergo bizarrely irregular increases in brightness. I have taken artistic license for the sake of the story, but I encourage readers to research the very real and very impressive science of star songs.

The Fading Storm
by Fred Phillips

"They based a comic book on me," the old man said wearily as the pool of water from his overturned cup spread across the bedside table. "Only I didn't need that silly amulet they gave him. Now, I'm reduced to this."

"It's OK, Papa." His teenage granddaughter grabbed the nearby towel to mop up the spill.

Suzy knew what would come next. She'd heard all his wild stories before. She loved her grandfather dearly, and in her younger days, the tales fascinated her. As she'd grown older, she realized how silly they were. Now, as he lay in a nursing home bed, unable to even grip a cup to drink from, it was almost impossible to see him as the superhero of her imaginings.

"I remember …" her grandfather began, but she just couldn't take it this afternoon.

"Sorry, Papa, I've got to go for today," she interrupted before he could get started. "I have lots of schoolwork to get done, but I'll see you again on Wednesday."

He trailed off, a disappointed look on his face, but then nodded.

"School comes first," he said. "Always."

"I promise I'll have longer to stay on Wednesday." Suzy plastered on a fake smile to hide the bit of guilt and pain she felt at that look of disappointment.

She quickly made her way to the door and into the hall, but a voice from behind her interrupted as she walked at a fast clip away from the room.

"You should show more respect for your elders."

Suzy spun on her heel to find a woman about her grandfather's age giving her a disapproving glare. Who did this woman think she was, and what business was it of hers?

"You know nothing about it," she snapped.

"Oh, I know a great deal about your grandfather," the woman said. "In fact, I'm here to pay my respects to him, but I didn't want to disturb you two. That was before I knew how rudely you were going to treat him."

"Listen, lady, I don't know who you think you are, but you don't know a thing about me." Suzy seethed at the audacity of this stranger. "I've listened patiently to his stories my entire life. I lived for them when I was a kid, but I know better now, and sometimes...sometimes I just can't take hearing those stories while I see him lying there like that."

A tear rolled down the girl's face, but she stared defiantly at her accuser.

"Oh dear." The woman's eyes widened. "Maybe I've misjudged the situation. I always did have trouble reading the room. Your grandfather could tell you that."

Suzy wiped her tears away with a quick brush of her fingers and turned to walk away, but the woman laid a strong hand on her shoulder.

"I'm sorry, child. I misunderstood."

Suzy jerked away.

"It's OK," she muttered. "I need to be going now."

She took off at a quick pace down the hall. She wanted to get away from the strange lady as fast as possible and get out of there before the dam broke and let out the flood of tears she was trying to hold back.

"We should talk sometime," the woman called behind her.

Suzy spun, ready to unleash another piece of her mind. The woman met her eyes, and though her lips didn't move, Suzy still heard her, somehow, inside her head.

There's more to your grandfather's stories than you may think.

At that, Suzy turned and dashed toward the front door, not worrying about what anyone else thought. She didn't stop until she was in her car and down the road, away from her grandfather and away from the strange woman. She pulled over in the parking lot of a fast-food joint and let the tears fall. She shook and sobbed. But underneath that was a nagging thought. What had just happened?

As promised, Suzy was at her grandfather's bedside again on Wednesday after school. It was not a good day for him. He had them sometimes. He mostly slept, and she would just sit there, maybe read a book, maybe just stare at the man who used to be her hero. She had believed in the tales of the Storm Guardian, had every single issue of the comic – even a few that would have brought a nice profit if she'd been willing to part with them. She never would. They reminded her of better days with her Papa.

Suzy assumed he'd chosen the character because the drawings bore a strong resemblance to the photos she'd seen of him as a young man, at least in the early runs. As time had gone on, new artists had put their own spin on it, and he'd changed to look less and less like her grandfather. There had even been a short-lived reboot with a female Storm Guardian a few years back. Every change in the character had saddened him, so she hadn't shared that.

The clock ticked away on the wall. Papa stirred in his sleep a few times but didn't wake up. Suzy shoved the novel she'd been reading into her backpack and shouldered it. It would be a few days before she could come and visit again, and she hoped that he'd be lucid then. Right now, she would have loved to hear some of his stories. It seemed like the bad days were becoming more and more frequent.

Suzy looked up to the door to find the woman who had accosted her in the hall a few days ago standing there, staring at the sleeping form of her grandfather. She began to wind herself up for another confrontation, but the woman looked at her with pleading eyes and held her hands out placatingly.

"I'm sorry that we got off on the wrong foot last time," she said. "Suzy, isn't it?"

"How do you know my name?"

"Daryl has spoken of you often over the past 17 years. Our visits have been less frequent of late." She gestured toward him with a rueful look. "It's quite a drive for me to visit, and he doesn't follow phone conversations well anymore. The last time I tried to call, he didn't know who I was and hung up on me."

Suzy nodded at that. She admitted she was intrigued by who this woman might be and what she might be able to share about her grandfather, but she was also still a little freaked out about their encounter earlier in the week.

"Well, I need to be going," Suzy said.

"I really am sorry about the other day, and I'd still like to talk to you when you have a chance. I knew your grandfather well, and I'd like to tell you about him."

"I don't even know who you are."

The woman smiled.

"No, I suppose you don't." She extended a hand. "Ruth Rogers, nice to meet you."

Suzy stared at her for a moment, dumbfounded. This had to be a bad joke.

"Ruth Rogers? As in Mindbender?"

The woman inclined her head. "The same, although I'm afraid I've been greatly exaggerated."

Great. Now, Suzy seemed to have another crazy person in her life who thought she was a comic book hero.

"I really have to be going." Suzy pushed past the nutty woman and into the hall.

"Please," Ruth said. "Just give me 15 minutes. Let me buy you a coffee, or whatever you want. If you don't like what I have to say, you'll never see me again."

Suzy sighed. She knew it was a mistake to continue this conversation, but she was also curious. She'd never had the chance to talk to anyone outside the family who had known her grandfather in his younger days, back when he was supposedly a superhero.

"OK," she said. "Fifteen minutes."

They settled down at a table by the window in Suzy's favorite coffee shop. Normally, she'd go for the quiet corner in the back, but she didn't quite trust Ruth, so she wanted to be very visible. The waitress delivered their coffees. Suzy took a sip and waited.

"Ooh, that's quite good," Ruth said as she set her cup on the table. "I'm glad you showed me this place. I've been getting my coffee at the Mickey D's down the street."

Suzy didn't respond.

"Well, then, I suppose we'll get on with it, shall we?"

Suzy nodded, still silent.

"I first worked with Daryl in 1964, and we worked off and on until the mid-1980s, when we were shuffled off and covered up."

Her grandfather would never talk about what he'd done for a living. He'd always pretended that it had been top secret, and then he'd told more Storm Guardian stories.

"So, you worked for the government, too?" she asked, testing the waters.

"In a manner of speaking," Ruth answered. "We were never official employees, but they hired us when they needed certain delicate problems solved. It paid well, and we were good at keeping quiet – well, most of us. I still remember how they freaked out when Steve published his first story."

"Steve?"

"Steven Parker."

"The guy who created Storm Guardian and Mindbender?"

"Oh, honey, he didn't create anything, just embellished it. We didn't use those silly names or dance around in bright spandex, of course. Imagine trying to blend in back then with green hair like my character had. And I don't think Daryl ever forgave him for that amulet thing."

She smiled at that, and Suzy couldn't help but let out a little giggle. That much was true. Her grandfather grumbled about that regularly when they talked about the comics.

"Every one of his characters was a real person. He changed the names, except for mine. I gave him permission – thought it would be cool to be a superhero. He exaggerated the powers for most of us. It would have been convenient if I could have taken control of people with my mind and made them do what I wanted, but not even close. Your grandfather, though, was by far the closest to his comic version. He was always the strongest of us all, in more ways than one."

Suzy just couldn't believe what she was hearing.

"You really expect me to believe that you and Papa were part of a superhero team? Superheroes don't exist."

"Not anymore, no. But they did, for a brief shining moment in time. I can prove it to you."

"Sure you can."

"What's the most famous Storm Guardian storyline?"

Suzy thought only for a split second.

"Invasion of Earth," she said. "When he stopped the aliens who wanted to enslave the human race."

"I was there."

"That's just silly. Now you're asking me to believe in superheroes *and* aliens?"

"The reason no one believes in aliens to this day is because of Daryl. He probably saved millions of people. He saved me."

Suzy stared skeptically.

It will be a little disorienting.

Suzy recoiled at the voice in her head, just like at the nursing home the other day.

It's OK, Ruth said again. *Yes, I'm using my powers to talk to you, mind-to-mind. What I'd like to do won't hurt, but it will be…strange for you. I'd like to show you what happened. Through my eyes.*

Suzy was reeling now. She didn't know what to think. Ruth switched back to speaking aloud.

"You've seen that I'm not lying about my powers. Surely, you're at least a little interested in what I might be able to show you?"

Trepidation weighed heavily on Suzy's decision, but she had to admit that she was fascinated with how Ruth was doing that little trick. After a few moments to consider, she nodded her head hesitantly. Then she was falling.

Suzy snapped open eyes that were not her own and found herself in a sterile meeting room. A dark-haired man in a military uniform stood at the head of the table, and four others were seated around it, including her. One of them looked very familiar, and it took her a moment to realize that she was staring at a younger version of her Papa. She tried to blink and shake her head to figure out what was going on, but she was not in control. She was just an observer.

"Gentlemen," the military man began, and Suzy heard a throat clearing that sounded like it was coming from her.

"And lady," he added with an acknowledging nod. That's when it clicked that she seemed to be seeing things through Ruth's eyes.

"You all know of our recent accomplishments with the Apollo 13 mission – the farthest we've ever traveled into space."

"That's a nice spin on a failure," said the man to her left, sandy-haired with geeky-looking heavy black glasses.

The commander gave him a glare before continuing.

"Let's leave opinions aside, Mr. Parker. Now, unfortunately, that mission not only caught the attention of the world, but something else as well."

A projector at the other end of the table flared to life, flashing rough images on a pull-down screen. Jerky footage showed what Suzy could best describe as hairless werewolves. They were roughly human-shaped with pale skin, but they had vicious teeth and claws. A group of four of them loped down a street after a fleeing family. The father turned to fight, trying to give the mother and child time to get away, but he was brutally taken down by one of the creatures. The other three overtook the rest of the family. The mother was left lying in the street, but one of the creatures dragged the child out of the shot.

Ruth looked away as that happened, and Suzy wished that she had turned her head much earlier. The three others at the table were all shaken as well. Steve Parker looked sick to his stomach. The other man, who hadn't been introduced yet, stared at the ceiling. Her grandfather studied his hands, knuckles white. On his face was a look of rage that she'd never seen or known he was capable of in her 17 years.

"That was Florida," the military man said into the uncomfortable silence. "We were lucky to have people on the ground investigating who intercepted the footage before it made it to the press. We believe they somehow traced the rocket back to Cape Kennedy. So far, there have been two attacks, both on small towns. Men and women killed. Children taken. The official story we've put out is that these are animal attacks. We've strongly suggested that there may be a rabies outbreak among wildlife in the local swamps. In reality, we believe they are raiding parties, testing the waters, perhaps for a full-scale attack."

"You need it handled efficiently and quietly," her grandfather said.

"Exactly. We've activated small squads of National Guard to patrol nearby towns looking for the rabid animals, but a larger military presence would raise eyebrows."

"Do we know where they may strike next?" Ruth asked.

"We believe the attacks were orchestrated by the same raiding party. The part about the attacks coming from the swamps is accurate, but we haven't been able to figure out where they're hiding."

"Which is why I'm here," said the man who had remained nameless to this point. "You need a tracker."

"If anyone can find them, you can."

The man nodded, and Suzy realized who it must be. She didn't know his real name, but the comic version was Dave Brown, the Bloodhound.

"Ruth's mission is to find out whatever she can about these aliens," the commander continued. "Get in their heads if you can and bring back any intelligence you can find on what they are or their plans.

"Steve will use his ability to amplify Daryl's powers and presence. I want these things to think there's an army just like him waiting for them if they decide to bring an attack. And Daryl, you know what to do."

Her grandfather simply nodded, the look of anger still twisting the face she'd known as kind and gentle into something she found a little scary.

"Good. We have an airplane waiting. We'll fly you into Orlando tonight and get you quietly to the site of the last attack. Make any preparations you need. We're wheels up in an hour and a half. You're going hunting."

The black sedan rolled down the same street they'd seen on the video in the pre-dawn. No one was around as they quietly exited the car and watched it drive away.

"You're up, Danny." Her grandfather nodded toward the Bloodhound.

Suzy halfway expected to see him sniff at the air or the ground as the character in the comics often did, but instead, he just closed his eyes, took a few deep breaths, and seemed to fall into a trance. He stayed that way for several minutes before his eyes popped open.

"This way." Without another word or gesture, he turned and walked into the nearby woods.

They slogged on for a few hours, the ground becoming softer and mushier beneath their feet. Danny paused occasionally, falling back into that trance, then leading them onward. Several times, they had to pick their way around stagnant pools of water, and more than once, one of them had taken a wrong step and ended up knee deep in sucking mud. Mosquitoes menaced them. Every patch of skin that wasn't covered was criss-crossed with briar scratches. The humidity pressed down on them. They were all filthy and tired when the Bloodhound called a halt.

"We're close," he said. "No more than a few hundred yards, I'd guess."

"Ruth," her Papa said. "Can you pick up anything? Steve, give her a little extra juice."

The next sensation Suzy felt was the strangest thing she'd ever experienced. She was in Ruth's head as she extended her power. The world shifted, and the people around her became glowing orbs. Ruth ignored their group and reached out further through the swamp. She could barely detect something out there, not blazing glows like the ones nearby, but very faint. There were maybe ten of them scattered around. Then there was another clump, brighter but still hard to detect, all gathered in the same place. The kidnapped children, Suzy guessed.

The vision bounced back to reality, and Ruth shook her head.

"They're different," she said. "And too far away, even with Steve's help. I need to be closer. There are about ten of them. The children are there and seem to be OK, so we need to be careful of them. If we can get near, maybe I can pick something up."

"Let's move out, then."

The Bloodhound again took the lead, with her grandfather second and Steve and Ruth bringing up the rear. They moved more slowly now, trying to be as stealthy as possible. After a couple hundred yards, Danny motioned them into some nearby brush, where they knelt and peered through the trees. In a small clearing, there was some sort of craft. It was shaped like a crescent moon, and the smooth metal glowed like none that Suzy had seen before.

Her vision was jarred again as Ruth reached out. She first went to the brighter glows, the children. She opened her mind, and Suzy could see into the heads of the kids. She couldn't hear their thoughts, exactly, but she got flashes of images and feelings. They were terrified and traumatized. They'd all seen at least one parent attacked. They couldn't understand the noises the horrific creatures made or what they planned to do with them. Suzy felt sick from the emotions Ruth was picking up. They were chained up in the spaceship but otherwise seemed to be well, aside from minor cuts and bruises. She felt relief at that.

Ruth came back to reality.

"The children are in the ship," she said. "They're scared, but not seriously hurt. There are five of them."

"That checks out with the number taken in the reports," Steve said. "We have them all."

Suzy saw relief in the faces of everyone there.

"What's the plan, boss?" Danny asked.

"Ruth will see what she can pick up from the aliens first. Then Steve will juice me up, and I'll hit them as hard as I can. Danny, you get the kids out of there while I have them occupied."

Nods all around, and Suzy was back into Ruth's power vision. On the third attempt, she'd gotten a little more used to it, and some of the disorientation was gone. Ruth reached out toward the nearest of the alien glows. Even this close, they were still muted compared to the others, a dull pearlescent white color next to the vibrant auras of the humans. She reached into the creature's mind, and both Ruth and Suzy reeled at what they found. It was a chaotic, snarling mess of thoughts and emotions, nothing like the relatively clear pictures she'd gotten from the children. There were flashes of others like them, a sort of pride in their success, an image of great rewards being heaped upon them for bringing the children back. Then, something changed. It was as if the creature noticed Ruth being there. As one, the auras of the aliens slowly turned dark, and it seemed to Suzy that they were turning toward Ruth.

She snapped her eyes open in a panic.

"Oh my God," she said. "They know I'm here. They're coming."

There was no time to prepare a defense as the aliens came bounding in, converging on their location. The first monster hit her like a freight train. Suzy felt Ruth's terror as she was thrown to the ground, 200 pounds-plus of muscle, claw, and tooth landing on top of her. She stared into rage-filled black eyes as teeth snapped at her throat. She managed to get an arm up to try to keep them at bay.

She felt the teeth sink in and tear, then searing pain.

Ruth felt a blast of wind and the crackle of electricity, and suddenly the weight disappeared with a sickening smell of singed flesh. Danny was there in an instant, checking on her and dragging her back from the battleground.

Steve lit up like a beacon. He sent out tendrils of light into her grandfather, and Suzy marveled at what happened next. Papa began to rise into the air, both arms extended to his sides just above his waist. Then two swirling balls of blue lightning coalesced in each hand. He hurled both at the alien that had just attacked Ruth and was attempting to rise. The thing yelped as they struck and was thrown several feet across the ground and into a tree trunk, where it lay still. The others began to pour through the trees, and her grandfather turned his attention to them, blasting lightning balls left and right at their attackers.

"Danny," he yelled over his shoulder. "Get the kids out."

The Bloodhound nodded and sprinted through the line of attackers with incredible speed toward the alien ship. Several of the beasts turned to follow him and caught bolts to the back from her grandfather. Then something even stranger happened. She saw at least ten versions of her grandfather in the skies, hurling death down on the aliens. Each of them was attached by a tendril to Steve, and she understood. As she watched, she realized each duplicate was making the exact same motions, and only the bolts from one of them were doing damage. Her grandfather alternated his attacks randomly to make sure they were hitting everywhere. In the chaos, the creatures didn't seem to realize that all but one of their enemies were projections.

That went on for a few moments, then Danny emerged from the spaceship, the five children in tow, and ushered them into the forest away from the battle.

"All clear," he yelled as he entered the trees last.

Then her Papa unleashed hell. Suzy remembered the battle scene where Storm Guardian took on the alien army. While, in reality, there were only ten aliens, not hundreds as in the comics, the artists couldn't do justice at all to what she witnessed. No cape and no amulet, of course, but her Papa glowed with wrath, and it rained down on the remaining monsters. One by one, they dropped under the onslaught and lay still, until there was a lone survivor running for the ship.

Suzy wanted to yell that it was getting away, but of course, she couldn't make Ruth form the words. Instead of attacking, her grandfather let the glow dissipate from him and floated slowly to the ground. As he touched, the duplicates blinked out of existence, and Steve slumped to the spongy marsh floor, exhausted. A high-pitched hum pierced the morning, then a blast of air as the ship lifted off and raced into the sky. Why had he let the one escape?

"That one will have a story to tell when he gets home," Steve said, and Suzy finally got it. The alien had seen an army of lightning-tossing superheroes protecting us.

Her grandfather nodded. "Let's hope it's good enough to keep the rest of them away."

Papa turned and sent three quick blasts of lightning into the sky, accompanied by cracking thunder, a storm from the clear blue. Then he turned his attention to Ruth, who was holding her bleeding and mutilated arm. He took bandages from Steve's pack and wrapped it as best he could.

It was about half an hour later when they heard the helicopter coming in over the swamp, responding to her grandfather's signal.

Suzy opened her eyes back in the coffee shop and stared in awe at Ruth.

"Was that real?"

In response, the woman across the table slid her sleeve back, showing a gnarled, deep scar on her forearm where the alien had torn a chunk of it away.

"They did what they could," she said. "But plastic surgery wasn't what it is now back then."

Suzy sat in stunned silence for a few minutes.

"So, what happened after that?"

Ruth shrugged.

"The usual. We were quietly commended and paid very well. The kids were processed and given happier memories in place of seeing their parents killed and being abducted by aliens.

"Oh, don't look at me like that. I didn't do it. Not in my skill set. It was for the best anyway. It allowed them to have a sort of normal life instead of becoming part of some government program. Most had grandparents who took them in. Danny adopted two of them, a brother and sister who had no next of kin they could find. They're the only ones I kept up with, and they've lived a mostly happy life."

"It's still hard to believe the Storm Guardian and all the others are real."

"Not really," Ruth said. "We weren't superheroes like in the comics. We were just a bunch of 20- and 30-somethings that happened to develop some strange powers around the same time. No one really knows why, and it never happened again. The government used us to take care of special problems, we got paid well, and eventually, we all got too old to do it. Many of us died early, a side effect of the powers, and even more had sharp declines when age caught up with them. Steve gave the world an idealized version of us in his comics, with powers far beyond what we had, but we were never those people."

"But you did save the world?"

"Oh, yes. We did that. A few times. But most of us did other things that we're not nearly as proud of. Those didn't make the comics. At the end of the day, we were just people – except for maybe Daryl. He truly was the best of us, and if ever there were a true superhero, it was him. That's why I still make the trip to visit when I can."

"Could you …" Suzy began, but trailed off and looked away.

"Go ahead. It's OK."

"Could you show me some more memories of my grandfather?"

Ruth smiled.

"Not today. I get tired quickly these days, and projecting my memories like I did is incredibly taxing. Maybe next time I'm in town, I'll share another."

The conversation was interrupted by the ring of Suzy's phone. She held up her hand to Ruth as she answered it.

"Hello?"

"Suzy Gordon?"

"Yes."

"Suzy, this is Nurse Johnston. It's your grandfather. Technically, I shouldn't be calling you, but I know how close you are to him, and I know you just left a little while ago…You may want to come back if you can. He's had an episode. I've informed your dad, too. He's on his way."

"Thank you. I-I'll be right there." Suzy hung up the phone and stared into space. Her shoulders slumped.

"What is it?" Ruth asked. "What's wrong?"

"It's Papa. He's had…the nurse called it an 'episode.' He's had them before, but she sounded like this one is different. She said I should come back."

"Then you should go now."

"Will you come with me?"

"I don't think that's appropriate. I'd be an intruder in your family's moment."

"You're just as much his family as we are. We've always thought his stories were just that. Someone who knows the truth should be there."

Ruth considered for a few seconds.

"If you think I'd be welcome, I'll go."

Nurses scurried around her grandfather's room when they arrived. Suzy's parents were not there yet. Nurse Johnston approached her with a sad look.

"We've done what we can to make him comfortable," she said. "But I think you should probably say your goodbyes."

She gave Suzy a quick hug and whispered in her ear to let her know if she could do anything. Then the nurses gave them the room. Her Papa looked more frail than ever, lying in the bed where she'd so often visited him. An IV ran into his arm, pumping in comforting drugs. A large bruise spread out from under the medical tape around it, another reminder of how far he was from the strong, proud man she'd seen in Ruth's memory. But when he opened his eyes and looked at her, they were clear and alert.

"I guess this is it." He looked more tired than she'd ever seen him.

"Don't talk like that, Papa," Suzy said, tears starting to fall from the corners of her eyes.

"It's time," he said firmly. "Past time, I think."

Then he looked up to Ruth.

"Ah, Ruth. I guess you'll be the last of us."

"There are a few others still out there," she said, tears also pouring down her face.

"Not any that matter. I'm guessing that you two have been talking?"

Suzy nodded, and he managed a wry smile.

"You were marvelous, Papa. Ruth showed me Invasion of Earth – the real version, not the comic. You were amazing."

"We were heroes," he said. "No matter what Ruth told you. Not all the powered were, but those don't matter. My teams, the people I surrounded myself with, were heroes to the end. Even Steve, I guess."

Ruth let out a chuckle at that.

"I'm sorry," Suzy said.

"For what?"

"I thought they were just silly stories. I had no idea."

He looked at her and gave a croaking laugh that turned into a cough.

"You think I didn't know that?" he said when it passed. "I knew you thought I was a silly old man. But you were here. You listened, and that means the world to me. I wish that I could pass my powers on to you because you would use them well, but it seems they'll die with me, whatever is left of them anyway. But know this, Suzy, you are just as much a hero as we were. Remember that, and it will serve you well."

"I'm not a hero."

"You are. You care, truly care, for the right reasons, and that's a power that most people in the world seem to have lost. Take that and use it, and you'll change the world far more than I did with my powers. Promise me."

"I promise," Suzy said through her tears.

"Good. Now, I hoped your dad would make it, but I don't think I have that long. Give him a hug for me and tell him that we'll see each other again one day."

"I will."

He took another long look at her, his face changing. All the weakness and frailty went out of that gaze. He smiled at her warmly, and she thought she saw a hint of blue light playing in his eyes. She blinked, thinking her mind was playing tricks on her. But no, there was a twinkle in those eyes she hadn't seen in years, and a storm of blue light roiled within them. He closed them then, and his body began to rise off the bed – only a few inches, but that was enough. Sparks of blue played down his arms and over his hands. Then he sank slowly back into the bed and took a last deep breath.

Outside, thunder rolled in the blue skies.

The Ballad of Cornman
by Colin Anderson

They were disgusting, yes, but the locusts were not dangerous. At least, not to people. Crops? That's a different story. Having arrived nearly three weeks ago, the locusts consumed nearly all the vegetation within a hundred-mile radius of town. While chaotic and concerning, the invasion hasn't caused significant panic yet. A rationing decree was enforced two weeks ago as a precautionary measure. Folks were hungry, but they were still eating. Trade has slowed down, largely due to merchants not wanting to brave the swarms. In the worst-case scenario, food reserves would still last at least six or seven months.

Most businesses and institutions were still running as normally as possible. Many provided makeshift solutions to allow patrons to spend as little time as possible outside, with an opportunity to de-bug before entering their establishments. Temporary vestibules built with tarps and fans enclosed nearly every building entrance in the village.

The village school was no exception, and it continued to operate through the bug situation. The clinks and clanks of locusts against the windows went unacknowledged, as they had since a few days after the insects' arrival. Everyone, including the students, quickly grew accustomed to the swarming pests. Morning class had just begun.

"There are no superheroes. They aren't real," Mrs. Cobb explained to the class as she walked desk to desk, demanding each student hand over their distracting comic books. She noticed the dejected faces and heard the growling stomachs before adding, "Well, not anymore."

Megan raised her hand. "What do you mean 'not anymore', Mrs. Cobb?"

"Yeah, what do you mean?" The rest of the class chimed in.

"Ok, ok, settle down. Maybe if everyone's good, we can talk about 'not anymore' at the end of class. We have a lot of material to cover on the agrarian revolution and not a lot of time to get through it. Everyone probably should have spent more time on their homework and less time with this stuff!" Mrs. Cobb waved the stack of confiscated media.

Irritated and impatient, Bobby interrupted, "We're not all gonna be farmers. All we learn about is farming, plant science, history of agriculture. I read comics because they are fun and aren't all about making vegetables."

"I get it. Everyone your age says the same thing." Mrs. Cobb replied in a tone practiced over the years, addressing the same complaints. "You'll never know when something you learn here will be important, but it will be." She paused. "Say, maybe, when a swarm of crop-eating insects comes to town. Everyone will have to pitch in to get crops growing again when the bugs leave. And if they don't leave… well, we'll have to be creative with what we know about plants and farming."

Bobby looked at the windows and shrugged. "Yeah, still," he trailed off without completing an argument. Ray and some of the others looked outside too and began murmuring concerns. Everyone already felt the possibilities of a dire future were becoming more and more likely every day the locusts stayed. Hearing their teacher say it out loud added more weight to the burden of reality.

Mrs. Cobb, worried she had upset the students with her assessment of what's happening outside, compromised. "I'll tell you what. If everyone promises to review the agrarian revolution chapters for homework tonight, so we can quickly review them tomorrow, we can talk about the 'not anymore' today."

The class perked up and unanimously agreed immediately. Mrs. Cobb activated the intercom microphone. "Mr. Brumsey, please send someone to my class with the story."

"It will be there in a moment." A solemn voice crackled through the speaker. "And… Thank you."

The teacher returned her attention to the class. "It's been a while since we've really needed to tell the story. With the way things are, though," she pointed to the windows, "it is time to read it and think about some of the things we've learned in class. Who will volunteer to read the story to everyone?"

After a few moments, Angie sheepishly raised her hand, the only student to do so. "Thank you, Angie. Please come on up, the story should be here in just a moment." Almost as soon as Mrs. Cobb said it, there was a knock on the door. She went to the door and accepted the delivery, then handed the small, leather-bound diary to Angie.

Angie unlatched a clasp on the book and opened it to the first page. She looked at the book, then looked to Mrs. Cobb, who gave an affirmative nod. "Remember, everyone, read your chapters tonight. Please, Angie, go ahead."

"Ok. Here we go." Angie confirmed before reading aloud.

Larrik, a faraway outpost
Sat nestled on the northern coast
But, for reasons unknown, dirt became stone
Seeds already sown were dried as a bone
The residents, alone, with no crops grown
Worry haunted thoughts as a ghost

Panic quickly descended
Unlikely to be mended,
"Pray," they said even as faith fled
"Save instead." remaining crumbs of bread
They followed the tread where hunger led
And found a legend where the trail ended...

This is the ballad of Cornman.

They finally began to recall
The sad story of old Larrik's fall
When the town was young, scarecrows were hung
Shovels were flung, covering seedlings with dung
Vegetation sprung, dinner bells rung
But, a villain came, ruining all

And then there came a terrible frost
All of the crops were tragically lost
The ferocious cold was unforetold
Magically bold, ancient, and old
Frozen black souled, demanding gold
Faminemancer exacted his cost

Townsfolk yearned to rid the cancer
Old Larrik's mad Faminemancer
No time to mourn, yet still forlorn

THE BALLAD OF CORNMAN

The sky torn and a hero born!
His suit of corn, used to adorn
Cornman gave prayers an answer

Is it nutritionally dense?
Not in the traditional sense.
Sure, it's not meat, but for those in the street
For workers on their feet, those who lie or cheat
Even the elite, all need food to eat
To repel hunger, corn was defense

As he descended from the sky
Cornman saw the dead gourds and rye
And the evil yob making the townsfolk sob
So he rammed a cob in the 'mancer's gob
No more curses to lob, no gold to rob
The Faminemancer and hunger die

Faithfully, they had thought
The salvation they sought
Surely would last, hunger in the past
Every curse cast, Cornman did blast
Much corn grew fast, which the townsfolk massed
Offsetting damage wrought

And with Cornman celebrated and praised
Crops were planted and successfully raised
With repaired ground, 'twas corn abound
Warmth did rebound, and commerce did sound
Yet townies frowned, Cornman wasn't found!
Yes, Cornman left, satisfied Larrik was maized

When things felt normal once more
Faminemancy became lore
Slowly, Cornman was forgotten with food begotten
Variety soughten as corn went spoiled rotten
Attention was caught in carrots, peas, even cotton!

Who could know what was in store

Who among the Larrik folk might truly say
What it meant, what it was, what they found this day?
Even if they could, was it understood?
In the wood under the canopy hood
They saw what should be their own force for good
Looking down where a skeleton of cob lay

But, once again, hope was reborn,
The memory of golden corn
Catching every mind of Larrik-kind
Faminemancy, the grind, how they resigned
How they would bind as a town so maligned
Enduring an era to mourn

Oh yes, a welcome hero came!
A time when problems were the same
For he did toil to fix their soil
Wouldn't recoil, he's hunger's foil
Larrik was loyal, Cornman was royal
Why have they forgotten his name?

There was what did remain
Of Faminemancer's bane
Laid piled, yet still beguiled
Townsfolk single-filed in the wild
Each softly smiled, happy as a child
Remembering how to ease their pain

They would understand
As Cornman planned
If they tried what Cornman did confide
If they had relied on their pride
Frozen or dried, soil could provide
and grow corn from the land

The return to town
As the sun went down
Would see spirits high, tears would dry
Steps were spry with salvation nigh
They would scry a successful try
Giving the king of crops back its crown

For they surely did begin
Conjuring magic within
Cornman's flare burned through the despair
Memories to share with each there
The skill thought rare, the will to care
Cornman's legacy is corn and kin

Angie closed the book and looked around. Her fellow students wore a look of confusion on their faces, a feeling she shared. The silence that permeated the room was soon greeted by a glow which grew more and more brilliant. The class looked to the windows, which were no longer crowded with locusts. A few bugs did linger, and many could be seen flying away. Sunlight replaced the dark swarms, and the windows let in the seemingly forgotten light. The students gathered around the windows and looked outside across sunlit fields they hadn't seen for so long.

"Mrs. Cobb, look!" Ray exclaimed, excited by the dissipating invaders. "The bugs are leaving! They are really leaving!" He looked to the teacher's desk and gasped.

The teacher's chair was spinning slowly to a stop. Upon it, sitting upright, was a bundle of corn stalks. Panic struck, and the students began screaming and crying. The intercom crackled. "Everyone, please be calm. You are all safe, and the bugs are gone now. Mrs. Cobb had to leave to get rid of the locusts. Please sit down at your desks. A substitute teacher will be there shortly to explain further."

Students obeyed and made their way back to their desks again, where their excited chatter slowly dwindled. As everyone sat in a shocked silence, Bobby wandered back to the window and watched the sparse remaining groups of locusts flying away. A hint of disappointment crept across his face as he placed his palm on the window. With his hand in place, a locust clinked onto the window and scurried to Bobby's finger, sensing him through the glass. Then, another. And six more. Bobby shook his head sadly. A locust crawled out of his sleeve and moved down his hand. He quickly redirected it back up his sleeve and cast glances around the room. Satisfied nobody witnessed his actions, he pulled his hand back from the window. The locusts on the window flew away a moment later.

Angie sat quietly contemplating the last month, the strange turn of recent events, and the seeming conclusion of sunlight. She opened the story again and flipped to the last lines she had read to the class. The story spanned six pages in a book with at least one hundred more. She flipped through the rest of the pages and found them all blank. She turned back to the last lines of the story and pulled a pen from her desk. Angie started writing on the next page.

A Faminemancer again arrived
Spewing locusts unhived
Skies grayed, sanity frayed
The town prayed to a hero who obeyed
A sacrifice made, the hero unswayed
And so into the void Cornman again dived

What could be next?
Are our people hexed?
Was famine beat? Did it retreat?
A hero's repeat? A foe's defeat?
A future to greet? A story complete?
Or another chapter indexed?

To Fly or Not to Fly
by Grigory Lukin

Lady Luck did a barrel roll right over our heads as we soaked up the warm September sun on the school's front steps.

"She. Is. So. Cool," Mike said as he stared in the direction she flew off.

"Yeah, well, anyone would be cool if they could fly," Sarah said, rolling her eyes.

"Not anyone," I cut in. "Do you remember Pterodactyle Pete?"

"The weird scientist guy?" Sarah scrunched her eyebrows.

Across the street, a bunch of kindergarteners played in the park. Must be a field trip day.

"Oh, yeah, I remember," Mike nodded. "The one that messed with his genes and came out all ugly."

"Yup, that's the one," I said. "He couldn't even get a TV show. I heard the League pays him to live underground now. He makes them look bad."

The three of us shook our heads, commiserating. Two blocks away, a couple of spandex-clad heroes leaned against the Starbucks wall, enjoying their free coffee.

"Wait. Is that...is that Frank Freedom?" Sarah said, her shaking hand pointing at the hero in a bright-red uniform with the golden "FF" logo on the chest.

"If that's him, then the other guy must be Mean Marine!" Mike said, his eyes wide.

"Should we go ask for their autographs?" I asked, just as star-struck as my best friends. When you're 13, this is literally the bestest thing that can happen to you.

"Nah," Mike said. "Let's just play it cool. If they see us acting like dumb groupies, there's no way we'll ever get into Super High."

Sarah and I made eye contact and shrugged, saying nothing. Across the street, the little kids started playing catch with a big blue ball.

No one really knew where the superheroes came from. Some said it was a great big secret government program. My crazy uncle Bob used to say it was all because of the nuclear power plant pollution, but then he got squished by a grand piano when Mad Musician started a street fight with Mighty Maestro. It was a closed-casket kind of funeral.

The only thing anyone could agree on was that almost everyone who attended Super High ended up with superpowers. Conspiracy theorists claimed there was something in their lunch food, some special "Compound S." Others said that powers could transfer through osmosis. Spend four years around superhero teachers, and some of that will rub off on you, too.

"What?" Mike said, finally noticing our silence. "We can absolutely get in. Just need to do more community service than anyone else, or intern as a sidekick, or..."

"Mike. Please. Stop." Sarah shook her head. "They admit less than one percent. You don't have what it takes. None of us do."

"Speak for yourself," Mike said, his face red as a tomato. "I just need 500 more hours of community service to be considered for the Bronze Tier. Or – hold on a minute," he said as he dug through his backpack for a bright but well-worn brochure. "Or do 'one truly selfless deed to help the world.'"

"What does that even mean?" Sarah asked.

"I think they mean something like rescuing kittens from high branches," I said. "Right?"

"Nah, Chris, stuck kittens are too cliché by now. Everyone's moved on." Mike chuckled. There was a kid – Bobby Smith – who tried to be clever about it, so he just threw the same kitten on high branches all weekend long, and then he'd 'rescue' it," Mike said, doing the air quotes with his fingers, "whenever someone walked by."

"That's...sociopathic," Sarah said slowly. "Tell me he didn't get into Super High with that?"

"No, eventually Cat Girl figured out what he was doing, and she scratched him up. A lot. Some kids said he got scars."

I gulped, trying to imagine the cat-obsessed antihero avenging that poor kitten.

"And he did all that just to get picked into Super High?" I asked.

"Worse," Sarah said. "For *just a chance* to get picked."

"Come on, though, wouldn't you take that chance if you could?" Mike said.

"I mean, just imagine… Flying around the city, fighting crime."

As if on cue, seven bright-colored heroes flew above us, their individual colors forming a rainbow.

"Whoooa," Sarah said. "The Rainbow Brigade! I've never seen them this clo–"

"Aiden, no!" A scream rang out from the park. We turned toward it, and…

It all happened at once. The big blue ball bouncing toward us. The laughing little kid – green shorts, pink shirt, unruly hair – running after the ball. Into the traffic.

I had no time to think. It felt like lightning, like some primal reaction deep in my brain.

Save.

Save the child.

Save him now.

Impetus, instinct, action. No thinking was involved.

I lunged toward the kid, who'd stopped right in the middle of the lane, unsure why his teacher had just screamed his name.

I reached him in two giant jumps, grabbed him by the shoulders, turned my back toward the approaching truck, braced myself, and…

The screech of tires. The smell of burning rubber. The strange sensation of something massive right behind me, an inch away from my back, as if a dragon had snuck up on you and stood there, waiting, contemplating.

The kid didn't die. I didn't die. This…this worked. My vision had contracted to a tiny cone, with the kid at its center, and now it slowly started getting back to normal. My hands shook.

Time snapped back to its usual pace, and that's when everybody started shouting.

"Aiden! Aiden, are you okay?"

"Miss Victoria, my ball!"

"Chris, dude, that was so cool!"

"Kid, what the hell do you think you're doing! My truck's AI woulda stopped just in time. Do you realize you coulda gotten yourself killed? You owe me new brakes."

"Look, everyone! It's Frank Freedom!"

The tall, athletic man, wearing tight, bright-red spandex with a flowing cape, descended from the sky, still holding onto his Starbucks cup. The famous FF logo glowed on his chest. His shoulder-length chestnut hair flowed in the wind.

"See, I told you it was him," Sarah whispered, her eyes as wide as saucers.

"And that's Mean Marine!" someone else yelled as a huge bearded guy wearing camo-colored spandex raced toward us with his super-speed, stopping right by his partner a few seconds later. His trademark machine gun was slung across his chest.

The street was getting crowded. I had no idea where all these people came from, but there they all were – on the sidewalk, in the park, gently pushing (or sometimes elbowing) each other out of the way to take a picture of their idols.

Frank Freedom and Mean Marine stepped between me and the kid. He was full-on crying now, his big green eyes staring at the heroes as snot ran down his face. He never did catch his ball.

The two men turned their backs on him as they smiled and waved at the cheering crowd. They ignored me, too, but I was just close enough to overhear their whispered conversation.

"This save is mine. I'm way behind on my quota this month. You know what Lucky does to underperformers."

"Frank, buddy, we're supposed to be partners. 50-50, remember?"

"If you don't back off, I'm going to laser you through the back of your dumb redneck head, right here and now. Do you think I'm bluffing? See if I'm bluffing."

"You're such an asshole," Mean Marine said as he spat on the ground and backed away.

Frank Freedom just smiled wider, waving with both hands as TV vans arrived and camera crews started setting up their equipment. He finally noticed me, still standing there in front of him, unable to move. My heart was beating like a colibri on cocaine, my hands were shaking, my mouth was dry like the Sahara, and my shirt was stuck to my sweaty back. Did I really just jump in front of a truck? And were they really...Holy crap, holy crap, holy crap.

"Get out of the camera shot, kid. And go see a medic or something. Tell them you've got a shock reaction. Now shoo," he said, still smiling, his perfect teeth glistening in sunlight like freshly fallen snow.

I still couldn't move. Was this real? Was any of this real?

"I said shoo," he repeated, and this time his blue eyes glowed red for just a fraction of a second. I ran.

Everything after that was a blur, with some labcoat people in the park poking and prodding me, giving me a soda and a bunch of candy, checking my blood sugar and heartbeat, and who knows what else. I couldn't make out half the stuff they were saying, so I just nodded and let them handle me. It all felt like a dream, so I kept dreaming and just went with the flow.

I was almost back to normal, reclining in the shade of a giant oak, when all the labcoat people stepped aside, making way for someone new. Someone important.

The tall woman was dressed in a gray skirt suit, and she walked confidently past the white-coated people, straight toward me. Instead of a tie, she wore a round obsidian talisman that accentuated her dark skin. I had no idea who she was, but I could just tell she had powers. You can tell by how confidently they all move, as if this world belonged to them. Maybe it did.

She strolled all the way up to me and kneeled on the grass, down to my eye level.

"Chris, do you know who I am?"

I shook my head, afraid to say anything. Was I in trouble? Was I in danger? Were the kid's parents going to sue me? Would I have to change my name? The sudden, scary questions overwhelmed me. I felt the familiar panic start to rise up. The stranger noticed none of that – or if she did, she chose to just ignore it.

"My name is Melissa, and I'm the chief legal liaison for the League." She smiled as she said that. A beautiful and practiced smile that didn't reach her eyes. "While that idiot out there is taking all the credit for the save," she pointed at Frank Freedom, still giving interviews, holding the now-laughing kid on his shoulders, "I want to make it clear we know it was you who saved that child. We saw the traffic camera footage."

She waited for some sort of reply. I nodded, too afraid to say anything at all. Uncle Bob had always said to stay quiet around lawyers.

"You're not in trouble." Another fake smile. An awkward pat on my shoulder, as if she were following some kind of instruction manual. "In fact, we think you have what it takes to join Super High. Exciting, right? Right?"

"Right."

"Right! So all we need you to do, Chris, is sign a couple of non-disclosure forms about today's incident, and then call this number, and we'll get you into our next class."

She reached into her jacket's inside pocket and took out a bunch of papers covered with tiny text on both sides. She also gave me a jet-black business card. The only thing on it was a phone number, printed in scarlet ink.

"So just sign here, here, here, initial here – no, don't bother reading, trust me – and you're all set!"

She took the papers and the pen back from me, stood up, gave one more big fake smile, and flew away with a little "whoosh."

"Whoooa. So cool," Mike and Sarah said in unison. I hadn't heard them approach.

"What did she talk to you about?" Sarah said.

"Nothing important," I lied, the business card clenched tight inside my fist. "Just a bunch of legal stuff from the League."

"So cool. So, so cool," Mike said, still looking at the trail the lawyer left in the sky.

"Anyway, I guess school is cancelled for today, huh?" I nodded at the hundreds of people surrounding Frank Freedom as he flexed and posed for the cameras. "Let's go get some ice cream."

"Great plan," Mike said.

"Awesome plan," Sarah agreed.

I let them lead the way as they laughed and argued about the best ice cream flavor. (Pistachio, obviously.)

Behind them, the afternoon wind ruffled the blades of the bright-green grass and carried away small pieces of jet-black paper.

Clap Back
by Jon Resnick

"Is there anything else you want me to get from the store today?" Theresa asked from our bed.

"Nah, I'm good," I said, slipping on my shirt. Looking myself over one last time in the mirror, I decided this was about as good as it'd get. "I'd say wait 'til the pharmacy calls and says her meds are ready. Avoid two trips, you know? If I think of anything else, I'll just text y-" I turned around and found quite the sight looking back at me.

My girlfriend was sitting against the headboard, her sleep shirt nowhere to be seen. The black comforter resting on her lap created a striking contrast to her porcelain skin and wavy, long blonde hair. Her seductive smile was quickly followed by a beckoning finger.

Don't have to tell me twice.

My hand grabbed the bottom of my shirt to rip it right the hell off, but my eyes caught the clock on the nightstand, and I groaned. If I didn't leave in the next five or six minutes, I'd miss the bus to work.

"No time, hun," I sighed, walking over to her. She playfully pouted as she pulled the comforter up to cover her breasts. I leaned in and gave her a passionate kiss, her hand finding the back of my head and pulling me in more.

When she pulled her lips from mine, her hand moved to my cheek and kept me close, her blue eyes staring into mine. "Are you gonna take the suit with you today?" She asked.

My head instantly dropped. "Why you gotta ruin the moment?"

I straightened back up and crossed my arms. I wasn't angry. Not at all. Just a little disappointed that she was bringing this up again.

"Because you make a difference when you're out there, babe," she said as I averted my eyes. "The people around here love 'The Nameless Hero of District

9.' Speaking of which, when are you gonna finally tell them your name is Clap-"

"I ain't using the name you came up with," I interrupted, my finger raised. "It's cringey as hell, and I was fine just being The Nameless Hero."

She rolled her eyes at me. "It's better than anything you came up wi- oh wait, that's right, you never came up with a name." Now it was my turn to roll my eyes.

"Anyways, people throughout the whole district talk about the people you've helped and even a few you've saved. Over in the alley near your bus stop, I even saw some graffiti art of you in a cool pose."

"Yeah...a few days ago, I walked past a few kids chilling on a stoop and one was bragging about how he saw me knock out a few guys who'd just held up the convenience store at Franklin and Southby," I admitted.

"See?" She asked excitedly. "You are a hero to the people here. You don't have to be as big as Valiant or the others, even though I think you could be."

I shook my head, and my gaze moved to the poster beside the window. On it, flying through the sky, was Valiant, leader of the Trinity–a hero that I, and every other man my age, have looked up to since he first came on the scene fifteen years ago.

"Look, I won't disagree with anything you said, other than the 'big as Valiant' part, because that shit's blasphemy–and I fully expect you to apologize to the poster at some point today–but I'm done, Theresa. I mean, the only reason I finally put on the suit a year ago is because you and my mom pushed me for so damn long to do it. I tried, but it ain't me. The only reason I didn't throw the suit out is because you two made it for me, and tossing it would be a dick move."

She deflated with my words.

"Look, at baseline, I'm a little stronger and a hell of a lot tougher than normal people. My powers could make me incredibly powerful, but it hurts me to get them going. Shit, the furthest I've ever charged them up was only to about nine or ten percent of what I think is my max. The idea of going much higher terrifies me. That's part one of why I gave up the whole hero thing." I held out my hand and stuck up my thumb.

"Part two," my index finger extended, "is that I don't want to lose my job. Since I put on that suit, I have constantly been late because I was out all night helping random people who were in trouble. If I get fired, it's just gonna be you working. My mom can't because of her condition, and you know we can't afford the rent and her medication on just one person's income. And do you know anyone who's hiring right now? Cause I don't. Especially not a twenty-year-old Black man with no college degree. And I've been looking for a second job for a year now. Even the guy working the drip over at On the Mark Coffee told me they won't hire anyone with anything less than a Bachelor's Degree. So, I'm damn lucky to be employed."

Theresa looked down at the bed, defeated.

I added another finger to the count. "Part three of why I gave it up is that I already did what every hero dreams of. I saved the world," I said.

She looked at me, confused, and I leaned my face toward hers again. "Because you are my world." Her face lit up, and I kissed her forehead goodbye. When I reached the bedroom door, I stopped and looked back. "Can I get one more for the road?" I asked with an impish grin.

Her eyes narrowed and her lips pursed, fighting a smile as she dropped the comforter to her lap again.

This is gonna be a good day.

"So...you're really firing me?"

This was the second time that I'd asked the question. Not because I hadn't heard the answer the first time, but because this happening right after I'd cut off a part of my life to focus more on my job, was just so damned ironic. *Maybe unfair would be a better word for it.*

Across the desk from me, Frank angled his head down and pinched the bridge of his nose. "Dom, again, yes. I'll send your last paycheck at the end of the week. Now take off. Let's not make this a thing."

I took a calming breath and placed my hands on the edge of the old wooden desk. "I'll admit," I began, "that my attendance hasn't been...ideal, but-"

"You're frequently late, exhausted, and half the time you look like you got the stupid beat out of you on your way to work!" The portly man snapped. For several seconds after, the only thing that broke the silence was the rickety ceiling fan spinning above us.

"When I'm here, I work harder than anyone else in this warehouse," I continued. "And these last two weeks, I've been on time, I've-I've stayed late, and helped the others meet their quotas. I mean, even today I-"

"I'll admit, you're good at what you do. Impressively so," Frank held up one hand to stop me while his other hand picked up a half-full glass of what I assumed was bourbon, going off the half-empty bottle on his filing cabinet. The sweat stain on the desk and the nearly melted ice cubes clinking in the glass were good indicators that this was not Frank's first pour.

"But that doesn't change the facts. You're unreliable, and I have no room here for someone like you." He drained what was left in the glass and set it back down.

I looked pleadingly at my boss. Maybe I should tell him the real reason why I had been late all those times. Why I always had fresh bruises on my face. And why it wouldn't happen again. But all that escaped my mouth was a pathetic, "Please... Frank, I need this job. You know why."

Frank stared at me, unmoving, for what seemed like an hour. The chair creaked in relief as he stood and waddled his rotund body toward the door. My heart sank further below the surface with every footfall and groan of the floor. He opened the door and pointed to the space beyond.

"The hell am I gonna do now?" I snatched another brick from the ground and threw it. The red missile whistled through the air for almost sixty yards before splashing into the bay.

My former employer was the only business still up and running within a mile of the docks, so abandoned factories and empty warehouses were the only witnesses to me launching bricks. At this point, even if someone did see me, I wouldn't care. As of two weeks ago, I didn't have a secret life to hide anymore. Right now, all that mattered was venting some frustration and clearing my head before I went home.

It took a few minutes–and almost forty bricks–before I calmed down enough to appreciate the final remnants of the pink and orange sky. The sun soon vanished beyond the horizon, and day transitioned to night. The lamps along the waterfront flickered to life, fighting back the darkness. A mile across the bay, the city lights all shone brightly and reflected across the undulating water.

With a heavy sigh and a slap to my cheeks, I decided it was time to head home and break the bad news. I slipped my hand back into my pocket and retrieved my phone to continue the job search I'd paused a little while ago.

I was serious when I told Theresa that no one in Mark City was hiring right now. Even if I did have a degree, the competition would be fierce with unemployment at an all-time high. It was doubtful that a hiring manager would count the month I'd spent at Mark City University, before having to drop out. But I didn't regret that decision. Family came first.

Unfortunately, that was a concept my Father never understood. He'd walked out on us when I was only eight, and Mom had to sacrifice everything to make sure I was taken care of. She worked two jobs and was always there when I needed her. So when the call came through that she'd collapsed at work and was in the hospital, I was at her bedside within minutes.

We thought we'd be okay, regardless of the horrible diagnosis, but then the bills came. Her insurance tried to get out of paying for her hospital stay, stating it hadn't been medically necessary. Then they refused to pay for the medication she would need every day for the rest of her life, telling us it was "still considered experimental" and "it didn't fall within her plan." Without those pills, she'd die. And it wouldn't be painless.

So I shifted gears without hesitation. I dropped out of school, and after months of interviews, I secured the warehouse job. Now, because of what I'd been doing in my off time, I was unemployed, and we were screwed.

I always told them it didn't pay to be a hero.

My thumb tapped the next icon on the job search, but an error message popped up.

[Unable to connect to the website. Signal lost.]

My phone had full bars only a second ago, and the waterfront wasn't near any dead zones, so why did-

The screen went black, and the phone died.

"Of course this piece of shi-" I trailed off, stopping in my tracks as the lamps died for as far as I could see. The distant sounds of car horns and crashes reached my ears. I walked to the edge of the walkway, and a cold wind blew in from the water and pierced through my jacket as I gripped the railing at the water's edge, watching the skyscrapers in Mark City go dark. The entire city had lost power. Even the lights on the suspension bridge were out, and nothing shone from the cars that had stopped on it.

My pulse accelerated, and the hair on my neck stood up as I took in the scene. "What the hell?"

Something major was happening. I could feel it in my bones. But, whatever it was, it wasn't my problem. I just wanted to get to the damn bus stop and, assuming the bus was still functional, go home to make sure Mom and Theresa were okay.

Even if I hadn't hung up the suit for good, this still wouldn't be my problem. Whatever was happening right now was probably way more than I could handle. This sort of thing was on the level of Valiant, or one of the other heroes in the Trinity. Not some low-level nobody like me.

Mom and Theresa were the only two people who knew my secret. Theresa discovered the truth the day we met back in junior high when I saved her life by diving into a lake and pulling her and her unconscious father free from a car that had sunk to the bottom. We've been inseparable ever since.

As I approached the edge of the grey industrial building that was once the Emerson Fishing Cannery, the sound of a car door slamming snapped me back to reality. Then came the sound of a panel van's side door sliding shut. It had been over a year since I'd seen anyone around these buildings, so this was unexpected, to say the least. Peeking around the edge of the building, my eyes went wide, and I instantly pulled myself back out of view, pressing my back tightly against the cracked bricks.

The men wore expensive black suits with a small red claw emblem over their hearts. Even if I hadn't recognized the outfits, their grey-tinged skin and glowing red eyes would have been a dead giveaway. The three henchmen walking into the building were enforcers of Maxis, one of the five most dangerous supervillains on the planet. He wasn't the strongest, not by a long shot, but the intellect and sadistic nature of the demonic creature and his cultists had cost several powerful heroes their lives over the last ten years.

What the hell are they doing here?

This was way above my pay grade. I needed to alert the authorities so they could contact the Trinity. There has to be a way to reach-

"Only a few more minutes until the slaughter begins. Are you all ready? Our lord awaits us." A gravelly voice said.

"To the beginning of a new world!" Another shouted, and they all cheered.

I froze in place as the door to the cannery squeaked shut behind them. I couldn't even breathe.

Maxis...is here? Slaughter?

The last time Maxis had surfaced was three years ago in Paris. The time before that was New York City, and Rio De Janeiro before that. Each time, a major city and the body count had been in the tens of thousands before he vanished again.

I stared at the darkened city in the distance. The one where Mom and Theresa were waiting for me at home.

"Oh no..."

Whatever was happening inside this building had just become something I couldn't walk away from. Even if it was a suicide mission.

It took only two minutes to find and scale the fire escape ladder to the roof of the old cannery. On my way up, I noticed that all the windows had been covered on the inside. Above me, with the light pollution from the city gone, stars dominated the night sky. It had been a long time since I'd seen them.

When I reached the top of the ladder, I carefully peered over the stone parapet and surveyed the roof. One enforcer was patrolling far on the other side. I'd almost missed him until he turned, two glowing red eyes cutting through the darkness. I ducked down and cursed. He hadn't reacted when he looked my way, so I didn't think he saw me. Which was good, because it was obvious the man was built like a brick shithouse.

Okay, so a minimum of four powered villains and one super villain, against a guy who's never fought anyone but unpowered street thugs. Should be a walk in the park.

Much slower than before, I peeked over the edge again. The enforcer was nowhere to be seen. The only things on the roof were rusted exhaust vents, rows of steam pipes running the length of the structure, and about three hundred feet away was an access shed. The door was slowly swinging shut.

With the coast clear, I hopped onto the rolled asphalt roof. Crouching low, I trotted between two long runs of pipe and headed toward the access shed. A short distance before my destination, I stopped. A light was shining up from the floor of the roof.

Wind blew against me as I high-stepped over an old steam pipe and crouched beside the skylight. Most of it had been covered by a black vinyl sheet, taped down at the edges–but a small corner had peeled back. Pulling it back a few inches further, I looked down into the building. Somehow, the entire interior of the old cannery still had power. Every light was on, illuminating the space. That was why they'd covered the windows. With every other building completely without power, this place would have become a beacon to every hero in the area.

Taking advantage of the opportunity, I tried to locate the four enforcers and-

A hand grabbed the back of my jacket and pulled. The air rushed by as I flew nearly thirty feet across the roof, crashing through several pipes. Metal shrieked as I collided with an exhaust vent, and the cold steel crumpled from the impact.

< 4% >

I collapsed to my hands and knees, shaking my head. "That sucked," I groaned.

Before I could collect myself, my attacker yanked me up to my feet and threw me back against the ruined vent. A fist flew forward, and I dove to the side as he punched straight through the steel, exactly where my head had been a millisecond prior. I stood up from my roll and faced the grey-skinned man, who was marching over with deadly intent.

Now, I wasn't a small man by any means. Excluding an inch of hair on top of my head, I stood six feet two inches and weighed a hair over two hundred pounds. So the fact that the guy coming my way made me feel small said a lot about him.

As soon as he was in range, I feinted a jab, slipped my head left, avoiding a punch, and landed a right counter squarely on the man's jaw. It felt like I'd just punched a brick wall, but I gritted my teeth and pressed on, throwing the strongest liver shot I could.

The punch found its mark, and the man grunted with the impact, but didn't drop back a single step. He didn't even look hurt. If anything, he just looked pissed. I moved to create some distance, a grey hand grabbed my jacket and wrenched me forward. The enforcer's forehead smashed into my own, and an ocean of twinkling lights exploded into existence.

< 10% >

The enforcer grunted as he twisted his body and, with one arm, swung me up over his head. The world inverted as I was slammed down onto the asphalt roof, the ground around me dented and cracked from the impact.

< 14% >

The wind was knocked out of me, and I lay there coughing. The enforcer laughed as he grabbed my jacket with both hands and lifted me to my feet.

As he did, I had three revelations.

The first was that these were the hardest hits I'd ever taken in a fight. It was no wonder powered people rarely used guns when they committed crimes. They didn't need them. This guy was strong as hell.

The second was that in just three hits, my power "battery" had already reached a higher charge than it ever had before. I stood there on wobbly legs, seemingly held up by the enforcer's grip on my jacket. He brought his right fist back and smiled.

"Wrong place and wrong time, kid," he said in a deep voice.

The fist shot forward like a missile, and a loud *crack* filled the air. His smile vanished as mine appeared, because the third thing I realized was that I was stronger than this asshole.

< 14% - 11% >

Heat flooded my body as I transferred the power from storage to active use.

My hand was wrapped around the fist I'd caught just inches before it hit my face. He tried to pull it back, but there was no give. My foot shot forward and connected with his crotch. Through my shin, I felt a crunching sensation as his testicles ruptured, and he released the grip he had on my jacket, stumbling backward and grabbing what was left of his manhood. It was time to end this.

< 11% - 0% >

My vision sharpened and the world slowed as my fists flew with inhuman speed, peppering his body with a storm of violence and shattering the bones in his face. He tried to defend at first, but after a few seconds, he fell to his knees, arms hanging limply. His one eye that could still open looked up at me, a furious red glow emanating from a face covered in blood.

"You're...already...too l-"

I threw one more punch, with every last bit of strength I still had from the charge, and his head whipped violently with the strike. He collapsed into a broken heap on the roof, and I knew that he wasn't going to get back up.

Pausing to swallow between heaving breaths, I whispered a quick, "Holy shit," trying to collect myself and mentally force my heart to slow the hell down. Revelling in the fact that I had just fought someone else with powers and won, would have to wait. Whatever these guys were up to needed to be stopped, and unfortunately, I was the only one who could do it.

But if I ran into another one of these bastards, I needed to have a charge built up ahead of time. Not establishing one before I scaled the fire escape ladder had been a stupid move on my part. But, in my defense, having to kick my own ass wasn't conducive to me wanting to use my powers. My body absorbed whatever kinetic energy and damage I received and multiplied it for me to send back at my opponents. Although if I ever received enough of a beating to achieve my full strength, I was pretty sure I'd die in the process.

As I walked toward the access shed, I knew that whatever charge I built up would vanish in about ten minutes. But it was better than going into this with nothing, so I started punching myself in the face. Hard.

< 3% >

A minute later, I was wiping blood from my lip as I crouched on the old, rusted catwalk, inspecting the scene. My brow furrowed. I didn't see Maxis or his enforcers. There was an old, broken-down conveyor system, a network of pipes and trash, and a few giant fire-tube boilers. I had expected to find stuff like that in the four-story building, but what I hadn't expected was the enormous machine in the middle.

It looked like a giant golden cylinder that stood nearly thirty feet tall. Three large, sharp mechanical talons came off the top. They angled out about ten feet and then pointed back in at the space just over the top of the machine. It reminded me of a grabber in the arcade game that picks up the stuffed animals.

Maybe if I can just sabotage that thing and then get the hell out of here, it'll buy enough time for the heroes to find this place.

I crept down to the ground floor much slower than I would have liked, but the damned walkways and narrow staircase creaked loudly if I didn't move with caution. While I couldn't see them, I knew there were some very dangerous people lurking around. Fighting those guys was firmly at the bottom of my to-do list.

My ears strained to catch any sound, but I caught nothing as I carefully navigated my way past a rusted steel boiler. The only sounds to be heard were my steps. A cold sweat started to bead across my forehead.

When I reached the golden cylinder, I gave it a quick once-over, looking for some way to sabotage it. I came up with nothing. This entire side was completely smooth, not a single access panel or blemish to the flawless metal structure, as if it had been moulded rather than built. Upon closer inspection, it didn't even look like metal. It almost looked organic.

I made sure I was still alone before circling to the far side. When I got there, I stumbled mid-step and looked at the horror before me. A large black circle full of runes was painted on the ground. In the middle of it, in a pile with their guts hanging out and looks of terror frozen onto their faces, lay the other three enforcers. A pool of blood was flowing away from the bodies and up the damn cylinder. As it ascended and was absorbed, red runes began to emerge and glow on the device. A heavy pulse vibrated away from the golden device, and the three metal talons on top began to spin around it. Small red arcs of electricity began dancing along them. A low hum filled the air, growing louder at an alarming rate.

"It took you long enough to commme downstairs. I was getting tired of waiting."

I froze, and my heart thundered at the sound of his grating voice. The *tap-tap-tap* of his shoes echoed throughout the building as he approached from behind me. The pressure he exuded was insane. Raw power and blood lust. My legs trembled as his aura pressed me toward the ground, but I steeled myself and spun around.

There was no one there.

"Youuuu actually, managed to move with that muccchhhh pressure upon you. Most people collapse on the spot, and some even die when they ffffeel my aura," Maxis hissed from only inches behind me. The heat of his breath coated my neck. I spun again, but he was ten feet away, sitting on the edge of a conveyor, one leg crossed over the other.

I'd seen images of him online before, and even those had been enough to send shivers down my spine. But here he was, in the crimson flesh. He didn't look as muscular as me, but I knew his strength eclipsed my own. The expensive suit he wore was as black as his hair and eyes. Three short black horns protruded from his forehead, and sharply clawed fingers stroked his goatee as he examined me. The man looked like Satan himself.

"I'mmm a man who believes in rewards and opportunitiesss," he said. "You're reward for overcoming the weight of myyy presence is the opportunity to live long enough to witness the barrier fall."

My heart was beating so hard now that I thought it might shatter my ribs. I had to get the fuck out of here. But instead of doing the sane thing and running, I asked, "What barrier?" I gulped as his smile grew.

"The one between worldsss. The more than fifty thousand soulsss I have collected now power this device, allowing my god and his kind to finally enter this world. Your speciesss shall fall."

My eyes darted to the cylinder that was almost entirely covered by glowing runes, and back to the demon before me. "The Trinity will stop you."

"They are following a falssse lead that I am about to commit mass murder in London. Valient has already begun his return, but even he won't be able to fly back before it's too late."

I brought my fists up as I slid a foot back.

< 3%- 0% >

I felt the power surge into my muscles as I declared, "Then I'm gonna take you down."

A heavy sigh left Maxis as he shook his head. "So you have chosennn... death." The conveyor he was sitting on shrieked and warped into twisted fragments of metal as he shot forward. I didn't even have time to block before his palm slammed into my chest. It felt like I'd been struck by a sledgehammer that got shot out of a cannon, and at least one rib broke. I rocketed backward like a missile, howling as I tore into and through an empty boiler, only stopping when I crashed into a brick wall. A pathetic cry flew from my mouth, and I fell to the floor, chunks of broken brick raining down on top of me.

< 36% >

The hum of the machine suddenly became a high-pitched screech. I looked and saw the talons had become a blur of motion and blood red light. A terrific *boom* rang out, shaking the building as a red beam shot up and ripped off half of the cannery's roof. High above, the beam slammed into an invisible ceiling. And then it tore that ceiling apart.

A hole in reality was ripped open, and what I saw on the other side of the rift could only be described as hell. A world of fire and death. Demonic creatures and mutants crawling over rocks and corpses. An orgy of violence and blood. There was only chaos, except for the one giant being who wore a crown of flames. Its six yellow eyes gazed down hungrily upon our world, and it smiled.

"Ssstill alive? I guess I shouldn't have held back."

My head snapped away from the approaching apocalypse and toward Maxis, who was holding a five-ton steel boiler over his head.

< 36% - 0%>

I pressed off the ground, high into the air with an explosive pushup, wincing in pain and watching the boiler slam through the wall where I'd been only a moment before. When I hit the ground, I dashed in. Maxis' smile grew, and he held his hands out wide. I gritted through the discomfort of a broken rib and unleashed a barrage of punches, hitting every vital point and knockout trigger I'd ever learned in my years of boxing. Maxis never stopped smiling. Never took a step back. He just stood there and took it while my power slowly depleted.

I threw another left hook, but before I could pull it back, he grabbed my wrist and tsked his tongue disapprovingly. "You are strong, annnd quite brave, but it seemsss you're out of time." With a sharp twist of his hand, both bones in my forearm snapped.

< 37% >

A horrific scream filled the air as he grabbed my face with his other hand and pulled me toward him, driving a knee into my stomach. I coughed up blood into his palm, just before he threw me skyward.

< 68% >

Before I reached the shattered roof, two fists slammed down into my back, and I felt several more ribs break. I blasted back down, and Maxis appeared below me again. A clawed hand opened, palm to the sky. Five razor-sharp claws plunged into my stomach and out from my back.

< 90%- 97% >

He gripped my hair with one hand and ripped his other free. Blood splattered across the concrete as he cast me aside, laughing. I watched him walk back toward his machine. He took a handkerchief from his suit and wiped the blood from his hands. The same blood that was pooling around me right now. The same blood I was coughing up.

Above me, winged beasts flew out of the rift and toward the city. The being with a crown of flames was nearing the gateway between worlds. And without a doubt, that beast was the size of the damn city. There would be no survivors if it got through. I couldn't let it end like this.

Images of Mom and Theresa flooded my mind, and the corners of my lips pulled up. This must be what they mean when they say your life flashes before your eyes right before you die. I knew that's what was happening because they were my life. My eyes shut, and my fists closed. I had to get home. I had to make sure Mom took her medicine. I still had to marry Theresa, god damnit!

I roared as I forced myself to roll over and onto my hands and knees. Blood flowed from the holes in my stomach and splashed the ground as I slammed my forehead onto the concrete.

< 98% >

"It seemsss you've lost your mind in these final moments." Maxis cackled, seeing what I was doing.

"No." I slammed down again.

< 99% >

"Is it the despairrr? Knowing that everyone you love is about to be a sacrificcccce."

"No!" I shouted, slamming down again.

< 100% >

"Then what's with the mmmasssichism?" He asked.

I yelled as I struggled to stand. Every movement sparked a new wave of pain. Every breath was agony. But I gritted my teeth and took a wobbly fighter's stance. Maxis laughed uncontrollably and pointed at me. Then he held his arms out. "I'll give you one final try. But before you die, just wwwwalking over here, perhaps tell me your nnnname. You put on quite the show."

"My name..." I could barely stay standing. Everything was turning black at the edges of my vision. And I was cold. God, I was so cold.

"Yesss?"

"Is Clap Back."

< 100% -0% >

The concrete shattered, and the air around me exploded outward as I shot forward. Maxis' eyes didn't have time to widen from the shock before my right fist crashed into his pointed chin like a meteor. His jaw shattered beneath my might, and it sounded like a shotgun as he exploded backward, crashing into his machine. His body was embedded so deeply in the cylinder that only his legs stuck out. They locked out and spasmed as red arcs of electricity consumed him, smoke pouring from the hole he'd made.

The golden machine shook violently and exploded. The shockwave slammed into me, and I crashed through the brick wall of the cannery and straight through the next two buildings beside it, before I rolled to a stop in the middle of an empty alley.

Above me, just as the king of demons reached the rift, the gateway between worlds snapped shut, trapping him on the other side. My vision was fading. I focused on having my final thoughts be about Theresa, but they ended up being about something else. A sound from high above me. It sounded like a sonic boom.

"Dom? He's waking up!" Theresa said, her voice pulling me closer to consciousness. I felt her hand rest over mine as people walked closer to me.

My eyes cracked open, and everything was blurry. I could tell there were a few figures near me, and some lights above. I felt drugged, and everything hurt like hell.

Am I supposed to hurt this badly if I'm dead?

"Sweety, can you hear me?" My mom asked.

My vision finally focused, but what I was seeing didn't make sense. Well, part of it didn't. The parts that did make sense were the hospital room, a dozen tubes and electrical wires connected to me, and Mom and Theresa standing on opposite sides of my bed. What didn't make sense was the figure standing beside my girlfriend. Wearing a black and red caped suit was Earth's mightiest hero, Valiant.

My eyes shot open wide, and I tried to sit up, but instantly regretted it as pain rocked my body. Theresa's hand found my shoulder and gently pressed me back.

"You need to rest, baby," Mom said, stroking her fingers across my forehead. She looked happy, but also sad for some reason.

"Dom," Theresa started, but stopped as tears ran down her face.

I'm alive, so why are you two so emotional?

Valiant must have registered my confusion because he said, "Their reactions are understandable, son. You were gravely wounded, and your heart stopped twice on the operating table. If I had been even a minute slower getting you here, they wouldn't have been able to save you."

His words hit me like a truck. I had died. Twice.

"After I saw to it that you were in good hands, I returned to the docks and figured out what happened. Dom, two weeks ago, you saved every single life in this world from a force that even I would have been powerless to stop. You have my thanks." He put a hand across his waist and bowed to me.

My head dropped back into the pillow. *Two weeks? I've been out for two fucking weeks?!*

"The public has been demanding to know who saved them. All I've said is that it was a hero of the highest caliber."

I shook my head in disbelief. This was all too much. My brutal fight with Maxis, dying, and the hero I'd looked up to since kindergarten just bowed to me. It took a few minutes, but I finally started coming to terms with everything. Then Valiant handed me a folded piece of paper.

"When they let you out, I would be honored to have you fighting by my side. What do you say? Will you join the Trinity in protecting this world?"

I lay there blinking for several seconds. At first, I thought I'd misheard him because I was still submerged in a fog of pain medications, but when I glanced at Theresa and Mom and saw their expressions, I knew I hadn't.

Theresa looked shocked at first, but then her lips pressed into a firm, nervous line. Her eyes met mine and practically screamed for me to decline the offer. Mom looked like she was about to launch over the bed and strangle Valiant. Which I got, because her only child had cheated death and was an absolute mess right now. But this wasn't their decision to make. It was mine. My path to walk and my burden to bear. And when I thought back to that grinning red asshole looking down on me, I didn't feel afraid. I felt like I needed to fight. Because monsters like him were out there, and I had the power to do something about that.

But in the end, it all came down to one thing. I looked back at Valiant and asked in a hoarse voice, "You guys offer a good family medical plan?"

Five Gold Rings
by Nicholas Samuel Stember

The creatures were in many shapes, some in the form of wild dogs, some as big as lions, or hippos, and there were even some which looked human…in a way…if they weren't all made up of pure electricity. They crackled and sparked as they rampaged through the city, blowing out windows and destroying vehicles and anything else that got in their path.

But still, the five members of Honor Wing fought on. Unlimited Power was in the lead with his blue cape billowing behind him, impervious to damage and super strong. At his side was Nuker, who could store energy of any sort and redirect it back to the source, which was precisely what he was doing to these electrical constructs. Zoomer was racing at super-speed, grabbing innocents who had been caught when this supervillain and her army appeared out of the vortex, which had just popped into the sky out of nowhere. She was struggling to make sure no one got hurt, and so far, she'd been mostly successful.

On the roof of one of the nearby apartment buildings, the last two members of the team had other concerns.

"Just let me help!" the youngest member of the team pleaded, but her words weren't swaying the older woman with large bird eyes and a costume to match.

"Zaplet," Thunderwren said, trying to calm down the teenager, "you've been doing fine against normal criminals, but these are something else, something we don't understand yet. We have no history with this villain and her constructs, who literally appeared out of nowhere."

"I'm calling her the Electrocution Woman," Zoomer said as she suddenly sped by them and vaulted into the air, easily clearing the distance to the next building over to save another bystander.

"I can handle these guys," the teen insisted. "My powers are electrical-based too!"

"And they haven't come in fully yet. You can create a few sparks, and it helps fighting against normal criminals…*normal* criminals, Zaplet."

"Stop calling me that!" she said as she folded her arms in a huff. "I want to be called Taser."

"A taser has the power to completely stop a foe," Unlimited Power said from high above them as he flew overhead and caught a huge chunk of the building next to theirs, preventing it from crushing them. "You're not quite there yet, Zaplet."

"Thanks, Power," Thunderwren said with an exasperated smile.

"Look, kid," the leader said while still floating above the pair. "We're just trying to protect you. One day you'll be a full-fledged member of Honor Wing, but for now, you're a sidekick and you do what we say, especially when Thunderwren says it."

"Why?"

"You know damn well why, young lady," Thunderwren said, her voice growing stern.

"Sorry to break this up, Wren," Unlimited Power said, "but we kinda need you down there. We're getting a handle on dissipating these electrical things, but still no sign of the supervillain. Saw her as we approached, but she must be hiding."

"Electrocution Woman," Zaplet said, the pout on her face still pronounced.

"Heh, I like it. Let's go, Wren."

"You stay here, out of trouble," Thunderwren said, this time quieter but still firm. "I know we just got here, but I feel like we've been fighting this battle forever. I'm exhausted and my patience is done, understood?"

The teen glanced down at her sapphire blue costume with a white spark pattern all over it, her voice growing quiet as well. "Yes…mom."

Unlimited Power swooped down and grabbed Thunderwren, and threw her into the air. She spread out her arms and wings formed as they both rejoined the fray.

Zaplet stood silently for a moment after they both were gone, listening to the sounds of the battle in the streets below. She knew her mother and the rest would win the day, they always did. No matter what villain popped up in the city, the Honor Wing's four members had always been there, and now that she was old enough and some of her own powers were beginning to emerge, they had allowed her to start to tag along, but this was her first supervillain.

She looked up over the commerce building at the large black and purple vortex, which was brimming with lightning and dark clouds that hadn't changed since it appeared, turning the bright summer afternoon into a veritable night. She carefully crept to the edge of the roof and glanced over, looking for her mother and the others. They weren't hard to find as they raced around the streets and above, using metal rods to short out the electrical creatures. So engrossed was she in watching them, she didn't hear the crackling behind her until it was almost upon her.

Spinning around, she saw one of the creatures…all white light and black eyes. It stood like a person, but it was pure energy, and it was coming right at her. Quickly, she raised her hands, and a shower of sparks erupted from her fingertips into the thing, but it easily absorbed the electrical output and was about to grab her when she felt a rush of air. Suddenly, she was moving fast off the roof and down to the alley below, as Zoomer let her go and shook her head.

"You've got to pay better attention, kid!" Then she was off again, leaving her alone between the two buildings.

For a moment, Zaplet just tried to calm her breathing as she silently berated herself for not paying better attention. She never liked being carried fast by Zoomer, and she was glad she didn't throw up…this time.

The wind was howling from the dark clouds above, and she had to steady herself as she watched objects flying back and forth in the street near her.

"I've got a bead on her!" she heard Unlimited Power's strong voice above the gale.

Zaplet glanced up, shielding her eyes as she tried to see what was going on, then she saw them. Unlimited Power high up in the air, facing off against a woman floating near the void, shrouded in dark electrical energy. He flew straight into her in his usual power move and Zaplet was sure that would be the end of it, but he vanished into the dark energy around her body for a moment, then came shooting back out the way he came, all covered in a violent static charge as he gave out a yell and went plummeting down behind another building. She saw a blur as Zoomer went after him to make sure he was alright.

Then she heard a booming yell and knew Nuker was up there too.

"Let's see you do that to me, Electrocution Woman!" and he leaped up to her, also vanishing into the darkness…then coming back out the same way Unlimited Power had, flailing wildly and going down rapidly.

She saw her mother swoop down after him to save him from the fall. Then glanced back up into the dark skies to see where the supervillain went, but there was no sign of her dark energy.

"Electrocution Woman is a dumb name," came a voice from behind Zaplet, her tone crackled and distorted.

Zaplet whirled and saw the supervillain ten feet behind her, floating off the ground. She tried to make out her face, but there was so much dark energy and electricity erupting around her, she couldn't make out much. However, her attention was drawn to her right hand, where she noticed each finger and her thumb had a glowing gold ring. They were mesmerizing.

The supervillain noticed the teen's attention and looked at her own hand. "I know, they are hard to resist. One ring was great, and two was more than enough, but I had to go and put on all five."

Zaplet didn't really know what to do; she knew she couldn't hurt this person. She wanted to yell for her team, her mother, but she was certain they were on their way and would save her at the last minute.

The wind was howling, the sounds of thunder were growing, and it was hard to make out Electrocution Woman's voice, but there was a sudden tone of worry in it.

"I'm not joking about the rings, Sandy, you have to listen to me this time!"

Zaplet's eyes blinked a few times. "How do you know my name?"

"You can't—" the supervillain started to explain, then an explosion above them cut her off as lightning hit a generator, and it sent a huge chunk of stonework down at them, straight above Zaplet.

"Dammit!" Electrocution Woman cursed, then dove right at her and shoved her back hard, just as the masonry came down in a crash, burying the supervillain.

Zaplet got back up from where she had been knocked down and coughed a few times, her body tingling from the electrical shove. Then she stumbled back to where the rubble was, searching for some sign of her unexpected savior. But all she uncovered was Electrocution Woman's right arm, which was broken and coated in blood and dust.

She heard the faintest of whispers from under the debris. "One...ring... two...at most." The voice died out, and the arm began to fade away to nothing, just as the dark clouds broke up above her and the late afternoon sun returned. Other than the destruction from the fight, all evidence of Electrocution Woman and her minions was gone. That...and the five gold rings lying on the debris.

Zaplet stared at them for a moment. Now that the person wearing them was no longer there, they stopped glowing and just looked like five plain gold bands. She picked them up, unsure at first what to do about them. What had Electrocution Woman meant with her cryptic warning?

She stared at them a bit longer, unsure what to do, then an impulse came over her and she took off her right glove and slid one of the rings on. It was warm and tingled, and she felt great. It was an indescribable sensation, almost like being wrapped in a hug which gave you confidence.

"Are you alright?" she heard Unlimited Power's voice from above.

Without thinking, she slipped her right glove back on and put the other four rings into her belt pouch.

"I'm fine, never better."

Her mother swooped down as she grabbed her daughter in her arms and hugged her tight, just as Zoomer raced up to them, followed by Nuker.

"I'm sorry I left you here," Zoomer said, her eyes showing her concern beneath her mask. "I had no idea this is where she'd go."

"It's okay," Zaplet said as she smiled at them all. "Really, not much happened. She appeared behind me and gave me a shove, and then was crushed by the falling building parts. I think she vanished when she died."

"A shove?" her mother asked as she inspected her.

"Mom, I think she was saving me. It could have been me under that pile of concrete."

The four members of Honor Wing stared at her in surprise.

"An honorable end to a villain," Nuker said as he nodded somberly. "Possibly hurting a child was where she drew the line."

"Possibly," Unlimited Power agreed. "I wish we knew more about who she was or where she came from, but our job is far from over for the day. The main villain and her minions are gone, but there are people to rescue and looters to stop from taking advantage of this chaos until the police and emergency services can get everything under control." He smiled at Zaplet. "You up to helping?"

His smile was so genuine that Zaplet decided to ignore the 'hurting a child' comment and nodded. "You bet."

Soon, the five of them were racing around the blasted city streets. The fight had been extreme, but hadn't spread more than five blocks from the vortex, which had vanished as quickly as it had appeared. At first, they worked together, but soon they encountered enough people in distress that they had to start splitting up. The last two to separate were Thunderwren and her daughter, who gave each other a smile and split up in a bank as they looked for people in trouble.

Zaplet found a couple who had become trapped in the stairwell, which had partially crumbled. She had been hoping for a chance to prove herself, and since the incident, she felt nothing but courage. In fact, she felt stronger than ever, and when she noticed one of the two had a pinned leg under a beam, she thought of slicing it with her sparkles, and was rewarded with a lightning arc which shot from her fingertips and blasted the concrete around the beam and allowed the person she was helping to escape.

For a moment, she stared at her own hand in shock, then a big smile began to spread across her lips.

It was then she heard a faint cry for help and some banging back in the main lobby of the bank. She made sure the couple was alright and ran back into the main room and was drawn to the vault. The door was half crumpled in, and there was a gap where she could see through into the vault at the five who were inside. They were hurt, and one was bleeding badly.

"We need a doctor, fast," one of the injured men called out.

Zaplet bit her lower lip in determination and tried her newfound stronger electricity to blast the molding of the door, but though it was stronger than ever before, it wasn't nearly enough. She glanced around quickly for help, but her mother and the others were nowhere to be seen, leaving her to deal with it herself.

One ring was great, and two was more than enough…

Zaplet remembered Electrocution Woman's words and nodded. Quickly taking off her right glove, she opened her pouch and grabbed a second of the gold rings and slipped it onto another finger. Instantly, she was rewarded with an even greater surge of power through her body, which crackled and sparked as little wisps of static power coursed along her limbs. She slipped her glove back on, and that's when she realized she was floating a foot off the ground.

"I'm flying…" she half said to herself, suddenly giddy. "I'm actually flying."

"That's great, but she still needs your help," the man in the vault angrily pleaded.

"Of course," Zaplet said with renewed determination and flew over to the vault door and grabbed it, and felt her strength surge. Sparks of electricity flowed along her arms, and her eyes began to glow white as she slowly, with great effort, pulled the door back and back until it fell off the broken hinges, freeing the bank employees.

They let out a cheer, and Zaplet had to try to contain her zeal as she looked behind her and saw her mother standing at the door of the bank, her mouth open in shock.

"San…Zaplet," her mother said. "What the heck?"

For some reason, she still didn't want to reveal the rings yet. Her mother was overly cautious, and she knew she'd want Unlimited Power to take the rings and secure them away in their base vault, where all the trinkets from past villains were kept.

"I don't know…Thunderwren, I guess my powers are finally coming in."

"Indeed, they are," Zoomer agreed as she suddenly appeared next to Thunderwren.

"We'll have to have a team meeting about this later," her mother said with a deep breath, "but for now, maybe you should return to base, and we'll finish up here."

"Why?" Zaplet said, her great mood suddenly soured. "I'm finally being a real member of this team, and you want me to stop?"

"No," Thunderwren said, her voice growing stern. "I want us to better understand your newfound powers and make sure you don't hurt yourself."

The explosion outside cut off any retort she had. All three of them raced outside as an ambulance arrived, and Zaplet pointed the EMTs to the vault.

They saw the explosion originated from the gas station at the end of the block, which had gone up in a ball of flame, and they could hear screams from inside the building.

Zoomer was there in a second, racing around the flames looking for people to pull out of the inferno.

"I'll get Power and Nuker," Thunderwren instructed. "You stay here and wait for us." In a flash, her arms were wings again as she took off in a run, vaulting herself into the sky to take to the air.

She knew she was supposed to stay put, but her zeal resurged, and she started to run towards the gas station, realizing she had taken to the air again, flying along a streak of electricity. She rose up over the flames and could see Zoomer running around inside the burning building…but suddenly she stopped. There had been a crash of some sort inside, and Zoomer was gone, out of sight.

For a moment, Zaplet blinked a few times, as a vision suddenly flashed in her mind. A premonition of Zoomer trapped in the basement…and suddenly her mother was there too, trying to free Zoomer…but the vision was gone in an instant.

"Wait…come back," she pleaded, trying to concentrate, hoping the vision would come back as her enthusiasm melted to panic. "What do I do? I need to see what happens…"

Suddenly deciding, she ripped off her glove and grabbed the remaining three rings and slipped one more on. The premonition returned, this time getting clearer, her mother was trapped in there too, but she couldn't see what happened next.

Another ring went on, and this time she could hear her mother screaming for help in the premonition.

Then she caught sight of her real mother flying in towards the blaze, heading straight in to save Zoomer, and vanished into the flames.

"Mom, NO!" she yelled, and knew she had to save her as panic took over.

She slipped the fifth gold ring on, and her body exploded in a flash of power and energy as she was enveloped by a dark field of lightning and storms. Suddenly, there was a crash in the sky, and the dark vortex reappeared where it had been before, and she felt herself pulled towards it uncontrollably.

"Mom!" she screamed as she fell into the raw power of the electricity and was enveloped by it.

Everything turned black, her body tingling and stinging all over. When she finally came too, she was hovering in the air next to the vortex, but something was wrong. All the damage which had been done by the fighting was gone. The city looked perfect.

That's when she spotted them. The five members of Honor Wing coming in fast.

Five...

She tried to scream, and instead electricity began jumping off her, forming into creatures made of pure energy; animals, people, things, all from her. The more she screamed, the more creatures she produced. Soon, they were spreading out, attacking the city.

"No, no, no," she tried to yell, but none of this made any sense...until she looked at her hand with the five glowing rings, and suddenly it did. She tried to frantically pull the rings off, but no matter how she tried, they wouldn't budge.

She looked down from behind the vortex and saw herself arguing with her mother on the rooftop.

"I have to stop her...have to stop this from happening again."

'I know we just got here, but I feel like we've been fighting this battle forever...' Her mother's words came back to her.

"Oh God," she whispered, "how long have we been doing this?" Then she glanced back at the roof and saw Zoomer saving Zaplet and taking her down to the alley. "I have to stop me...have to stop me NOW!"

She was about to fly down when Unlimited Power struck, though she tried to warn him. Soon he was tossed away, and Nuker right after. Then she mustered up all her strength and quickly went down to the alley to face herself, certain that this time she could convince herself not to use the rings.

Well...not all of them at least. Maybe one or two would be alright.

Villain Emeritus
by Ross Tuohy

The warm, lilting notes of Bach's Cello Suite No. 1 in G Major drifted through the palatial dining room. Doctor Stephen Werner pulled a chair from beneath the huge black oak table and eased his wife down into the seat. She wore an emerald green dress that flowed over her pale shoulders and down to the floor; the material bunched around her pronounced baby bump. An intricate plate of her long black hair hung down the centre of her back with a huge crystal hair clip in the shape of a butterfly at the bottom.

The Doctor kissed the top of her head and brushed his fingers down her arms.

"Tonight, my dear Carmen, we have roast duck in plum sauce alongside creamed potatoes and buttered spinach." He reached into the pocket of his jacket and activated a remote control.

A small pool of shimmering blue-white light appeared in the centre of her place setting, and a plate of exquisite food rose from the centre alongside two bottles of fine French wine.

"Non-alcoholic, of course."

"Of course." Carmen giggled.

She clapped her hands in delight and turned her face up to kiss the underside of his chin. The Doctor smiled and returned the kiss.

"This reminds me of our first date," said Carmen. "Our anniversary isn't for months. What are we celebrating?"

"All in good time, my love." He replied, then sat across from her and conjured his own plate. The Doctor picked up a silver knife and fork and was about to make the first cut when a far-off boom of thunder drew his attention to the window.

"He's early," sighed the Doctor. He crossed his cutlery over the top of his plate and looked towards his wife.

"Stephen?" she asked, her first forkful of food already halfway to her mouth.

"I have some business matters to attend to, love."

Carmen paled.

"It's him, isn't it?"

"I'm afraid so. I do wish he'd keep to MY time once in a while. Is a man not allowed a moment's peace?"

Carmen threw down her fork, which bounced off her plate with a clatter and sailed into the centre of the table. Her neck and face were already red with anger.

"Why won't he leave us alone?!" she hissed, hot tears sprang into her eyes, and she slammed a fist against the tabletop.

"Darling, darling, shh, shh, it's alright, don't upset yourself."

"Oh, to hell with upset, I'll kill him myself!" she spat. "Can't he see your inventions are doing a far better job than he ever could?"

"I know love, I know." He sighed. "I hate to see you like this, but we have little time. You know how he-"

The world exploded before he could finish his sentence. With desperate speed, he pressed the remote control, opening a portal, and pushed his wife's chair backward into the void, then closed the entrance.

The immense window of his dining room that had once overlooked a rather splendid view of the Lake District now lay shattered across the plush carpeted floor in a thousand pieces. A cool night breeze rippled through the shredded remnants of the curtains. The long table of polished black oak was now fit for nothing but firewood, wrapped in a torn and stained tablecloth of what had been the finest Egyptian cotton. Chairs littered the wreckage in all manner of odd positions.

He righted his own chair and sat back down. He pressed the button again, and a fresh cup of tea appeared in his hand.

The Doctor sipped it. The warm liquid trickled down his throat, and his shoulders settled back in his chair. Despite the devastation, a wave of calm swept over him.

He sipped his tea again and paid no mind to the pieces of glass perched on the shoulders of his jacket. His small brown eyes flickered toward the source of the destruction.

A statuesque figure of a man, tall, bronze, and blonde with eyes of the deepest blue, floated before him. He hovered a few inches off the floor and seemed to balance on an invisible pedestal that accentuated his Herculean features. He bore a stylised Lion crest across his leather-clad chest. Its noble face seemed to invite both scorn and challenge. It carried a sword in one mighty paw and a spear in the other. A long white cape trimmed with red spilled across his shoulders and down to the middle of his back.

Major Tom.

Even the name was ridiculous. A David Bowie reference? The man before him was meant to be a symbol to light the way into Britain's new golden age in the super-heroic arms race. Instead, he was nothing but a propaganda tool. A cardboard cutout blessed with the power to juggle the moon.

Laughable.

The Doctor set the cup down on the floor next to him and fixed the floating man with a rather disinterested glare.

"Sit please," he said. "Would you care for some tea or coffee?"

"Neither," the hero replied.

"Something stronger perhaps?"

"No!" The single word reverberated around the room, but the Doctor's expression did not change.

His hand motioned toward one of the upturned chairs on the far side of the room.

"I'd rather not," replied Major Tom. The once-perfect quaff of the hero's slick blonde hair was now peppered with dust and flecks of debris.

"SIT! Daniel."

The major's eyes widened, "What did you say?"

"Daniel Hawthorne. That's your name, isn't it? Your real name, not that jingoistic nom de guerre the Ministry of Defence christened you with."

The Major sagged for a moment, and the hem of his cape brushed the floor.

"How did you -?"

"Royal Marines Corporal Daniel James Hawthorne, born to Lisa and Brian Hawthorne of Solihull, England, February 6th, 1997, older brother Dexter, younger sister Alice. Enough pretence, Tom. I am telling you to sit down so we may have a frank and honest discussion."

The Major bristled, his hands curling into fists to keep them from shaking. He flipped a chair upright, swept off the layer of dust, and sat down.

"At last," the Doctor said with a long sigh. His eyes lingered on the space where his wife had sat, "She's pregnant, you know." He suppressed a bark of a laugh, "What am I saying? Of course you know".

"Five months?" asked Major Tom.

"Six." The Doctor picked up the cup and sipped his tea again.

"Congratulations," said Major Tom.

"Thank you very much," said the Doctor.

"She should not experience any undue stress, and I must say that smashing through the window and allowing shards of glass to scatter in her food is simply unacceptable. I've sequestered her in a pocket dimension until we conclude our business here."

Tom's shoulders slumped. "I apologise."

"I would much rather you apologise to my wife, though given how you ruined our evening, I very much doubt she would appreciate it. " The Doctor glared at the hero over the rim of the cup.

"Why do you insist on never keeping time?" Asked the Doctor. "The flood in Tsushima, the alien mind parasites in Times Square, and the nuclear missile in Korea should have given me at least forty minutes, perhaps an hour?" He rubbed his thumb and forefinger against the bridge of his nose, "Doesn't matter now, you're here."

"I've decided to retire." He announced. The clock on the wall ticked on.

"I- What?" Tom blurted out. "I- You- This isn't something you retire from! You-"

The Doctor raised his hand to quiet him.

"What with Carmen, the lecture tours, and the contracts between your own government and myself...Well, I just do not have the time to play along with you anymore."

The Doctor took a steadying breath and smoothed out imperceptible creases in the arms and legs of his elegant Prussian blue suit.

"February 5th, 1948, meeting in a small public house in Sutton Coldfield that has the potential to change the world. Of course, the rather pedestrian minds in that room had no idea what they would create. They just needed something to impress the warmongers and bureaucrats in Westminster. I assume you're aware of Operation Hurricane, yes?"

Major Tom's eyes narrowed, "One of Britain's first nuclear tests after the war?"

The Doctor smiled and tipped his teacup towards the floating figure. "A student of history! Top marks, young man. After the Americans rescinded their cooperation in the development of nuclear weapons, the British struck out on their own and attempted to match the stockpile of the US and the Russians; however, that was only half true. The real target was a formula developed by a coalition of American, German, Russian, and French scientists that they hoped would turn ordinary infantry into superhumans. Of course, by that time, all those countries were allies, but that didn't stop a British spy from pilfering an untested sample. It took them until 1956 before the test subjects' bodies stopped exploding."

Major Tom swallowed, "Are you saying you had a hand in what made me into this?"

The Doctor let out a short bark of a laugh.

"You're more intelligent than that, Daniel, and this isn't a comic book. No, I undertook extensive research while at university, which drew the attention of some…unsavoury individuals, but my vast intelligence and ability to decipher a small flaw that remained within the concoction granted me an esteemed position in the British government's top secret research and development division, Project Parzival. I undermined them, of course," the Doctor allowed himself a chuckle. "How could I not? They were hamstrung by a lack of resources and narrow vision."

He sneered, "Super soldiers? Men with the power of the gods being told who to kill, what country to destabilise by men who sat behind desks all day? What a farce! I wanted no part of some superhuman arms race, so I gathered what pertinent information I could and left to pursue my own ends."

"It wasn't until the 1970s that they sent the first real challenge. By that time, I had consolidated my hold on Europe. I was part of the silver age, obsessed with atomic power, metal, machines, and science, a child playing with matches really until my mentor found me and showed me how to wield power with a deft hand and focus my intellect in ways you couldn't conceive of. Now? After so many years, I am tired of the constant ebb and flow, the ceaseless battle for superiority. In short, the whole affair has lost its allure. I resign."

The Doctor steepled his fingers, "The game is over. Well done, Major."

Tom made to speak, but the Doctor flexed his fingers.

"Given my knowledge of your civilian life, you must understand that I am no longer interested in this garish pantomime of ours. I've created extensive files on you and all your costumed associates, which includes a list of all significant persons in their lives. Should any harm come to me or my wife, or god forbid if there are complications in the birth of my future son or daughter from your actions tonight, the destruction I bring down upon you and yours will be absolute. There will be no schemes, there will be no ultimate plans to conquer the world. It will not be death, rather I will destroy them piece by piece like a child that plucks the petals off a daisy. Anything you value, even in the slightest, will come to ruin, and that goes double for the members of your little cabaret act. I will watch while they lose their homes, their livelihoods, and soon enough their minds. There will be nothing you or anyone else could do to stop it."

"You wouldn't," the hero hissed through gritted teeth.

"You know me better than that." The Doctor's eyes flashed, "How's your father? Does he still suffer from that terrible cough? Did he manage to find another job? I do hope the Hawthornes can still put food on the table."

The hero flew from his chair. His eyes blazed with a black fury and glared across the room.

"Fix my home, then get out of my sight." The Doctor spat, "If I even sense you or anyone else get close to me..."

"I understand," replied the Major.

The Doctor's features relaxed, yet his eyes still smouldered with malicious intent.

"For what it's worth, Daniel, thank you for your constant challenges in this old man's life."

"It was my pleasure," he sneered.

The Doctor's home was back in pristine order in a rush of wind and a blur of colour and speed.

He rose from his chair and listened for a moment. A far-off boom of thunder allowed him to relax at last. He took the small remote control from the inside of his jacket, pressed the button, and stepped through the shimmering rift in the fabric of reality to embrace his wife.

Ratcatcher Versus The Spring Heeled Fiend
by David Turnbull

Take a walk across the bridge to the Surrey side of the Thames. This is the north end of Lambeth. The severed stump of London's amputated foot. Hobbled by its abject poverty. This is my world. By day, I'm known as Charlie Figgins. I work as a porter on the Necropolis Railway, helping load coffins onto carriages bound for Brookwood Cemetery. By night, I have fashioned myself a vigilante. My people have given me the name, Ratcatcher.

Perched on my rooftop vantage point, I maintain my vigil. I have no fear of heights. No worry that I might lose my balance and tumble to the street below. I grew up in a circus family, The Flying Figgins. From an early age, I was introduced to the high wire, the trapeze, and the athletic skills of the acrobat.

I was orphaned at fourteen, when the proprietor of the circus we worked for, on the verge of bankruptcy, burned down his big top for the insurance. My parents and my elder sister were rehearsing a new act. They died in that dreadful blaze. The corrupt circus impresario became the first criminal I brought to justice. All it took was the surreptitious turn of the brass key in the lock of the lion's cage.

I fended for myself. Living, at first, amongst the homeless community sleeping rough in the arches behind Waterloo train station. Then, when I began to obtain regular casual work at the Necropolis, I rented a garret from old Mrs. Pearson on Oakley Street. My room is hardly big enough to fit a bed and a closet, but its narrow window opens onto the grimy world of slate rooftops and brick chimneys that has become my nocturnal domain.

When I first took on my self-appointed role as guardian of the poor, I used a plain woolen muffler pulled up over my mouth and nose and a cloth cap pulled low on my brow to disguise my identity. My acrobatic prowess allowed me to access the gilded homes of those committing crimes against hard-working folk. My targets were cowards at heart. Pressure on them was easy to apply.

I had some success in achieving my ends. A slum landlord forced to lower his rent. The owner of a jam factory persuaded to place protective guards on his dangerous machinery. The cutting of extortionate interest rates by a ruthless money lender. The reigning in of the methods of his brutal debt collectors.

Word of my deeds spread fast through the slums. My legend grew. I was taking down the filthiest of the rats who had thrived in the sewers of their own creating. And so, they gave me my name. When the Necropolis took me on in full-time employment, I was able to afford the means to construct the fighting costume I now wear in honor of that name.

Breeches and a vest fashioned from the skinned hides of dead stray cats found in alleyways and courtyards. The vest worn over a cotton shirt I purchased from a second-hand clothes shop. A neckerchief of braided rat tails. A slightly battered Derby hat, a mourner had left this behind on the Necropolis platform when a funeral train departed. I took it to Stamford Street and had a felt trimmer restore it, and finish it off with a pair of preserved cat's ears attached to either side above its brim.

Now, each night after a modest dinner, I use the greasepaints I inherited from my parents and watch my reflection in the cracked mirror as I deftly transform my features from human to those of a fierce battle-torn tomcat.

I began as an angry young man, and an idealist to boot. I attended lectures by firebrands from the Social Democratic Federation. Inspired by their vision of a utopian future, I targeted those I hoped might be coerced into mending their corrupt and exploitative ways. Those who heartlessly preyed upon the poor and defenseless. Those who became rich on the backs of their victims.

But one night, not long ago, I had an encounter that changed my outlook by revealing to me that there are far worse monsters out there in the night than those born of the excesses of capitalism.

I was on the roof of the local library, watching as the crowds alighted the trams and gathered for a night of music hall entertainment at the Royal Victoria Theatre on the other side of Waterloo Road. A gang of urchins, boys and girls no older than nine or ten, were weaving in and out of the crowd, picking pockets as they went. I made no move to intervene. This wasn't a crime in my eyes. It was an act of wealth distribution.

I saw Lil, the flower seller, her red hair tied up under her straw hat, proffering bunches of colorful posies to courting couples. My heart began to flutter. I thought Lil Hargreaves was the most beautiful thing I'd ever seen. I would have given anything to walk out with her. But I never seemed able to pluck up the courage to ask her outright.

Then I saw him. A gent in a top hat and cape, partially concealed within the shadows of a nearby doorway. He seemed to be looking in Lil's direction. Paying her an unhealthy amount of attention. Lil began to move up the street. I could hear her call above the din of the throng. "Flowers. Flowers. Lovely flowers for sale."

I saw the gent step from the doorway and begin walking slowly and deliberately toward Lil. My heart went from a besotted flutter to a drumbeat tattoo. I rose to my feet and made a rapid descent from the rooftop, leaping from drainpipe to window ledge, dashing across the road, dodging through the crowd.

Lil was holding out her bunches of posies and calling out her wares. The gent in the top hat was almost upon her. I saw a long, pale arm snake out from beneath his cape. His crooked, claw-like fingers made a grab for her. I snatched at his wrist. His flesh felt sickeningly cold. He gasped, withdrew his arm, and fled back along the pavement, heading in the direction of the Elephant and Castle.

I gave chase. Lil cried out in confusion. One of the juvenile pickpockets saw me and yelled. "Blimey! Ratcatcher is after a rat." The crowd parted as I chased my quarry. I was almost upon him when he couched low and vaulted on his heels, springing high over a nearby gas lamp and landing on the roof of a passing tram.

It was an impressive vault. My father was famed within the circus community for the height he could reach from a standing jump. But even he would have been hard pushed to match this feat. Undeterred, I leapt from the pavement to the side of the tram and scrambled monkey-style up to the roof.

As soon as I gained my balance, the man turned to face me. What I saw would haunt my dreams for nights to come. Beneath his top hat, his face was gaunt, almost skeletal. His demonic eyes burned red like hot coals in a pottery furnace. His wide lips were studded with what appeared to be rows of spiky little teeth. A fat, purple tongue squirmed like a bloated slug within the dark maw of his mouth. He crouched and sprang on his heels once more. This time, he went higher and faster, coming to land on the rooftop of a building on the opposite side of the road.

I leapt from the tram to the wall of the building. Managing to grasp the drainpipe, I scrambled upwards hand over foot. By the time I hauled myself onto the roof, he was gone, no more than a blur dashing into the grey fugue caused by the stacks of smoking chimneys.

I frequently went without breakfast. But occasionally, if I was flush, I would treat myself to a cup of tea and two slices of bread and butter in the little cafe near my garret. These were the cheapest items on their modest menu. That demonic face staring at me from under its top hat had kept me awake all night. I needed sustenance to prevent me from collapsing from exhaustion once I started lugging coffins.

I had just collected my order at the counter when I noticed that Lil was seated alone at one of the tables, nibbling away at some toast and marmalade. "Mind if I join you?" I asked, feeling the butterfly flutter of my heart once more.

"It's a free country," she replied, dabbing her upper lip with a napkin.

"I heard you had a bit of bother last night," I said, sitting down opposite her.

She held up a copy of the South London Press. "It's all over the papers. Have a read if you like."

I busied myself with my tea and bread. "I can't read," came my mumbled confession. "Never had no teachers in the circus."

Lil smiled sympathetically. "The headline reads *'Police Hunt for Spring Heeled Fiend.'* It says they want Ratcatcher to reveal his identity and turn himself in."

"Really?" I felt the color drain from my face.

"I reckon it's a ruse to get their grubby hands on him," said Lil. "He's ruffled feathers. Them what thinks they're above the law are willing to press handsome bribes into the sweaty palms of them what are supposed to enforce the law."

I took a sip of my tea and nodded my agreement. "What does it say about this spring heeled fellow?"

"Say's the police think him and Ratcatcher might be in cahoots," replied Lil.

"Bloody hell," I gasped.

"I hope he keeps clear of the police station," said Lil. "I owe him a big, sloppy kiss for what he did last night. I bet he's a handsome bugger beneath all that greasepaint.'

Although she was talking about me, I was almost overwhelmed by the pang of illogical jealousy I felt against my alter ego. "How would you fancy coming with me to see Dan Leno one night at the Royal Surrey?" I blurted before I had a moment to consider what I was saying.

Lil narrowed her eyes. "How are you going to afford seats at the Surrey, Charlie?"

"Sometimes when a wealthy family hires a first-class funeral carriage, they leave a big tip for the porters to share," I replied. "It would be the stalls, though. Not a fancy box nor nothing."

Lil gave me a flirtatious wink that caused my pulse to race. "Ask me again when you have enough money set aside. If you behave yourself, I might teach you to read."

That night, I decided to pay a visit to the one person who might have inside knowledge on the direction of the police investigation. He was known locally as Upright Johnny, a name given to him by a judge who commended him for his honesty when he appeared as a witness in the trial of an alleged felon. He was a former member of the Metropolitan police. His real name was William Thicke. He'd been a sergeant over in Whitechapel at the time of the investigations into the Ripper murders.

Dressed in my Ratcatcher costume, I entered his study through an open window.

"Can't you just knock on the door?" he asked, not bothering to look up from the copy of the London Illustrated News he was reading.

"Climbing drainpipes keeps me in shape," I said, taking a seat in the armchair opposite him.

He folded the newspaper on his lap and ran his finger and thumb over his thick walrus moustache. "Probably just as well. I wouldn't want my former associates on the force knowing that you pay me a little visit every now and then."

"What do I need to know?" I asked.

"Two things," he replied, picking up his tobacco pouch and beginning to stuff his smoking pipe. He struck a match to light the pipe. For a moment, he was concealed in a swirling fug of smoke.

"Firstly," he said, drawing a long puff, "they're out to bring you down. You're interfering with the status quo. You've made enemies of rich and powerful men who are exerting their considerable influence. I warned you that you can't operate in the margins of the law without eventually coming a cropper."

Lil was right, I thought, recalling our conversation that morning.

"They haven't caught me yet," I said.

"They will," he said and drew another puff on his pipe.

"You said there were two things," I said. "What's the second?"

Upright Johnny lifted the pipe stem away from his mouth and looked straight over at me. "The man you chased last night is a murder suspect."

"Murder?"

"There have been two murders in the past fortnight. Both women. One was pulled out of the Thames near Waterloo Bridge two weeks ago. The other was found by the railway sidings near Vauxhall. It's being kept hush hush. They don't want to cause a panic."

"What makes them think they're connected?" I asked.

"Both victims had circular wounds on their chests. The circumferences were littered with dozens of tiny puncture marks. Both had lost a lot of blood. They think the murderer has some sort of device with which he draws the blood of his victims for some sort of nefarious purpose."

Realizing what a narrow escape Lil had had, I felt my fingers tremble on the armrests of the chair as a cold shiver ran through me.

"If you know something," said Upright Johnny. "If you saw something you think might be important, you should report it to the police."

I rose to my feet. "I have to go."

"You'll be caught in the end," he called as I climbed back through the window. "Mark my words. The rats are closing in. When they get you, don't you dare drag my name into it."

I crossed the rooftops of Roupell Street and Theed Street and climbed to the top of the W.H. Smith printworks on Stamford Street. My head was full of *what-ifs. What if I hadn't been there last night and the Spring Heeled Fiend got Lil in his clutches? What if the police caught me now and tossed me into a cell? What if I had caught up with the Fiend? Would I have been a match for him?*

It was up to me to protect Lil and everyone else from this malevolent predator who was abroad in our midst. The police could not be relied upon, nor trusted. Given the choice between protecting powerful, wealthy men from me and powerless, working-class girls from the murderous fiend, I knew toward which cause their efforts and resources would be directed.

A sudden cry echoed into the night, snapping me out of my thoughts. It seemed to come from the direction of Coin Street. I set off to investigate. Zigzagging down via drainpipes and ledges in the agile manner I had perfected. At street level, I found myself enveloped in the sluggish green mist that was rolling lethargically in from the Thames. Crouching low, I sank into it, hoping to avoid running into any constables on their night beat.

As I entered Coin Street, I could make out the outlines of a dark, hunched figure to the front of the tenements. I approached cautiously. My foot crunched on a broken beer bottle. The figure froze. Its head snapped round to face me. Once more, I gazed into the demonic eyes of the fiend. Blood was dripping from the spiky teeth studding the ragged circle of his lips. Beneath him lay the unconscious body of a young woman, bodice ripped open, chest bone bleeding from the punctures that perforated a horrific round wound.

"Surrender yourself," I demanded, mustering as much authority as I could into the tone of my voice.

The creature sprayed sour spittle as it let out a foul screech of frustration. It rose to its full height, which I estimated to be at least seven feet tall. Without another sound, it made a break for it, trampling over the young woman, cutting into the thickening mist with a violent bound and leap. I broke into a chase, seized once more with a debilitating doubt about my prowess. If I caught up with him, would I be his match? Or could he overpower me with ease?

A low quivering groan from the tremulous lips of the unfortunate young woman gave me my excuse to pause. "You're safe," I whispered, peering down on her as I slowed to a halt.

Her eyes flickered, then popped wide with shock when she saw me. "You?" She gasped the word like an accusation. "Why?"

From the direction of Stamford Street, there came the sound of raised voices. Someone blew a police whistle. The young woman sat upright. She touched the wound on her chest, saw blood on her fingers, and screamed at the top of her lungs.

Heavy footsteps came running toward us.

"Help is coming,' I told her, making a desperate dive for the nearest drainpipe.

I made the newspaper headlines again. One of my fellow porters read them out when we were on tea break from platform duty. *'Ratcatcher Named as Accomplice to the Spring Heeled Fiend.'* The article told how the female victim, Tilly Richards, had positively identified Ratcatcher the moment she regained consciousness. Two constables who had arrived on the gory scene moments later said they had witnessed Ratcatcher scaling a drainpipe to make his escape. The article also revealed for the first time the details of the two murders Upright Johnny had told me about. I was suspected of being complicit in both these crimes.

That night, mentally floored by the notion that powerful men were conspiring to frame me, I found I was not motivated to don my cat costume and my greasepaint. I sat dejected on the lumpy mattress in my garret, staring forlornly out through the open window at a fingernail moon in a starless sky.

If I went out onto the streets as Ratcatcher, I would be forever glancing over my shoulder in case the police were waiting to seize me and shackle me in handcuffs. If I turned my attention back to the robber barons and slum landlords I had previously focused on, they might be far less inclined to succumb to my persuasions now that they knew they'd successfully made me the prime suspect in a murder investigation.

I ruled out paying a visit to Upright Johnny. His counsel and inside knowledge had been invaluable to me in the past. But his mood the previous night had not filled me with confidence. He hadn't been given the name Upright for nothing. If I entered his apartments, I had a sickening hunch that he would attempt to restrain me in order to hand me over to the police.

I felt that Lil at least could be relied on not to have turned her back on Ratcatcher. But if she saw me again in my costume and greasepaint, her infatuation with my alter-ego might grow. Poor old Charlie Figgins might never get a second look.

More to the point, I had to come to terms with the fact that I was in the grip of fear. I had encountered the fiend twice now. What I had seen chilled me to the bone. When I was twelve, my father had engaged the services of the circus strongman. He taught me the arts of wrestling, pugilism, and close-quarter grappling. The purpose was to improve my core body strength for the rigors of high wire acrobatics. As a consequence, I had the skills and speed to outmaneuver and bring down the most hardened street fighter. But I doubted that I could do so with the fiend.

My community was facing a huge threat from some murderous blood sucking entity. And I was a complete loss. No use to them whatsoever. So much for my delusional self-appointment as their protector. Had I not been so focused on wallowing in my self-pity, I may have been able to attempt something that would have prevented the fiend from committing his third murder.

This time, the police immediately released the victim's name, hoping that it might encourage witnesses to come forward with important details about her movements, as well as any information which may lead to the apprehension of Ratcatcher. There was no mention now of the Spring Heeled Fiend. They were taking full advantage of this opportunity and totally ignoring the true perpetrator.

The victim's name was Bess McTigan. Her body, replete with a circular wound on her exposed chest, had been found by a lamplighter taking a shortcut home under the railway arch near Hercules Road. Trains from the Necropolis passed over that arch daily. The murder had happened a stone's throw from the platform where I worked.

I knew Bess. She'd been a trick horse rider in the circus. She went by the name of Bareback Bessie. Once, she'd attempted to teach me how to balance upright on the back of a speckled mare as it trotted around the ring. She'd laughed like a drain when I'd fallen flat on my face in the sawdust and almost bit through my tongue. Since the fire, she'd been working as a groom in the stables where some of the local handsome cab drivers housed their horses overnight.

I felt responsible for her death. If I'd had the courage of my convictions and tackled the fiend two nights earlier, I might have had a chance to end his reign of terror. Conversely, had I gone out onto the streets the previous night, I might have at least scared him off and saved Bess's life the way I had managed with Tilly Richards in Coin Street. It was the kick up the behind I needed to shake myself out of my debilitating mood.

That night, I reverted to my original costume. The police were hunting me in my Ratcatcher persona. They were not on the lookout for someone in a cloth cap with a muffler pulled up over his nose.

Using a route via the Necropolis, I climbed up onto the vast steel and glass rooftop of Waterloo Station. Some weeks earlier, I had picked up a pair of a lady's theatrical binoculars that had been accidentally dropped near the Royal Victoria. I'd hoped they might prove of value one day. Now, balanced on one of the huge girders, I scanned the area, north, south, east, and west, for signs of a prowling, hunched figure in a top hat.

Luckily, there was no mist that night. Turning on my heels, rotating slowly. I watched the area transform from dusk to nocturnal life. Trams and carriages passing along Waterloo and Westminster Bridge Roads. People drifting in and out of pubs and ale houses. Queues beginning to form outside theatres and music halls. Steam trains with multiple passenger carriages crawling like gigantic caterpillars in and out of the station.

Through the binoculars, I looked toward the white pillars of St John's Church and then on to Waterloo Bridge, where pedestrian and horse-drawn traffic was milling back and forth. I traced the length of York Road and spied someone in a top hat scuttling across the road. He parked himself on the corner. Although he remained hunched over, I knew that if he rose to his full height, he would stand seven feet tall. I knew that the Spring Heeled Fiend was on the hunt for his next victim.

Balancing as if I were on the high wire, I moved deftly along the girder. When I reached the York Road end of the station roof, I launched myself into a leap, tumbling midair to give myself the extra momentum needed to reach the rooftop of a neighboring building. From there, I swung myself over the guttering and down the drainpipe to reach over to the brass pole of a gas lamp with which to complete my descent. I hit the ground running, heading straight for the corner.

The fiend stood there, intently watching those who were passing by. I shouted no warning as I ran at him, hoping the element of surprise would help me tackle him to the ground. However, as if he was imbued with some type of sixth sense, his head jerked instantly in my direction.

He took off. Recklessly running into the middle of York Road, turning to face an oncoming carriage, rising monstrously, flailing his spindly arms, spiky lips spread wide. The horse pulling the carriage reared up at the sight of him, almost toppling the carriage as it turned to flee. This set off a chain reaction. Several other horses took fright. Passengers in the carriages screamed, pedestrians on the pavements scattered.

It took all of my agility to dodge through the ensuing mayhem. Somehow, though, he had not managed to evade me. I pushed myself harder as he ran headlong toward the riverside wharves and timber yards. As the gap closed between us, I noticed for the first time elements of him I hadn't quite noticed before.

His cloak, unfurled and fluttering behind him, was not in fact an item of clothing. It appeared to be a dark, fleshy membrane growing organically from the back of his neck. His boots, too, looked to be part of him. Hooves, somehow fashioned into a mimicry of human footwear. No springs concealed within those heels, just extraordinary muscle tissue.

I chased him over stacks of sawn timber, across jetties and barges, leaping inlets, clattering over chain-fenced walkways. For a moment, at the Hungerford Railway Bridge, I thought I'd managed to corner him. But, with an audible hiss of defiance, he began to scale the side bridge as if he were a scampering spider.

I continued my chase. I had no idea what I was going to do if I caught up with him, but there was fire in my belly. The bridge rumbled and shook as I climbed in pursuit of the creature. A train departing Charing Cross gushed steam as it crossed noisily over to the south side.

The fiend climbed higher, and I followed. Soon, he was standing upright on the railings. Moments later, we were face-to-face. The wind from the river was gusting so hard that it was a huge challenge to keep my balance. My cloth cap was snatched from my head and went tumbling through the air. Despite its imposing height, the fiend's top hat did not budge. I saw now that, like his cloak, it too was an organic extension of his body. Its black color was marbled with hints of mildewed grey, like the flesh of a cadaver in the advanced stages of decomposition.

"What in God's name are you?" I demanded, over the banshee howl of the wind.

The fiend's tooth-studded mouth curved to a hideous grin. "A bloated corpse tossed and rolled on the river currents. Imbued and reanimated by the alchemy of effluence from the sewers and toxic discharges from the factories. A new life form. One with an insatiable hunger that needs to be fed."

I trembled as he spoke those words, but it wasn't the time for a faint heart. "It's over now," I said. "Surrender yourself. Perhaps someone, a doctor or such, could help you."

The fiend issued a throaty, phlegm-heavy wheeze of laughter. "No one can help me. I do not desire help. Whoever I was died long ago down there in that filthy river." He took a step toward me, eyes blazing. "Embrace me. Plunge into the cold waters. Be born anew. You think this is the only form I can take? There have been many before this. There are many yet to come. I am a fungal parasite. I adapt and grow wantonly."

I crouched to one knee, ready to dodge clear if he tried to grab me.

"Afraid?" he mocked. "So be it."

Without another word, he stepped over the edge and dropped like a stone toward the brown surge of the Thames. As I looked down, he looked back up at me. "I shall return to feast anew." Then he was swallowed by the churning swell.

I heard a whistle being blown. The trains at Charing Cross and Waterloo Junction had been suspended. From either side of the bridge, police patrols, with wooden truncheons drawn, were about to converge on me. I swung myself over the side of the bridge and scrambled to its underbelly, seeking out handholds and footholds on its cold steel girders till I was once more back at the timber yards where I executed my escape.

Now I have a new vantage point, high above the river, perched on top of the huge Coade stone lion statue, which itself sits on the rooftop of the Lion Brewery next to Waterloo Bridge. I am once more in my Ratcatcher costume and face paint. I have studied the police patrols in the area. I know them by heart. Although I remain a wanted man, I can move through the streets without fear of apprehension.

I have almost saved enough money to buy two dress circle tickets to see Dan Leno at the Royal Surrey. Any day now, Charlie Figgins will pluck up the courage to ask Lil, the flower seller, if she would give him the honor of accompanying him. For now, I scan the wharves and timber yards with my theatrical binoculars. When the rat comes crawling out of the river, whatever form he decides to take this time, I will be waiting.

Good Intentions
by Nicholas Leamy

Standing in front of the building, Chris looked it over with trepidation. It could have been any nondescript government building with its concrete walls and bland rectangular windows. The one thing that set it apart was the statues decorating the roof. Each one depicted a superhero in action. One was of a woman wearing a bow and quiver catching a child from what was implied to have been a great height. Another was an overly large and beefy man in position to suggest they were pushing back a rampaging train or some other powerful calamity. The one closest to the entrance was leaping into the air, their cape billowing out behind them.

Chris looked down, frowning at his button-down shirt, the hole in his jeans, and the grass stains on the sneakers he used for yard work. Shoving his hands into his pockets, he turned around and took three steps away before stopping. Closing his eyes, he took slow, deep breaths, shook his head, and turned back to the entrance. Walking through the door, he passed under the large sign stating, "Heroic Registration Offices."

As he approached the main desk, the attendant on duty asked, "Good afternoon! May I ask what service we can help you with today?"

Chris paused for a moment before saying, "Umm, stipends?"

"Of course, sir." He typed an entry into his system, and a ticket with the number 34 popped out. Handing the ticket to Chris, he said, "Here you go, sir. If you would please have a seat over to the right. Once your number is called, you will see it above your assigned auditor office. Thank you!"

The seats were plastic benches. Others ahead of him sat waiting for their turn. He sat down with a space between him and a man in a blazer. Their eyes met long enough that he nervously said, "Hi, it's my first time." The blazer man gave a polite and awkward nod and went back to his phone. Chris's anxiety spiked. He looked at his watch, then the front door, and had his attention pulled back to the moment when a loud ding went off. Looking up, he saw a counter turn to 32, then blazer man got up and headed toward a desk.

Letting out a breath he didn't know he was holding, Chris clenched his hands together, focused on his breathing, and said to himself, "You can do this. You belong here. Just wait your turn, and this either works or it doesn't." After a few more breaths, he opened his eyes, saw he had missed the last counter tick, and then heard the next ding indicating it was his turn.

A woman stood up from her auditor's desk to greet him as he entered her office. Wearing business casual pants and a jacket, she extended her hand and said, "Hello, I'm Auditor Lynda Wagner, but you can just call me Lynda."

Chris reached out his hand to be polite, saying, "Hi Lynda, thanks for your time, but I think I may have made a mistake coming..."

As her hand took his, all his anxiety washed away. His shoulders relaxed. A weight he had not noticed on his chest dropped away. In this moment, all he wanted was to sit back and just hang with this total stranger.

Lynda saw the look in his eyes and smiled. "Please, have a seat. I should be up front with you. What you're feeling now is a result of my ability. I'm able to put people at ease just by touching them. The larger effects should wear off any second now, but I hope it lingers long enough to make this a relatively painless transaction for you."

Sitting down, Chris looked her in the eyes and said, "That was amazing! How is it someone like you is working a desk job and not out doing bigger things... I mean... not that what you do isn't..."

With a smile, Lynda raised a hand and interjected, "I see I'm starting to wear off already. First, I'm not offended. I understand that office work is different from saving the city from alien invaders. In answer to your question, though, I've considered what I could do to diffuse difficult situations to save lives, but when that only works if you can touch the person, well, I'm not going to be stopping any bank robberies or hostage situations any time soon. Anyway, you'd be surprised how many people we get every day that come in here on edge. While I may not have a massive impact, I at least get to use my ability for good. Now, how can I help you, mister...?"

Chris shifted in his seat and said, "Bixby. Christopher Bixby. Please, just call me Chris. I was under the impression that this is where we can request a stipend.

Could you please explain that to me?"

"My pleasure. As I'm sure you are aware, over the last few decades, empowered humans have been increasing in frequency. Twelve years ago, the government wanted to help direct the use of these abilities towards the greater good. As such, a city ordinance was enacted stating that if a person could prove that by use of an empowered ability they successfully prevented felonies such as murder, property damage, or theft, then they would be entitled to a stipend based on a percentage of the value saved, or set amounts for situations where no value could be attributed, such as the life of a person. In short, if you are able to supply me with proof of your successful use of an empowered ability in such a case, I will be able to award you an appropriate stipend."

"Well, you see, that's where things get tricky. My ability has always been hard to... explain."

"Is it a physical ability?"

"I guess. I don't need any gadgets or anything to make it happen."

"I'm sorry, I mean, is this an ability such as super strength, personal size manipulation..."

"Oh, no. It's just all in my head."

"A psychic ability like telekinesis, or pyrokinesis?"

"Ok. So, I get these hunches, you see. I suddenly get the notion that if I do some particular action in the moment, it will be good. Then, I get a sensation that the good of my actions has happened. Does that make sense?"

"Um, not exactly. Could you be more specific? I'll be honest, it just sounds like you're describing morality right now."

"Fair. Ok. I don't know this for certain, but it feels like dominoes to me. I get a sudden compulsion saying I should push this first domino, and then it will knock down the next, and then the next, and then the next, and finally, the last domino is something positive. I've done things in the past that, days later, I'll have a feeling of resolution. I'll start watching the news, and if I'm lucky, I'll find an event that I just know I'm responsible for. Now, I'm sure in general there is no way I could take credit for these events, but today is different. Today is the first time I've ever done something that I could feel the results of my actions on the same day. I think today may be my one and only chance to possibly earn my stipend."

Lynda sat back, steepled her fingers, and thought to herself for a moment before saying, "I think I get it. This is some low-level precognition thing, where you can predict the possibility of a positive impact and nudge it into being. We can work with this. If we can take your initial action, map out the chain reaction that took place from it, and connect that to the final result, then we could get your stipend approved. It helps that you know the beginning and end of the chain."

Pulling out a report form, Lynda started filling out the details of the request. "Now, we'll need to do a bit of fieldwork here to determine the connections, since you yourself are uncertain of the exact chain you created. I'll hit up every stage of the chain, get witness statements, and submit the report. Due to the freshness of this, we'll want to get started immediately. Could you please tell me your initiating action and the resulting good from it?"

Chris looked down and rubbed his temple before replying, "Um, it may be easier if we just start from the good and work backwards. Let's start with the robbery I stopped and… we'll work back to me."

Lynda looked at the worry creasing his face, gave a comforting smile, and said, "I think we can work with that."

Approaching Marco's Bodega, people passed on the sidewalk like any other day, except for a man in an apron out front sweeping up metal scraps around a small blood stain in the concrete. As Lynda and Chris approached him, she signaled for Chris to hold back.

"Hello, sir! My name is Auditor Lynda Wagner from the HRO. Is there any chance you are the owner of this establishment and have time for a few questions?"

"A pleasure to meet you. Yes, I'm Marco, and this is my store. How can I help you?"

"I just wanted to ask you about the robbery earlier today. I'm told you had a stroke of luck hit you today."

With a chuckle, Marco replied, "Well, I'm not the one it hit. But yeah. I was running the store earlier today when I was held up at gunpoint. He walked right up to me and put the gun in my face. It's a risk of the job in any city, of course, but still, it rarely happens to me, much less during the middle of the day. Not sure what his problem was, but he had a desperate look in his eyes. He seemed unstable, and I had no interest in taking any risks, so I filled a bag with all the cash in the cash register and from the safe. $2000, he was walking out the door with. On his way out, I was doing my best to memorize his clothes and any other descriptive details I could, so I could give them to the cops when it happened. He paused for just a second out front of the store when I saw the air conditioning unit from the 3rd floor come crashing down on his head!"

All three of them paused, looking up at the empty third-floor window and then back down at the blood stain on the ground. Lynda replied, "Wow! Did he survive the impact?"

"Oh yeah! Not sure how. Probably bounced off a ledge or something. He started to regain consciousness shortly after the police and ambulance showed up. It was the damnedest thing. I know it was me he threatened, but I still hope he gets whatever help he needs."

"You're a good man, Marco. Thank you for your time."

Walking out of earshot, Lynda said to Chris, "Ok, so you're stating your ability is responsible for the foiling of this robbery. I'm going to say right now, you need to be ready to deal with the fact that there is a real possibility we may not be able to connect this to you. If you are somehow responsible for whatever caused him to pause outside the store, we're basically done, as there is no way to tell which of a hundred possibilities that was. But I'm going to continue to follow the more direct path of the AC unit and see where that takes us. Does that sound fair to you?"

"That sounds reasonable to me. Thank you."

"My pleasure. Now, let's see what is going on with the 3rd floor."

Opening the door as far as the chain would allow, Molly from the third floor apartment asked the pair, "Can I help you?"

"Hello ma'am, my name is Auditor Lynda Wagner from the HRO. We're following up concerning the fall of your AC unit earlier today. We wanted to ask…"

"I had nothing to do with that! I can't be held responsible for the fellow it landed on! I was actively trying to avoid something like this!"

"Please, I promise you. If you could just give me a few moments of your time, I intend to fully blame this man for the entire incident."

Chris stared slack-jawed at Lynda as she was ushered into the apartment and the door closed behind her.

Walking back to Lynda's car, Chris finally said, "I can't believe you said that to her!"

"Said what?"

"That thing about trying to blame me for the AC unit!"

"I mean, think about it. We are actively trying to associate this situation with your actions, right? So was I incorrect?"

"I mean… no…but.. It's just that… I think it's you using the word blame that has me all torn up inside for some reason."

"I understand. You're surprisingly hesitant about this whole situation already, and any implied negativity from me is going to be a trigger for you. That being said, that woman was terrified we were there to prosecute her in some way for the injured man. I felt the fastest way to get into her confidence was to show we meant her no ill intentions, and the best way to do that was to point the blame she was feeling directly at you. Look, we're potentially on the clock here, so I made a decision in the moment. That being said, you are still a person and not just a case, so my apologies."

After a moment of quiet contemplation, Chris nodded his head and said, "Thank you... And I get it. I'm sorry for being defensive. This just has me all sorts of nervous. All of this is very new to me. Where are we going now?"

"Well, after introducing myself to Molly and explaining why I was there, I learned that the AC unit has been wobbly and poorly secured for some time now. She was telling the truth about wanting to prevent something like this from happening, though. In fact, she had an appointment today to have a technician out to look it over."

"How does that help us? Is this a dead end? How do we connect me to making the unit finally topple out?"

"Oh, I don't think you made it fall?"

"I didn't?"

"Nope. I think you are somehow responsible for the technician being thirty minutes late for his appointment. Guess when the unit decided to finally give up the ghost."

"My name is Ethan, and I perform HVAC work for several buildings in the area."

"Excellent! It's a pleasure to meet you. We've been told by a Molly Godowsky that you were called in earlier today to work on her AC unit, but you were delayed in reaching her?"

"Oh yeah! The unit that fell out the window. Kicking myself that I couldn't get there any sooner to stop it from falling. I was driving there when I got stuck behind a bus accident. It suddenly screeched out and swerved to a stop, blocking traffic. I think they ended up having to change the tire before it could get moving again. Whatever it was, there was no way around, and too many people behind me to consider backing up. About half an hour later, I was back on the road, but it was already too late."

"Thank you so much for your time, Ethan. Don't beat yourself up too much about this. I'm fairly certain there was no way you could have seen this coming. We'll be off…" Lynda turned back to include Chris with her goodbye to find him already out the door. Giving Ethan one final smile, she left the office.

Chris was waiting outside, pacing. Stopping when Lynda left the building, he said, "You know, maybe none of this is actually worth it. I mean, how much money do I even stand to make for this if we're successful?"

Lynda reached out for him, and he pulled back. Respecting his desire to not be calmed, she replied, "At a 1% compensation rate, and the return of the $2000 to Marco's, you're looking at a $20 stipend."

Returning to his pacing, he continued, "$20 bucks. I've dragged you all over town for $20. This is ridiculous. I've wasted yours and everyone else's time. Why are we even doing this?"

"Chris!" Her sharp response stopped him dead, and she caught his eyes. "We're doing this because you did something good today. And if we're lucky, we'll be able to prove that it was Marco not losing $2000 that you are responsible for. And a disturbed individual finally getting a chance for some resources to be funneled his way. Also, that you took some of the blame off a woman's shoulders for her AC unit. Even the little things we do deserve to be seen and recognized. It's all those little things that add up to a better world. It's only right that we should sing their praises."

Chris looked down, his cheeks slightly blushing. Lynda continued with a smirk, "And as for me, I get paid by the hour. You got me out of the office for the day. This has been nothing but win for me."

Chris had a small chuckle escape from him before looking up. "Thank you."

"Don't thank me yet, we still need to find out what happened to this bus. Now, we can contact the bus depot to get a statement from the driver. This will help us determine what caused their mishap and determine the location of the breakdown…"

"No need."

"What?"

"Come on. I know where we need to go."

They came to stop at a random spot in the road. Getting out of the car, Lynda looked around and saw nothing of interest. She turned to Chris as he got out, and he said, "If we wait here just a moment longer, you'll have everything you need."

They stood there for a few minutes. Lynda turned to say something when a deep voice from across the street bellowed, "That son of a bitch came back!"

A burly man came lumbering towards them. He crossed the road, looking either way just long enough to make quick eye contact with an oncoming driver and make it clear between both of them that he had the right of way. He barrelled towards Chris with murder in his eyes. Chris didn't move. He stood completely still, his eyes staring back heavy with guilt, waiting for the train of a man to mow him down.

Within a handful of feet of reaching Chris, he raised his hand to grab him by the throat when Lynda's hand landed on his shoulder. Coming to a stuttering halt, the brute deflated and stood there blinking something out of his eyes.

Lynda gently took him by the arm and turned him to face her. "Hi there. My name is Auditor Lynda Wagner from the HRO. You should know that what you're feeling now is a result of my ability. I'm currently putting you at ease with my touch. The larger effects should wear off when I let go of you. I am concerned you may do my associate harm here, so I will be maintaining contact until we get this sorted out. Who do I have the pleasure of talking to today?"

"Hi, Lynda. I'm Paul."

"Hi, Paul. You seem very upset with this man, and I'm guessing it has something to do with why I'm here today. Why don't you tell me everything about your anger, and I'll do everything in my power to fix the situation for you."

Lynda continued to maintain direct contact with him. With a dreamy expression, Paul said, "I appreciate that, Lynda. It's been a hard day for me. I'm a stay-at-home dad. I take care of my daughter, Elisa. She's five years old and cute as a button. Her mom works for the Capital, so we're lucky we can afford for me to stay home and raise her. It's a lot of work, but worth every second. Witnessing how she grows and changes has been nothing short of a blessing. In fact, today, we took her training wheels off. She was riding her bike for the first time down the sidewalk all on her own. I watched her ride off ahead of me when suddenly this monster came out of nowhere, pulled her off her bike, and flung it under a bus as it drove by. Popped its tire, destroyed the bike, and left my daughter traumatized and crying. I handed her off to a neighbor and chased him down three blocks before I lost him."

Lynda turned a raised eyebrow to Chris. He was shifting side to side, eyes flickering back and forth, brow furrowed. After a moment, he threw his hands up in the air and declared, "I swear I meant well!"

Lynda placed her hand on her face and turned away thoughtful, when in reality she was desperately trying not to burst out laughing. After composing herself, she turned back to Paul and asked, "How much was the bike?"

"I bought it for $140."

"Ok, Paul, here's what we're going to do. I'm going to let go of you now. You'll still remain pretty calm for a bit, but I'm going to ask you to try and hold onto that as long as possible." He nodded his head, and she released him. She reached into her pocket and pulled out a card. "This is my contact information. You are going to call me tomorrow, and I am going to have the Heroic Registration Office fully reimburse you for the loss of your bike. Please know that it is the HRO's official stance that the destruction of your bike was an unfortunate consequence of actions performed in the means of stopping a felony. Now, I'll be happy to fully detail how that is the case if you want to know tomorrow, but I am afraid I need to finish up the rest of my report today. Does all of this sound reasonable to you?"

"Yes, thank you."

"Thank you, Paul. Have a wonderful day." Turning to Chris, she said, "Walk with me for a second."

Walking down the block, Chris broke the silence first. With tears brimming, he said, "I can't believe what I did to that little girl. You have to believe me, I wouldn't have done it if I hadn't thought..."

Cutting him off, Lynda said, "Chris, it's alright. We have made it pretty clear today you only have the best intentions in mind. All the collective good you've done along the way barely balances out in your head what you did to that girl, and that's enough to tell me what kind of person you are."

"I appreciate that, but after seeing him again. After hearing it all replayed, I don't think I could possibly accept the $20 stipend."

"Oh, you're not getting the stipend."

Chris came to a sudden halt, and Lynda met his eyes. "What? But I thought..."

"Oh, we definitely satisfied the conditions for your audit. I'm going to write up how you were responsible for thwarting the bodega robbery and submit you into the official record as a hero of the state."

"I'm confused."

"I'm awarding you full credit for your actions, but your $20 is going towards the bike reimbursement. Also, I expect you to be at the office early tomorrow morning. I don't care what plans or employment you have. We have a lot of work to do. You're going to document every impulse you can remember following, and we're going to connect the dots to all of the confirmed results you've linked with. We'll tally up any damages you're responsible for, issue reimbursements for those losses, and then compare that with whatever stipends you are entitled to. If you happen to come out in the black, I'll issue you the check myself. If not, well, we'll work out some way for you to balance the scales. I'm sure we could find something for you to do at the HRO."

Chris stood there for a moment, digesting it all. Slowly, a relieved smile began to creep up his face. Glancing back up at Lynda, he said, "Yeah. I think I like that."

Fear of Reprisal: Blood Will Have Blood
by Michael Joseph Tharnish Roby

Reprisal: Volume Two, Issue Fifteen

He stole from a hospital, snatching life-giving medicine away from mothers and children. That's just today, never mind what he's done before. Never mind the rest of his crimes. Never mind what he's done to you.

I sat, cross-legged, on the rafters of a long-abandoned canning factory. The cold, metal paneling and the wide-open space carried the words of the hired guns gathered below up to me, but I hardly paid them any mind. Reprisal kept hissing in my ear, it spoke in Halloway's voice, like it always did.

This could be the night; we can finally put him out of his misery. He's gone too far; now it's time we go with him.

Halloway told me I could try talking to it if I wanted to, but it wasn't a person; it couldn't really understand or reason. After five years on the job, I stuck to the affirmations my therapist gave me. So quiet even the factory couldn't carry my voice, I recited, "My name is Allie Greene. I am the one in control. I choose to be focused. I am my own woman. I can feel anger and not lose myself."

The sound of Reprisal, my whispers, and the group below were all cut off by a rhythmic *beep beep beep* from a semi-truck as it backed into the factory. My blood ran hot, I clenched my fists, and rose. On quick, quiet steps, I approached the docking bay entrance. Nine big, burly mercenaries in Kevlar armor stood around a shorter man in a suit and tie. The way he obviously wasn't as fit or dressed for combat marked him as the buyer. Reprisal whispered to me about contract killers and culpability in overdoses, as if I needed to be reminded. I pushed its thoughts away and kept my focus on the truck as two figures emerged from the cabin. One was familiar to me, one wasn't. The one I hadn't seen before stepped out of the passenger's side; he wore a tight, high-collared black jacket which buttoned on the right. A lightning bolt symbol zig-zagged down from the collar along his coat's side, and a pair of goggles in a similar yellow covered his eyes. Black curls helped obstruct the rest of his face, and he kept his hands slipped into his pockets.

Out from the driver's side came a much older man, his blond hair just starting to gray. A tan trench coat covered a gaudy orange suit replete with decals of intertwined locks and keys. His name was Grant Greene, the Key Keeper. And, once upon a time, I called him, "Dad."

"About time you got here." The buyer approached my father and his underling and glared. "Who's this with you, Key Keeper?"

"He's newly discovered talent." My father patted his compatriot on the shoulder. "Calling himself Current, idn't you, bud?"

His partner said nothing; he just nodded.

The buyer turned his attention toward the truck. "And it's all there? Three thousand units of Type C?"

Type C is a chemical derived from the blood of the empowered population. Even those with minor latent abilities couldn't accept Type A or Type B blood, so they called the chemical abnormality Type C. The empowered could metabolize it lightning-fast, and it gave the powerless a drug-like rush. Hence, its value among thieves, and why Reprisal kept castigating me for waiting.

"Depends on what you're ready to pay for." My father smirked. "There's three thousand units if you're paying for three thousand units."

The man who approached him grunted and called, "Dickson, you go count the goods." As one of his mercenaries approached the truck, he continued, "Reiley, start counting his money." Again, he leveled a glare at the delivery pair. "And you're certain you weren't followed?"

My father scoffed and showed a leer of his own. "You're from out of town, Johnno, so I don't expect you to know this. But you don't ask questions like that around here. Not when—" he stopped and smirked, "—you fear Reprisal."

Ever the furious reactionary, Reprisal demanded, *End him, end him now!*

I couldn't tell what my father hoped to accomplish by invoking its name. But it was as good a time as any to step in. I projected my voice as I commanded, "Freeze, dirtbags!" A clichéd line, I knew, it was a carry-over from being a theatre kid. But the bad guys always knew just how to react.

The buyer jerked his head around, shouted, "What the—" and, I assume, got his first distant look at me in the shadows. As if to prove what an out-of-towner he was, he commanded his men, "Open fire! Kill that—that thing!"

My father probably shouted at them to stop, but I dealt with goons like those all the time. I still stood a ways off, and they couldn't aim well, but I spread my arms out wide to make myself a bigger target. My armor absorbed the shock of the barrage that struck me, but little jolts of pain still ran through my stomach, chest, and arms. Which was good, because I needed extra fuel for the next step in my dramatic entrance.

I leapt over the catwalk's guardrail and hit the ground a moment later. The Reprisal armor absorbs and redistributes kinetic energy, so it took just a little of the impact it absorbed from those bullets to cushion my fall. Nervous calls of "What is that thing?" joined more vulgar variants in a chorus as I stood up straight. The first night I ever saw Halloway in the suit, even as kind as she'd been, still gave me nightmares. Scaley crimson armor covered every inch of my body, interrupted only by a hooded mantle formed of dark, inky tendrils. The openings for my eyes were a haunting, pure white from the outside, and down from my mask descended finer, scarlet tendrils, a holdover of Halloway's red hair.

I prepared to give my "Your crimes have invited Reprisal" speech, but the mercenaries had already started reloading their weapons. Just as well, I wanted to cut to the chase anyway.

Another round of gunfire smashed into my armor, and I accepted it for just a few seconds before I redistributed the force and ran. I was never much of an athlete as a kid, and the early years on hormones made me feel off-balance, but Reprisal sent power rushing through my whole body. My feet carried me hard and fast; I blurred as I closed the distance to my nearest assailant. My fists may as well have been hammers when I smashed him in the face and knocked him to the floor in one punch. That constant bash of bullets against my armor would leave bruises later, but each burst strengthened me. The barrage of gunfire slowed as, one by one, I knocked out the opposition. A nose-breaking thrust to the face for this one, a twist and a kick to the skull for that one, a two-handed smash to the back for yet another. Less than thirty seconds later, I stood surrounded by floored, groaning bodies.

The buyer scrambled backwards and hid behind my father. "This is the freak your city's been fighting all these years?"

My father chuckled. "She's knocked out a few of my teeth, I know the feeling."

That was Halloway, not me, but he didn't know. None of the city's criminal element knew of the original Reprisal's passing.

He motioned toward his underling. "Current, enough's enough. Time to earn your keep. Take care of this."

I turned to face his partner, but Current didn't drop into a stance; he just stepped forward and thrust out a finger. A bolt of lightning blasted from his fingertips and threw me backwards, a shout slipped from my lips as I fell. He took another step forward and stuck out his hand again. I leapt from where I fell—no amount of kinetic energy from bullets could get Reprisal to dodge lightning, but I only had to outrun his point. Another blast tore a hole in the concrete floor. I made out a little smirk on his face under his high collar as he hopped on his toes like we were in a boxing match.

Insolent worm, Reprisal said. *He dares use lightning on us? We kill him — we must kill him.*

I had to shake out my arms and legs. Reprisal couldn't convert electricity, even a lowlife crook like my father knew that, and he'd brought a lightning conductor. With my sight fixed on his hands in anticipation of another attack, I ran again in a spiral path. Twice more, Current threw out pointed hands. Sudden bursts of power shredded right through the floor, but my feet remained quicker than his gestures. As I closed the distance between us, he clapped his hands together, and sparks flew from his palms.

Kill him, kill him! Reprisal flooded my gloved fist with power, but I willed it back. I reared back for just a moment before I smashed into Current's face, determined to end the fight in a single punch.

He stumbled, shouted, and grabbed at his nose. It was a much higher cry of pain than I anticipated. The thought of how young he might be made me sick. My hit broke his goggles, and blood from his nose seeped through his fingers. I almost stopped right there to ask if he was alright.

Then the cry of pain shifted to an angry howl. With lightning still crackling at his fingertips, Current threw himself forward and grabbed ahold of me by my elbows. Electricity surged through my body, every one of my muscles went still, and I felt like I was burning from the inside. Reprisal cursed him in my head. I could feel my reserves of energy slipping away. My arms and legs blazed as I pushed through the pain, like forcing movement in the depths of sleep paralysis. With enough struggle, I tore myself off him and leapt away.

Current's heavy breaths told me his attack took a lot out of him, too. We stood, for the moment, at an impasse.

A gunshot rang out and bounced off my armor. I turned and saw the buyer with a pistol in his hand. My father gawked at him and, if I could hear, probably slipped into a tirade about how he'd just ruined everything. The out-of-towners could never get it through their heads—don't shoot Reprisal, it just makes her stronger.

They couldn't see, but I flashed a smirk as, empowered again, I ran and caught my father in a chokehold. He yelped and struggled as I turned back toward Current, whose eyes went wide.

"I don't know what he's paying you," I said. "But you can't collect if I take him out."

Current's mouth slipped open in surprise and fear as he looked between the two of us.

I wanted to ask, "What's it gonna be?" But his terrified shout cut me off.

"Dad!"

For the second time, paralysis overwhelmed me. What? What did I just hear? Did he—

"Dad, what do I do?"

Another jolt ran through me and crippled my power supply. My father had an empowered-grade taser pressed to my side, I had to release him and lunge away before he burned out the last of Reprisal's power.

"Your old man knows how to take care of himself," my father said. "As long as there's no more gunshots from the peanut gallery."

I needed to escape, regroup, and digest this insane revelation. But first, I had to interrupt the deal taking place. If I could steal the truck, I could get the Type C back to the people who needed it, but any of my enemies could shoot the tires before I escaped. Next to one of the hired guns lay a briefcase. It would have to do.

I took off at a dash and zig-zagged to dodge Current's lightning strikes. With a scoop and a leap, I grabbed the briefcase and jumped back to the catwalk. Indistinct voices below shouted that I was escaping. With another leap, I slipped out a long-broken window in the ceiling. After a quick peek to confirm the briefcase held the night's payment, I sprinted into the darkness to decide my next step.

Reprisal: Volume Two, Issue Sixteen

"Halloway... did you know?"

I threw the briefcase on my bed, stood in the kitchen of one of Halloway's Southside safehouses, and tried to get my breathing under control. As anticipated, little purple bruises ran up and down my body; even hours later, it felt like the ligaments in my arms and legs hadn't fully reconnected. And Current's shout played on constant repeat in my head.

My whole life, I'd been an only child. Heck, most of it, I'd been a single-parent child. How old was he? All at once, I felt like I lowballed the numbers—sixteen? Seventeen? If so, he'd be half my age, only a little older than when I first encountered Halloway. Was she trying to protect me? Protect him? Or was this an echo of what she'd always said about blood coming up again?

Flashback to Reprisal: Volume One, Issue One Forty-Three

At two thirty in the morning on a Wednesday in March, life thrust me into my first experience with costumed crimefighting. Mom and I lived in a townhouse she inherited from Grandpa. But even without a mortgage, she needed constant late shifts at the gas station to keep us above water. I didn't really know where my father was most of the time, just that he wasn't contributing to the family. Mom expected me to go to bed at a reasonable hour even if she was out, but I sat at my desk, wide awake. She loved me, but she wouldn't understand. Late at night was the only time I could wear the thrift store nightdress I kept crumpled under the bed, or paint my nails blue with a bottle from the dollar store. I'd scrub it off and be her dutiful son again by morning.

A sustained creak interrupted my ritual. We had a backdoor right underneath my bedroom nobody in the house ever used, and the noise carried up to me. A pit formed in my stomach. There was no reason for it to be Mom down there. Were we being burgled? I wanted to just hide underneath my covers, but I could almost hear my father saying, "Let them get away, did you? You never were man enough to protect anything." His projected criticism pushed me to stand. I dug around in the closet until I found a baseball bat I hadn't used since middle school. That had to be good enough.

I crept downstairs with the quiet movements of a theatrical run crew. The lights were still out, so I barely made out a body when I spotted the intruder in the living room, rifling through a bookcase. I was only gonna get one shot, so with the bat pulled back, I took in a deep breath and ran. I smashed the bat across the back of the crook's head. A *crack* reverberated through the living room, but it didn't come from the stranger's skull. With a flinch, I stared at the bat. A long, splintering line ran down the point of impact. My lips slid open, and I shook in horror as the masked figure turned to face me. Those two white pits at the center of the mask felt like they pierced right through my soul. I knew this intruder from the TV and the papers. I felt so scared I could throw up. After an instant, I found enough nerve to scream and swung again.

Reprisal caught the bat at the cracked point, clenched her hand, and the weapon shattered. I stumbled backwards right onto the couch. The intruder tossed the end of the bat aside, but then raised her hands. In a voice that might have been gentle if not for the distortion, she said, "It's all right, I'm not here for you."

"What do you want?" My voice cracked as I put up my hands in supplication. "Don't—I don't—it's not my fault! I'll—I'll never do it again—"

"What are you talking about?" Again, it might have been kindly if the mask hadn't been interfering.

"You're an avenging angel, right?" I shut my eyes tight to keep tears from flowing. "You think I'm messed up because I pretend I'm a girl—I swear, that's all I'm doing! I'm just pretending, I'm an actor—I—I—"

Her demeanor changed; she tensed up for a moment. Reprisal came no closer; she just kept her hands up and, eventually, said, "I'm no angel. And I'm not here to hurt you." After another pause, she added, "Miss."

Her words made my stomach churn; even with all her effort, it sounded like she mocked me. "What—what do you want?"

"I'm tracking the case of a criminal calling himself the Key Keeper." After I gave her a blank stare, she added, "And I recently learned his real name is Grant Greene."

It took a hard swallow for me to find my words. Eventually, I asked, "My—my dad? My dad is a bad guy?"

"I'm sorry," Reprisal said. "This must be difficult."

A rueful laugh slipped past my lips. "Dunno, might explain a lot, maybe." My gaze fell back to my calloused hands and the cheap blue on my nails.

I hadn't seen my father in weeks, but I remembered Mom telling him I got cast in the spring play. He scoffed and said, "Quit coddling him, he'll never be a real man if you keep letting him go out for that fairy stuff."

With slow, deliberate movements, Reprisal sat down in the recliner across from me. She looked ridiculous and jarring, but I felt like she wanted to be comforting. "Has he hurt you?"

My throat tightened. "I… why do you care?"

"I'm a warrior of retribution," she said. "Do you deserve retribution as well?" When I couldn't form words, she drew her own conclusion. "Family can be so cruel, I know."

I swallowed. "You do?"

"My aunt wore this suit before I did," Reprisal said. "It's been around for centuries now, the wearers battled evil from the shadows. You only know I exist thanks to news broadcasts and video cameras and the like." She shook her head, as if to recenter and return to her point. "She pushed me so hard, beat me for my failures, and she just kept acting like it was her right. That being of my blood meant I just had to accept it, and I had to love and be loyal to her no matter what." Reprisal shook her head. "It's a lie, kid. Blood can't demand loyalty, and it doesn't justify pain."

I didn't need her to tell me any of that, yet I listened with rapt attention.

"You know what else I understand?" She gestured at her mask. "That sometimes we need to adjust who we are on the outside to reflect what's within. I don't feel like I can save people without wearing this suit." She took a masterful dramatic pause. "And you don't feel like you can be yourself in a body that's betraying you."

I couldn't keep the tears back anymore. The suit still made Reprisal too intimidating, I didn't dare approach her, but I hugged myself. Someone finally put it into words. "Are... are you just trying to get me to help you?"

"No. I just want to save one more person tonight."

When I found the fortitude to wipe my eyes and stop blubbering, I led her first to the basement, then to a manhole cover in the corner. "There's a cistern down there," I said. "Dad always screamed at me to keep away. It's really heavy, I don't think I can open it."

Reprisal bent down and tore it aside. I later learned my father kept a hoard of stolen cash and equipment down there. Mom and I scraped by to pay for the house, and he had so much money stashed right under our noses.

When she emerged from the pit, Reprisal laid a reassuring hand on my shoulder. "Thank you," she said. "I know payback is usually only considered an act of vengeance. But you've helped me tonight, and I promise I will repay you many times." With a squeeze of my shoulder, she again said, "Is it Miss Greene, then?"

Choked up, I nodded. "I, uh... I haven't picked out a new first name yet."

"Then I'm going to take it upon myself to ensure you get to do so."

Within ten days, I heard my father was in prison again. The same evening, I received a letter in the mail for a grant from Halloway Industries that I had never applied for. Halloway's first gift of many.

Present Day

So much remained left unsaid between us when stomach cancer claimed Adeline Halloway years later. She trained me just enough to know how to take up the Reprisal armor—passed aunt to niece through the centuries, in spirit, if not in blood, she said. I got a crash course in how to access her records of the city's criminal element. I'd seen my father's file; Mom and I were his only documented relations. But she always kept secrets, always said anything she didn't tell me, it was only because it didn't matter. And she had so much contempt for the idea of blood, could that mean—

An explosion of force and sound tore through the safehouse's front door. I knocked against the kitchen wall like a ragdoll and stared out through the wreckage. Current stood beyond the blazing remnants of the entryway. An empty bag of Type C stuck out of his lips, he raised two fingers and squeezed the rest into his mouth. They'd found me, the briefcase must have been bugged. I scrambled into the den, scooped my armor off the couch, and ran into the bedroom.

"You're too late," he said. "I hear where you're going, and I have more than enough C to power me through this."

"Don't come any closer." I yanked on my armor and ran for the safe under my bed.

"I'm not afraid of you." Current projected his voice. "My old man told me how your powers work, my tank is full, and you're all burned out."

After a quick feel around my nightstand, I found the key and shoved it in the lockbox. "I'm warning you, you don't wanna be in here for this."

Current stepped into the entryway just as I pulled the pin off of a grenade. Even behind his broken goggles, I saw as his eyes bugged out, his hands rose in defense, and a shout slipped past his lips. I fell on the bomb to maximize the effect as an explosion engulfed me.

Reprisal: Volume Two, Issue Seventeen

Nothing but an erupting sound made it past the armor. When I stood back up, the force of an explosion flowed through me. Current held his hands over his ears, and I lunged forward to resume our battle.

He is weak, defenseless! Reprisal's voice came out raw and distorted with all the power we suddenly shared. *Throttle him, crush his neck, kill, kill, kill!*

My haymaker burst open Current's nose and knocked him off-balance; he stumbled backwards into my den. When I threw a kick toward him, he rolled out of my path, grabbed hold of the leg, and a channel of lightning coursed through me. I suppressed a shriek as energy ran like pins and needles before I ripped it away and fell back into the kitchen.

The two of us shared a glare as we both shook out our limbs. "I could end you right now," I said. "This thing in my head is screaming at me to do it."

"You won't." He sounded certain. "You're too soft-hearted. Dad says you always have been."

I clenched my fists. "You're not like him. Or you don't have to be."

For just a moment, a troubled look passed my brother's face. "You couldn't understand. He's all I have." And he stuck out two fingers again.

I leapt and rolled out of the lightning bolt's path. Reprisal screeched, *He's made his choice, now we make ours!* Current took aim again; I grabbed my cast iron and flung it at his head. With a heavy projectile coming at his face, he redirected his fingers and atomized the skillet. That gave me the opening I needed—I rushed at him, got ahold of one arm, kicked him behind a knee, and knocked him to the floor.

Rip it off, let him bleed out!

I didn't give in, but I indulged. One fierce twist and one solid punch to the elbow was all it took to force out a *crack* and a scream. Electricity sparked off of Current's body; flayed, frantic bursts jabbed me like tiny daggers. A shriek of my own slipped loose and forced me to retreat.

Current writhed on the floor, the sight made my stomach turn, as Reprisal kept hissing at me to finish him. "That could have been your neck," I said. "But I don't want it to be."

"Screw you." He spoke through gnashed teeth.

"Listen to me, I don't want you arrested. I can help you. I—"

A pair of tiny spears cut into me. I winced and looked down; the points of an empowered-grade stun gun pricked me a moment before a blast of electricity racked my body. I fell to the ground, quivering.

"That's enough of that." My father laughed as he stepped into the safehouse and took his place at Current's side. In his hand, he held a packet of Type C he tossed next to his protégé. "This is finally it, my boy. The night the great Reprisal finally meets her end. Let's tear that armor off and put a bullet in her."

Idiot girl, he has you cornered now!

"Don't do it." I started talking through my teeth, "Current—listen to me— you don't want this."

He scowled as he reached for the pack with his good arm. "What would you know about what I want?" He tore it open with his teeth.

I reached up and took hold of my mask. It wasn't a good answer, but it felt like the only one I could think of. "I know because he almost ruined me, too." I tore the cover away and looked at him, face to face. "My name is Allie Greene. I'm your big sister." Bitter and rueful, I looked toward my father. "Hey there, Dad."

Current froze up with the packet still lingering next to his lips. Probably because, for all of Halloway's money I spent on surgery and hair removal, he saw it just like I did: I still had our father's face.

For his part, the old man gawked before, trembling, confused, and as a question, he uttered one word: my deadname. A moment later, voice tinged by disgust and fury, he said it again, before, with all the hate he could muster, he said, "You always were such a disappointing son."

I turned my focus squarely back to my dumbfounded brother. Halloway was right, blood and biology didn't matter between us. What we shared ran much deeper. "He could have ruined me, but when I needed it most, Reprisal saved me. I want to save you, too."

"You should have kept your mask on and your mouth shut, boy. Now I've got a clean shot." Our father took a step forward and drew a pistol from his gaudy suit. "Guess I just never could set you straight."

My blood ran cold, and I tried to push upward, but the latest electrical blast reduced the Reprisal suit to dead weight. As the corrupted copy of Halloway's voice rang in my head, I turned a sad look toward Current. As if reciting affirmations to myself, I said, "You deserve to be happy. You deserve to be free."

Our father pointed the gun at my face.

"And you deserve a family who will look out for you."

Reprisal screamed a last insult

Our father fingered the trigger.

But the old man wasn't faster than lightning.

Current turned a blast of electricity at him, Grant Greene shrieked, lost hold of his gun, and collapsed to the floor.

With quakes running through his body, Current pushed up, looked down at him, stepped over to the fallen pistol, and kicked it toward me.

After a little fumbling, I got ahold of the weapon, pressed the muzzle against one hand, and fired. My suit had strength again, so I got up and stepped to his side.

After a moment to collect myself, I said, "Thank you."

His eyes remained downcast toward our father, who still lay trembling and beaten on the ground. "You said you'd help me?"

"As far as I'm concerned, him and those thieves were the only ones stealing Type C tonight," I said. "But I have to get that shipment back to the hospital."

He nodded slowly. A quiet moment passed between us before he said, "He told me he had another kid... a son, but..." It seemed his initial question died on his tongue. Instead, he asked, "Your name's Allie?"

I nodded. "Yours?"

"Carlos." After a last hesitation, he turned to face me. "You're... you're really my sister?"

"By blood, yes. But that doesn't really matter." I raised a gentle hand toward him. "I will be by choice, too, if you want me to be."

Carlos looked at my hand, as if he didn't know what to do with it, before he fell forward, and I caught him in an embrace. I didn't know what he struggled with most, but with effort, he said, "You got what you wanted. You saved one more person tonight."

What the Gargoyle Knew
by Brian Gibson

Michael Travers, aka "The Apparition," crouched atop the county courthouse, his gaze fixed on the bell tower of the Saint James Episcopal Church across the street. This late at night, the pairs of empty arches that pierced each face of the square-sided structure, just below the peaked roof, were shrouded in nearly impenetrable darkness. Nonetheless, he could sense, with crystal clarity, that nothing moved within the bell chamber that the shadows concealed.

This sense, which informed him of the size, shape, and location of every physical object in his vicinity, was just one of the gifts bestowed by the teleporter accident he'd been caught in the year before. That same accident had claimed his father's life and blinded his younger brother. Since then, his life had undergone radical changes, and the fact that he sometimes patrolled the rooftops at night clad in the blue, gray, and red uniform he'd adopted in his alter ego as a protector of the city's people was just one of them.

Tonight, though, was not just some random patrol; he'd been searching for something specific for several nights running and believed he'd find it arriving at this bell tower sometime tonight. While he waited, he mentally reviewed the events that had brought him here.

He'd arrived in Detective Serena Blake's apartment by the usual means, materializing in the center of her living room with a "WHUMP!" of displaced air.

"Is it just me," she'd drawled from her position on the couch, "or is that getting quieter?"

"I'm getting better at swapping the volume of air where I arrive with what my body occupied where I left. If I can get it exactly right, I think I can eliminate the sound altogether." He'd smiled down at her over the glass coffee table that separated them, before moving toward the leather upholstered chair sitting catty-corner to the couch. "So what's up?"

"Straight to it, huh, kid?" Her white teeth flashed against dark brown skin as she smiled back at him, and a wave of one elegantly manicured hand approved his move to take a seat. She was still dressed in the slacks from her work pantsuit, but had sloughed the jacket, tie, and shoulder holster here in her own home. The top button of her blouse collar was undone, the greatest concession to comfortable informality he'd ever known her to make.

Once he'd settled into his seat, she'd leaned forward and her fine-featured face had taken on a more serious expression. "We've had some interesting hospitalizations in the last few weeks. The descriptions remind me a bit of The Creature's attacks from last summer, except for the lack of poison or body count. But all these victims talk about something inhuman attacking them, something stronger than any mere man." There had been a hard edge to her voice as she'd recalled the attacks that had all but crippled the Lancaster Police Department the year before and had put her partner in the hospital.

"No shit?"

"None, indeed," she'd smiled sardonically, her mask of humorous detachment slipping back into place. Stopping The Creature had put him in the hospital, too, and he still sometimes had nightmares about it. Knowing how deeply those events had affected her, the seeming ease with which she adopted a tough exterior had always intimidated him just a little – that, and the fact that she had a couple of inches of height and at least a decade of experience on him. "And since, during the last go-around, you were the only one able to do anything to stop him, I'd like to bring you in on this."

"Not," she'd continued, "that I want you tangling with this thing the same way. I don't want you getting torn up again or killed. I just figure that, with what you can do, you have the best chance of anyone I know of finding this thing and getting away with your skin intact."

"So, what can you tell me?"

That's how he came to spend the last several nights looking over crime scene photos, reading police reports, and lurking on rooftops hoping to catch a glimpse of the latest horror of the modern age. Unlike The Creature, which had murdered its way through a sizable chunk of both the criminal underworld and the Lancaster Police Department, this particular horror hadn't caused any fatalities yet. It had, however, left a trail of broken bones and nearly religious terror through that selfsame underworld.

Religious terror wasn't surprising, though; the thing they described sounded an awful lot like a gargoyle to him.

A little internet research had initially led him to the Keiper-Long Mansion on Duke Street, which featured gargoyles on its roof. That had turned out to be a bust. While cool, the decorations on the mansion had been nothing more than ordinary grotesques.

And so, he'd taken to lurking on rooftops around the East Lancaster neighborhoods where the attacks had been taking place – an easy enough thing to do when you could not only teleport, but stand on sheer walls, and even ceilings, as though they were level ground. In so doing, he'd caught sight of what he believed to be his target flying overhead several times.

Well, not sight, exactly. He'd picked it out of the night sky thanks to that mysterious other sense he'd acquired (and he was increasingly thinking he'd have to come up with a name for it – he made a mental note to do some research on something appropriate). Several nights of teleporting about Lancaster rooftops, following that distant form, had led him to the belfry of Saint James.

Now, he was lurking in the shadow of the massive air conditioning unit on the courthouse roof, keeping an eye out to see if the gargoyle would return and confirm its hiding place. The deep blue and gray of the uniform he wore while 'on the job' helped him to blend into the darkness, so he wasn't concerned about being spotted when he sensed the creature winging toward him from over the Marriott hotel to his southwest. If it was, indeed, heading for the belfry, it seemed like it would pass directly over him. He shrank deeper into the shadows and waited for it to come into sight overhead.

As it approached the courthouse, it began to climb, losing speed as it did. By the time it cleared the edge of the looming environmental machinery, it was high overhead and nearly at a complete standstill with its wings outstretched, affording the Apparition his first really clear look at the object of his hunt.

It was shaped like a powerfully built man, though one only about three feet in height. The heavy musculature was sharply defined, which, combined with the dark gray color and rough texture of its hide, gave it the appearance of being carved from stone. Hands and feet alike, while human-like in shape, ended in sharp talons, and a long tail snaked out from the base of its spine. From behind its shoulders spread a pair of bat-like wings that easily spanned ten feet. Its head was brutish in appearance, with sharp tusks jutting up from a powerful lower jaw, part of a short muzzle that extended from beneath heavy brows studded with short spikes. A pair of large horns curled back from its brow and down to either side of its face, reminiscent of a ram.

It had only just dawned on The Apparition that the dark eyes beneath those heavy brows were staring directly at him when the creature flipped over in midair, folded its wings, and plummeted straight for him.

It streaked through the distance between them in an instant, and The Apparition had barely enough time to raise his force field before an impact like a meteor strike drove him down to the rough surface of the roof. He had little doubt it would have broken ribs without that added protection; as it was, he knew he'd be feeling it in the morning. He tried to raise his arms to fend off his attacker, but they were swiftly pinned down by the crushing grip of the beast's clawed hands. The power and weight of the thing belied by its small stature, and he could hardly draw breath against the mass of it on his chest.

It lowered its head to glare into his eyes. The reflection of the reddish glow that The Apparition's own eyes gave off when actively using his powers added an even more demonic aspect to its appearance. Its jaw dropped open, and, much to The Apparition's shock, spoke in a voice like rocks grinding together.

"Who are you?!" it demanded. "Did Reverend Terror send you?!"

The Apparition teleported.

WHUMP!

From across the street, standing on the steep slope of the St. James steeple roof, The Apparition looked back toward the courthouse and his attacker. He could easily make it out despite the deep shadows shrouding the area he'd just vacated – the darkness made no difference at all to his peculiar extra sense. It was picking itself off the roof, where it had sprawled upon The Apparition's abrupt departure, and looking around with quick jerks of its bestial head. After a moment, it paused, looking up, then suddenly spun around to glare directly at him.

The gargoyle (at this point, he really couldn't think of it as anything else) dropped to all fours and charged toward him across the courthouse roof. When it reached the edge, it leapt powerfully out into the space above Duke Street, its wings snapping out to turn the leap into a glide that bore it unerringly towards him. At the last second, the wings thrust back, adding an extra burst of momentum to the aerial charge.

The Apparition teleported again – *WHUMP!* – and almost immediately heard a crash as the gargoyle slammed into the steeple roof with shingle-shattering force. From his new position at the peak of the church roof near the rear, he watched the creature wrench its clawed hands free of the splintered wood and shuddered at the thought of what that impact might have done to him if he'd still been there.

Once again, after only a moment's pause, his attacker oriented on him with startling speed. But this time, rather than launch into another headlong charge, it clenched its fists in obvious frustration and bellowed a challenge.

"Stand still and fight me, villain, if you dare!"

The Apparition blinked in surprise.

"Villain?"

"Don't play dumb with me! You're clearly one of Reverend Terror's minions!" It crouched as if preparing to spring again, the claws on its feet and one hand digging into the steeple to maintain its purchase on the steep slope.

The Apparition was starting to feel like he'd lost the thread, but, as long as he had the thing talking, maybe he could de-escalate the situation and get some answers. He tried straightening from his own defensive crouch and spreading his hands in a mollifying gesture.

"I don't even know who that is!"

Now it was the gargoyle's turn to look uncertain.

"Reverend Terror! The biggest human trafficker in this part of the country! If you're not working for him, then why are you following me around?"

"Umm… because you've been attacking people all over the city."

"Harrumph," the creature rumbled. It dug the claws of its feet more deeply into the roof and straightened to cross its arms over its broad chest. "If you want to call them 'people.'"

The Apparition was encouraged by the gargoyle's willingness to talk and was beginning to feel like they might not actually be on opposing sides here, even if he was a little uncomfortable with its casual dismissal of the humanity of its victims.

"What do you mean?"

"They've all trafficked people to Reverend Terror, the pieces of crap. I've been trying to get information on where to find him!" The gargoyle hopped down from the steeple to the same roof level where The Apparition stood, using its wings to make the landing much softer than it otherwise would have been. "I was pretty sure I had it figured out when I noticed you following me around. Guessed the Reverend had heard I was after him and sent you to deal with me." It began walking toward him, and The Apparition stood his ground. Since its posture seemed to have lost the coiled tension of moments before, he was pretty sure it was approaching to make talking easier rather than to resume its attack.

"Nah," The Apparition responded, doing his best to sound casual and non-threatening. "A contact in the police asked me to find out who or what was attacking people."

"Pfft! Cops!" It practically spat the word as an epithet.

"Hey, they're not all bad."

"Not all good, either. But all dangerous." Its fanged muzzle curled in the first approximation of a smile he'd seen from it. "Well, not so much to me. But neither here nor there; they aren't part of my business." By now, it was only a couple of paces away, its wings slightly unfolded and held loosely just around the sides of its shoulders so that they cast much of its body in shadow from the streetlights beyond.

"So, about your business; what comes next?"

"Go after the Reverend, of course."

"And, by 'go after,' you mean...?"

In response, the gargoyle turned away from him and crouched, spreading its wings in clear preparation to take off. It glanced back at him over its shoulder. "I mean 'go after,' and you'd better stay out of my way. You and the cops."

The Apparition clenched his fists in frustration as the gargoyle launched itself into space and started to climb away with powerful beats of its wings. This thing didn't seem indiscriminately vicious, and it hadn't killed anybody yet, that he knew of, but it's possible it was saving up the real violence for the object of its hunt. For all he knew, letting it carry out its plan could still be a bloodbath. He couldn't let that happen.

WHUMP!

He appeared on the gargoyle's back, directly between its wings, and wrapped his arms tightly around its neck. "Not so fast! You're not going after this guy without me!"

The sudden addition of his weight caused the gargoyle's flight to falter, and it immediately started to lose altitude. It seized The Apparition's forearms in its claws, and pried them from around its neck without much seeming effort – he was once again surprised by the sheer strength contained in the small frame.

"Get off!"

A wingbeat brought their descent to a halt, and the gargoyle flung him over its head and straight toward the asphalt and passing cars below.

WHUMP!

This time, he materialized in front of the gargoyle, and again he wrapped his arms around the creature's neck. "We go together, or not at all!"

He once again had to activate his force field to keep the beast from biting his face in reaction. Since the gargoyle was too short for him to wrap his legs around as well, they dangled awkwardly beneath the pair, but his opponent had no such problem. It pulled its legs up to plant clawed feet on his chest and thrust him away, again breaking his grip with ease.

"Leave me alone!"

The Apparition fell away, a wry smile forming on his lips, and…

WHUMP!

…landed on the gargoyle's back. "I can go all night."

"Alright!" the gargoyle bellowed in defeat. "Just let me land and I'll tell you where we're going!"

In the end, it wasn't a long trip to their destination. After all, Lancaster wasn't a very big city and was lousy with churches. And where else were you going to find some schmuck who styles himself "Reverend Terror?"

The pair crouched on a rooftop across Orange Street from the cathedral. It was a soaring structure, more than a century old, and, knowing what they did of what was contained in its basement, seemingly sinister in its grandeur. The parking lot to the west of the building was almost empty, but for the church's passenger van and a single nondescript sedan. Despite his extraordinary senses, he couldn't tell much about the interior; most of the building was stone, and too much mass in the way tended to obscure his perceptions. The reluctant companions kept to the shadows where the mismatch between the roofs of two buildings, metastasized into each other over the decades, created a hollow that was shielded from any eyes that might be keeping watch.

Though in The Apparition's experience, people rarely looked up.

"In there, huh?" he whispered to his unwilling companion.

"Where else?" the gargoyle growled back.

"Alright. So, how're you planning to get in?"

"Break a window and walk in."

The Apparition glanced down at the gargoyle, a note of levity creeping into his voice. "Not very subtle, is it?"

The gargoyle merely shrugged and grunted.

"I could just teleport inside, then let you in. Quieter, and won't leave any broken bits for any guards to find."

"How do I know you won't just leave me outside?

The Apparition shrugged. "If I don't let you in after three seconds, you can just do your plan."

The gargoyle's stony lips spread in a toothy grin. "Sounds fair."

The Apparition started to rise from his crouch, but then stopped and looked down at his companion. "By the way, what should I call you?"

"Gargoyle is fine."

The Apparition and The Gargoyle headed together into Reverend Terror's lair. Getting in was just as easy as he'd explained it on the rooftop. He'd teleported through one of the cathedral's rear entrances and simply opened the door from the inside to let The Gargoyle walk right through. The diminutive beast's rock-like claws clacked rhythmically against the tiled floor as they made their way through the darkened halls inside. This portion of the building was newer than the cathedral edifice, a modern addition that appeared to house offices and activity spaces. Though light was sparse, The Apparition could navigate easily, and his companion didn't seem to suffer any from the darkness either.

It was The Gargoyle who sensed their quarry first. They had come to a T intersection – one hall leading toward the sanctuary, and the other further into the more secular spaces – when the creature suddenly stopped and lifted a hand in a gesture calling for a halt. He cocked his head to one side as if listening to something in the distance, then pointed up the hall to the sanctuary.

The Apparition shot him a questioning look. He couldn't hear a thing moving in the entire place, but The Gargoyle headed in his chosen direction with a confidence that brooked no argument. He followed, and by the time they reached the heavy wooden door that gave access to the original cathedral building, even he could hear the voices beyond. More importantly, he could sense them - well enough to know there was a guard just on the other side of the door.

The Gargoyle seemed ready to bull right through the door, but The Apparition dropped a hand on his shoulder to hold him back. When The Gargoyle looked up at him, he exaggeratedly pointed at a spot on the floor and mouthed, "Wait here!" After getting a nod, he focused on a point just behind the guard, and...

WHUMP!

One arm around the guard's chest, the other snaking around to clamp a hand over his mouth.

WHUMP!

They appeared right in front of The Gargoyle, where The Apparition threw the hapless guard to the ground. Both were surprised, but The Gargoyle recovered first and slammed one of his stony fists into the side of the guard's head. The guard collapsed to the floor like a sack of potatoes.

The Apparition stooped to verify that the man was still breathing and to take his weapon. It was some kind of wicked-looking rifle – maybe an AR-15 or something similar; he wasn't any kind of firearms expert. He handed the weapon to The Gargoyle and whispered, "Can you do something with this?"

The Gargoyle took the weapon between his hands and, seemingly without much effort, bent the barrel.

The Apparition's eyebrows rose behind his mask. The strength of this thing continued to surprise him, and he was increasingly glad they hadn't come to serious blows.

"Alright," he knelt to whisper to his companion, "Door's clear. I can sense through the structure here; there's nobody else between us and where these rooms lead out onto the stage behind the pulpit. There's a guy standing there, and a group of people in the first couple pews. I'm guessing the guy behind the pulpit is your Reverend Terror?"

"Yeah," The Gargoyle growled, a bestial and unsettling sound. "I can hear him."

"Not gonna rip him apart, are ya?"

"He'll live."

The Apparition regarded The Gargoyle for a moment before nodding. "OK. Let's go." He started to rise, but a vice-like grip on his forearm stalled the movement.

"Take him down quick, or he'll put things in your head. Make you terrified of things that aren't even there. Practically paralyzes you that way. Don't give him the chance."

It didn't take long for them to get through the door, by the same means they'd gotten into the building in the first place, and make their way to the sanctuary. Well before they reached the final portal, even the Apparition could hear the reverend haranguing his captive audience in a booming, sermon-like cadence. He could sense that there were three men with guns similar to the one they'd taken off the guard ranged around the sanctuary.

"Hell is very real, my children. The Devil is very real, and his agents are all around you," he was intoning from his position behind the podium. "Yes, this sinful society has weakened you, isolated you from the men who are your rightful spiritual protectors by making you think you can stand on your own. That only means you stand alone! Alone against adversaries you couldn't even see until God brought you to me, so that I could show you what you truly face!"

He could hear sobs from the cluster of women gathered in the pews. His speech was occasionally punctuated by small flinches and shrieks from members of his audience, as though they were reacting to some unseen thing lunging at them. Up to this point, he'd felt just a little bit of excitement and trepidation for the upcoming confrontation, but now a seething anger was building in his gut.

"Three guards," and now his own whisper now had an edge of a growl to it. "Two at the back of the room, one at the front of the stage, between us and the Rev."

The Gargoyle nodded. "Reverend first. Guys with guns I can handle, but if he gets in our heads, we're cooked."

The Apparition raised a hand with his index finger extended to indicate "one." He raised his middle and ring fingers in succession to count of "two," then "three," and then…

WHUMP!

He appeared behind the Reverend and immediately lashed out. He heard the Gargoyle crash through the door in the same moment his fist connected with the back of the villain's head and drove him forward against the podium.

But Reverend Terror didn't go down.

Something he had neither seen nor sensed lunged at him from the corner of his vision, and a spike of terror rammed through him.

WHUMP!

He appeared on the sanctuary ceiling, crouching upside-down next to one of the arches that supported it. From there, he looked down (up, from his perspective) on the scene as The Gargoyle crashed into the guard on the stage and hurled him over the heads of the cowering young women to crash among the empty pews. The other guards were a little slow on the uptake, so The Gargoyle was halfway to the Reverend before they opened fire. Bullets sparked off its stony hide without slowing it at all.

The Gargoyle leapt with a roar, claws extended toward the Reverend, but at the last second its wings snapped out and spun it careening across the stage. It rolled across the planks and back to its feet, only to throw itself to one side as if dodging some unseen attack. For a few seconds, it leapt and spun across the stage before collapsing and curling into a twitching ball on the floor with its arms and wings wrapped protectively around it.

"The fool says in his heart that there is no terror!" the Reverend bellowed, standing with arms stretched to either side above his head. His black robes and priestly stole hung loose on him, the billowing fabric making him seem larger than he was. "But I am fear's instrument, and you will bow down!"

The Gargoyle gave every appearance of helplessness as the two remaining guards approached, their weapons trained on its shuddering form. The Gargoyle whimpered, and Reverend Terror turned a slow circle with his arms still extended.

"But where is your friend? Do you think he will watch as my children find your weak spots and take you apart? Or has he abandoned you altogether? Has terror mastered him, as well?"

The fear had melted away as The Apparition watched, and now the anger was back. He clenched his fists, focused on the rage, and...

WHUMP!

He appeared directly in front of the villain, his fist already in motion towards the Reverend's face.

His bowels turned to ice water as a hideous form coalesced between him and his target. Sheathed in shadow and flame, it towered over him, its massive scaled frame rendered even larger by the bat-like wings that spread out behind it. It lunged at him with a roar, moving far faster than anything of its bulk had any right to do. On instinct, The Apparition snapped his force field around himself even as he sprawled back flat on the stage floor.

The demon vanished, and the terror with it.

The Apparition gaped up at the empty space where the creature had been a mere moment before, then focused on the gloating face of the villain beyond. A slow smile spread across his face.

"Well, doubleplus spiffy!"

He lunged up from the floor toward the astonished Reverend and seized him in one hand by the front of his robe. He pulled back his other hand in a fist, and now it was the villain's turn to stare gape-mouthed.

"Reverend Terror? Think I'll call you 'Jareth,' instead."

"Wha...?"

"'Cause you have no power over me."

This time, when The Apparition hit him, Reverend Terror went down.

A few minutes later, a recovered Gargoyle stood with fists on hips atop the unconscious forms of one of the guards he'd just dispatched, glaring at the Apparition. The former captives were gathered at the opposite end of the sanctuary, soothing each other's trauma while waiting in the quiet for the police and paramedics to arrive. They didn't seem at all keen to be near their rescuers, particularly The Gargoyle.

"You almost blew it, kid." He could tell The Gargoyle was working to suppress his anger and tried for an apologetic tone.

"It worked out OK in the end."

"I told you to take him out quick. You gave him an opening with that weak punch of yours, and we could've been killed."

"Sorry. I'm pretty new at this, actually, and I still kinda suck at the hitty parts."

The Gargoyle glared at him for a moment, but then its angry demeanor cracked. A smile spread across its muzzle. "By the way, cute quote. But you realize you cast yourself as the teenage girl in that scene?"

"Meh," The Apparition shrugged, and returned the smile. "I'm secure in my masculinity."

Uncle Sam's Angels
by Eric Remington

Captain Justice spun in the air and dove out of the way of yet another plasma bolt. This one came close enough to singe the cloth of his sleeve. He added an extra spin into his turn and reversed direction hard as his red-white-and-blue cape fluttered behind him. The trooper pursuing flew past, unable to match Captain Justice's maneuverability. A flare of energy surrounded Captain Justice's hand as it tore through the trooper's jetpack. The trooper frantically tried to correct the incipient spin before dropping his pack and activating his parachute.

On the ground below, the battle continued to rage all around the National Mall, the final line of defense before the occupied White House. Squinting for a moment, Captain Justice could see his sister, Captain Truth, her American flag uniform starting to show the strain of the battle. She threw all the force she could muster from her deceptively small frame and punched the trooper in front of her hard enough to send him flying into a tank, knocking him unconscious and severely damaging the tank. "That's the way, sis! Every day is Punch a Nazi Day!" Captain Justice called over the team radio.

Captain Truth glanced up at her brother, hovering above the battlefield, "You say that in every fight. You can't use that as your catchphrase. What happens when we have to fight somebody else? The Legion of Awfulness escaped the last time."

Captain Justice turned hard as a flock of birds sped across in front of him, momentarily blocking his vision. It streaked past into the face of another jet trooper, blinding him and causing him to crash into the branches of a high tree near the edge of the Mall.

"Perhaps thinking of catchphrases and sibling bickering can wait for the end of the current hostilities? My eagle sees another group of troopers approaching from the north," Faunia allowed only some of the amusement she felt into her voice as she called out from the out-of-the-way park bench she'd chosen as her vantage point. Being blind, she stayed out of the way of the main fighters, but helped immensely by splitting her mind into pieces and controlling a vast array of animals. She winced as a stray plasma bolt cooked one of her sparrows, "Will someone please take out that last jet trooper?"

Across the Mall, the battle-scarred, mottled green and brown mechanical form of Armored Cavalry turned a sensor dome skyward as the jet trooper streaked by overhead. "Yes," his flat, metallic voice replied over the radio. He steadied himself, a hatch cover on his back opened, and the nose of a rocket poked out for a moment before streaking up, followed by a plume of exhaust. The missile homed for a moment before detonating, sending the last flyer to the ground, "Handled."

Captain Justice spent another moment surveying the field, "Guys, let's get this wrapped up. Can we find the C&C and get a good target for Lumina? Faun, do you see anything?" he winced at the unintentional joke.

The barb's recipient smiled slightly beneath the dark glasses covering her eyes, "Not since birth, but my eagle might see somebody of interest just shy of the Memorial. Looks like he's got binoculars and a big radio setup. He's definitely their Command and Control. Let me point him out." An eagle dove from the sky, screeching loudly. A volley of plasma bolts completely failed to hit it on the way down.

"Got it! He looks nice. Pretty far, need another moment to gather the power. Don't look like ah've been spotted yet, but keep 'em distracted a moment longer, would you, hon?" Lumina's southern accent always bled through when she was preparing a difficult shot. She smiled as she aimed the shot from her position atop the Holocaust Museum at her target in front of the World War II Memorial, just under half a mile away. She felt the individual photons in the air all around her, felt their power. She began to channel them into a ball of energy inside of her, bending them the same way she bent them around her to maintain her invisibility. The charge building was a growing pressure in her body before the release of the laser that connected the two of them briefly. The target's armor vaporized in a moment, and he dropped, a smoking hole in his chest plate. "Target down."

The troops of the American Nazi Reich paused for a moment, briefly falling into disarray as their leadership faltered. The team paused, hoping for a surrender. An amplified voice rang out from behind the ANR's lines, "Enough of this. It is time for the true leaders to take the stage." A path formed as the lower-level troops made way for a group of hulking, armored cyborgs.

The three combat members of Uncle Sam's Angels gathered at a discreet distance away. Captain Justice drifted down from the sky to join Captain Truth, and Armored Cavalry stomped up behind them. His multi-ton bulk left divots in the soft grass. Captain Truth cracked her knuckles and settled into an easy, at-ready position. Armored Cavalry flipped the covers off a pair of chain guns under his vambraces. Captain Justice just tried to look menacing as the four figures approached.

"We are the Übermensch!" the lead figure boomed out, "No pathetic display of force will dissuade us from our glorious purpose! This country is ours by right of conquest; do not challenge us! We have wiped away your military with the cleansing power of the blood of our martyrs! Your precious American freedom ends now!"

The four cyborgs squared off, facing the three heroes. They had a swastika-on-stripes blazoned across their chests, and each wore a plasma gun on their arms, bringing them to bear on the heroes arrayed in front of them. Their optics glowed red; exposed hoses pumped a sickly green fluid around their bodies.

The heroes looked unimpressed. "Are you finished?" Captain Justice asked mockingly, "Hitler's speeches were shorter. We've seen your kind before. Truth, remind me, is this the fourth Nazi resurgence we've taken down, or the fifth?"

"This'll be the fifth. And they don't even have a clone of Hitler. Or Hitler's brain in a mech-suit. And aren't you South African, not German?"

The taunting had its desired effect as the four cyborgs charged. A bright flash tagged the head of one, destroying his helmet and dropping him to the ground. Lumina's joyous shout over the radio of "First!" was drowned out quickly by the snarl of a pack of wolves burying a second in a pile of fur and claws, coolant sprayed into the air, an amplified cry of "Kak!" before he stopped moving, and Faunia's frustrated, "Dammit, second!" over the team radio.

The final cyborg, thinking Captain Truth to be the easier target, found himself flying backward from a palm strike that shattered his chest plate and left him dazed on a pile of crushed troopers.

The ANR leader aimed his charge straight for Armored Cavalry, the two bulky war machines grappling for a moment, seemingly evenly matched. The ANR leader's strained grunts echoed over the suddenly quiet battlefield, the other troops visibly reluctant to interfere in this honor duel.

Armored Cavalry remained silent.

The leader's arms bulged, fluid pumping more and more vigorously through the tubing around his body, pulsing in time with more and more strained grunting.

Armored Cavalry remained silent.

With a final roar of rage, the leader slipped back to re-double his charge, pushing with so much power that several vents opened on the back of his suit to release overpressure in his systems.

Armored Cavalry remained silent.

Captain Truth watched impassively, her initial rage turning to pity, "Cav, just put the poor guy out of his misery, please? This is pathetic." Armored Cavalry's head swiveled to her, his mechanical face impassive. He turned back and, with an almost contemptuous ease, shoved the cyborg to his knees, forced his arms nearly to the breaking point, and then headbutted him. The cyborg collapsed on the ground, unconscious.

Watching their leader's ignominious defeat took the fight out of the rest of the enemy group. Only a few remained. The team left them to the approaching regular Army forces that arrived to reinforce the team's position.

This fight over, the Angels turned their attention to the White House itself, readying themselves for the final push. A single ANR soldier, one of the last in the main defense line, struggled forward, pulling himself along with his fingertips, striving for the rifle that remained just out of reach. The wound in his side caused him to grimace with each pull of his hand. An armored foot mashing it into the dirt took the last of the fight out of him. "Don't," Armored Cavalry said in a metallic voice.

A pair of US Army soldiers rushed up and took the defeated nazi under their arms. He slumped between them, submitting to being led away as a prisoner. Armored Cavalry surveyed the remaining battleground. Here and there, across a broad perimeter, sporadic resistance was still popping up, the occasional muzzle flash denoting the brief skirmishes, but overall, this battle had been won. He turned further to gaze at the White House across the Ellipse, the Reich flag still flying proudly on the flagpole above.

"Don't you hate that sight?" Captain Truth asked from his left. She squinted at the House, hate twisting her face into a grimace. His only response was a rumbling grunt of assent as he turned back to survey the various lines of attack.

"Don't like the view? I think I can fix that," Lumina's voice came over the comm, followed by a brief flash of fire as her laser shot burning through the hoist-side of the flag, and it fell, flaming, to the lawn below.

"Much better, thanks, Lume. Now, let's get that good old Stars and Stripes back up there!" Captain Truth replied, a smile in her voice.

Captain Justice joined them, surveying the Park through a pair of binoculars, "Resistance still looks pretty stiff. I see plenty of gun emplacements and possibly even a few snipers. We've got everything buttoned up right to Constitution Avenue. The Ellipse is still in their hands."

"Lumina, anything you can do about the guys inside the fence?" Captain Justice asked over the team radio.

"They haven't spotted me yet, but the angles are all wrong from here. I can relocate, but there's not much high ground I can get to quickly," she paused a moment, "Wait, I might be able to blind them if you can get me down there fast enough?"

"No sooner said," Captain Justice replied, skimmed the treetops, and paused a moment while she let her invisibility cloak fade, grabbed her from her rooftop perch, and returned her to the group.

"Oof, I'll never get used to that. Okay, let's see here," she gestured, and a piece of air in front of her formed a window that zoomed in on the distant emplacements. With detail, the full scale of the problem was clear: a dozen heavy guns, nearly a hundred regular troops, and the tell-tale signs of snipers on the roof of the White House itself. "So, if I were to get close enough, I think I can blind them all simultaneously with one of my big flares."

Captain Justice edged over, gazing through the zoom window, "That's got to be at least a quarter mile. Are you sure you can maintain your cloak for that long?"

"With a little help. Can you three organize a distraction? I need to end up right in the middle there to be effective, but if I cut across from the side, I should be able to get there fairly quickly. What's left of those trees should help for a while," she waved again, dismissing the view.

Wordlessly, Armored Cavalry strode between the group, pushing past into the opening onto the road. His turret-like head rotated towards Lumina, "Go," issued from the speaker on his chest before he strode into the road, planted both feet, opened an array of hatches and covers, and anchored himself to the concrete with a pair of spikes from his calves.

Lumina turned and ran, covering the distance to 15th street quickly, before ducking through the tree line, sprinting across Constitution, and taking cover behind the shattered remains of a van. Slowing her breathing, she concentrated, feeling the photons all around her, pulling and pushing them, convincing them to avoid her, to bend around her, in the process fading from view. After a moment, she called on the radio, "All set."

"Faunia, anything you've got to help?" Captain Truth asked, moving into position next to Armored Cavalry, weighing a chunk of stone in one hand.

"Unfortunately, I can do little in this case save reconnaissance. For that, my eagle continues to circle. Lumina's initial assessment seems correct, though I see fewer snipers than her. I would caution that several of the heavy weapons appear to be big enough to possibly damage even you, Truth."

"Well, nothing ventured, nothing gained. Let's show these South Africans what real apartheid feels like!" Captain Justice gave her a look. "Yeah, it sounded better in my head. Cav! Hit it!"

Illegals

by Jon Negroni

It had been sixteen years since Ignacio Garvey stopped using his real name, and seven since he last set foot on the skybridge between the El Puente district and the Beacon Core. Such a short distance, really, between utter squalor and extravagant power, the beating authorial heart of the entire city. He'd walked the bridge once as a child, hand in hand with his mother, before the Sanctum classified their family as a "high-visibility risk." That was the phrase stamped across the redacted custody record, alongside "Subject unrecovered."

The bridge itself hadn't changed. It still arched like a spinal column over the artificial bay, its metal bones glinting with blue municipal runes and broken prayer beads from vigils long disbanded. The cables hummed when the air shifted, like something dying trying to remember its own throat.

Tonight, the whole bridge shimmered in fog, smeared with the flicker of patrol drones circling above the perimeter fence. Below, the glowgutter canals bubbled with factory runoff, and the neon signs of El Puente, the city's underbelly, blinked in weary indifference.

Ignacio — known throughout the city of Vireluna only as *Azul* — stepped onto the middle spine of the bridge like a ghost trespassing in his own afterlife. His boots made no sound. His coat held no color. His pulse bent the light itself.

Behind him came Aris Zamudio, skating along an electromagnetic rail she conjured from the bridge's grounding rods, sparks trailing like sequins from her boot rims. Her body moved with the grace of paper in air. One arm extended, and on it curled a slender hoverboard etched with old symbols. Her only relic from before the Registry Years, the turning point when the Sanctum started turning people into data. Data that could be erased without question or argument.

"Three units patrolling the Zona Edge," she murmured, voice cool in his comm. "Marked for extraction. No civilian backup."

Ignacio nodded once. The Zona Edge was a jagged, militarized border between the Beacon Core and the sprawling outer districts. For a place teeming with drones and Redwing marshals, it was easily the most lawless territory in the city.

Beneath Ignacio's skin, his power stirred. An ache, a thirst, a wound that never fully closed. Eclipse-walking. His power, his only recourse. Its name given by those who had watched him vanish into light, then reemerge through concrete, blinking and breathless, yet also changed.

The truth was uglier. When he phased, he could feel the world forget him. A name like his meant nothing when vanishing. Neither did his body nor his blood. He became memory's absence, where a young man should have been, where a family once backed him. The law could not track him, but neither could the people he loved. It was a miracle. It was a curse. It was everything survival on the fringes required.

"So, are we doing this or not?" came a third voice, younger, trembling beneath the practiced cadence.

Martí. The boy squatted low and quiet, flames curling around his knuckles, casting halos that didn't belong to any saint. He couldn't be older than fifteen. Maybe not even that. His face was obscured by the scarf he wore year-round, not for cold, but to hide the split along his jaw. An old surgical scar from the clinics that preyed on spirit-children born outside Sanctum bounds. He'd once told Ignacio he lit his palms when he dreamed of his mother. The fire, he said, wasn't his. It was hers, trying to reach back.

Ignacio signaled with two fingers. Showtime.

They dropped together. Three figures, carved from the shadows of the erased, falling like ash into the brightest part of Vireluna. The fall wasn't far, but it felt like eternity unfolding sideways.

Ignacio phased as he dropped, skin dimming to a blur and breath tucked between molecules. His invisibility was more like a subtraction of himself. He shed his own substance like sorrow, leaking memory into the air, letting the world forget him for just long enough to pass through it.

He landed in a crouch on the edge of a shipping container stacked with others like bricks in a commerce graveyard. Below, the Zona Sagrada — or Sacred Zone — boiled in soft blue light, its halogen domes arranged like prayer circles, each centered on a Redwing enforcement pod. Four drones hovered low, angular and cruel in design. More like shrikes than drones. Their wings buzzed with an eerie resonance. They didn't need eyes to scan. They had frequencies. They could practically smell guilt.

Two children knelt in the dirt between pods, hands zip-bound, heads bare in the cold. Between them stood a Redwing marshal in full Sanctum plate: cobalt armor, reinforced jaw mesh, and a rifle tall as the girl's spine. Marshals thought themselves judges, really. The kind who passed sentence before names were even exchanged.

"No registry chip. No embassy. No claims." The voice from the helmet rang flat across the loudspeaker, as if synthesized from a thousand recordings. "As per Civic Mandate Twelve, Section 4, both are hereby designated untethered biologicals. Extraction for relocation will proceed immediately. You have no rights."

Ignacio blinked. The phrase "untethered biologicals" made his teeth flare. It meant the same thing it always did. No documentation. No representation. No proof you were real.

Below, one of the children sobbed. The other didn't make a sound. Just looked up. Directly at him. Directly at Azul. She…saw him. Even while he was phased. Even while he was unmade.

He inhaled sharply and moved.

Sliding down the container's edge, he released the phase. Gravity kissed his skin again, weight returned, and his boots hit earth with a dull *thok*.

The drones chirped. Their field broke, just enough to make a difference.

Aris came in next. A whip of magnetic current spiraled ahead of her, knocking two drones sideways like leaves on a griddle. The air snapped with static, and the drones tumbled in arcs of scorched red.

Martí landed last. Not so much landed as collapsed. His knees hit pavement, his hands lit up like votive candles, and the scream that tore from his mouth came not from fear, but belief. He threw both arms forward, fire coiling outward in wide, mournful ribbons.

The Redwing marshal raised his rifle.

Too slow.

Ignacio phased forward. Once, twice. Then reemerged behind him. He didn't bother with flair. He struck the back of the man's helmet with the butt of a stolen baton, watched him crumple, and caught the rifle mid-fall before it hit the dirt.

The boy and girl stared at him.

Ignacio turned, letting the eclipse wrap around him again. When he spoke, his voice carried like stone dragged across water.

"No one here is untethered," he said.

Above them, the Redwing pods recalibrated. One began charging an arc pulse.

Martí saw it first. "I can take it," the boy said, coughing ash. "But it's gonna hurt."

"No," said Ignacio, "it's going to work." He tossed the rifle aside. Raised both hands. And vanished.

He reappeared inside the arc pod's outer paneling. The air was cramped, electric, suffocating. He screamed from the pressure but held form just long enough to shove both palms into the core and will the field to rupture. His body glitched — half here, half not. Metal sliced through his side. Memory thinned.

The pulse failed. The pod exploded outward in harmless, beautiful fragments. When he tumbled out of the debris, the kids were already gone, swept away by Aris, who was skating across a recharged magnetic rail, her board pulsing low and wild.

Martí met him at the edge of the blast radius. He offered a trembling hand. His fingers flickered with flame. Ignacio took it. And for a moment, the fire did not burn.

No time to waste.

In minutes, they were moving beneath the city, through heat tunnels and rust-veined sewer vaults that carried more filth than water. The children clung to Aris's coat, coughing softly, coated in soot and adrenaline. No one spoke. It wasn't safe to talk down here. Sound echoed in strange ways.

Martí walked beside Ignacio, quiet as a hum. His fire had gone cold, burnt itself out somewhere between that last flare and the moment Ignacio collapsed in his arms.

They reached an access point. An iron hatch disguised as a broken vent behind the old Evangelista shrine. Ignacio tapped the rhythm. Three slow. One fast. Two slow. A mechanical hiss followed. The hatch opened to reveal a steep staircase lit by red filaments, leading into the bowels of La Hondonada. The *Hollow*. It had once been a foundry for airships, back when the people of Vireluna still believed in escape. Now it served as a safehouse. One of the last. The city's maps no longer acknowledged it, and that was the point.

Inside, warm eyes greeted them. A woman with braids like rivers. A boy missing an eye. An elder who no longer walked but still judged every arrival like he was reading a book only he could interpret.

The children were pulled away, then fed, wrapped, and comforted. Martí collapsed on a bench, but Ignacio didn't make it that far. He staggered once, caught the wall with a hand, and went down on one knee. The pain came suddenly. After the mission, after the adrenaline, that was always how it worked. Power was never free. Not for him. Not for any of them.

Aris was there before he fell further, arms under his shoulder. Her eyes narrowed when she saw the shimmer on his skin. The glitch. *His* glitch.

"You phased too far," she said.

"It was worth it," he murmured.

"You say that every time." Her fingers pressed along his ribs. They passed through a patch of flesh that didn't quite hold shape, like water trying to remember how to be solid. "One day, you won't come back all the way."

He looked up at her. "By then, it won't matter if I do."

Her jaw clenched. The lights above them flickered.

Martí stirred from the bench. "Well, I thought it was beautiful," he chirped. "When you slammed that marshal in the head. Ha! How could you vanish forever after doing something that badass?"

Ignacio rolled his eyes and clutched his side. From the far wall, a shape peeled away from shadow, catching his attention. Tenoch. The boy was thin as wire and twice as dangerous. His face was always painted in old resistance sigils, his eyes almost too calm. He didn't speak. He never did. Instead, he approached the cracked concrete pillar that held up the western arch of the Hollow, lifted his brush, and began to write.

Ignacio watched as the message formed:

THE ERASED SHALL BECOME LEGEND.

Beneath it, a signature mark: a spiral with no center. The mark of the Illegals.

By morning, the Hollow had taken on the hush of a fever dream. Rain slicked the district in sheets of bio-light, running down vents and railings, a chemical baptism. Somewhere above them, the Beacon towers blinked on and off. Processing, calculating, listening. Down here, where the official maps curled inward and tore, where names wore out faster than boots, the world smelled like melted copper and dry blood.

Ignacio sat on a crate near the air scrubber column, the metal still warm from overnight use. His coat was draped over one knee. His body pulsed with low-grade nausea. It always did after a hard glitch.

He held out his hand. His fingers flickered. Subtle, but visible. The phase wasn't settled. His atoms still remembered being somewhere else. Maybe nowhere else.

From across the room, Aris watched him. She didn't interrupt. Her silence was sharper than pity. It meant she knew what it was to fall apart piece by piece and pretend you were whole just because the world needed a name like "Azul" to chant.

The children they'd rescued now slept in the chapel corner, curled under waxcloth and thermal mesh, guarded by a woman named Yara Luperón. Yara was reading from a book with no title, her voice low, musical, and crackling like vinyl.

"The Sanctum will try to convince you that your story belongs to them. But it doesn't. It never did. The moment you put your body in the way of their forgetting, you are a writer of legend."

Ignacio couldn't tell if the words were for the kids or for the Hollow itself. He decided not to care. Too much else to worry about. A job coming up, for one thing. An important job.

Someone moved near him. A girl, maybe seventeen, all elbows and haunted eyes. She wore the mark on her sleeve: Tenoch's spiral, spray-painted in pale yellow. Faded.

"I heard about what you did," the girl said. Her accent placed her deep South. Candelaria quadrant, likely. A ghetto built over old salt fields. "The kids said you walked *through* the light."

Ignacio didn't look up. "I was just passing through."

"You made a choice." The girl stepped closer. "You could've run. You could've waited. But you stepped in. That makes you the kind of story they try to erase."

Ignacio lifted his gaze then. "I'm no story," he said, voice sandpapered by fatigue. "I'm a broken lightbulb, fading fast."

"You're a legend," the girl said. The way she said the word implied a softer description. Not to praise him, but to rebuke him.

Ignacio shook his head. "Legends don't look like this." He lifted his shirt slightly. The glitch wound had spread: a small bloom of phase rot, like heat shimmer warping a memory. It hadn't closed. It wouldn't.

The girl refused to flinch. "And just how would you know if you were or weren't a legend?" She scoffed and walked away without waiting for approval. Just dropped the words at Ignacio's feet like an altar.

That strangely astute girl terrified him. What she just said was the real danger, he knew. Not the glitch. Not the Sanctum. But hope. Hope meant others might follow. And if they followed, and he failed…it wouldn't be just Ignacio Garvey who disappeared this time.

It was always morning inside the Assembly.

Not by sun — Vireluna's upper Beacon Core hadn't seen real daylight since the domes went up — but by algorithm. A calculated warmth. A tactical luminescence. The overhead panels bathed the Sanctum chamber in golden light meant to evoke trust, renewal, and civility.

Warden Vexal sat at the head of the causeway, where data stalked like predators behind his eyes. His skin bore no sweat. His heart bore no variation. In the Sanctum medical file, his profile listed "sub-synthetic regulatory enhancements." In practice, this meant he smiled only when the math allowed it.

Today, the math gave him reason. He watched the footage again. Five seconds looped in crisp, multi-angle resolution. The Zona Sagrada raid. The interference. The anomaly.

Frame 217: A blue-cloaked figure dropped between two Redwing pods and vanished into light.

Frame 221: An electromagnetic cascade flattened three drones at once.

Frame 228: Controlled fire rippled from a boy's fingers.

Warden Vexal clicked his jaw, and the data split into nodes. Cross-referenced, undocumented bio-variants. 14.7% match to pre-Sanction SinLuz census files. Gene signature, partial, with a drift factor of 0.03. Strong enough for identification.

"Subject likely born Ignacio C. Garvey," the voiceprint AI offered from its perch above the screen. "Erased from systems twelve years ago via unauthorized null-chip phasing. Current alias unknown. Powers include temporo-material displacement via non-tech interface. Classification: Myth-Risk."

Vexal murmured the term aloud. "Myth-Risk." It was a newer way to put it. Invented last cycle. Applied only when the state feared violence less and narrative contagions far more.

"Have we scrubbed the footage?" he asked.

"Yes, Warden," came the obedient reply. "BeaconNet servers replaced the anomaly with environmental static. News tags attribute the event to a heat bloom and criminal sabotage. Civilian memory edits in progress."

"Good." He exhaled with precision.

Across the causeway, behind reinforced glass, a figure stood waiting. She wore white. Not the white of hope or peace. The kind used in sanitariums. The kind that blinded cameras.

Lexicon Mirth. The 19th success in the Sanctum's Sentiment Weaponization Initiative. Her presence in a room altered the way people dreamed. Her voice could extinguish grief. Her touch could make a child forget the face of their mother.

"What do you feel?" Vexal asked the Lexicon.

Mirth tilted her head. "His pain," she said. "It tastes bitter and cold like resistance."

"Do you even know what resistance is, Mirth?"

She smiled. It did not reach her eyes. "Resistance is a noise. A noise I was made to silence."

Vexal allowed himself to smile. "Then silence it."

They arrived beneath the Central Identity Archive just before the first curfew bells. The sewer corridor was narrow, slick with condensation, and smelled of ozone. Above them, the city's upper quadrant pulsed with security drones, while the Archive itself — a massive slab of hexagonal architecture — hovered on hydraulic stabilizers. It had no doors or windows. Only a single ramp connected it to the Zone Edge, guarded by biometric sentries and algorithmic locks.

Thankfully, they had access to old maps. Forgotten tunnels. Places where ghosts could walk.

Martí crawled through the grate first, his hands lit with soft embers, just enough to see but not burn. Behind him, Aris unspooled a tether of magnetic wire, feeding it into the wall panel beside her. Sparks danced up her arm, seeking the node.

"Fifteen seconds to breach," she whispered.

Ignacio sighed, heart heavy but steady. He reached into his coat, fingers brushing the chip Yara had ripped out of a salvaged drone some years ago. It held hundreds of names. Children erased by Sanctum raids. Names like his.

The plan was simple: inject the chip into the Archive's core, forcing a synchronization disruption. The system would see the erased entries as ghost files, then, in attempting to purge them, create a feedback loop, causing a full reboot. Which meant for thirty seconds, all records would be visible. Unfiltered. Unredacted. No more "untethered biologicals." Only names, listed plainly for all to see. And remember.

Martí counted down from five. The grate lifted. The breach opened. And the air changed.

Ignacio felt it first. A bleak stillness. A memory that didn't belong. His vacant eyes fell on a woman in white. *A damn Lexicon.* There weren't many of them, thank hell. This particular Lexicon hadn't broken in through a wall or descended from above to ambush them. No, she was simply there. Waiting. Pale, barefoot, clad in the sterile robes of the state's weaponized silence. Her white-blonde hair hung like wet string. Her eyes shimmered like screens waiting to load.

Aris stepped forward instinctively, but the moment the Lexicon turned her head, sound died.

Ignacio opened his mouth. Nothing. Martí reached for flame. Nothing. The Hollow's crew staggered. Pulse monitors failed. Neural links stuttered. Language itself trembled.

The Lexicon smiled. She walked toward Ignacio, her steps soft as regret. In her wake, graffiti peeled from the walls. Names on the chip scrambled. Even the power of Tenoch's prophecy, written in the micro-etches of Ignacio's coat, dissolved letter by letter.

Aris dropped to one knee, gasping. The tether sparked and died, rendering her powerless. Martí whimpered. "I—I can't remember her name—I can't—"

Ignacio stumbled backward as the Lexicon's eyes fixed on him. "You are the original echo," she said, voice like nothing, like the moment after a scream. "You are misfiled. Unnamed."

He tried to phase, but his body remained solid, real, and all too vulnerable.

She reached for his chest as he burst out his name. Loud. As loudly as possible.

"I…I…I am…IGNACIO!"

The phase returned, if only for the briefest moment. He screamed and vanished. Inside her.

For one terrible second, he passed through the Lexicon like static through flesh, through circuitry, through memory itself. He saw visions. Files, prisons, voices. His mother's voice. His sister's name. He felt every child the state had scraped from the record, heard their cries knotted into code.

He emerged on the other side of her, coughing blood, every nerve raw. But the Lexicon shuddered. Her pupils dilated. Her breath hitched. She stepped back, face cracked with hairline fractures of light.

Before anyone could speak, the Archive lit up. Alarms, red strobes, and data streams erupted from the core as the injected names surged through the system. The core overloaded. Ignacio fell. Aris caught him, shaking, eyes wild.

"It…it worked," Martí whispered.

Above them, inside the Archive's translucent wall, thousands of names bloomed like fireflies in code. Some still lived. Others hadn't for years. And one name hovered for Ignacio the longest: Isabel Garvey. His sister. He'd almost forgotten her name.

It started with a flicker. Not the kind you see, but the kind you feel when your atoms shift and your body forgets which world it's supposed to be in. Ignacio woke up to that feeling again, same as after every deep phase. A kind of reverse birth, wet and raw and gasping. His body had returned before his breath had.

He was alive. Hopefully. Still glitched, though. A slow throb pulsed in his spine like a bad song on loop. His skin jittered every few seconds, stuttering in the light. When he moved, parts of him didn't follow.

They'd dragged him back through the tunnels after the Archive went ablaze. Aris had done the heavy lifting. She wasn't talking, and Martí hadn't said anything either, though the kid had barely stopped shaking. The fire in his palms had gone out sometime on the walk home. Yara led them through a side route to avoid scannets. Ignacio remembered the way she looked back at him, once. Not like he was hurt. Like he was deadly.

Now, Ignacio lay on a stained mattress inside one of the Hollow's old maintenance rooms. Someone had wrapped his chest in gauze and hooked him to a jerry-rigged monitor that blinked nonsense. His name glowed above him on a wall screen. IGNACIO C. GARVEY. He shuddered. Not erased. Not hidden. They'd put his name back into the system. They'd lit a signal fire over his own grave.

Aris leaned against the doorframe, arms crossed, jaw tight. "You shouldn't be alive, Azul."

Ignacio cracked a smile. "Not the first time I've heard that."

"It's not a joke. You phased through a Lexicon. That's not supposed to be possible. She's not just a person, she's the Sanctum's firewall given skin."

He rolled onto his side, grimacing. "Felt like diving headfirst into a two-foot pool."

Aris stepped closer. "Well, people are talking. They think you actually managed to hurt her. Maybe even change her."

He blinked. "Did I?"

"You tell me. You were inside her head."

Ignacio didn't answer.

Martí sat on a crate nearby, eyes dark, watching Ignacio like a kid studies fire when it first burns him. He opened his mouth, then closed it again. Finally, "I saw you vanish, Azul, and honestly, I prayed you wouldn't come back."

Ignacio wasn't sure what to say to that. "OK…thanks. Real nice of you, Martí. But…can I ask why?"

"Because then you'd be a martyr. Martyrs are easier to love. And safer."

Ignacio let the words hang there. They gave him an idea. A powerful one. A dangerous one.

A soft sound caught his ear. Spraypaint. Tenoch was working again. He'd chosen the outer hallway this time, on the far side of the Hollow's metal underbelly. A flickering floodlamp swung back and forth like a slow pendulum, casting long shadows on the boy's back. His strokes were harsher tonight, less prophecy, more curse.

Aris followed Ignacio's eyes to the brushwork. She didn't ask. Didn't have to.

The Mark lives. The Mark bleeds.

Under it: a spiral with a cracked line through the center. Half-complete.

Ignacio turned his face toward the ceiling. The air smelled like old coolant and rotten fruit.

"They'll come harder next time," Aris said.

"I know."

"They'll send more Lexicons. They might use that last one to bait you. Or whatever comes after her."

"I know."

She crouched beside him. "And you're still willing to keep going?"

He looked at her, one eye glitching faintly in its socket. "You don't stop a story once it starts telling itself."

Martí laughed, short and bitter. "What are we, then? Supporting characters?"

"Hell no," Ignacio said. "You're the next few chapters. I'm just a footnote. And I know exactly how to finish the page."

From the hallway, Tenoch finished the final stroke. Sparks fizzled across the metal wall.

THE ILLEGALS LIVE TWICE.

It began with the sound of music.

A soft sound. Almost broken, really. A woman on a rooftop plucked strings from a guitar she made out of salvage wire and shattered drone casings. She didn't even use an amp. Just fingers and calluses and the kind of voice you only learn from living beneath someone else's boot.

The melody drifted up into the smoke-hazed dawn like an unforgiven apology. Quiet, but somehow still loud enough to hear. First in the Hollow. Then across the entire underbelly. Then on into the other districts and through the starlight panels of the Beacon Core itself. Finally, all of Vireluna could likely hear the song.

That's when they began to rise.

Not with guns or war cries or beating drums. With paint.

On every wall, every pillar, every rusted tram. Spirals bloomed like constellations in the wilderness. Half-finished. Cracked. Absolutely beautiful. The mark of the Illegals. Not so hidden anymore.

The Sanctum tried to scrub them in real time. Sent out drones to repaint, re-code, and reframe the narrative. But every patch they erased returned within minutes, bolder, brighter, burning with names long thought dead.

Isabel Garvey. Jesús Calderón. Ana Loba. Ernesto Días. Zuleika Ramos. A choir of the forgotten etched back into the bones of the city. And seeing all this, the people came. Quickly.

From every tier and trench, every undocumented block, every forgotten stairwell. Kids too young to remember the first registry sweeps. Old women who still wore glasses to hide the barcodes etched into their eyes. Men who hadn't spoken aloud in a decade chanted like saints. All of them moved in a hushed rhythm. All of them marked.

They wore blue and copper and gray and brown, or nothing at all but their faces, bare and unafraid. Above them, the Beacon Core's dome roared to life. Redwings shrieked overhead, hundreds of them, dark and sleek, the will of the Sanctum made steel. Below, over a dozen Lexicons emerged in formation. Mirth stood at the front, untouched by the glitch that had cracked her. But there was something in her eyes now.

Recognition. She saw Ignacio in the crowd. But for some reason, he did not hide. No, he walked forward alone. No mask. No alias. No Azul. His phase shimmer had gone quiet, barely visible now. His body bent under the weight of a myth being born in real time.

He reached into his coat. It was a flare. Blue fire shot skyward, piercing the dome's illusion of control.

In response, the Lexicons advanced. But thousands of citizens rushed forward, vanishing Ignacio in the crowd. Almost all of them wearing his mark. Which meant the system couldn't distinguish him now. Couldn't isolate. Couldn't erase. He had become too many.

Mirth hesitated before raising her hand. She paused. Lowered it. Across the sky, the Redwings fell still. In that silence, she finally caught a glimpse of Ignacio once more. But just as soon as he revealed himself, he vanished yet again. Not with his power, not through light. He was simply gone. All that remained was a spiral burned into the concrete beneath where he stood.

Another, the prophet they called Tenoch, stepped out of the crowd. He lifted his brush. And began to write, desperately and hopelessly into the concrete.

THE ERASED HAVE SPOKEN. THE ILLEGALS WALK AMONG YOU.

Too invincible
by Michael Penncavage

He looked up at the X-ray. "Are you certain?"

The doctor took her pencil and pointed to the dark spot between the two ribs. Placing two additional X-rays onto the overhead light, she pointed to similar areas. "We took three just in case there was a mistake."

The man walked over to the room's window. It looked out over the city. *His city.* Crossing his arms, his white T-shirt stretched to the point where the seams began to separate. "How long do I have?"

"We have no way of knowing if it is malignant or benign until we perform a biopsy."

The man turned to her, glaring. "Was that supposed to be a joke, doctor?"

The woman felt a trickle of sweat run down her side. Clearing her throat, she steadied her voice. "*No.* But currently, there is no way of knowing. All that we are certain of is that it has grown since last month."

"It's because of the cigarettes, isn't it?"

"That's a possibility."

"If it's..." he stated.

The doctor clicked off the viewer. "*If* the tumor is malignant and keeps growing at its current rate, I estimate you have six months...a year at most."

The man banged his fist into the windowsill. Wood chips flew onto the floor. "Are there any medications you know of...perhaps in other countries that aren't allowed here?" he asked. A silly question – though desperation had set in.

"Not that I'm aware, but it is something we shouldn't rule out."

He frowned. A crease formed on his brow. It was something new. Further testament, like his graying temples, to his age. "All that I've done for this city... and *this* happens."

All the doctor could do was look sympathetic.

Tugging the painted window open, Captain Invincible flew out of the room and into the moonless night.

"I just can't believe there is nothing the doctors can do! They don't have *anything* strong enough?" asked the Privateer as they met for lunch the following day.

They sat at a corner table. They were rarely noticed in the always-crowded restaurant. The benefits of living in the big city. Everyone minded their own business, not caring if they were lunching next to superheroes. Though with the Privateer's Clark Gable mustache, he did sometimes stand out.

"No. If a chainsaw can't hurt me, how are they going to break skin with a scalpel?" he answered, picking indiscriminately at his Caesar Salad.

"Have you told anyone else, Roy?"

Staring at a piece of lettuce like it was poisonous, he placed his fork down. "Just my family. I don't want this getting out. The press would have a field day. I can just see the headlines: *Captain Invincible – A Little Too Invincible?* Or some similar line of bullshit."

"Does anyone else from the Team know?" The Privateer asked.

"Just Sam. He's the only other person I could trust to keep his mouth shut."

Paul started laughing. "Well, considering robots don't gossip, that was a safe choice!"

Roy started laughing as well. They drew a few curious glances, but none made the connection between the two men and their alter egos.

The waiter brought over The Privateer's sandwich and Captain Invincibles' three. They ate in silence for several minutes. "There is one way, Paul."

The Privateer looked up at him.

"Nefarious."

Choking slightly, the Privateer cleared his throat with some wine. "What do you mean?" he asked in a low voice.

"We never found his workshop."

"He's been in jail for what…ten years?"

"Thirteen."

"He's a murderer, Roy."

"I'm aware of that. We both saw first-hand what he did."

The Privateer placed his sandwich down. "What are you suggesting?"

"The weapons he used were more advanced than anyone else's. There is a chance he might have developed something strong enough that I could use."

"Don't you think that if he did have something, he would have used it *against* us?"

Captain Invincible shrugged. "He could have thought one up since being incarcerated. Thirteen years in Solitary, a man has plenty of free time to ponder past mistakes."

"What are you planning to do, Roy?"

"It's not so much as…"

"*What* are you planning to do, Roy?"

Paul's mustache, which usually accentuated his smile, now only added to the frown.

It had been years since Roy had a reason to visit the Barion Correctional Facility. *Not long enough,* he thought, landing in front of the guard's booth.

The flabbergasted officer rang up the Warden's Office.

Warden Joe Smith looked much the same as how Roy remembered. A little wider in the midsection, but he still appeared fit. He was an honest, by-the-books man who always got frustrated when Roy dropped criminals he had captured into the prison courtyard instead of the police station.

They exchanged courtesies and sat down.

"How has *he* been, Warden?"

"Over the years, I've seen many men rehabilitated, many men not, and even more pretending to be, just as a way of obtaining early parole. I've gotten to know Leonard well. I believe he's the real deal." The Warden scratched his head as he sat back. The chair squeaked loudly in protest. "We've put him in one of the conjugal rooms."

Captain Invincible nodded. "Thank you, Warden."

"Do you want a guard in the room with you for protection?"

Roy looked at him curiously.

"I'm required to say that. You know…lawsuits."

Captain Invincible smiled. They shook hands goodbye.

A table, two chairs, and a bed were the room's complete furnishings. Considering the room's function, that was enough. A small, wiry man with a gray, balding head and thick glasses sat behind the table. His hands were folded together as if praying.

Mister Nefarious.

"You've gotten gray, Captain."

"It's good to see you, too, Leonard."

"Gave up on the Spandex, I see?" he said, with a grin of missing, stained teeth.

"Several years ago."

Leonard swept a dust mite off the table. "The years tick by slow in here, Captain."

"Must give you time to think."

"Yes. That it does."

"Regrets?"

"Not a day goes by without them."

"What types?"

Leonard opened his mouth to answer, but stopped himself. He stared across the table for a moment. "Why are you here, Roy?"

"Even though the prosecutor was willing to take five years from your sentence if you divulged the location of your Workshop, you never did."

"Five years off of *Life* really doesn't amount to much."

"We thought you had more weapons hidden."

Leonard lit up a cigarette. Offering one to Roy, he accepted. "Wife. Three kids. Plus the day job – I was a busy man back then."

"Yes, Leonard. Yes, you were."

A stream of smoke passed through his nose. "It was a horrible mistake. What happened to those people."

Roy stared at his lit cigarette, the stream of smoke drifting upwards to the *No Smoking sign*. "Five people died when the gold depository's wall collapsed onto the Brownstone across the street."

Leonard nodded. "Now you know my regrets." Removing his glasses, he wiped them with a tissue. "Back then, I prided myself on committing those crimes and making sure no one got hurt. These days, I watch the news and see the animals that are running loose around the city. I give you credit for not being judge, jury, and executioner all in one. I know I sure couldn't."

They sat in silence as they finished their cigarettes.

The second hand on the wall clock ticked softly.

"You hate me?"

"What for?"

"For capturing you."

"At first." He rubbed his temple. "But after a while, I realized if it wasn't you, it would have been someone else…The Horseman…Billy Zero…The Privateer… or even the police."

"But it was *me*."

"Yes. Captain Invincible," he looked at Roy. "The Displacer Gun. The Gamma Blaster. The Terror Ray. Nothing I built ever affected you. Towards the end, I *was* getting better at making my weapons, though the most harm I did was give you a migraine with The Radiation Rifle."

Roy smirked. "Did you ever think up anything more powerful?" He paused, choosing his words carefully. "Anything that could cause more than a headache?"

Leonard lit up another cigarette. "I had created sketches for a Pulse Gun that I had high hopes for. It would fire a pulse-ray that the further it traveled, the stronger it became – still with pinpoint accuracy."

"You still have those sketches?"

Leonard slid Roy the pack of cigarettes. "What's the matter? Superhero work gotten too boring? You want to take up robbing banks instead?"

"You're pretty sure that your Pulse-Ray Gun could have beaten me?" asked Roy with just the right amount of smugness.

"It should have been able to disable you at least."

"How old are you, Leonard?"

"I just turned fifty-eight."

"You miss your wife and sons?"

"Wouldn't any father? Doris took my going to prison very hard. It took almost a year after I was incarcerated for her to start writing to me. Another year after that to visit." Leonard sighed. "I just received a letter from her. My son, Matthew, received his MBA from NYU last month."

"So slow in here, so quick outside," remarked Roy.

"That it does, Captain."

"How would you like to be paroled?"

His eyebrows raised; Leonard snuffed out his cigarette. "To tell you the truth, I wasn't expecting *that*."

"What do you mean?"

"Did you really believe I thought you came here to talk about old times?"

Roy pulled out another cigarette. He held it up. "It's about these, Leonard. I trust you've seen the commercials."

It took Nefarious several moments to realize what he was talking about. "Well, I'll be damned." He handed Roy the matchbook. "Cancer?"

"They're pretty certain."

"How long did they give you?"

"A couple of months." Captain Invincible stared at the unlit cigarette and matchbook for a moment. "How precise do you think the gun would be?"

"If my calculations are correct - very." Leonard looked at him seriously. "Could you really get me out?"

"Can I trust you, Leonard?"

Leonard sat back against the chair. "I'm tired, Captain. I just want to get a job and see if I can get Doris to stop hating me for what I have done."

"If you're a stand-up guy through this, I'll make sure you get a job that will keep that mind of yours busy."

Roy stood up - his massive frame looking like an eclipse had passed under the light.

"How long would it take to get me released?" asked Leonard.

"How long do you need to pack?"

Landing onto the roof of his apartment building several days later, Roy was confident that Nefarious had changed. He was putting all his eggs in one basket, but he felt certain that Nefarious had the skills. His gut told him that he was trustworthy, and since mind-reading was not among his abilities, the gut would have to do.

He walked down the hallway and arrived at his apartment. Crime fighting had not quite made him rich enough to live in a mansion as in the comic books, but he was still able to save up enough money to invest in a penthouse co-op.

Opening the door, he saw his refrigerator being hurtled towards him.

Though getting on in years, his reflexes were still lightning. He grabbed the appliance in mid-air and carefully placed it onto the wooden floor to avoid scratching the finish.

He didn't anticipate the kitchen table that came next.

Striking his lower back, the oak table shattered into several pieces.

A tall, shapely woman stood at the kitchen entrance. Dressed in a business suit and heels, her once-done hair was now tussled about – the obvious result of tossing refrigerators.

"Son of a bitch!" she hollered, her face flushed with anger. "When were you planning to tell me?!"

"Denise…what…who told…?" he asked, picking up pieces of wood - using it as an excuse not to look at her.

"Paul told The Saber, and The Saber blabbed it to everyone else - including me."

Roy shook his head. Denise became even more annoyed. "When was I going to find out? When I got the call from the funeral home asking me if I wanted to stop by and pay last respects?"

Roy opened his mouth, but Denise cut him off. "*Now* I find out at work that you had Nefarious released from prison. A killer, Roy! What were you thinking?"

"He took us to his workshop, Denise. You have no idea what we found there. If that's not a sign of good faith, I don't know what is."

"So what exactly are you and your newfound friend up to?"

"He's constructing a…machine from one of his sketches."

Denise pinched her brow. "I'm getting a headache listening to this. I have a murder trial starting tomorrow morning, and I still have to prep my questions for the jury selection. I'm going to leave now before my temper gets the best of me." Grabbing her attaché off the counter, she began walking out. She turned around at the door. "Where is he building it?"

"At the Complex. Under intense supervision," he quickly added. Roy wasn't in the mood to be hit with the piano.

She sighed, shaking her head. "I'll call you in a day or two."

"How is it coming along?" Roy asked, walking in. The room was bare save for a large drafting table, an overhead lamp, empty coffee cups, and balls of crumpled paper peppering the floor. Nefarious looked tired, his back arched in a way that made him look like he had been hunched over all day.

He rubbed his eyes. "It's taking longer than I had planned. I should be able to start construction in a week, though." He placed his pencil down. "There is machinery back in my Workshop that I'm going to need."

"Sure."

"I'll write up a list of things."

"No. I'll bring it all."

"There's a lot of stuff."

"Later today, I will go and bring the entire building here for you. The front lawn should be large enough to fit it."

Leonard stared at him for a moment. "Very convenient," he looked at his watch and ran his fingers through his graying hair. Getting off the chair, he put on his jeans jacket.

"Where are you going?"

"What day is it, Captain?"

"Friday."

"That's right. Friday. Friday night. Have you gotten so old that you don't remember what Friday nights are for?"

"Well, I…" Roy was at a loss.

"Friday is date night. Do you realize it has been over twenty-five years since I've been on a date?"

"Who are you going out with?"

"Doris."

"Your wife?"

"That's right. After thirteen years, she's making me start from the beginning."

"How is she?"

Leonard paused for a moment as he contemplated his answer. "Angry." Roy looked at him questionably. "It's hard to explain." He watched as Leonard walked towards the exit. "Of course, you're welcome to come along. You can jump in if there are any lulls in the conversation."

"Leonard, if you run out of things to say after being away all these years, you have more problems than I could fix. Besides, I have plans already."

He nodded and walked outside. Roy looked absentmindedly at the blueprints.

Plans?

A lie.

That night Leonard and Doris ate at *Southern Lou's.* Being a former resident of the Crescent City, Lou specialized in Cajun and Creole cuisine. Since his release, Leonard had acquired an insatiable appetite for hot, spicy dishes. *Lou's* was a short drive away, and the gumbo was served with a money-back guarantee to make his customers break out in a sweat.

Leonard sent his back, complaining that it was too mild.

Doris informed him of things that had passed – minor events that never made their way into her letters.

Doris mixed the ice cubes around in her empty glass. "So what exactly are you working on with *him?*"

"A Pulse-Ray Gun."

"You realize that sounds like something out of a science fiction movie," she paused for a moment, smiling. "How does it work?"

Leonard flipped over his paper placemat and pulled a pen from his pocket. A half-hour later, he had fully explained the process.

"So you think it will be powerful enough to break Captain Invincible's skin?"

"It should be."

"That will let the doctors operate?"

"Yes."

"Which would, in turn, save his life."

"If the tumors are malignant. Yes."

"You're being very generous to the man who robbed my children of a father."

Leonard was shocked to hear her say such a comment. "You can't blame him, Doris. He was doing his job."

Doris' face turned bright red as she said nothing in response. Picking up her fork, she continued eating.

*

After dinner, they saw a re-release of Vertigo. Doris had always been a big fan of Jimmy Stewart. It was strange seeing such an old movie playing at a theater that showed big-budget action pictures.

Strangely, it made him feel less old.

Like he hadn't wasted so many years in prison.

The call came five weeks later - a day after the message from the doctor stating his tumor had again doubled in size.

Captain Invincible was in his study watching the morning events on Headline News when the phone started beeping. As he picked up the receiver, he knew who it would be.

"It's finished, Captain."

Roy held the phone, saying nothing.

"I tested it late last night." He could hear Leonard's voice trembling with excitement. "I shot a pinpoint hole through four feet of reinforced steel."

Silence at the other end.

"Captain, are you still there?"

"Yes."

"I can have the machine ready by tonight. Does that give you enough time to make arrangements?"

"Yes."

Leonard was inhaling in short, rapid breaths. "My crowning achievement, Captain. Until tonight."

And then a dial tone.

His crowning achievement.

Nefarious.

The gun looked like a cross between a telescope and a flame-thrower. It was bolted to a conveyor belt with a dentist-type chair placed at the bottom.

Roy wished cavities were the extent of his problem.

Leonard was ready by eight o'clock. The doctors had been summoned, skeptical of the thin, wiry man darting about, making last-minute adjustments to knobs and levers that no one else could comprehend. The doctors who were performing the surgery had the operating area sterilized.

Perfectly useless measures for a man who was immune to infection.

Though the media had not been tipped off, word of his condition had spread through his teammates, and they had come. Roy had not heard from many of them in years; there were faces to whom he could link recent news articles to. The Bobcat had become a Wall Street Commodities trader; Mister Proper a spokesman for a pharmaceutical company; Tommy-Two-Tone an assemblyman in Connecticut; The Mist Man a CFO of an internet company; The Hurricane had obtained his CPA license and was an auditor for the New York City Comptroller's Office.

Finally, he looked at Leonard, who was standing alongside his weapon.

Mister Nefarious was ready.

The machine turned on with a dull, electric hum. Leonard flipped a second switch, and a thin red line, no wider than a pinpoint, beamed down onto Roy's arm.

Nefarious looked at the weapon's gauge. "It's on the lowest setting. Right now, the beam is strong enough to pierce a half inch of steel." He pushed a lever, and the machine started moving upwards on the conveyor, away from Roy. "The further the machine gets, the stronger the beam becomes. Once it penetrates your skin, the doctors can operate at that intensity to burn away the tumor."

Roy looked at the long track that the gun was on. "That's some amplification."

Nefarious smiled. "At maximum power, we could burn a hole straight through to China."

He looked questionably at Nefarious, who shrugged. "Just a joke, Captain. A little levity never hurts." He pushed the lever, and the machine moved. "Do you feel any sensation?"

"No."

The doctors edged nearer.

Nefarious moved the machine another two feet, the beam remaining steady on Roy's arm.

The crowd looked on.

"How about now?"

"A little prickle."

Nefarious shook his head in disbelief. "It's good you never acquired an affinity for tattoos."

He raised the machine again.

"Yes, I think I feel something." Nefarious nodded and slowly began to increase the power, while monitoring Roy's arm.

The machine inched forward. Suddenly, the skin broke.

The beam sliced through his arm and burned itself into the floor.

Roy winced. "Ouch."

Nefarious quickly switched off the machine. He watched as a sliver of blood trickled down Roy's arm, making its way along the contours of his muscles.

Eyebrows raised. Several people gasped. No one was more surprised than Roy.

Though he had been bruised and felt pain before, he had never bled..

The machine suddenly powered back on. The beam wavered slightly, cutting another incision about an inch wide into Roy's arm before shutting back off. He hollered in pain.

Nefarious turned to see Doris standing by the controls, her eyes wide with anger. "Doris!" He stepped forward but stopped after seeing the fury on his wife's face.

Roy clamped his hand over his wound in an attempt to ebb the flow of blood. The wound was small enough and had missed any major veins that he felt confident it would heal. He did not know how the wound would heal if it were any larger. Having invincible skin meant the doctors did not possess the instruments capable of suturing. He kept still, knowing any sudden moves might cause the woman to turn the machine back on. Movement from the corner of his eye made him yell out in alarm.

"No! Bradley, put the gun down!"

The Rook slowly lowered his weapon. The terse tone of Roy's voice made everyone else back down as well.

He looked back at Doris. There had to be a better way. Saving his own life at the expense of hers would make all of this in vain.

"Doris, step away from the controls," pleaded Nefarious. Not much time was left.

"How can *you*, of all people, say that?" Doris glared at him, then back at Roy. "*He* destroyed our family, and you want to save him?"

"No, Doris. He didn't ruin anything. If you want to blame someone, blame me. I knew what I was doing back then. I take responsibility for my actions." Doris' finger was still poised over the power switch. "For God's sake, Doris! Can't you see that I've been given a second chance? Can't you see that *we've* been given a second chance? Kill him, and we will not get a third."

"How do you know…" Tears began to form in Doris' eyes. Her voice faltered. "How do you know that this is going to work?"

"I don't. I don't know if the procedure will work." He pointed to Roy. "I don't know if I will be able to save him. Hell, I don't even know if I can regain your respect or win back the love of my son. But I have to hope. I have to hope that it will get better, that it will work out. At the end of the day, hope is all that any of us really have."

Doris contemplated what he said for a moment. Then slowly, she lifted her hand from the controls. Sighs of relief followed as she took a step back. Two figures suddenly moved in, and she was escorted away.

Nefarious looked on with concern.

"Don't worry, Leonard. She won't be charged."

He watched Doris disappear through one of the exits.

"You have my word, Leonard," added Roy, as if sensing his thoughts. "She will be released when the operation is over."

"Thank you." Nefarious sighed and looked at the machine for a moment before turning to him. "It's all about hope, isn't it, Roy?"

Captain Invincible grinned. "That it is, Leonard. That it is."

Civic Guardian
by John Haas

"What are we unloadin' tonight, Jimmy?" the new kid asked.

Jimmy, lead hand on this late-night unloading, gave the kid a glare that said, "you shouldn't be asking questions if you want to do these kinds of jobs." Then he shook himself and gave a quick laugh. What was the saying? Occupational hazard?

"I think this truck's full of furniture."

"Furniture?" The kid said it in a way like maybe Jimmy had said old lady's underpants or some other item, which was beneath him.

"What's wrong with furniture?" Jimmy asked. The four others stood waiting for the truck's back door to open, glancing up toward the nearby rooftops. He looked to them, wondering if he was missing something.

He'd worked with these other guys before. There was Lance, with his thick biceps, perfect for the really heavy stuff. Moose, who you would think from the name would be the big guy, but he was really just the dumb one. Still, he was a good worker, did what he was told. Then the Miller twins, who didn't look the least bit alike. One was blond, short, and chunky, while the other was tall and brunette. Len and Ben—why were twins always named like that?

Lance shrugged. The Millers just looked ready to get to work. Belatedly, Moose shrugged too, a full fifteen seconds after everyone else reacted.

"Nah," the kid said, "it's just, I dunno, I expected TVs or computers. Somethin' like that."

"We get the job, we unload, then we go home," Moose said, repeating a mantra he'd heard Jimmy say, looking pleased with himself for remembering.

"Yeah, yeah, yeah. It's cool. Just electronics are cooler, you know? I like that kinda stuff. I worked with one guy who told me all sorts of stuff about it…"

Great. The kid was a talker. By the time tonight was over, they'd hear every stray thought that passed through his head.

"Go unlock the loading bay, okay?"

The kid nodded enthusiastically and sprinted off to do just that. He disappeared through the side door, and after about thirty seconds of silence, the door rolled up, as if of its own accord. Once up, Jimmy and the guys went in and scoped out where to drop the items. There was one area that had been left free for a load. Not much in the way of choices.

A clipboard with shipping papers sat on one of the pallets, left behind by their employer who couldn't be bothered to show up and supervise. Well, that's why Jimmy got an extra buck an hour. He grabbed the manifest, scanning it while heading back to the truck. Yep, furniture. A bunch of those put-it-together-at-home pieces. Moose and Lance brought the ramp over and got it set up.

"Let's get to it," Jimmy said, placing the clipboard under the ramp.

The kid was a talker, all right. Each one of the guys shot Jimmy a look of rolling eyes, even Moose, who usually didn't notice much of anything. All Jimmy could do was shrug.

Most places, this kind of unloading would be done with a forklift, and during the day, but this forty-foot container came in late and needed a hastily assembled crew. Jimmy was lucky to get the guys he did... and the kid who'd just been kind of hanging around looking for work.

Jimmy had a soft spot for possibly homeless kids.

An hour later, the truck was half unloaded, and there was more room to get deeper inside. Ben and Len took a long piece out and down the ramp, exposing an odd-shaped box in the next row, not the usual... well, box shape. Some kind of table by the picture on it.

"Lance, come here."

Lance came back up the ramp, followed by Moose. The Millers continued on into the warehouse.

"Let me and Moose get this box out of the way, Lance, then you and the kid get that weird-shaped one, okay?"

Lance shot a quick glance at the kid, sighed, then gave a nod.

Before anyone could move, a hard thump came from above, and they all looked up. Whatever had landed on the roof was heavy, the noise echoing through the cramped space. It probably echoed up and down the alley and out to the street, too.

"Aw, crap," Lance said, looking up.

"What?" the kid said. His enthusiastic smile edged over into curiosity.

"Yo!" one of the Millers called. "CG! It's CG."

CG. The Civic Guardian, self-appointed defender of their fair city. A supposed hero, but Jimmy knew far too many friends who'd been put into the hospital by this bone-breaking thug. As far as he was concerned, there was little difference between CG, as the papers called him, and an enforcer who'd show up to bust your kneecaps.

"Hey," the other Miller called, "I thought—"

Whatever he thought stayed inside of his skull as a ball-shaped projectile connected with his forehead. This was CG's weapon of choice, a solid metal ball coated with a thin layer of rubber, roughly the size of a squash ball. You could find them all over the city, anywhere CG had attacked. Ben was off to dreamland while Len spun around to run, but CG launched himself from the truck's roof and landed on the poor guy, feet first. One unnecessary punch and Len was out too.

CG turned back toward the truck. "Come out of there." The voice was deep and gravelly, like someone trying to disguise what they really sounded like. "Let's get this over with."

Everyone looked to Jimmy for direction.

"We have no weapons," Jimmy called. "We don't want to fight you."

"You're just giving up?" CG said. "These two had more backbone than that."

Lance gave a low growl, never one to be called chicken. Jimmy placed a hand in front of him and shook his head.

"Yeah, we're serious. What's the point in fighting? Last time one of my guys met up with you, they lost teeth. We don't get dental, you know."

"Dental." Civic Guardian huffed out a derisive laugh. "Fine. Come out."

"Only if you promise you aren't going to pummel my crew."

The sigh that came was loud and meant to reach them. They were ruining this guy's night by not fighting back. Was he some kind of 'roid rager?

"Fine. Whatever."

Jimmy went down the ramp first. This was his crew, and if something went wrong, he should at least be the first one to take a hit. He stood there, looking at the man in his leather combat armor. How did he even move in that stuff? It all looked so stiff. The mask came down halfway to cover the front of his nose, but kept his mouth free. Up close like this, Jimmy could see the guy had some sort of makeup around the eyes to keep it from showing any skin. These guys were so weird. A belt which held all kinds of items for bodily damage sat around his middle. CG even now held two of his rubber-wrapped balls, ready to throw.

One thing to say about the guy, he had wicked aim.

Jimmy made sure to keep his hands where they could be seen. The kid came out next and stood close to Jimmy.

"Whoa! It's really you! I can't believe I'm meetin' you, man."

The kid looked ready to rush forward and hug CG, which would probably result in the kid eating meals through a straw for a month. Would that stop the incessant chatter? Jimmy placed a hand on the kid's shoulder and kept him from doing anything fatal, while Moose and Lance came out next. They stood in a row at the bottom of the ramp, like those guys in The Usual Suspects. Jimmy loved that movie.

CG looked from face to face, as if unsure what to do with guys who surrendered. "Who's in charge?" he said. "Give him up."

The three still conscious looked at Jimmy.

"Great," he muttered, then louder. "I'm lead hand on this job."

"Not you, small potatoes," CG said. "Not interested in you and these other losers."

Jimmy placed a hand in front of Lance, though it apparently wasn't necessary. Lance's hot button was being called a chicken, not a loser.

"You the tough guy?" CG said to Lance. "Want to take a swing at me?"

Lance looked like he might be convinced of doing just that.

"Go on," CG said. "I'll let you have one punch free."

"Lance, you can't afford the time off work," Jimmy said.

The other man deflated. None of them could afford time off from their day jobs. Most had the kind of jobs without sick pay.

"Don't worry about your jobs," CG said. "You'll all still be in jail tomorrow morning."

"Aw, man," Moose said. "Lisa will be pissed."

"Hold up," Jimmy said. "Wait a minute!"

CG looked ready to put a fist through Jimmy for telling him to *hold up*.

Jimmy bent and grabbed the clipboard under the edge of the ramp. When he turned back, he saw CG had one arm cocked and ready to throw. Jimmy brought the clipboard up, knowing it would make a crap shield, but seeing no better option. The blow never came. He lowered the makeshift protection and saw the squinted glare of CG, evaluating.

"Look," Jimmy said. "This is a valid order we're unloading. Our boss, who owns this warehouse, bought it legally."

"Legal?" Lance said. "Really?" Then he looked at the supposed hero. "Oh, I mean, yeah. Of course it is."

CG snorted his own disbelief.

"Here," Jimmy said, holding out the clipboard. "Just look for yourself."

The hero stomped closer, looking as if he hoped one of them would try something. He grabbed the clipboard from Jimmy's hand and scanned it. The longer he looked, the deeper the scowl on his face became.

"Huh, it all *looks* on the up and up."

"It is."

The leather-clad man tossed the clipboard toward Jimmy with another sigh. "Well, carry on, I suppose."

CG turned to leave, and Jimmy's jaw dropped open. It took a lot to rile him, but those five words did it. He couldn't believe the attitude of this entitled thug.

"Car… Carry on?" Jimmy exploded, taking a step toward the man. He felt Lance's hand on his shoulder, and some small part of him marvelled at the transfer of roles. "*Carry on?* That's all you have to say?"

Civic Guardian stopped and took a second before turning to stare at Jimmy, arms across his chest.

Jimmy gestured at the Millers. "You just beat two of my men unconscious and would have done the same to the rest, all for unloading a truck!"

"Legally," Moose added. Once in a while, he actually said the right words at the right moment.

"That's messed up," Lance said.

"You looked suspicious," CG said.

"We were unloading a truck!" Jimmy spat. "What's suspicious about that?"

"Middle of the night in a back alley," CG said.

"That's the time we were given for the job."

"You should get better jobs, make better choices in life."

"Better choices?" Jimmy said. "How many choices do you think we have?"

"Everyone has choices."

"What do you know about choices? You ever have to choose between going to work sick or losing your job?"

"Or between food and clothing ?" Lance added.

"Sleeping inside for the night or eating?" the kid said.

CG didn't answer, his eyes darting to one side. He didn't need to answer. Only a guy with excess money and time could run around like a big kid on Halloween.

"Do you even know what minimum wage is?" Jimmy asked.

CG gave his head one quick shake and looked up for the roof he wanted to leave by.

"Hey guys," Moose said, "we gotta finish unloading or we don't get paid, right?"

Two great observations by Moose in one night. That was a new record. They did need to get back to work.

"How we going to finish on time without the Millers?" Lance asked.

"That's right. You knocked out two of our guys," Jimmy said. "They aren't coming around any time soon. I doubt they'd be up for continuing even if they did."

The kid said. "Isn't that assault?"

CG and Jimmy both looked at him.

"I mean, 'cause we weren't doing anything illegal… and…" his voice trailed off.

"You're not suggesting I help you unload?" CG asked.

"That's exactly what I'm suggesting," Jimmy said.

Civic Guardian turned and glanced at the two unconscious Miller twins, then toward the kid, maybe replaying what had been said about assault. He threw up his hands. "Fine! Just make it quick."

"Sure, sure," Jimmy looked back toward the truck. "CG, you and the kid get that awkward-shaped box. Kid, I'm counting on you to tell him *everything* he needs to know."

"Oh, yeah. You bet, Jimmy. C'mon, CG."

As the two climbed the ramp into the truck, the kid's chattering becoming less distinct, Lance came up beside Jimmy and said in a low voice. "That's just mean."

Best Friends
by Jay T. Levy

"I can't wait to tell Mom," Chris said, pulling into the driveway. "She'll be so excited."

"Only about half as excited as you," Lloyd, his father, patted him on the shoulder. "Congratulations again on passing. We practiced a lot, and I'm proud of you. Let's go show off your license."

As they both exited, a man dropped from the sky, landing on his feet at the end of the driveway and shaking the ground—just enough to rattle the mailbox and vibrate the sedan next to Chris and his father.

Chris's eyes widened in amazement. "Oh, my god! It's The Ultimate." A superhero was right in front of him—the protector of the city, the people, even the world at times. The Ultimate was a dark-haired, large-smiled, muscle-bodied champion of truth and justice, whose tight black suit did little to hide his massive physique. On his chest was a stylized, chrome-colored U symbol, which matched in color to his bracers, boots, and belt.

In the superhero's arms was a skinny, unshaven, and haggard-looking blond man wearing a long, old-fashioned sports jacket with patches on the elbows. Unlike The Ultimate's chrome boots, the skinny man's sneakers were dirty and worn.

Chris was so excited—a superhero stood in his driveway. He couldn't wait to tell his friends.

The blond man pointed at Lloyd. "That's him. That's the guy."

"Wait a minute, I'm not sure I understand. How do you want me to fulfill your debt?" The Ultimate frowned. "I know you said I 'owe you everything,' but what does this citizen have to do with it?"

"You're going to take care of him," the blond man said as The Ultimate lowered him to his feet.

"Jared, is that you?" Lloyd nodded, confusion hinted in his eyes. "It's been a long time. How've you been?" He stepped forward as if to shake Jared's hand.

"The worst ever," Jared spat on the ground, not accepting the handshake. "Thanks to you!"

"Dad, who's that guy with The Ultimate?" Chris looked between the hero and his father.

"He's why we had to buy this." Lloyd patted the sedan. "You remember that auto accident I was in last year? Well, it was with Jared and me."

"At least you could afford a new car." Jared's tone was venomous, and he folded his arms. "My life's been ruined since the accident."

"I'm… so sorry," Lloyd said. "Chris, why don't you run inside? Tell your mother the good news about your driver's license. I'll be right behind you."

Chris's brow furrowed, and he shook his head. "I… I don't think I should." He looked at the confusion on the superhero's face, and mirrored it himself.

"My leg was broken in three places. I had to learn to walk again. I couldn't work," Jared said through clenched teeth. "I lost my job cause of you. It was humiliating, being drummed out like that. No one would hire me afterwards."

"I'm very sorry I hit your car," Lloyd held up a hand; his tone, apologetic. "And I'm sorry you got hurt. I assumed the insurance covered it. They told me it was all taken care of. I know, or at least I assumed, a person couldn't lose their job over being hurt like that, but if you did, it sounds like you needed to get a lawyer involved. That part's on you."

"You assume too much, and now it's going to cost you. You're going to feel my pain in kind." Jared scowled. "Get him, Ultimate."

"What?" The Ultimate took a step back. "What'd you mean, 'get him?' Buddy, this guy's obviously not a threat. You promised this was about a threat. This is… it's not right. He's just a guy."

"He's my threat!" Jared screamed. "He ruined my life!" He puffed out his chest, which paled in comparison to The Ultimate's. "Do you remember the playground, back at school, when we were just kids, long before your *powers*? When you were that skinny, stuttering, weakling, and how the other guys pushed you around? Do you?"

"I-I-I… r-r-remember," The Ultimate stuttered, looking suddenly shorter, as if weights had piled upon his shoulders.

"And who stood up for you?" Jared raised his voice. "Who gave them black eyes and fat lips? Who was there to fight *your* battles, right *your* wrongs, huh?"

"Y-y-you were…"

Chris had seen the hero on TV many times, and had never once heard The Ultimate stutter, who suddenly seemed timid, small, and weak compared to his shorter friend.

"Yeah, me, and only me." Jared thumped his chest. "Without me, you'd have never survived. I remember you talking about ending it, too. Do you remember that, *buddy?* If it weren't for me, you wouldn't be here today, and never would've been chosen to get your powers. You owe me everything!"

"B-b-but there has to be a b-b-better way," The Ultimate said. "W-w-we can f-f-figure this out d-d-differently."

Jared stood face to face with The Ultimate. "You will do this for me. It's part of being best friends; it's our code. Remember the pinky swear? We'd do anything for each other."

The Ultimate lowered his shoulders, closed his eyes, and scrunched his face. "I-I-I can't…"

"You will. A promise is a promise. Or are you a liar?"

Chris knew that look on his favorite superhero's face — playground politics and acquiescence to your bully. A tear slid down The Ultimate's cheek; he looked crushed.

Jared pointed to Lloyd again. "Ultimate, break his leg. Teach him a lesson."

"Wait, what?" Lloyd took a step back. "Ultimate, you're a hero. You don't hurt people. Snap out of it."

"I-I-I'm truly s-s-sorry." The Ultimate's shoulders sagged even more. "I-I-I'm a man of m-m-my word, and I-I-I made a p-p-promise." He looked at Lloyd and nodded sheepishly. In the blink of an eye, The Ultimate rushed Lloyd, grabbing his leg. He flipped the man upside down and paused.

Lloyd hung in silence for a mere moment. Chris drew a breath; his father looked dumbfounded.

The Ultimate snapped Lloyd's lower leg, exposing his fibula and tibia.

Lloyd screamed and passed out.

Hearing his father's howl of pain, Chris' knees weakened, and he fell against the car.

Jared cackled like a villain getting his revenge.

"It's d-d-done." The Ultimate scowled and cradled Lloyd in his arms. He took a deep breath, held it, and let it out slowly, like a therapeutic breathing technique.

"My debt is paid," The Ultimate said, sans stutter. "I don't owe you ever again." He lifted off, floating just a few feet above the ground.

"Where're you going?" Jared demanded.

"I'm still The Ultimate. This man now *needs* my help. I'm getting him to a hospital." He pointed a finger at Jared and raised his voice. "You stay here. You'll need to explain to this kid's mother. I'll be back for you."

"Are you kidding me?" Jared pointed at Chris. "Stay here with this loser?"

The Ultimate turned his back to his 'best friend' and zoomed forward, as though propelled by some invisible jet. The pair was out of sight within seconds.

"You're the loser." Chris ran up to Jared, punched him in the mouth, and knocked The Ultimate's best friend to the ground. "You need your friend to fight your battles. You're nothing but a bully!" With tears in his eyes, Chris ran inside to tell his mother. It just wasn't the news he'd hoped to share.

Jared stood, wiped blood from his mouth, then looked around before flipping off Chris's house and hobbling away, despite being told to stay put.

Rooftop Interviews with the Man of Might
by Steve Gillies

I wasn't trying to kill myself that night, but I understand how he made that mistake. It was the top of a fifteen-story building, there was no guard rail, and I stood a little too close to the edge. It couldn't have looked great to a person who could see me up there, alone in the dark. And not that even he would know, but there was a family history (my mother, found in the garage with the car engine running).

I had been in the city for a few months with vague ambitions of being some kind of writer. I bounced from temp job to temp job, lived in a sketchy apartment that I couldn't really afford, and spent my nights stuck inside those moldy walls, staring blankly at a blank computer screen. That night, I got restless. I didn't have anyone to talk to or anywhere to go. So, I went up to the roof. It was one of those still, clear nights where you could see the city stretch out in front of you for miles. I gazed out at the lights, the buildings, the people. It all meant a little less to me than maybe it should have. No, I wasn't trying to kill myself that night. But how many nights like this had my mother had?

Then he appeared, clinging to the sky above me. I said nothing. What was there to say?

"Don't do it," he said in that powerful voice we'd all come to know so well.

"Uh," I said.

"There's so much to live for." Again, that voice. Booming and mighty. "Don't kill yourself."

"I just came up for some fresh air," I said.

"Oh," he said.

Suddenly, he didn't sound so super. He sounded more like one of my weird neighbors. I ignored that he was hovering above me and looked closer at him. It was, in fact, one of my weird neighbors. Maybe my weirdest neighbor. The building I lived in was littered with people muttering to themselves and stinking out the elevators. Amid all the junkies, weirdoes, and depressives, there was one guy with perfect hair, great posture, and freshly laundered clothes. Maybe the most normal-looking person I'd ever seen. In that building, a total weirdo. Now, for some reason, he was wearing white tights and a golden cape. For some reason, he could fly.

"What are you doing up there?" I asked.

"I usually manage to time it better. After people jump," he said. "I catch them, they're so grateful. They think I'm an angel. No one ever thinks to ask questions."

"No, what are you – how are you even in the air?"

"Don't tell anyone about me," he said. "I just want to help."

"I wouldn't even know what to tell them," I said. I started walking back to the stairwell. I stopped at the door and looked back. "The jumpers. They're always happy when you catch them?"

"Always," he said. Then he flew back into the night.

I didn't tell anyone what I saw that night, but I did some research. I went to churches, soup kitchens, shelters, guys hanging around the corner store, and asked if anyone had seen an angel. I got a lot of blank looks, a few threats, but also a couple of stories. It wasn't only jumpers, though I talked to more than a few of them. I also heard about armed robberies, assaults, gang fights. I wrote it all down. Soon, I had a feature article for what could be a great Sunday Magazine piece about a new urban myth – a yellow and white angel here to save the neighborhood. I kept it factual. I quoted eyewitnesses. It got laughed at or met with total silence when I pitched it to some of the bigger papers. I sold it to a free weekly. They cut it down to 200 words and put it in one of the back pages next to the police blotter and classified ads for hookers. It was my first piece of professional writing. It went largely ignored except for one person.

We met on the roof again. He told me to stop. He pleaded with me. He told me that my article would draw unwanted attention. But before long, he was telling me his whole story. I barely even had to ask him a question.

He grew up in a small town, a lot like me. He'd been a high school sports star, gotten a scholarship to a respectable state school. He was a team player, worked hard, and got good grades. At various team functions, he impressed alumni with his maturity and integrity. That led to a job with a management consulting firm in the city. It had a good salary and a generous signing bonus – far more than he was ever taught to want. He didn't go out drinking, didn't spend his money foolishly, and sent a good portion of it back home. On weekends, when he wasn't catching up on work, he volunteered, coaching at-risk kids in sports. Went to church every Sunday. Like I said, a total weirdo.

One long weekend, he went back home for a visit. Instead of the yard where he threw his first ball, the sidewalk where he learned to ride a bike, the house where he grew up, he found a giant, glowing green crater. Something unexplainable had fallen from the sky and left a gaping hole where his world used to be. He stood at the edge of the crater, not knowing what to do, when he heard the faintest echo of a voice. It sounded familiar – like the most familiar thing in the world.

"Do something," the Voice said.

There may have been more, but he couldn't make it out. It was tough to say if they were really words at all. It was just something he could feel.

"Do something."

In a life spent following instructions, it was the vaguest – and maybe most important – one he'd ever received.

The incident passed with barely a mention on the news. Maybe nobody knew how to describe it. Maybe it was just flyover country, so nobody cared. He stayed in town to settle his parents' affairs. He had frustrating conversations with insurance companies. He took condolences from friends and neighbors. He endured the sympathetic looks, the unhelpful kindnesses, for as long as he could. Then he went back to the city, back to work.

The Voice didn't stop, though. He knew he wasn't crazy. He knew he had to do something. He would. Just as soon as he figured out what "something" was. He sat in his cubicle reading emails or staring at spreadsheets. He went to meetings and pointed at things on PowerPoint. He wrote reports, attended webinars, had conference calls that could have been emails. He stayed busy, but he didn't feel like he was doing much of anything at all.

Finally, he couldn't stand sitting at his desk another minute. So he did something he'd never done before. He took a lunch break. Not feeling particularly hungry, he gave a homeless man his sandwich. He walked out of the financial district, into one of those neighborhoods where he coached kids on weekends. By one o'clock, when he should have been back in the office, he was carrying groceries to homebound senior citizens. No matter how full they packed the bags, he didn't feel the weight. By 5:30, he was breaking up bar fights. He didn't get a scratch on him. By six o'clock, he phoned in his resignation. By nightfall, he was flying.

"Just like that?" I asked.

"It wasn't just like that," he told me. He had incredible powers, but they had come at a terrible cost. Everything he had ever known was gone. But he had power given from on high. He had to do something. He had to help people. He had to follow the Voice.

Angels. On high. The Voice. The way he talked reminded me of the Bible beaters back in my hometown. That worried me. Most of what I knew about faith was the damage it did. This story wasn't something I was comfortable putting out into the world.

I wrote other stories, though. After talking to so many people about the Angel, I actually had a pretty good handle on the neighborhood. Living where I lived, that quickly turned into steady stringer work on the crime beat for some of those papers would have that laughed my Angel story out of the room. I didn't make enough to move into a nicer place, but I didn't have to work as many temp jobs.

I still went to the rooftop. I'm not sure why he kept coming back. I guess I got a few scoops out of it. I started telling him about things going on in the city, laid out some of the more intricate and police-baffling details of the criminal organizations in town. He started acting on my information, focusing less on petty thieves and going after some of the most dangerous criminals in the city. I'd be ready to get the story; the police got a ton of arrests, and people started to notice him.

Grainy video footage of him in action became a fixture on the news. Comedians asked gross questions about his possible superpowers. Street vendors sold bootleg t-shirts. People wore them with varying degrees of irony. Young reporters were combing through the city, trying to be the first to officially get the scoop on what they'd dubbed the Hero Guy. It was a stupid name, I'd been pitching the Man of Might at reporter bars, but at least it wasn't the Angel. Still, I kept his origin story to myself.

Then, one day Hero Guy stopped a giant, killer robot from destroying the city, and everything changed.

That night, I waited on the rooftop past midnight before I realized Hero Guy wasn't going to show. I went out. The streets were quiet, though unusually active for that time of night. Groups of people would walk by. Or couples. Nobody was going anywhere alone except me. I ducked into a reporter bar where people squinted at the closed captioning on the TV while scrolling through their phones for leads. The attack played over and over again. The anchors imagined what might have happened if it weren't for Hero Guy. They waited for breaking developments, some explanation on who or what attacked their city. They were desperately looking for any information on the hero who saved us all. Nobody at the bar was having much luck either. The drinking got heavier and the mood gloomier. There could be more killer robots out there right now, and all the reporting in the world wasn't going to stop it. This was my moment. I could have talked to one of the dozens of people in the bar who worked for a news network. I could have landed a job that would have gotten me out of that shithole apartment right there. But I was drinking next to a very pretty girl and didn't want to be anywhere else.

"Pretty crazy, huh?" I said to her.

"All this time, my money was on some dumb publicity stunt," she said.

"No, he's for real, all right," I said.

Suddenly sweaty guy with a beard tapped her on the shoulder. "I've got a red hot lead and I can't get hold of Jenna. I need someone to do a quick remote," he said.

"I'd do a way better remote than Jenna, but I just put in twelve hours, and your leads are always garbage. Besides, I'm having a drink right with a nice gentleman right now, so beat it."

She turned back to me. "You've seen him?"

"Yeah," I said, but then I realized I had to be careful. "We're counsellors at the same church camp."

"If that were remotely true, you'd be in church right now," she said.

"Good point," I said. "But he seems like the type, right?"

"Sure," she said. "He must be a total choir boy."

"I guess I'm glad the guy with the superpowers has something in his life showing him how to be a good person."

She took a drink. "I try to think that we're all basically good people. Except for the giant killer robots and the men who build them." We burst out laughing. Her name was Suzanne, and she was a woman who laughed at danger.

Others didn't laugh. This Hero Guy thing turned deadly serious. I caught up with him on the rooftop early the next morning. He told me about The Mad Inventor, a brilliant but disturbed scientist who built the robot that attacked the city. Hero Guy tracked the Mad Inventor down and listened to a long speech about his motivations. The Mad Inventor wanted to show that an ordinary human could compete with Hero Guy. He considered Hero Guy's powers an unearthly abomination, a test for his superior human intelligence. After listening carefully to his perspective, Hero Guy decided the best course of action was to punch him in the face and turn him in to the authorities.

This was the start of something, and there was no telling where it would end. People dressed in costumes and prevented crimes. People dressed in costumes and committed crimes. Some people had superpowers, some people had enough technology at their disposal that you couldn't tell if they didn't; a lot were just crazy people who liked to dress up. Talking heads shouted at us on TV about Hero Guy. They blamed him for all this superhuman mayhem. They thanked him for saving us from it. Politicians crusaded against him. Politicians tacitly claimed his endorsement. Successful politicians somehow did both. People started discussion groups devoted to upholding the values that Hero Guy represented, and then they fought about what those values were. T-shirt sales skyrocketed, and almost nobody wore them ironically anymore.

All this meant I saw less and less of Hero Guy on the rooftop. When I did see him, it was always, "Can't stop to chat too long, there's some kind of crisis at City Hall. I wish we could catch up more. I'm really sorry."

I didn't have as much time anymore, either. I was seeing a lot more of Suzanne Jones. She didn't have superpowers that I knew of, but when I was around her, I was suddenly aware of how much more exciting and interesting the world seemed. She was smart, brave, funny, and amazing at her job. We both worked bizarre hours, but we spent time together every chance we got. Soon our lives became a blur of sleep and sex and work and lack of sleep and day-drinking and work and takeout food. It was exhilarating. It was exhausting. It was getting serious. At least that's how I interpreted it when she asked how come she'd never seen my place or met any of my friends.

"I don't really have friends," I said, trying to make it sound like a joke. "And my place is barely big enough for me."

"I'd like to see it," she said. "I never really minded a tight fit." I couldn't tell if she was being sexy or not. With her, it was usually best to assume she was being sexy.

So, one night after I hit a deadline and she finished a spot on the 11 o'clock news, we met up at a dive in my neighborhood. I knew the bartender working that night. I dropped in occasionally to follow up on some local beat leads. I hoped the bartender knowing my name gave me some semblance of crime reporter legitimacy, but in that place, maybe it just made me come off like a low-life.

"Not exactly a lot of anchor material hanging around here," I said.

"No, no," Suzanne said. "I like it. It's got . . ." hesitating a little too long to come up with a word, "character."

"Yeah, you probably don't want to drink anything on tap," I said.

It was mostly empty around us, except for an old man sleeping facedown on the bar and a table of red-faced men shouting at each other loudly while a jukebox played Foreigner. We couldn't hear each other, and I couldn't think of anything to talk about anyway. I just looked at her, dressed down in jeans and a t-shirt, but still in her newslady makeup, imagining what she thought of this place.

After a drink, I told her my place was right around the corner. Luckily, we didn't run into any weirdos in the building, and the elevator was at just a regular level of stink. As we entered my apartment, I made a show of giving her the grand tour, pointing to the sink, the stove, the desk, and the bed, all within a few feet of the front door. After that, there wasn't a lot to say. One thing worse than being pent up in those four walls with myself was being there with someone else. It was hard to look at her looking at my place, and it seemed like she couldn't look at me. So, I did the only thing I could think of. I took her up to the roof.

Silently, I scanned the skies for signs of the Hero Guy. Would he show up if someone else was here? Did I want that? Maybe it would make me look cool in front of Suzanne, knowing the guy that most of the city was obsessed with. On the other hand, what would the reporter in her think about it, sitting on the story of the century and doing nothing? She'd try to convince me to break the story, insisting it's what a real reporter would do. She'd be shocked at my lack of ambition. This story was my ticket out of a tiny studio; it was my chance to really make it in the city, in the world, even. Maybe she'd even scoop me on the story and leave me all alone in my tiny apartment. I stood there, staring at the sky.

"Well, this is nice, but what are we doing up here?" she said. "Like, anything you want to talk about?"

"Look, I know my apartment sucks. I'm not like you, OK. I got to the city. I got away. I don't get why that can't be enough."

"Whoa," she said. "I thought we were going to make out up here, but now

I'm kind of losing the mood."

"I'm not chasing some big life. I don't want to be famous. I don't want to be rich. I can see you looking around the place. I know you want more from me, but this is what I've got."

"All I wanted from you - I just kind of wanted to know about you. Like, for starters, where the hell this line of bullshit might be coming from. But it's late, I have work in the morning, and I think I should go," she said, making her way to the fire escape. "If you ever want to tell me anything about yourself, you know how to find me. Christ, you're an idiot."

I didn't talk to anyone about much of anything for a few days. I stayed in my apartment, avoided work, and thought about what she said. I never told people much about me, where I came from, what happened. I didn't want them to look at me differently. Sometimes I didn't want people to look at me at all. Sitting in my room, staring at the walls, seems like I had accomplished that mission. Realizing that wasn't getting me anywhere, I went back to the rooftop. There was an early fall chill in the air. It wasn't long before Hero Guy came. He seemed tired.

He fought off a group of bank robbers who were armed with super-powered weaponry and backed up by several robots. He saved the passengers on a commuter train that derailed after a mysterious technical glitch. He dealt with an incident at a high school science fair where a group of robots some kids had made went out of control and almost caused a cataclysmic explosion at an alternate energy exhibition.

"These things. They seem connected. Somehow. Something's coming. I can feel it," he said. "Have you heard anything from any of your contacts?"

"No, I haven't been uh, out in the field much," I said.

"What have you been doing?" he asked.

"Nothing," I said. "Just nothing."

"Well, that seems like a poor way to spend your time."

"Have you ever screwed something up irredeemably?" I asked. "Well, that's dumb, look who I'm talking to."

"No, I've screwed plenty of things up," he said. "I screwed up the night you met me. If you screw up as many things as I do, you'll find that very few things are irredeemable."

I wasn't sure about that, but I called her anyway. We talked a bit. I told her things about my life, the things I hadn't been telling people. I told her I did have someone I wanted to meet. She said she'd like that. So, I called my dad.

Dad was glad to hear from me. We'd spoken since I moved to the city, but not frequently or at length, and never at my initiative. Maybe enough time had passed that I could think of him and think about more than just my mother. My dad decided to come to the city. I surprised myself with how much I looked forward to seeing him. I even went shopping for new clothes. I'd been wearing the same scruffy thrift store gear since college. I didn't want my father to see me that way. I wanted to be seen as an adult. I was starting to feel like one.

Suzanne tagged along to help with style advice, but mostly to make jokes at my expense. She followed me around the department store with a pair of polka-dotted briefs, claiming to have found the missing ingredient to our love life. People turned and laughed. If it had been anyone else, they'd be annoyed. She engaged strangers in really long conversations about my fashion choices and the broader topic of my more endearing personality quirks. Then she wanted me to try on a pair of $500 jeans.

"I'm not even shopping for jeans," I said. "And no way I can pay for $500 anythings. You know that. I just, maybe this is a big mistake."

"We don't need to have this conversation again," said Suzanne. "Nobody needs you to pay for anything. I just need all these people to see how good you look in ridonkulous cocknocker jeans for five minutes."

"Were any of those words just then?" I said.

"Don't deny me this."

She barely waited a beat before pushing me towards the changing room.

"OK. OK. I'll do it," I said.

I was just putting the pants on when I heard a loud crash outside. I ran out of the stall to look for Suzanne. People screamed. People ran. Panic reigned. For a moment, I didn't notice the giant robot foot where Suzanne used to be.

"Suzanne! Suzanne!" I called out.

The robot's foot rose above me. I stood there, I just stood there and screamed my girlfriend's name. Another loud noise, and the giant robot foot lurched backwards, a giant robot torso crashed through the ceiling. Behind the fallen giant robot hovered Hero Guy, a look of determination on his face that didn't leave until I called out again.

"Suzanne!"

Hero Guy looked at me, first with confusion, and then like he wanted to say something. Before he could, a mechanized, claw-like hand grabbed him. Exhaust came screaming out of the robot's feet, and they took off, leaving a hole in the ceiling and debris everywhere.

"Suzanne!"

I saw her. A bald man was on the ground. He held her slumped figure by the cash register. She didn't respond as I shouted her name. The man who held her looked at me. He shook his head. "I'm sorry. I'm sorry. I'm sorry." I heard it over and over again until I realized that it was me saying it. Blood trickled out of her ears, and her eyes were open, wide fucking open.

She had gone quickly, they told me. She probably never even knew it was happening. It wasn't a comfort to me; the idea that she didn't even know it when she was thinking her last thought. She was in a better place now, they told me. I nodded politely. You don't argue when somebody says that, no matter how little you believe it. I wasn't looking for Hero Guy that night on the rooftop. I just wanted to stare and not think about anything. Still, I wasn't surprised when he swooped down from the sky and put a hand on my shoulder.

"Thank goodness you're alright," he said. "I started to worry when I saw you. Maybe you were worried about me, too. But it turned out you left me with a perfect opportunity to play possum."

I moved away from Hero Guy and stood at the corner of the rooftop. Hero Guy continued to narrate, oblivious. Once the robot had Hero Guy in his clutches, he brought him back to his home base. It turned out that the original Mad Inventor had a twin brother. There had always been a sibling rivalry, and this most recent wave of robot attacks was his way of trying to prove he was the superior inventor. "But don't worry," Hero Guy said. "They have a jail cell big enough for both of them, ha-ha! By the way, those jeans look fantastic on you!"

I didn't say a thing.

"What's wrong?" Hero Guy asked finally.

"You don't even know? I thought you'd at least know."

"Know?" asked Hero Guy.

"There was a girl in the department store. When the robot landed, its foot… It… She. . . " I said. I paused. I would have to get used to saying it. "She's dead now. Her name was Suzanne. That girl was everything."

"What can I do to help?"

It was such a superhero thing to say. The last thing I needed was a superhero.

"Can you bring people back from the dead?" I asked. "Can you time-travel? Can you send me back so that I just try on those jeans without being a dick about it? What about alternate universes? Can you assure me there's a place out there where I died and she lived? If so, I'd like to know about it because it would be a much better universe for everyone."

Hero Guy just kept quietly apologizing.

"Are you sorry?" I snapped. "Really? I had to get her cell phone from the police and call her mom. She was driving, and I told her to call me back, but she knew. She just knew. Do you have any idea what that was like?"

"I've had some experience with grief," Hero Guy said quietly.

Below, people walked the sidewalks or stood clustered in doorways, bracing themselves against the cold. The bus made its stop on the corner, its automated announcement called out to unlistening streets. Pigeons nibbled at the sludge in the gutters.

"I know it's not your fault. But every time you're there for someone, in the right place, the right time; every person you save, don't ask me to believe there's any reason for it. Don't ask me to believe there's any reason for you. You're just dumb luck. If you were anything other than that, I'd have to hate you, and I'd prefer to just ignore you."

That was basically goodbye. I quit the crime beat. I took some copy-editing jobs, fact-checked obituaries, any work I could get from the dwindling newspaper world without doing any actual reporting, without anything that would make me go back up to that rooftop.

In the years that followed, Hero Guy wasn't easy to ignore. I saw him everywhere except our building. Every time I turned on a TV or walked past a newspaper stand, there he was. He stopped genocides in Africa, he fought off alien invasions, he went on cosmic missions to preserve the very fabric of space and time, he helped old ladies across the street. On the news, they'd debate what the increased activity from Hero Guy meant. Despite all he'd accomplished, was Hero Guy more in demand now than ever before? What did that say about his effect on the world? Or was this simply the next step in the evolution of Hero Guy? Had he moved beyond the need to eat or sleep, and now he could devote all of his time to heroism? It didn't matter. People still died stupid deaths every single day.

I tried to do what I could. I volunteered to tutor writing at an after-school Community Center. Eventually, I got a low-paying job as a program coordinator there. I threw myself into my work. The place was run by a group of local churches, but I never set foot in one of them. That raised eyebrows. They'd ask me why someone without faith would do this job. All I could do was shrug and make jokes about the big bucks they paid me.

I never moved out of that building. I lived alone and was polite to neighbors but never particularly friendly or social. I didn't have friends. I didn't go on dates.

I kept the same basic profile as a serial killer. Or a superhero. I'm not sure which is worse. The only exception was the weekly dinner date I kept with my father. He retired and moved to the city shortly after Suzanne's death. We never cried or had a big dramatic scene, but we each knew we'd have at least one conversation a week.

My life. It hadn't turned out like I expected. But if I had times when I wasn't sure what to do with myself, if I didn't know what to make of long Saturday afternoons that turned into empty evenings, lonely nights, didn't everyone? It didn't have any purpose or plan to it, but it was a life. Did I have the right to expect anything more? Still, some evenings I found myself wandering.

One of those nights, I pretended to not know where I was going and ended up in the bar where Suzanne and I met. It hadn't changed at all. Hero Guy was even still fighting a giant, killer robot on TV. This time, I didn't have Suzanne there to laugh with me. This time, Hero Guy was losing.

"Is this live?" I asked the bartender.

The bartender grunted. "This look live to you?"

"How did it turn out? I mean, he beats the robot in the end, right?"

The bartender just grunted again.

"Right?"

"Who knows? They both fell off the Center Building. Practically left a crater in the middle of the parkway. People went down there. Didn't find anything but robot parts and blood."

Blood?

I paid my tab quickly. He was kneeling down against the ledge in the corner of the rooftop. His hair stuck together in matted clumps, his head slumped, a puddle of darkness spread beneath him. For all the years he helped people, I hoped Hero Guy had somewhere else to go. He deserved better. This was what he got.

"When I do bleed, I bleed a lot," said Hero Guy. "Apparently." I had never heard his voice so calm. "I'm going to die."

"What happened?" I asked.

"The Mad Inventors. They teamed up," he said.

"Did they find some kind of hidden weakness?" I asked.

"No," said Hero Guy. "It's much worse than that. They figured me out."

Hero Guy's powers were slowly killing him. People aren't made for so much possibility. Every time he used his powers, it damaged him. He looked fine, but on a cellular level, he was breaking apart. And what's more, he was clinically mad. There was no Voice. There never had been. As a side effect of his powers, he started hearing his own thoughts. The Mad Inventors had been sending out probes, collecting information about him. They'd discovered all this, and now, somehow, the Mad Inventors had figured out a way to use this radiation against him?

"No. They just think it's funny, knowing that I'm dying," said Hero Guy. "They've been emailing me about it for years."

Years?

"They told me if I stopped and behaved like a human being, I could have a long and happy life. Otherwise, they'd be there when I was at my weakest and take credit for my demise," Hero Guy said.

"But you beat them," I said. "Can't you just retire now? We can get you to a hospital, you can stop using your powers, and then live that long and happy life."

"I can't," said Hero Guy. He groaned as he struggled to his feet. Blood flowed down his face. "They picked a really good time to attack. Something is coming. It's up there in the dark, moving this way faster than any human instrument can detect. It might be the end of everything. Or it might take out some kid's house."

"Or some kid's parents' house," I said.

"This will be my last flight."

"Don't say that," I said.

"No. This is all I have left," said Hero Guy. His voice still sounded calm, but I thought I could detect a slight quiver. Was Hero Guy scared? Or was it just me? "I'm glad you came, though. I'm glad I get to say goodbye. And sorry. I'm so sorry for all the people I couldn't save."

I wanted to say something comforting and redemptive. All I could think of was the thing that people always said to me. The thing I didn't believe.

"You'll be seeing them soon enough."

"I'm a superhero, Steve," said Hero Guy. "I can tell when you're lying."

"Just because I don't believe it doesn't mean it's a lie," I said.

"I've seen too much to believe in anything like that," said Hero Guy. "Not since I found out about the Voice."

But he kept going all this time. He went even faster; he did even more.

"You could stay here," I said. "If the world ends, let it. What would we do without you anyway? The next time. And if the world doesn't end, you get to live. Why bother sacrificing yourself if there's no…"

Hero Guy didn't answer. He flew away. Shortly after, the sky exploded for a moment, and the night returned to calm.

Nobody believed the Mad Inventors. They had all seen the pile of rubble he made of their robot. And besides, it was more fun for people to believe their own crackpot theories. Those abounded in the years that followed. His powers had increased. He was with us still, moving faster than ever before, faster than the human eye could see, but he was here, always, keeping us safe from harm. He got tired of it all and left the heroics to younger men. He was working in a gas station in Newport. He lived in a retirement community in Tucson. He was holed up in a Vegas hotel suite playing poker with Elvis and Tupac. Some remembered the flash of light and tried to put it together. He ascended to a higher plane of existence. He'd been given his reward for all the good he'd done. The worthy would one day rise with him, too.

I never told his story. Not to anyone. I went about my life the best I could. I worked at the Community Center, got passed over for the Director position more than once. I went out to dinner with my father until he couldn't go out to dinner anymore. Then we ate dinner in the assisted living facility until he just couldn't eat, or do much of anything else anymore, and I sat by his bedside, not eating with him. I was out in the hallway, getting a drink of water, when it happened.

A flash of light in the sky. A giant robot foot and department store calamity. Police lights outside my family's home. This. As with all the people that mattered to me, I wasn't there the moment he passed. It wouldn't matter if I had been. I couldn't help, and I wouldn't learn a single thing I didn't already know about what death leaves behind. Still, I wish I was there.

From the hospital, I walked back home, back up to the old rooftop. I don't know why I keep coming here. I don't care much for the superheroes anymore. There are so many these days they're barely amazing. At any given moment, they fill the sky. Displays of power, daring, and impossibility. And every single one of them will be gone too. Still, I come up here. Even though I know I'm not any more alone than anyone else, still I come up here to think about my father, to think about Suzanne. Still, I look to the sky and think about that last question I had for Hero Guy. Why he did what he did? I think about my mom, why she did what she did. I know there's nothing new for me up here anymore, but still I come up here and look to the sky like there's an answer up there somewhere. Still, I come up here and look to the sky and . . . oh, I don't know, maybe I just miss everyone.

Saving the World
by Katie Kent

"You're a weak, pathetic dyke." The girls circle me as my heart races. "It's no wonder your mom left you."

Despite hearing words like this many times before, it still feels like someone has punched me in my gut. "L.. leave me alone." My voice is barely a whisper, but it shakes anyway.

One of the girls cups her hand to her ear. "Did you hear something, girls? It sounded like the squeak of a mouse." They break out into laughter.

"Let her go." Jess' voice, from outside the circle, is much louder and surer than mine. "What's she ever done to you?"

Another one of the girls sneers. "Looks like your girlfriend has come to rescue you, again." Smirking, they walk away, leaving me staring at their backs.

"You've got to learn to stand up for yourself, Liv." Jess sighs. As I look at her blonde hair cascading over her shoulders, warmth floods through me. Contrary to what the bullies said, she's *not* my girlfriend, but I wish she was. I don't know if she knows that, and I don't know if she feels the same way. She's the only one I can talk to, but I *can't* tell her how I feel. I need her in my corner; I have no one else. I can't risk scaring her away.

I just shrug, and she sighs again. "If they knew who you really were, they'd leave you alone."

"Maybe. Maybe not. But you know I couldn't handle the attention."

"Good job you've got a talented best friend who can make *really* good costumes and build *really* good apps." She elbows me in the side, winking. "You know, to preserve your anonymity and everything."

I can't help but smile. Jess is the only one who can make me smile these days. It's been a long time since I smiled at anything else. Dad does his best with me, but Mom's departure affected him as much as it did me. I hear him pacing his room at night, when I'm lying awake in bed. I don't want to add to his stress. My social anxiety means that I can't properly talk to anyone except Dad and Jess, who has been my best friend since I was tiny, and the bullying has been going on for so long that I can't remember a time when I wasn't hassled at school.

"You look pretty when you smile." She coughs, her cheeks taking on a slight reddish tinge. There are enough comments like this to make me think there could be a chance for us, but my brain always convinces me that I've read too much into innocent statements. And I've never been one to take a risk, at least not outside of my costume.

We're just walking down our road towards our houses – we've lived next door to each other ever since we were little – when our phones buzz simultaneously. I rub my eyes as Jess pulls her phone out of her pocket.

"You know, you don't have to respond to every alert," she says, obviously picking up on my weariness. "You look like you could use a rest."

"I'm okay." I open up the app on my phone and scan the map for the location. "Are you alright to drive?"

"Yep." That's another benefit that Jess brings; she took her test as soon as she was able to and passed the first time. I've never even bothered to take lessons. The whole idea of it brings me out in a cold sweat. Having Jess as my driver means we have to spend a lot of time together, which brings both benefits and drawbacks. I can't get enough of her company, but my feelings for her get stronger every day. I can deal with it, though. I'm a superhero, for God's sake. Not that that helps when the negative thoughts bombard my brain on a daily basis.

Jess pulls her keys out of her bag and opens the driver's door, whilst I fold myself into the back seat. As she drives, I manoeuvre myself into my costume: a purple top with an 'M' embroidered on the front, and a pair of purple leggings, with a purple mask obscuring my face. Despite how it looks in the TV programmes, it's not easy, even though the costume just slips on over my usual clothes.

A few minutes later, she brings the car to a stop at the side of the road and kills the engine. "That must be the culprit." She nods, and I follow her line of sight down the road, where a man and woman are struggling.

I open the door and sprint down the road, any weariness instantly gone. The woman is facing in my direction, and I see the relief in her eyes when she notices me.

"Mighty Girl!" she shouts. "Help me!"

The man turns around, frowning when he sees me. "Stay out of this! This doesn't need to concern you." He turns back and lunges at the woman.

I've seen enough. If there's one thing I really hate, it's men who think they own women. I aim a kick at the man's bottom, and when it connects, he goes flying into a dumpster full of rubbish.

He pulls himself to his feet and comes running back towards me, but I punch him square in the gut, and when he stands up, he's clutching his stomach.

"L.. leave," I say, and with one last look at us, he flees.

"Thanks," the woman says, and I just nod. She looks a bit dishevelled, but there's no mistaking that she's gorgeous, and my legs shake even more than they usually do around people. I look down at my feet, feeling suddenly like a kid playing dress-up in my costume as she stands in front of me in her navy power suit.

"I'm glad you came," she says, taking something out of her pocket and handing it to me, "I'd like you to have this."

Is she giving me her number? She's got to be a few years older than me, and I'm hardly a catch. Other than the super strength, of course. But when I look down, I'm holding what looks like a business card with a name, job title, number, and email address on it. Her name is Marianne Clements, and underneath it is written the word 'Reporter'.

I look back up, and she smiles at me. "I'd love to tell your story."

"I… I…" I stammer.

"Who's behind the mask, Mighty Girl?" she asks, slipping seamlessly into a professional persona, all evidence of her earlier struggle gone. "Who are you in real life? Everyone is desperate to know, but even though you've saved countless people from attackers, no one's ever heard you say more than a few words. Don't you want the chance to tell your story?"

"N… no." I look down at my feet again.

"Well, you know where to find me if you change your mind."

I nod, then turn and run back to the car, getting into the front seat next to Jess.

She looks at me quizzically as I slam the door shut. "She was cute."

I shrug. "Was she? I didn't notice." Okay, so that's a little bit of a lie. I *did* notice. But there's only one girl for me, and she's sitting right next to me. "She's a reporter. She wants to interview me."

"Oh, so that's why she gave you her number." Relief washes over her face, and before I have a chance to question it, she continues, "You should do it."

My hands start to shake. "You know I can't. I wouldn't be able to get the words out."

She puts her hand on my arm, and it comforts me. "I'm sure she's interviewed nervous people before. She'll know what to do to put you at ease."

I just shake my head.

"Liv." She reaches out and tucks a stray hair behind my ear. "Maybe you should think about coming out."

"The kids at school already know I'm gay," I say.

She frowns. "That's not what I meant. I meant maybe it's time to reveal to the world who you really are."

I grip onto the handle of the door, my palms sweaty. "No way. That's like my worst nightmare. Why would you suggest that?"

"Think about it. Number one," she holds up one finger. "Those kids who are bullying you might stop. If they don't respect you when they know who you really are, they'll at least fear you. Either way, I can't imagine they'll ever bother you again."

"You know I can't talk to her." I count to ten in my head, trying to banish the rage I can feel building up in me. Jess *knows* I can't do this. I thought she got it.

She holds up another finger. "That brings me to reason number two. If you talk about your anxiety and depression, you can raise mental health awareness. This is a way to combine your two personas to help other kids. I mean, you're a badass superhero. Imagine how great it would feel to another kid who's struggling, to know that even Mighty Girl suffers from mental illness?"

"You think I'm badass?" I joke.

"The baddest." She looks into my eyes, and suddenly it's like we're the only two people in the world. "It's super hot." A blush spreads across her face, and it's reassuring to know that even my confident best friend, the most attractive girl in the whole school, can get nervous. Suddenly, I get what she's been saying about how I can inspire others with mental health problems. I know how much it would have helped me, growing up, if I'd had someone like me sharing their story.

I take a deep breath. "Alright, I'll do it." It'll probably be the hardest thing I've ever done, but she's right; it might change things for me, and for other people.

She smiles. "Awesome. I'm so proud of you, Liv." She leans her head closer to mine and, oh God, is she going to kiss me? I've dreamt of this moment for so long, but now that it's happening, I have no idea how to handle it.

Don't over-analyse everything, a voice in my head says. *For once in your life, just go with the flow.* I shut my eyes and lean into her. As our lips touch, fireworks go off in my body, and it's the most alive I've felt in months. Saving the world is one thing, but this is on a completely different level.

As we finally pull away from each other, she leans back in her seat, a grin on her face. "I've wanted to do that for ages."

"Me too," I admit.

"Give me that card." She holds her hand out. "You need to call her now, before you lose your nerve."

I swallow a lump in my throat and open my mouth to protest, but she quickly puts a finger across my mouth. My lips tingle.

"No buts. Strike while the iron is hot."

I take a deep breath. Pulling the card out of my pocket, I take my phone out of the glove compartment.

"Want me to do it?" she asks, but I shake my head.

"May as well start as I mean to go on."

She squeezes my thigh as I dial the number on the card, and I almost drop the phone.

Marianne answers immediately. "Marianne Clements?"

"H… hi." I grip the phone tightly in my sweaty hand. "We… we met earlier. It's Mighty Girl. I… if it's okay, I'd l… I'd like to take you up on your offer of an in… interview." I drum the fingers of my left hand against my knee. "Y… yes, tomorrow n.. night is f… fine."

Jess pounces on me as soon as I've hung up, planting kisses all down my neck. I shiver as I link my fingers with hers. As our lips touch again, our phones buzz in unison.

I pull away, reaching for my phone, and she moans. "Talk about bad timing."

"I don't have to answer them all," I say. "That's what you said earlier."

"You want to, though." It's not a question, but I nod anyway. The thought of ignoring someone in need just doesn't sit well with me.

She turns the key in the engine. "You want to help people. I love that about you." She clears her throat as her cheeks turn pink. "Let's go and save the world."

Memories of a Demon
by Daniel Medrano

The smell of dust and old sweat hit my nose hard as I entered the old building. The years hadn't been kind, but I do whatever I can to keep it from crumbling over my head; too much history to allow that to happen.

I hit the lights, and that old familiar hum followed. People complain a bit, but I can't get rid of it. I don't think I even want to, really. It's one of those constants I would miss if it were actually gone… Feh. I turn my gaze to the ring in the center of the gym, remembering the old times and what they led to.

It was the end of the sixth round, and I was fighting Maurice "Machine Gun" Manzanares. He was good, definitely better than the scrubs I had fought before; it was a title shot after all. I went to my corner and heard Sly, in his old, cracked voice, as he tried to tell me not to follow my plan.

I didn't pay attention to Sly while he tried his hardest to dissuade me. I didn't care. There were only two things that mattered to me at that point.

The smell still stung my nose when I remembered that damn cheap cig Jimmy smoked while he told me what he wanted.

"The seventh starts, you hit the mat and you *don't* get back up."

That was the second thing.

Then there was the voice. I looked out to the stands, past Sly, and saw her, Maria, my little Scrapper. She had her mother's blazing hair, dazzling smile, definitely her eyes, all the way down to the fire that shone in them. I never did right by her, but lord knows that I tried.

She was always the first thing.

She'd been to every fight. She was the only one who cheered against the others who brushed me off in the beginning. As they grew to like me, she grew louder, just to make sure I heard her. I always did.

The bell rang, and so she yelled. It was the only thing I heard through that round. Not the spectator's yells, not my own grunts, not even the dull thud of Maurice's punches as they worked my body. It didn't matter, though, I heard her and that was it.

I must've blacked out at some point, because the next thing I heard was the ending bell, and I was being called the winner. I won. I defied the threats of the fixers, and I won. I hoped she'd forgive me.

I needed to get out of there quickly if I was to have a chance for her to be safe. Cleaned out my locker and got Maria. I spooked her. I had to, but it was good for her to be scared, made her quicker, and was supposed to get us out of there sooner. We almost made it, too.

They caught up with us. Took both of us into the alley and beat me while my daughter watched. I couldn't fight back, but she didn't cry a single tear. That fire in her eyes dimmed, though, that's what killed me. They almost did, too, but we were lucky enough that some flatfoot was nearby and interrupted them.

He wanted to help, but I told him not to worry about it. He was the one good cop in a town where Jimmy's boss went to dinner with the chief. Didn't want to drag him into my mess.

I looked at my little Scrapper. She was still, quiet, and I could tell all she wanted to do was go home. I let her down. Again.

I sent her away. I had a cousin upstate who owed me a favor, and she didn't ask too many questions while I finally did something right by my Scrapper for once.

You could argue I was being angry, spiteful, and all that bull, but they beat me within an inch of my life, and made my daughter watch. No little girl deserved to see anything like that, and I knew I wasn't the only one they did it to. I was going to be the last.

Sly hid me in the gym, and I went to work.

I was a shadow; no one saw me. I paid anyone I talked to more than enough to keep my name out of their mouths. Helped that I didn't use my real name. Had to learn how to use a camera, too. Words were one thing, but pictures had so much more power. That was all before that Photoshop mess changed everything.

I'd gotten it all. What was sent, where it all went, and who it went to. All I needed was the right time. My title fight seemed good enough. Sly made sure it was still on, and I knew they would be there. I wanted to make sure they were watching.

I decided a few things that night: Let them know I was still there, and they wouldn't get rid of me, but I was going to get rid of them.

I fought for three rounds. Three rounds against Frank "The Falcon" Mathis. He hit hard, but I had bigger fish to fry, and he was just an opening act. I probably could've ended it in two, but I wanted to give them a show.

I caught them when they tried to run. Found them in the same alley. They had muscle with them, of course, they always did in those days. They must've thought that Mathis wore me out. I proved them wrong. I never fought as hard as I did that night, and according to them, I wasn't even human.

The finishing touch was a certain flatfoot who happened to receive a parcel with more than enough info to make sure none of them ever did to anyone else what they did to me again.

When they went in, I got my daughter back, and people got an idea of someone protecting downtown. Guess one of the muscle heads let slip that they fought a "demon". So, the Demon of Downtown was born. I thought it was corny, but it got me started.

I still shake my head when I think about it. It was a strange time, but it makes me smile.

Things were simpler back then. Throw on a costume, beat up some dealers, and people believed The Demon was real. He was real in a way, for the time when I wore the mask anyway.

It wasn't much. Didn't have to be, really. A simple black mask with the design of a fanged skull. A costume, throw a decent punch, and want to do some good. None of these aliens and mystic arts that they have these days. Hell, when times were good, you could do it all by yourself.

Teams are a whole different beast, though.

18 years ago

I did a lot of good by myself, but it was when I was with The Guardians that I was shown a new world. I was sitting in the same chair when Exairetos himself asked me to join. He was the first real super. His story was complicated, and I never fully understood it. All I knew was aliens were involved, and there were more like him.

He somehow found out who I was and popped up at the gym. I debated joining at first. I was already pushing the whole hero gig with Maria. I didn't know what would happen if I joined some team that would take me to fight lord knows what.

It was a good deal, with a shot to do some actual, wide-scale good, but I told him I'd think about it. Funny thing was, I didn't get to. What cinched it was when she came bolting out and said quickly, "Yes! Yes, he'll do it!" She had been hiding in the office closet when he came by.

She stood right in front of that golden boy, who was supposed to be older than me, but looked 30, locked eyes, and I swore that I saw her mother in her again. That damned fire.

I joined that day and, just like that, the world opened up in ways I couldn't have imagined. There were monsters and magic. I traveled to outer space. Hell, I even traveled back in time and fought in WW2.

It took me a lot of places, a lot of faraway places, away from her. I look at the lockers and I think about it. I think about all I did at her cost.

I was gone a lot, but she never got angry about it. I had no idea why for a long time. I had missed birthdays, dances, all the mess a father should be there for. There was one night when I found out why.

10 years ago

I was in the lockers. I had just gotten done with a Guardians mission, and fought some guy who called himself Samael. Fancied himself some sort of apostle of the devil or some crap like that. Singled me out, didn't like me using the name of his ilk as a "mockery". A couple of jabs, and some help from the others, and he was out like a light.

Jade brought me home. Her super speed always astounded me, as did everything else about her. I was in no mood to entertain, though. So, I thanked her and let her take off. I went to work patching myself up when I heard footsteps. They were heels. I turned quickly, and there she was.

Black and blue gown and cap. It was her graduation and I had missed it.

"Scrapper…" I said slowly, my eyes began to well up. I wondered if I had fallen that far that one of the most important days of my daughter's life happened, and I had completely forgotten because I was fighting some maniac?

She walked up, took the kit, and sat me down with that same smile she had the day I got her back from my cousin's. "My god dad, you never listen when they tell you to watch for your side, do you?" She sat me down, and I looked at her in awe.

"Why aren't you angry?" I asked like a child waiting for a parent to scold them,

"Why should I be?"

"I missed your graduation," I said. I could feel my eyes begin to well up. "I miss everything important to-." She held up a hand and cut me off.

"The only reason I was able to have a graduation is because of what you and the Guardians do." She told me with that same smile. "The reason that I'm still alive, or anyone else for that matter, is because of what you guys do." She added. "Anytime you're not there, I know it's because of what you do, and that at least I know where I'll be able to find you."

I couldn't hold back the tears that day. I held her close and cried, like a damn baby. I cried, and she just held me. I had never done right by her, lord knows I tried.

After that, she went to college, and I was by myself. Not for long anyway. I still have the picture on my desk. Jade looked so beautiful in that dress that day. She made my girl her maid of honor. I was as surprised as anyone. I had Yale as my best man. The guy died for me once. That's a weird story for another time.

It was around that time things began to change. The villains had changed, and the world had changed. It was one of the times I felt like I was truly out of it. The doctor's telling me that my still standing was nothing short of a miracle was definitely another.

Jade hopped right on it, wanted me to quit. We were set with her job as a biologist, and I was actually seeing a fair bit of change from the money we got from the gym. More and more people were coming. A lot recommended by friends in the Guardians. I had taught Terry when he was starting out, and in turn, he sent me Jasper, the second Cub. Kid had promise, but they seemed to start getting younger or older depending on whenever the seasons started. The younger they were, though, the shorter they lasted, just like Jasper.

The young guys all wanted the flash. The glitz. Everything that made them dress up for the completely wrong reasons. I've seen them all: The gaudy costumes, the convoluted powers and origins. Then came all the pouches and shoulder pads. My god, the pouches, and don't you even get me started on the damn belts-on-belts thing they did back then either. Who was that even for? What did it even do?

Like I said, it had become a young kid's game, and it was all too much at the time for an old man like me. Not made any easier by what happened.

My Scrapper came back to town with a friend of hers. Well, I thought she was a friend.

4 years ago

Her name was Lilith, lovely girl. She was TA in her school, and it turned out they were dating. She had brought her there to meet me; they were that serious. She was scared when she showed up with her, admittedly, and I was kind of blind until it was made clear to me.

I was shocked, sure, but I thought I handled it well. No yelling, nothing got broken at least. She was my kid, who was I to tell her who she can or can't love? I had to get out of there, though. Just another example of how out of touch I was.

I went to the gym. It was my haven.

"Dad?" Hers too. "Are you mad at me?" She asked, "Do you not like Lilith?"

"Oh, Scrapper," I said, and took her in my arms. "Of course I'm not mad," I told her. "She is nice and she's trying desperately to impress us. A bit perkier than I imagined you getting with." I said with a laugh. "Obviously, she doesn't know everything, I take it?"

"Of course not." She replied with a smile. "That's actually what I wanted to talk to you about."

"You want to tell her?" I asked, concerned at the implication of a normal person beyond Sly (bless the old bastard) and some others knowing what I do, or did, would've been the more operative term.

"Not yet, but I wanted to show you something." I hadn't noticed she brought a bag with her. She reached in and pulled out a mask. It looked like mine, or at least a version of it. "Dad?"

That was when I decided that breaking things was allowed. We argued, I yelled, I broke a lot more than I intended, and she said the one thing I was scared of.

"There are other people out there," she said. "You don't think I can't find someone to train me?"

My blood went cold.

She was right. There were others. Hundreds more than what we had when I started. She would find one, and with my luck, it would be the ones I hated. Or even worse, Titan.

"The Demon has been asleep for too long, Pop." She said, "Can we bring it back?"

I only catch the last few steps, but then I hear her call me back from that memory.

"Dad?" She asks. I turn, and she's already prepped. Her hair in a ponytail, dressed for a workout. It had been a couple years since she put on the mask, and she had already been accepted into the Guardians. I made a promise not to help her with that one. Even made sure that Titan was on the selection board, I had to make sure no one questioned her being there.

"There's my Scrapper," I say with a smile, hugging her tight in my arms. "How you feeling?"

"Good." She replies.

"Liar," I say with a chuckle. "I caught your fight with those Ouroboros nuts." I take my seat while I talk. "You've got, I'm guessing, a fractured rib, and your left shoulder seems messed up," I added, and she shrank after realizing that I caught her. "You're running drills until I'm tired."

"But dad-" I hold up a finger.

"You got fluked by scrubs, and I trained you better than that. Drills." I ordered with a smirk.

Some hours pass as we work. She's amazing, she got her mother's looks, but if I had given her anything, it's that right hook.

We work on focus mitts before her alarm goes off. The ground shaking also clues us in. She picks it up, and I know what's coming next.

Prison transfer. Bunch of inmates, some with abilities. She's the closest Guardian, and she needs to go. I watch her and I go tense. She looks at me and says those words that always make me go cold.

"I have to get ready." She tells me.

I will never get used to her leaving in that costume, I'm just glad Jade helped in getting her something actually good. After I was done being furious that she helped her behind my back, we made up for it. I go back to my seat and turn on the

TV to watch the coverage. My phone goes off, and Jade is on the other end. "Jade? What's up?" I ask after I pick up.

"Please tell me she isn't going to the bridge?" Her tone makes me tense again.

"Jade, what's wrong?"

"Call her, and get her away from the bridge now!"

"Jade, she already left, she doesn't take her phone with her," I stated. "I taught her that it would be a distraction."

"Samael is there!" She yells, and my blood is ice. "Find some way to get her out of there! She's not ready for him!"

"She's already there," I say as I finally move. I head to my office. "She's gonna be there and he's gonna notice her," I add.

"Honey, please don't do it." She pleads. "You can't go after him like you-"

"I'll come home, baby," I tell her as I pull the phone away from my ear. She yells for me not to do what I'm about to. Though I might be guessing that last bit. I hang up and set my phone down as I look at my old poster, the one for my title fight against Mathis. My Scrapper had it framed as a gift.

"..."

The bridge is chaos. People screaming, running, all hell breaking loose. She does her best. Focus on the people, don't let the monsters get close to them.

"Get to safety!" She yells with authority. "Get as far as you can, and get hidden now!" She turns and catches several escapees as they try to bum rush her. They're cake. I'm not worried about that. It's what comes next.

A blast hits her in the back.

She's down, and he walks up with that damn glowing claw of his. "Another angel trying to demean my kind?!" He yells. "I won't stand for it!" He's manic as he yells again and blasts her. She screams as he cackles loudly. "A woman in the guise this time?" He asks. "Has the original profaner run home to hide?"

"He would never hide from a punk like you!" She growls as she moves to look at him. "You're just another little nutjob with-" She cries out when she's blasted again.

"Hush, child," he says with another blast firing off. "I have no time for the prattle of children."

"Good, I always hated talking!" He turns and doesn't even notice me until he's on the ground, clutching his jaw with a scared look. "Why do the ones with the biblical gimmicks always have to be the talkers?" He looks up and sees me in my armored costume.

Reinforced joints, some type of metal weave that Exairetos brought back from his planet, all I knew was that it was strong and didn't slow me down, even got a nifty new mask that kept the original look, but gave me some nice goggles that let me see everything about a person. Like Samael's racing heartbeat when he looks at me.

"It's been a long time due, nut-bag, but I am gonna enjoy this... Get you some!"

Captain Power

by Zacheriah Tucker

Papa drove the car, while Mama did her crochet in the passenger seat, June's brother Harry read his comic books in the back of the station wagon, and June herself played dolls with Emily. All of them were wearing their nice clothes, even though it was Saturday and church wasn't until tomorrow.

June had on her blue dress with all the little buttons (which was her favorite), her red shoes (which were uncomfortable, but pretty), and the sacred amulet given to her by Captain Power. They were all wearing their best clothes on account of how they were visiting the new exhibit on ancient Egypt at the history museum in the city, featuring the Sarcophagus of the Unknown Pharaoh.

Mama and Papa were talking about that nice Mr. Kennedy running for president, whom they both planned to vote for. Papa liked what he had to say about the missile gap. "We need a president who isn't asleep at the wheel against the Russians."

Mama was glad they were all able to watch the debates on their new television set as a family together. "You could really see just how articulate and intelligent he is up close."

Harry was absorbed in the latest issue of The One-Gun Kid. June liked comics, but her brother only read westerns, war, and science fiction monster stories. Her favorites were the funny fashion comics like Mary Ann the Model or Adeline the Adolescent Hurricane. She *hated* the sappy romance comics, but she liked superheroes- especially the elegant lady detectives in domino masks and evening dresses. She loved looking at them in their beautiful clothes, but she also liked the big muscled super-heroines in their swimsuits.

June refocused her attention back on her game of house with Emily, the neighbor girl, and June's best friend in the whole world. June's daddy doll had just come home from work and was kissing Emily's mommy doll before dinner.

Emily wasn't, strictly speaking, part of their family, but June loved her so much she considered her family.

"We're here!" Papa announced to his passengers. "Everybody out."

Papa always knew just where to park downtown because his law office was only a few blocks away. When Mama drove them into town for groceries, it always took her forever to park the car.

Everyone hopped out, and they only needed to walk a few blocks to the museum. It was nice and warm, and June was enjoying the sun. The museum was a big marble building with a huge colonnade in front. She, Emily, and Harry raced up the stairs to the top. Her older brother was faster, but the girls both got a head start before they challenged him to the race, and June won in the end.

Past the main doors, they got into the line for entrance. June noticed her teacher, Ms. Winters, was there ahead of them, and she frantically waved 'hello' until Ms. Winters saw and waved back.

Ms. Winters might have been the most beautiful woman June knew, excepting Ms. Marilyn Monroe, but June only really knew her through the movies. She knew Ms. Winters in real life, and thought she was gorgeous. June usually finished her schoolwork faster than the rest of her class (on account of her being a straight A student), and after finishing, she liked just looking at Ms. Winters and thinking about how pretty she was.

Holding Mama's hand and being guided through the slow ticket queue was hypnotically dull. June was soon lost in thought, thinking about Ms. Winters wearing all kinds of beautiful dresses, when she felt her amulet trembling.

Captain Power was trying to contact her through the sacred Power Amulet; she could feel the crystal vibrating against her chest. Why did hero business always come up at the worst time?

It didn't matter. She had a responsibility. But she needed to get away from the others in order to transform without revealing her secret identity, for no one must ever discover that mild-mannered June Jordan of Claremont Middle School was also Captain Power, defender of the innocent, crimefighter, and founding member of the new Champions League of America.

"I need to go to the bathroom, Mama."

"You already went before we left home, sweetheart."

"I need to go again, Mama. And I should go now before we get our tickets, shouldn't I?"

"Do you need me to go with you, dear?"

"Mama, I'm practically grown up now. I can go to the bathroom alone."

Normally, June never liked leaving her family when she was in a public place, ever since the amusement park debacle. But that particular catastrophe happened back in grade school. She was in middle school now. And she had also become Captain Power since then.

"Alright, come right back here when you're done."

June rushed right past Ms. Winters into the restroom, of course it was full. Why were women's rooms always full? She was sure Black-wing and Fusion-man never had this problem…

Yet, it was she that fate had chosen to give these abilities so long ago- in her previous grade, at the elementary school. She and Emily were on a camping trip then, with their Girl Scout troop, when they witnessed the most incredible meteor shower June had ever seen. The next morning, she and Emily were fishing when they saw a man floating in the water.

He was face down, and they pulled him out at once. He was very big and was wearing a strange crimson uniform. Only June had earned her medicine merit badge, so she sent Emily to get their scout leader, Mrs. Crenshaw, while she performed first aid.

She tried to give the man CPR, but she was scared that he was already dead. That certainly would have been a terrible initial outing for her first aid skills. No one wanted a nurse whose only previous patient was dead.

He was still weakly alive, though, and he clasped her hand tightly. "I can see in your heart that you are brave and virtuous," he whispered. "I have been sent here from my home world, but this body has been critically wounded. I must revert to an energy form."

June didn't understand much of what he said, but she did like to think of herself as brave and virtuous. "Is there anything I can do to help?"

"Your planet faces grave peril. I came to help, but I was attacked by the Hidden Masters in the atmosphere, high above your world. Now I must pass on my power, and soon! Will you accept the mantle, and the burden, of Captain Power?"

"I will."

In an instant, the man was gone. And she held the sacred Power Amulet.

Mrs. Crenshaw was very cross at her and Emily for playing pranks when she arrived, but they both got an apology later, once the newspapers started reporting on Captain Power. The man was really an alien, a Pow'rellian. He was still alive inside the amulet, but as an energy form, he could only manifest with the aid of a human host. They had been working together to defeat the Hidden masters ever since.

Finally, a stall was available. June snatched it at once and locked it, just ahead of a large woman with a sunhat who tried to force her way in. Then she pulled out the Power Amulet and held the crystal to her forehead where she could get the best telepathic reception.

What is it, Captain Power?

"Danger, June. Ever since Dr. Agon escaped from the insane asylum earlier this week, I have been monitoring the communication frequencies the Hidden Masters used to send their messages to him in our previous battles. My search has just borne fruit."

Oh, what kind of fruit? We're going to lunch after the museum, but I'm already hungry.

"The richest Centauri kumquats, June. The fruit of success. Dr. Agon has been ordered to steal the Apophis Stone on display at this very museum."

Dr. Agon was one of her most dangerous nemeses. He was once a brilliant scientist, but a terrible lab accident left him horribly deformed. His eyes became reptilian, his hands turned into scaley claws, and he started breathing fire. The accident also left him incurably insane.

It was unclear if that was a direct result of the radiation he was exposed to, or a consequence of developing powers so ironically appropriate to his portmanteau of a title and name. Whatever the reason for it, he had turned to crime and eventually began aiding the Hidden Masters in their scheme for world domination.

As if on cue, June heard a commotion from out in the main hall, and the bathroom began to empty in a general confusion.

"Hurry, June! Make the transformation into Captain Power."

June held the sacred crystal in her amulet over her heart. She focused all her spiritual energy into it until it was throbbing with power. Then she said the magic Pow'rellian word, "Rael'cun!"

At once, June was transformed into Captain Power. The little girl was replaced by a man in a red Power-suit, with bulging biceps, huge quadriceps, and pectoral muscles so massive they put Ms. Marilyn Monroe's chest to shame. Her long brown hair was now short and blond. Her eyes turned from hazel to blue as her perspective expanded beyond the human visual spectrum.

June took a moment to refamiliarize herself with her new body and broader senses. It always took her some time to get used to being so much taller and stronger than usual.

"Quickly, June. Although your human archaeologists are unaware of this, the Apophis Stone is an ancient extraterrestrial weapon lost on your world by my people during the time of Atlantis. It must not be allowed to fall into the hands of Dr. Agon and the Hidden Masters. It was the greatest treasure of the Unknown Pharaoh, and buried with him in his sarcophagus."

Wait! Everyone knows I came in here. And we don't want anyone to know that Captain Power uses the ladies' room.

"Hold the top of the stall and use the shrinking beam on yourself. Then we may traverse through that vent on the wall into the ductwork."

Good thinking, Captain Power.

June held her own shrinking beam on herself and reduced until she was small enough to sit criss cross applesauce on a dime. She hoisted herself up and ran along the top of the stall to the ventilation duct. It was an enormous ten or twelve inches above her on the wall, but she activated the sticky suction devices in her gloves and boots.

The tile wall was simple to scale. She had just reached the vent when the bathroom door was kicked open. A man dressed like a cheap ruffian and wearing a Halloween mask resembling a reptile came in holding a shotgun. One of Dr. Agon's men.

Fortunately, the room was nearly empty. Only the heavy-set woman in the sunhat was left, and she fainted straight away when she saw the gun. The goon was just standing over his unconscious hostage, and probably wondering how on earth he could even budge her, when June blasted him with her stasis beam.

Each second of exposure to the stasis beam equated to a minute of complete paralysis. She kept him under the beam for a minute by the reading on her wrist-mounted chronometer. That should be long enough, and more than ninety seconds of exposure risked instantaneous combustion.

It was strictly against the Champions of America's charter to ever take a human life. Also, even if he was a bad guy, June didn't want to see anyone splattered all over the bathroom like her snowman test subjects ended up over Christmas break.

With that one dealt with, she started her voyage through the museum's ventilation system. Through another outlet, she could see into the main hall. More of Dr. Agon's henchmen were there, and they had grouped all their hostages in front of the Indigenous America exhibit. June could see Mama, Papa, and Harry there, but not Emily or Ms. Winters. She hoped that meant they had gotten away.

Have the police been alerted yet, Captain Power?

"*Yes, several people escaped and called the emergency services, including your loved one Emily. The authorities are currently cordoning the area, but according to their radio transmissions, they fear endangering the hostages' lives.*"

I fear endangering them too! That's my Mama, and Papa, and my big brother down there.

"*You must remain focused, June of Earth. Fear will not aid you in the rescue of your family unit. Climb down and surround the civilians in your invulnerability field generators, that will keep them safe while we deal with Dr. Agon's underlings.*"

You're right, Captain Power.

There were six goons in the main hall, all armed with tommy guns, but there was no sign of Dr. Agon. June was still micro-sized, so no one saw her as she was climbing down the wall. It was a good thing that Pow'rellian technology was designed to work just as efficiently regardless of size.

Once she was certain the museum goers were safe, June used her growth ray to expand back to normal size. Normal size for Captain Power, that is. Seven foot and two hundred fifty pounds was rather larger than June's real size.

"Look, it's Captain Power! We're saved!"

"It's Captain Power! Boss said to ice the hostages if he turns up!"

The two thugs nearest to the hostages turned their guns on them and fired. A few of the more panicky hostages screamed and dived for the floor, but there was no need. The bullets ricocheted off in all directions, but no one inside the invulnerability field could be harmed. One of the hostage-takers did manage to wing himself in the arm when a bullet deflected back at him, though. Soon their guns clicked empty.

"He's got them in some kind of forcefield or somethin'."

"Well, blast him then."

June activated the null velocity device on her belt. "Surrender, you ne'er-do-wells." Her voice was deeper as Captain Power, but she also tried to speak from her chest as much as possible, because she thought it made her sound more heroic. "Your weapons are useless."

"We'll see about that, do-gooder!"

The four who still held loaded weapons opened fire. They needn't have bothered. The null velocity effect halted the bullets in midair around her in four distinct groupings. Suspended there, they couldn't even manage the acceleration to fall.

June stepped out from the middle of them, and the bullets clinked to the ground in little piles once they were out of range from the null velocity effect. "I told you your weapons were useless. Now surrender to the po-"

"He can't stop us all! Rush him!"

She ought to have expected as much. Once all else failed, criminals like these always resorted to the bum rush. June turned off the null velocity device so they wouldn't accidentally tear themselves apart by moving into and out of it, then put up her dukes. She wasn't much of a fighter, but she was super-strong, and Captain Power was trying to teach her the basics of Pow'rellian boxing.

The nearest man to her wore an Iguana mask and tried throwing short hooks to her solar plexus. They landed like feathers. June countered with one big haymaker (Bam!) that set him flying into the prehistoric era… of the museum.

The Champions had turned over the time machine that sent all of them back into the real dinosaur times, to their science officer, Dr. Zedd, for disassembly and study a month ago. Unlike the museum models, real prehistoric dinosaurs actually had feathers instead of scales, just like the surviving dinosaurs living in Antarctica.

The next one, wearing a turtle mask, swung at her head by using his gun as a bat. It hit with the impact of paper confetti. June decided to rely on her old favorite, the single big haymaker. (Wump!) He was sent flying across the Delaware and into the Revolutionary War.

In a rash endeavor, two of the robbers tried to grab each of her arms. She picked them up and knocked their heads together. (Clunk!)

The biggest member of their gang wore a frog mask, and it had been he issuing most of the orders to the others. He was the only one who almost matched her in size, so June decided to practice her boxing with a few jabs that quickly sent him reeling. (Biff, biff, biff!)

"Don't you know that frogs are amphibians, not reptiles?" she asked.

He climbed back to his feet; the other four she had knocked down were out for the count. This one was obviously a higher pay grade. "It was the only mask they had left."

June decided to stop messing around with the giant and went back to her signature strike, the big haymaker. (Sock!) He went to visit the Civil War and met his Sayler's Creek.

The last gangster was wearing a snake mask. He was smaller than the others, but he held back from their attack. June hoped that meant he would surrender peacefully, because she didn't really like fighting. Though when she approached, he took a karate stance.

"Why don't you just give up?" she asked.

By way of answer, he threw himself at her with a leaping head kick. It felt like when her big brother tapped her on the forehead. She tried to counter with the big haymaker, but it missed! He squirmed out of the way, just like a snake.

She tried another and another, but he kept moving. And all the while, he just kept kicking her in the head, over and over. It didn't hurt exactly, but the fact that she couldn't stop him was just as aggravating as when Harry was being obnoxious.

Finally, she got ahold of him. She decided to hoist him into the air and spin around with him until he got dizzy. As Captain Power, her own inner ear was superhumanly stable.

"June, I believe throwing him should be sufficient."

No. He needs to go for a ride.

"June of Earth, do not forget that our true goal is to prevent Dr. Agon from escaping with the Apophis Stone."

Oh, alright.

June stopped. This ninja-wannabe didn't deserve to land in an interesting exhibit, so she tossed him into the broom closet. Then she went immediately to the Egyptology area, she didn't like being too close to her family when she was Captain Power.

"Be wary, June. I have shifted my energy field to protect you from Dr. Agon's recently acquired powers of mesmerism, but he may still have placed others under his control."

In their most recent battle, Dr. Agon had hypnotized her through his weird snake eyes and turned her against the other Champions of America. Fortunately, the other Champs were eventually able to free her, and together they defeated Dr. Agon.

The new Egypt exhibition looked spectacular; it was a shame the museum would probably be closed for the rest of the day. In the center of it, she found Dr. Agon with Ms. Winters beside him, a blank look on her face. The focal point of the exhibit was the massive Sarcophagus of the Unknown Pharaoh on a raised dais. The smaller showcases were in a starburst pattern of surrounding corridors.

A coalition of the museum security guards were struggling to push open the heavy stone lid of the sarcophagus. With a terrific grinding sound, they tipped it open just as June arrived, sending the lid crashing to the ground.

"That's an important cultural artifact of the Egyptian people on loan to our museum! How dare you damage it so carelessly?!"

Dr. Agon turned to face her. "Ah, Captain Power. I presumed that noise out in the main hall must be you. I dare all in pursuit of my research, as you well know."

"You're sick, Dr. Agon. Let me take you back to the asylum where the therapists can help you."

"You think I'm mad. But could a madman develop a device to harness the power of the Apophis Stone into a laser blaster capable of annihilating a small European country!? No. It's the world that is mad." He slipped his long tongue out of his mouth and licked his own eyes. "Only I remain sane. Guards, kill him."

The security guards drew their revolvers mechanically. June activated the null velocity effect around herself, so she had nothing to fear. But the guards were innocent, so she preferred not to get rough with them, and she wasn't sure what to do.

Dr. Agon grabbed Ms. Winters. "Come with me, dear. I suspect I shall need a hostage once Captain Power deals with these pawns, and you'll do nicely."

"Yes, master," intoned Ms. Winters.

They went to the sarcophagus where Dr. Agon drew forth a shimmering crystal like the one in her Power Amulet, then ran for the emergency exit.

"Quickly, June! He must not escape. Use the sonic cannon to temporarily incapacitate these men and pursue Dr. Agon."

Clever plan, Captain Power.

June donned her auditory eliminating headgear and activated her sonic cannon. It was more than enough to disable such sluggish and uncommitted opponents. She rushed past the guards after Dr. Agon.

The emergency exit led out into the loading area where Dr. Agon was waiting for her. "…" he said.

"What?"

"…"

"Just a minute." June deactivated the sonic cannon and took off her headgear.

"At last! My god, that sound was irritating! As I said, take one more step and I charbroil this lovely young woman's head!" Dr. Agon was having trouble regulating his speaking volume after exposure to the sonic cannon. "Such a pretty face, don't you think!? Charming hair! Such a shame to see it all go up like the wick of a candle!"

"There's no escape, Dr. Agon. The police have already surrounded us. Why don't you just let her go?"

"Once again, Captain Power, you underestimate my brilliance!"

June noticed a helicopter approaching. She realized that it bore the official logo of the Hidden Masters- a massive fist grasping a globe of earth, while a second massive hand drove a dagger into it. They weren't terribly subtle about their intentions.

"All I want is the Apophis Stone, Captain! If you give me your word of honor that you'll let me board the helicopter and take off unobstructed, I'll free the woman unharmed!"

What do we do, Captain Power?

"*Remain calm, June of Earth. I have a plan.*"

"Alright, Dr. Agon, you slime. I give you my word that I'll let you board the helicopter and take off again."

"Aha! You foolish heroes will never win, because you are constantly hampered by your weak morality! I release you, woman. Enjoy your petty freedom, brief as it may be, before I make all the world my slaves!"

Dr. Agon shoved Ms. Winters over to her, and his helicopter came in for a landing. The doctor's control over Ms. Winters appeared to have been broken. "You aren't going to just let him go, are you?" she asked June.

"I have to," June replied. "I gave my word. And a hero always keeps their word."

Dr. Agon boarded the helicopter and held the Apophis Stone aloft in victory, laughing maniacally. The helicopter lifted off, and June waited until she considered the take-off complete. Then she activated her magnetic anchor before they could fly away.

The helicopter strained against the magnetic pull holding it in place, but to no effect. "Curse you, Captain Power! You lied to me!"

"Don't curse me, doctor. There's a lady present. And I never lie. I let you board and take off, I never said anything about letting you fly away."

The pilot pushed the vehicle harder, but that only burnt out the engine. It started to sputter, and the helicopter spiraled back down to earth. Dr. Agon emerged, literally spitting fire. "I'll kill you, Captain! I'll kill you!"

June activated her null ignition field and went back into her boxer's stance. When Dr. Agon realized his flames couldn't reach her, he resorted to his claws, like some savage beast. He scratched at her Power-suit, but the armor was impenetrable.

In his vicious attack, however, he had left himself open to her patented finishing maneuver, the single big haymaker punch. (Pow!) Dr. Agon crashed into the dumpsters where he belonged, and the police arrived at last to arrest the pilot.

"Oh, Captain Power!" Ms. Winters threw herself into June's embrace. "You were wonderful!" She kissed June's cheek. "So dashing!"

"I- er- thank-you, Ms. W- thank-you, miss. I- uh- must go now. To consult with your government's authorities, you understand?"

"Of course. I hope to see you again sometime, Captain Power."

"I'd- ah- like that too. Miss?"

"Susan, Susan Winters."

"I'd like that too, Ms. Winters."

June was still flushed and fluttered when she explained everything to Emily's father, who was the commissioner of police. She told them that the Champions would be taking custody of the Apophis Stone for safekeeping, but that Professor Magick would be happy to help restore the Sarcophagus of the Unknown Pharaoh for the Egyptians.

"Good work here, Captain Power. I've told my men to take the utmost caution with Dr. Agon. I can assure you, there will be no seventh escape for the good doctor."

"I'm sure there won't, sir. But if you'll excuse me, I have some pressing business."

"I understand. Thank you for your help, Captain."

"It was no trouble at all. Give my regards to your wife and daughter, commissioner." June hoped the commissioner didn't think she was being rude, but she really wanted to get back to being herself before her parents started to worry.

She passed Emily on her way, who was incidentally being brought to her daddy now that the danger was over. June said, "Hello."

Emily just stared at her wonderstruck, and went all gaga the way girls sometimes got with boys. June wasn't sure why girls did that. She certainly never acted that way with boys.

June just hurried on and micro-sized herself to return to the restrooms in secret. The large woman with the hat was just coming to when June left the stall as herself. A pair of police women were sent in to retrieve the paralyzed prisoner.

When she came out of the bathroom, June rushed straight to Mama, who was very worried about her, as expected. She lavished in both Mama and Papa's attention over lunch, which they shared with Emily's daddy, as he was already nearby.

Harry was very excited to tell the story of Captain Power's battle over and over again during lunch and on their drive back. "It's a shame you never seem to get to see any of Captain Power's battles, sis. He's really something else."

"I'm just unlucky, I guess."

"He's so dreamy," said Emily. "You should have seen him, Junie. He was just so dreamy."

And they would go around like this, with Harry retelling his favorite parts again, and Emily pining away with all her heart.

Well, it may have been Captain Power she was yearning for, but it was June that Emily was cuddled up with in the back of the station wagon. And June was all smiles the whole drive home.

Inmate_382A4L
by Andrew Leslie

"Piss off, brat! Your face is making me sick," I shouted at a nearby child while avoiding the clubbing blows of a robotic prison guard.

As she ran off, she spat in my direction and called me a monster.

People in the city of Westwood have bestowed upon me various names throughout the generations, but the only one that's stuck is the one I'm best known for: Lowlife.

I'd remained hidden on Earth for decades after being marooned here as punishment for my alleged crimes, per the Arbiters' decree. On Eonz, my home planet, I was hated by the wrong people, and the irony of where my prison lies is not lost on me. I spent those first few weeks hating myself for being so foolish, so prideful. I could have avoided this fate had I simply bent a knee to the ones in power, even though I knew they didn't deserve it. After the first month on Earth, I found myself able to fly. This was abnormal even for my people, and I mistakenly attributed it to the new atmosphere.

The first time I made my presence known to the human race was after the radio became a household item. Curiosity overtook me, and I stole one from a local store. I overheard a broadcast warning everyone that a dam had burst and the townspeople should evacuate immediately. Of course, they'd all be washed away before they had a chance to escape. I flew above them, hidden by the night sky, and saw the fear and horror on everyone's faces. The power I needed to save them all did not course through my veins then, though bitterness did. Perhaps fueled by loneliness and self-loathing, I landed near a crowd and addressed them all.

"Look at you, pathetic humans! Why bother trying to save yourselves? Just let your children drown and finally end your sad, whimpering bloodlines for good!"

They gazed at my figure, cloaked by a hooded overcoat I found in the cave where I made my home. At first, they weren't sure what to make of me as my form looked very much like their own. When I removed my hood, they instantly knew I wasn't one of them. Some of them made the erroneous connection that I was the one who burst their dam, and that I was here to gloat about their doom. It's true, I was gloating, but I didn't wish them to die. I suppose something inside of me knew what I was doing. What I would become.

The crowd's fear and panic transformed into revulsion and vitriol. I stood there, surrounded by these cowering humans, as their hate filled me up. The more they jeered at me, the stronger I felt. The more they hissed and decried me, the more keen my senses became. An awakening happened that was as new to me as I was to them. Overwhelmed by the power flowing through me, I manically laughed in their direction. This only made them angrier, which, in turn, made me feel more powerful. I shot into the air faster than I ever had before. Though the dam was miles away, I arrived there in an instant. The water poured out of the widening crack, and there were mere moments before it burst wide open, drowning countless lives into the black nothingness. In another millisecond, I located the closest building to the dam - the historic town hall, a source of pride for the fledgling city at that time. To my own surprise, I was able to smash it to rubble with my bare hands! At the speed of light, I carried as much of it as I could back to the dam, where I pummeled it into the hole, sealing the crack and saving the town from certain destruction.

The next day, the radio broadcast a message that the expert engineering of the dam allowed it to seal itself off when the pressure reached a certain level. Whoever was in charge here couldn't explain what happened and knew that a helpful lie would go much further than the inexplicable truth. It was for the best, in the end. The people needn't know who saved them. The citizens mourned the loss of their town hall and cursed the cloaked figure who destroyed it while mocking them in their time of desperation. The newspaper dubbed me "Lowlife" after a young girl called me that in an interview.

It took me some time to put the pieces together. The hate I directed at myself granted me the ability to fly, but meagerly so. The hatred others directed at me gave me unimaginable speed, power, and reflexes. That day, I realized my time on this planet could be for more than just self-loathing and bitterness. These Earthlings needed me, and I needed something more than just revenge against the Arbiters to live for.

As generations passed, I always found a way to keep their ire up, even when

I was helping them. The town grew into a bustling city, and its problems grew in tandem. When invaders from the Circinus galaxy claimed Earth as the newest hub in their intergalactic slave trade, Westwood was their first stop. I abducted the chief of police, the homecoming queen, the proprietor of an animal sanctuary, and several others. After breaking into the news station during a live broadcast, I announced that as a "gesture of goodwill" to the Circinusians, I would be handing a dozen of Westwood's finest over to them.

"Coward!" "Spineless!" "Traitor!"

Oh, how they loathed me. Luckily for them, their hatred gave me the strength necessary to destroy the entire fleet of Circinusian warships, ending their millennia-long reign of terror over the universe. The chief of police, who had been suffering from a cold at the time, took credit for their downfall. He explained in an exclusive interview that he infected their alien computers with his human virus, causing them all to malfunction and self-destruct. He also regaled them with how I gifted them to the Circinusians on bended knee and then disappeared in fear and cowardice. The first part was true, but I wasn't bending my knee in fealty; I was preparing to propel myself upward, straight through their interstellar reactors. My "gift' was simply a ruse to grant me access to the Circinusian's inner sanctum. As I shuttled the Westwood citizens back to Earth, I announced to everyone within earshot that I didn't care either way who won or who lost as long as my backside was covered.

My reputation as Lowlife was cemented worldwide that day.

The timing was propitious, as my self-hatred began to wane around this time. It's difficult to look inward and see something horrible when you've saved galaxies full of sentient beings. My powers didn't falter as I was nourished with the disdain of millions, but I was still very much alone. The punishment for my crimes took on a new dimension when I realized that no matter how much I tried to help them, there wasn't a single person here I could confide in. A companionless, friendless, lonely existence was all I could expect for the duration of my sentence. That was until the Arbiters who handed down judgment on me sent a guard to check up on me.

This came on the heels of my battle against the warlock Javeus. Originally from the Drifting Realm, Javeus came to Earth in search of a lost gemstone. Completely useless to humans, it granted people from the Drifting Realm the kind of unlimited power that would allow an evil warlock to overthrow a dimension like this one. Javeus found the gemstone embedded in the necklace of an elderly woman who was just about to gift it to her granddaughter on her wedding day.

During the ceremony, he cast a spell of invisibility on himself and attempted to steal the necklace. I was there to stop him, but to the onlookers of the wedding, it seemed I was the one who stole the bride's beloved keepsake. The reception was completely destroyed during our ensuing battle. Despite the waves of hatred from the wedding party that empowered me, that slippery spellcaster escaped my clutches and disappeared back to the Drifting Realm. I decided to hold on to the necklace for safekeeping, in case he ever returned.

While I flew away, something flashed in my peripheral vision. As it grew closer, I saw its human-sized metallic form keeping pace with me. It appeared to be a robot of some kind, with a large domed head and oversized limbs. When I glanced at its chest plate, I recognized an insignia I hadn't seen in centuries: The Arbiters' Crest. The robot had watched over my battle with Javeus and decided to confront me about these strange, new powers.

"Inmate 382A4L, I am Sentranought – a guardian from Eonz's Correctional Sector. An anomaly in your physiology has been detected," the robot vocalized. "The Arbiters will demand an explanation for this. You will come with me back to Eonz for further judgment."

"So you're my prison guard. Well, guard, I'm not here to do the Arbiters' dirty work. That's your job," I replied before flying away.

Sentranought powered up its thrusters and pursued me. The technology responsible for this machine must have been beyond what I thought capable of my home world. Despite my near-light-speed flight, it matched my pace. My supernaturally keen senses weren't sharp enough to outmaneuver it. If it came down to a fight, I'd need all the hate I could salvage. My first instinct was to get this monstrosity away from Westwood and into the open countryside surrounding the city. I quickly realized that would rob me of the power I desperately needed to stop this armor-plated sentry from taking me away from those whom I'd undertaken the role of protector. My mind raced with possibilities. Where could I take this potentially dangerous battle to a place with a small group of people who hated so purely?

My namesake smacked me in the face when the answer finally came: the elementary school on the outskirts of town. It was a dangerous gambit, but one I thought worth the risk. Who knows what menace or natural disaster would be next in line to try and wipe out humanity? Javeus was still out there, waiting for his opportunity to strike. I landed just outside the playground and was in luck, the children were at recess. Before I could get their attention and throw some childish insult their way, Sentranought rammed its metallic shoulder into my chest, sending me tumbling away from the school.

"Oh, cool, a robot!" a curly-haired child exclaimed from the swing set. That got them all running to see what the commotion was about. Nearly three dozen kids crowded against the chain-link fence that outlined their play area. They all stared in amazement at Sentranought's stature.

"What are you?" a child shouted from the crowd.

"I am Sentranought from the planet -," the digitized voice emanated from its head. As it was speaking, I unleashed a right hook that sent it barreling towards a water tower located a half mile from the school. I turned to face the children, and over my left shoulder, they could see Sentranought smash into the tower, water cascading down into the field below.

"He's just another victim," I scowled at the young boys and girls whose faces were pressed against the fence. "Of the Lowlife."

The children all booed and jeered at me with a purity that only youth can provide.

"My grandpa says you tried to blow up the dam!"

"My daddy says you're a meanie!"

"You're stinky!"

Imbued with their hatred, I felt emboldened to put a stop to the Arbiter's lapdog. As I turned to locate this metallic menace, my vision filled with steely silver. Sentranought's clubbing blow nearly collided with my head. Luckily, I was able to dodge it in time. I wasn't as fortunate with the next one. It sent me rolling toward the fence line where a little girl stared down at me. Too close to the action, I thought.

"Piss off, brat! Your face is making me sick," I said, leaping away from an incoming blow. Out of the corner of my eye, I saw her curse at me while running to safety. Sentranought caught up to me near the ruined water tower, where I grabbed each of its clawed fists with my hands. I could hear the mechanisms working fervently inside, attempting to compensate for my newfound strength.

"How..are..you...doing...this?" Sentranought's vocal processor must have been rerouting its power somewhere else; the voice almost sounded strained.

"Oh, you mean this?" I said, rearing my head back and unleashing all my power into a headbutt that could split Earth's moon in two. A thunderous clang rang out, causing the schoolchildren to cover their ears. Sentranought went flying through a hillside and out of sight. The children all groaned in disappointment, and a new chorus of boos erupted. I flew back to the school and slowly descended into the fenced area. Shame overtook me. I wanted nothing more than to apologize for putting them in danger and explain that it was the only way to ensure their survival. Of course, they wouldn't understand, and even if they could, it would be the end of my ability to protect them. A small child threw a teddy bear at me, which bounced off my chest and landed on the ground. I bent down to pick it up. My first instinct was to hand it back to the child, but I knew better. Instead, I flung it casually into the next county.

"Never forget," I said, placing my hand on the metal slide situated next to me. "The Lowlife will never leave you Earthlings alone."

I ripped the slide out of the ground and flew off to find Sentranought hearing the jibes of the children growing softer in the distance.

The trail of destruction I'd caused wasn't hard to follow. It ended with the top half of Sentranought's body buried in the ground and its head a few kilometers away. I landed near the domed, metallic head and reached down to pick it up. Curiously, it was hollow. It wasn't a head at all, it was a helmet! I flew over to the body and began to dig it out of the ground.

By the time Sentranought woke up, they were back at my cave away in the mountains where I'd lived for centuries. After removing them from their robot armor, I fashioned the children's slide into a makeshift straitjacket to keep them from doing anything dangerous. It had been so long since I'd seen another Eonzian that I didn't recognize them as one of my own.

"Inmate 382A4L, I demand you release me and accompany me back to Eonz, by decree of the Arbiters!" They struggled against their restraints to no avail.

Whatever gave me power from the humans' hatred didn't work with Eonzians. Sentranought clearly hated me, but I felt no boon of power from it.

"I'm not going anywhere," I said. "And neither are you."

"If you think killing me will stop them from sending others, you're wrong, Wren Clovis!"

My Eonzian name. I'd forgotten what it sounded like.

"That's not my name," I said, sitting on the floor across from Sentranought.

"I've been monitoring your activity on this planet," Sentranought said. "I know what these Earthlings call you. I know what it means. Based on how you acted around those younglings and at that betrothal ceremony, it seems to fit."

"Why are you even here, guard?" I asked.

"To pass judgment!"

This meant my reprieve was potentially approaching. My sentence was nearing its end, and Sentranought was here to assess whether or not I was fit to rejoin the peaceful people of Eonz.

"But, I cannot allow you to remain," Sentranought said. "You are terrorizing these people. That was not why you were sent here to watch this fledgling society work together to grow, in hopes you'll understand why you were punished. On top of that, you've gained some very extraordinary powers. We must find out how you attained them and how to strip them away from you."

"Because I'm far too dangerous to be trusted with them. Is that your assessment, guard?"

"It is my duty to ensure your humility to the Arbiters' will and that these innocents are not harmed," Sentranought's steely glare made me smile. Their resolve and honor were a beacon of light in a lonely world.

At that time, I had no notion of what to do with this noble, if naive, Eonzian. Unfortunately, it would have to wait as an emergency siren sounded from far away. Something was very wrong deep in the heart of Westwood.

"Come with me, guard," I said, grabbing him by the metal straitjacket and flying away. "I'll show you my humility."

I rocketed towards the source of the disturbance, with Sentranought in tow. The city center was abandoned, under the assumption that some kind of weather anomaly was tearing down buildings. As we came closer to the ruckus, I saw nothing but could tell Javeus had cloaked himself again. He was tearing down one building at a time, in search of the gemstone I had on me. I could feel it pulsating with power. I tossed Sentranought down in the city street so he could see what I already knew to be true.

"Javeus!" I bellowed. "I have what you want. Come at me, if you dare."

I couldn't get a bead on the wizard, and before I realized what was happening, he enveloped me in a spell that froze me in time. Not frozen, actually, but slowed to a crawl. For every inch I moved, he could move a dozen feet. This kind of sorcery could only come from the Drifting Realm! Javeus uncloaked himself right in front of me and procured the gemstone from my cloak.

"I heard you calling to me," he said, holding it up for me to see. It was pulsing very quickly. I had felt this previously but didn't realize the implication - the gemstone pulsed faster the closer it was to someone who could properly use it. "And now, I'll repay you for your trespasses against this realm's newest ruler!"

The wizard proceeded to cast spell after spell. The void of space was put into my lungs, sucking the air out of me. Fire from a hellish realm scorched my skin. Pressure from the surface of a distant planet compressed my chest. I was beginning to black out. As I faded away, my vision filled with steely gray. It collided with Javeus's face, sending him crashing into a nearby building. After I shook off the effects of his spell, I realized that Sentranought had somehow gotten back into their armor. Magic, it seemed, was susceptible to Eonzian technology.

"Go on, inmate," the digital voice intoned from his mask as they handed me the gemstone that had fallen from Javeus's grasp. "I think you've got it from here."

I looked around, but the wizard was nowhere to be seen. He'd cloaked himself again. The pulsing gemstone grew stronger as the invisible warlock approached me. Once the pulsing was at a fever pitch, I knew he was within arm's length. I reached out and grabbed him by the neck, squeezing just enough for the desired effect. His power waned briefly, showing his true form to me and Sentranought.

"Oh, hello, Javeus," I said to the frightened warlock. "You were saying something about becoming this realm's new ruler?"

Javeus was in no position to answer with my hand tightening around his windpipe. I pulled him close so we were nose to nose.

"Listen, wizard. This realm is under my protection. All who reside in it are under my protection." I produced the pulsing gemstone from my pocket and held it up for him to see. "And all its contents are under my protection. This is as close as you'll ever come to it, again. Do we have an understanding?"

I squeezed just a touch harder to make my point clear. Javeus nodded his head furiously. However different the Drifting Realm was from my home, the need for oxygen was one thing we had in common. I dropped the wizard with a flop onto the ground next to Sentranought.

Between gasps for breath, he summoned a portal back to his world.

"I don't know the source of your power, Lowlife, or why you act like you care about this realm. One day I'll figure it out and rest assured I'll return for what's mine," Javeus said as he disappeared into the portal.

The siren had stopped ringing, and people were coming back to assess the damage. Buildings lay in rubble around me, and they made the obvious, mistaken connection. Within moments, the jeers and cries of hatred erupted from all around. Sentranought started to say something in my defense, but I held up my hand letting the guard know it was pointless. Instead, I flew into the air, hovering just above the newly formed mob.

"Build it back up, humans, so I can knock it down again," I sneered at them, dashing off in a blur.

Sentranought followed me back to my cave and removed their helmet to show they were not looking to restart our fight.

"My robotic armor can get a fix on my location and autopilot back to me when we're separated," they said, answering my unasked question.

"So, what happens now?" I asked. "Are you still intent on taking me back to the Arbiters?"

"Tell me, Wren Clovis, why do you protect these Earthlings?"

This was something I'd never really thought about, but the answer came to me naturally.

"It's their resolve. No matter what fate throws at them, they never give up," I said.

Sentranought grinned.

"Perhaps I've rushed to judgment, inmate. I think I'll stay a bit longer and reassess your parole. It seems this planet needs all the help it can get."

Sentranought slid their helmet back into place. They stepped to the mouth of the cave and fired up their boosters.

"There aren't many friendly places for our kind out there, guard," I said over the low rumble of his thrusters. "But if you ever need a place of respite, I'd welcome the company."

As Sentranought rocketed away, I looked out into the vastness of my newly adopted home world. For the first time in nearly a century, I smiled to myself at the prospect of being stuck here on Earth.

Walk Through Fire
by Marlaina Cockcroft

Fireflower had nearly burned her way through the vault's wall to rescue the hostages when her phone buzzed. She mouthed curses and kept her hands steady, directing the flame. The school *always* called while she was at work.

And this was the volunteer job. The school called her at the marketing firm all the time, too.

She left the phone in its fireproof hip pouch and burst into the vault, eyes and hair blazing to match her red skintight suit, flames crackling from her outstretched fingers. Before she could growl, "Drop your weapons," the robbers had done it, one of them batting at his smoking hair. Robbers and hostages alike cowered on the floor, whimpering.

Fireflower knew she ought to expect such reactions. She had an effect on people.

Still, no one ever said *thank you*. Not lately.

She ducked back through the hole as bank security and police came swarming in. They wouldn't arrest her—she did get her little stipend from the PD, though they'd never admit it—but they liked to be territorial. "You're welcome," she called, tossing the words behind her as she sped out of the building. Alleys were her friend.

She closed her eyes, opened her fists, counted to ten, and there she was, quiet little Brooke Bloome. Never got to talk in staff meetings. Always nudged out of line at the elevator. Usually expected to clean the microwave.

Her new flats were already scuffed. Brooke sighed and pulled out her phone.

She played the voicemail, groaned, and hit call-back while jogging to her car. "Hi, it's Pol's mom. I got your message. Is anyone hurt?"

"Yes, hello." The counselor's voice was frosty. "He's here. Everyone's fine. But Mrs. Bloome—"

Ms., thought Brooke, for the twentieth time or the two hundredth, she wasn't sure. Pol's school didn't seem to comprehend single motherhood.

"—This is the third such incident this week, and it's lucky that no one has gotten hurt. Your son needs to better manage his emotions."

Brooke was about to apologize, promise to talk to him, swear it wouldn't happen again. The usual. But she'd been doing the usual for so long, and she couldn't say it anymore. Her eyes glinted beneath her drugstore sunglasses, and Fireflower spoke up instead. "Maybe you should try managing my son."

"Excuse me?"

"You said he didn't qualify for behavioral help. Maybe the school should rethink that decision, since during school hours he's your responsibility. Legally."

She could feel the guidance counselor flinch through the phone. School officials didn't like the word *legally*.

Fireflower smirked, but knew she'd regret that little swipe.

Pol slumped in the folding chair that touched the wall outside Dr. Reza's office. Reza and Mrs. Winderman, the guidance counselor, were finding new ways to tell Brooke why she was a bad parent. Pol was too emotional. Pol was too aggressive. Pol shouldn't throw things.

"Then those other kids should stop harassing him," said Brooke, though Fireflower hovered, keeping the edges of her voice sharp. She could see her son through the open doorway. His legs sprawled crookedly across the linoleum.

Reza and Winderman bulldozed right past her, taking turns in their eagerness. "Whatever the other students may be saying to him, it is not acceptable to throw chairs at them."

"We're getting calls from other parents."

"Are there problems at home?"

"The smoking is also a concern. You know, of course, this is a smoke-free building."

"What?" said Brooke, suddenly interested in the conversation again.

Reza glowered. "I *said*, Mrs. Bloome—"

"Ms." She wondered if he'd notice the spark in her eyes.

"—that on top of everything else, he seems to be smoking on school property. I don't need to tell you he's far too young for this."

"Where was the smoke coming from?" Was it possible? He was old enough.

"His fingers," Reza said impatiently, "where else would you hide a cigarette?

This is beside the point."

Brooke's hair glowed the tiniest bit. Maybe she'd let Fireflower wrap things up. Reza and Winderman, looking uneasily at her face, shifted further backward in their wooden chairs.

"*Legally* speaking," she said, "I don't have to come collect my son, and next time, I won't. Handle his nasty classmates, or I get a lawyer."

She knew Pol had heard her, but he kept quiet as they walked to her gently rusting brown sedan. No *thank you* from him, either, and she certainly didn't have to defend him for throwing furniture around, no matter how vile his overentitled, over-tutored, overachieving classmates were. The car was on Cypress Highway when she finally said, "You mind telling me what you were thinking?"

"They were laughing," Pol mumbled from the back seat. "They're always laughing."

"Sweetie, throwing chairs does not stop people from laughing at you." She couldn't see his eyes in the rearview mirror.

"It does while they're running away from the chairs." He was overdue for a haircut again, dark curls spiraling out, so unlike her own straw-colored wisps. His face was thinner than she'd realized, his cheekbones sharper. He looked like his father. Brooke didn't want to think about that too much.

"Were your fingers smoking?"

He blinked, looking up. His eyes were still green, Brooke saw, no hints of red. "*That's* a weird question," he said.

"Just answer it."

Show me something. Give me a reason. I'll tell you who you really are.

"You're so weird, Mom." He flicked his fingers at her, consciously or not, she wasn't sure. They were regular teenage boy fingers, with ragged nails and cuticles. No sign of flames. Brooke's next words died away.

Was she disappointed, or relieved?

A particular light on the car's dashboard blinked on. Brooke bit back a groan. People always picked the most inconvenient times to be criminals.

Her sister. She could leave Pol with her sister. Again.

It was a shootout downtown. Fireflower ignited the guns, and their owners screamed at what the explosions did to their hands. Grimly, the EMTs moved in to clean up.

She headed for the nearest alley, a boarded-over back loading dock for some forgotten business. The man standing in the shadows applauded dryly. "Our Fireflower saves the day."

She stopped short. Of course he knew all the city's private dark spaces as well as she did. "Doc? Are you breaking parole?"

He clutched his hands to his chest, staggering. He always did have a touch of the theatrical, even during battles. Sometimes she had to stifle a laugh while punching him. "You *wound* me, you do. I've kept parole. I'm thoroughly reformed. I helped you, remember?"

"Once," she agreed. "Because Captain Creature was using your Earthquaker to wreck the city. So noble of you to clean up your own mess."

"Willingly," he said, "willingly. I want some credit here." He was smiling, but his eyes weren't. There was a sadness about him now that suited him. He seemed more dignified, matching the gray streaks along his temples.

"I'm not Dr. Destruction anymore," he said. "Just a concerned citizen. Used to be, you'd get the guns away from people first, *then* blow them up."

She flushed. "They were shooting. It was faster. You're seriously questioning my methods? How many people did you send to the hospital, Doc?"

"George," he said. "Please." He stared at the ground as he said it, hands shoved into the pockets of his rumpled khakis, as though there were something interesting among the broken bottles and fast-food wrappers. Then he looked at Fireflower, and she was struck again by his eyes—so dark, so intense. Her own began to lose their red. "My point is, those methods were appropriate for Captain Creature. Or the Worm. Or me." He smiled ruefully. "Not a bunch of scared teenagers. Can't you hold back the fire a little?"

Her straw-colored hair lay limp across her shoulders. She pointed to it. "If I lose my anger, I lose my flame. You know that."

"Doesn't it seem like you need to get angrier and angrier to get the job done?"

Of course not, you're exaggerating, but she didn't say it aloud.

He paused, then added, "I watch the videos of you online. You look more like you're in pain. Like being Fireflower hurts you."

Brooke stood shivering in the brown pants and white button-down she'd been wearing when she left work for lunch and, for various reasons, never returned. She was always cold when the flame left. Always huddling away from her other, stronger self.

"Just trying to help people," she muttered.

He took a tentative step toward her. "Want to talk about it? Get a drink?"

"We're archenemies. No." Her eyes glinted again, briefly.

"We're not archenemies anymore." But he sighed.

She needed to pick up Pol. She walked past George, wincing as her thin-soled shoes crunched over glass shards. Then she stopped. She'd never asked, and always wondered. "Why did you become a villain?"

She could hear the shrug in his voice. "I didn't think I had better options." Then he said, "How's your son?"

She hugged herself. There was no one else to tell. "He might have my powers. I'm afraid he'll hurt someone."

His hand gently touched her shoulder. "Is there anything you can do about it?"

She paused for a long moment. Then kept walking.

"Why do you always send me to Aunt Barb's place?" grumbled Pol as they pulled into the driveway. It was the first thing he'd said since they left her sister's downtown apartment. "She takes my phone, and she never lets me watch anything."

Barb thought Pol had anger issues because Brooke let him watch violent videos. Barb thought many things about Brooke's parenting skills. Barb's theoretical children would've been better behaved.

"There was something I had to do." Brooke opened the door, aware of him shuffling behind her. When had he gotten this tall? "What do you want for dinner?"

"Aunt Barb made stuffed cabbages." Her sister liked having a reason to cook. Brooke was more of a defroster. She grabbed a French bread pizza from the freezer and stuck it in the oven.

"Wait, can I have one?" Pol said. "I didn't know we had pizza." Brooke couldn't help grinning as she reopened the freezer. Teenagers and their appetites.

They sat on the couch, chewing absently, neither one focused on the TV. Brooke would have to finish her market research study after dinner to make up for skipping out of work again. At least the school meeting gave her a better-than-usual excuse. *Poor Brooke and her troubled son, she works so hard.* Her co-workers had no idea how hard she worked when she wasn't stuck being Brooke.

She studied her surroundings. Everything in her living room, from the couch to the carpet to the wall, was brown or beige, tastefully matching, blending together into nothingness. Brooke had always tried to make her little house into a calm space, but she'd made it boring instead. Nothing here matched Fireflower.

Pol switched off the TV but kept squeezing the remote with both hands. He said, "Mom? Where do you go? What is it you have to do?" Then exhaled softly.

There was so much she wouldn't talk to him about. So many gulfs in their conversations. He must have thought he wouldn't get answers.

She studied the greasy remains of her pizza. He was thirteen. Powers or not, this was his birthright.

"Mom?" he pressed.

She nodded. "Come with me."

In the basement, with its peeling walls and stacked boxes of old toys and clothes, she pressed her thumb into a worn gray button, and a door appeared. The next room was littered with torn-up costumes, stacks of criminal records, secret maps of the city, and most satisfyingly, a pinned-up poster of all her archnemeses: Captain Creature, the Worm, Dr. Destruction. Each villain's face had been Xed out, checked off the list.

Pol stared. "What is this stuff?"

"My headquarters." When he didn't say anything, she added, "My other office." It needed dusting, she noticed, and the records needed updating, but she could barely keep the rest of the house clean.

"Soooo, you run a superhero fan club?"

She'd been fighting his teachers and principals since second grade, fighting to raise him alone, fighting to keep her career going, and he couldn't translate any of that to fighting crime.

He of all people should take her seriously!

Pol gasped. She'd become Fireflower, and she didn't remember doing it.

She held a hand out so Pol could see the tiny flames sparking from her fingers. "This is the real me, Pol."

His face was white. Slowly, he held a hand up to match hers. Tendrils of smoke, barely there, rose from his fingers. "I thought it was in my head," he said hoarsely. "I thought I was crazy."

"I *knew* you had my power," she said. "We need to train."

He didn't seem to hear her. "Does Dad know about you?"

Her hand snapped shut, extinguishing the flame. "He knows."

"Is that why he went back to Greece?" He took a step back. "Mom? Stop glowing."

Fireflower closed her eyes, breathed deep, but her hair still flamed around her head. "He didn't approve," she said finally.

"And he just left me with you anyway?"

Something about his tone clawed at Fireflower. Why shouldn't he live with her? Was she the one who'd destroyed the family? She was so angry that she said it out loud. "I warned him if he took you away from me. He listened. That's all."

Pol's legs bowed out from under him, and he sat on the concrete floor. "You told him you'd set him on fire. Right? You threatened to burn my dad if he took me. I watch you online, and all you do is burn things." His tears reflected her firelight gleam. "I thought Dad hated me. He's just scared of you."

Fireflower felt herself fizzle. "I would never have done it. I was angry. Just angry."

"So you get to be angry and I don't?" His voice was raw and scratched-over, but she heard every word. "I'm the bad kid, and you're the good mom? You set people on *fire*."

"I fight crime," Fireflower said, except she was Brooke again, swaying slightly, all beige and no spark.

He gulped a few breaths. His hand shot upward, and thin jets of flame arched toward her.

She dodged them easily, but he might as well have punched her or thrown her into a wall. She'd said regrettable things but never thrown flame at her husband. Attacked by her own *son*—she felt the betrayal in her bones. She staggered.

He shook all over, staring at his hands, then bolted out of the basement.

The front door was wide open by the time she got to it. "Wait. Pol! Apollo! Wait, *please*." But he was gone.

By 3 a.m., she'd driven around the neighborhood five times and no Pol. All her texts were unread, and the tracking app couldn't find him. He could've taken the bus to anywhere. Alone in her house, she gritted her teeth as the brownness closed in on her. She darted to her secret office and hauled out the red shining scraps, the costumes ruined in fights or shredded from overuse, and draped them over the couch, the counter, the kitchen chairs. Color was better. *I'm going to paint this whole house red,* she thought wildly. Orange. *Something bright.*

She sank onto the red-striped couch to catch her breath.

At 3:30, her buzzing phone woke her. She scooped it off the coffee table. "Pol?"

"No," said a sad voice. "Just me."

"George?" Brooke said. The voice attempted a dramatic laugh.

"Dr. Destruction," she said. "What did you *do*?"

"I'm sorry." His breath was ragged.

She let Fireflower take over. "Doc, stop whatever it is. I'm coming right now."

After years of crisscrossing the city, Fireflower knew the quickest ways to everywhere. Dr. Destruction's old lab was nestled into the top floor of a converted slaughterhouse, five floors above a nightclub. He'd always coexisted well with the nightclub. "They're good cover," he said, even after Fireflower discovered his location. Occasionally, he admitted once, he'd toss the lab coat and mask aside and wander down for a drink. He didn't make a good loner.

He'd always been quirky, even for a supervillain. That was one of the things she'd secretly liked about him.

Fireflower could have shot flames straight at the ground, blasted herself up to the roof. Instead, mindful of the neighbors, she climbed the fire escape.

He was on the roof, slumped against a rectangular thing covered with a tarp. "You beat the buyer here," he said, staring down at those gaudy silver boots of his. "I knew you would." Fireflower hadn't seen his lab coat and mask since before he'd served time, and her heart ached to see them now.

"What's the machine?" she asked. She thought she heard a rustling, a clank from the fire escape. Was that the buyer?

"We upset the order of things," he said. "You had no archenemies left, so you started maiming teenage gunmen. I didn't have a purpose, so I made another nefarious machine."

She didn't know whether to laugh or yell. He reached up to pat the machine, like it was a good puppy.

"I tried so hard to be normal," he said. "No one hires a supervillain for anything, believe me. I was chased out of a few places." His look turned dreamy. "I had *such* power. I was fearsome. Wasn't I?"

"You were," she said quietly.

He nodded. "But I don't want this machine in circulation, either. It amplifies abilities. If you used it, you could immolate a building three states away. I don't know what the buyer wants it for, and that scares me. I just realized that."

She couldn't think of a thing to say. She stood over him, wishing it were the old days and they'd have a good rousing fight before she foiled his dastardly plot.

"Brooke," he said, "I wish you'd had that drink with me."

She couldn't cry; she'd lose her fire. She closed her eyes and heard herself whispering, "I do too."

Helicopter blades whirred in the distance. If that was the buyer, who'd been creeping on the fire escape? Either way, time was up. She held out a hand to Dr. Destruction.

George smiled crookedly and took it.

Then he reared back as the bullets hit.

Fireflower pulled him down and away, throwing a quick flame to melt the next few rounds of gunfire. The buyer, apparently, hadn't been planning on paying; she could see the man leaning out the open door of the copter, holding a semiautomatic. Thugs, common *thugs,* to deal this way with Dr. Destruction. She shot an arc of flame at them.

The copter exploded, lighting the night, sending flaming shards everywhere.

Too late, Fireflower realized her carelessness. There were screams from the surrounding buildings, screams from the street, blending with the sound of shattering glass and screeching car tires. So many ways to take down a helicopter, and she'd picked the worst one.

"Fireflower," whispered Dr. Destruction, "what did you do?"

She stared at the space where the copter had been. "I don't know." She clenched her fists, trying to douse her flame, but her body was roiling with the heat of it. Giving up, she lifted his lab coat to check for a wound.

"Bulletproof vest," he said. "Do you think I'm an idiot?"

"Lucky they didn't hit your head," she muttered, furious with herself. She'd avenged a death that hadn't happened. But she'd stopped the buyers. That mattered.

Didn't it?

"Am I still the hero?" she asked.

Groaning, he pushed himself to his knees. "Well, it isn't *me.*"

They both froze at the sound of beeping behind them. The fire escape—whoever was on it had gotten to the machine. Fireflower whirled, flames arching toward the intruder.

Pol stood there, shivering in a thin hoodie, bathing in the rays' orange glow. She pulled her hands backward, and the flames went wide, missing their target, but he'd seen. Fury twisted his face as his eyes began to spark red. He lifted his hands...

Fireflower threw hers out to block him, but the force of his flame pushed her across the roof.

"I followed you so I could help you, and look what you did," he shouted as she struggled to her feet. "You can't scare me now, I'm as strong as you are, you killer! You made me just like you, and I *hate* you." He blasted at her again, and she dove away.

Sirens wailed from the street. The police couldn't get involved in this. Too many people might be hurt already.

She could stop Pol. But she might kill him. The thought chilled her.

They could throw flame at each other until they destroyed each other and everything around them, and it wouldn't solve anything. All these years of trying, and she couldn't save him.

Clanging noises across the roof. Dr. Destruction was rewiring his machine. Dodging flame, she ran back over.

Pol screamed incoherently, blasting fire, eyes blazing, hair swirling, like a beautiful avenging angel. Fireflower flicked a flame at him, and he jumped back. Dr. Destruction called, "That's your son?"

She nodded, tense, watching for Pol's next move.

"I'm so sorry," said Dr. Destruction. He slammed the panel cover shut. "I reversed the polarity. You can neutralize him."

Pol was coming closer. She needed to stop him. She needed him to control his anger.

She needed to show him how.

"Turn it on," she told Dr. Destruction, and, dodging his attempt to block her, she ran through the orange glow. She felt it dimming her power as he switched the machine off. Her flame was half gone. Her mind cleared.

Brooke, a redheaded Brooke with brown eyes, held her hands out to her son.

A blast of fire blew her over.

George screamed. So did Pol.

Fireflower wouldn't burn. Brooke would die. This in-between Brooke, halfway superpowered? She opened her eyes. Singed all over. No flame in her fingers.

Pol peered down at her, breathing raggedly. "Mom—I didn't see you'd changed back—I thought you'd made yourself stronger. I'm sorry, I'm sorry, please be okay."

Unflappable George babbled into his phone. Pol cried. Her heart twisted to see them both.

"I hurt you," Pol said.

Brooke reached to touch his cheek. "You stopped your flame when it mattered. Remember that control. Hold on to it."

The sky was lightening into dawn as George bent, draping his lab coat over her. "EMTs are on their way up."

Brooke attempted to shake her head. "They should help everyone else first." The burns were little fires on her skin. *So this is what it feels like.*

"You can't turn," he said, his face etched in grief. "You're stuck. I did this to you."

"I chose this, George," she said. "I don't want to be two people anymore. Just myself."

George managed a shaky laugh. "Then teach me how. Please."

There was shouting and the stamp of feet. "Pol," Brooke said, straining to be heard. "Be who you are. Be exactly who you are."

As the EMTs lifted her stretcher and the police flanked them, she mouthed, *Pick a name.* Pol nodded, still teary-eyed.

He'd make her proud, she knew it.

She still had a core of anger burning within her. A *little* anger.

Just enough.

Darklight
by Scott Kinkade

"Aroo?" The werewolves gaped at the elevator doors, their noses upturned as they tried to work out the mystery of what lay beyond. Their intelligence in this form could be charitably described as lacking; so, whatever lay behind the doors held the same air of mystery as the edge of the known universe.

One thing they did know: something was coming. Something both familiar and alien. It had the same scent as them, yet it reeked of humanity. If they had been in their human forms, they would have recognized the presence of their greatest adversary.

The elevator *dinged,* and the doors swished open. The unlucky lycanthropes enjoyed a split-second of dual muzzle flashes before their minds were literally blown.

He swaggered out of the elevator as nothing less than a white-hot vision of Hell itself. His black duster coat—made from the hide of Cerberus, Satan's beloved pooch, and covered in stitches drawn from the devil dog's intestines—flapped stylishly in the breeze created by the gunshots.

Atop his head sat a black fedora. A bandana, covered in mystic runes, obscured his face. He twirled his guns and pointed them left and right to draw a bead on any other demonic denizens of the tower that might be lurking about. Nothing. But that would soon change. The explosive rapport of two Colt Single Action Army pistols unleashing fire-and-brimstone rounds was sure to draw the attention of anyone in the area.

Sarah Bilderback, the wealthy heiress of Gothopolis, had taken great care in designing this building. She had ensured one couldn't just ride one elevator to the top floor. Instead, ten different elevators went up ten floors each. That meant anyone seeking to stop her ritual tonight faced a laborious journey to the top. And of course, each floor was guarded by forces both human and otherwise. Thankfully, only one elevator remained.

He stepped over the bloody werewolf carcasses and headed down the red-carpeted hallway with its brick veneer. Ostensibly a hotel, each room was, in fact, empty. Bilderback funded the construction of Bilderback Tower throughout the early 1940s, but it had only one purpose: to focus demonic energy on a single point. And now, in 1945, enough energy had been gathered to open a portal to Hell itself.

As his eyes burned with literal hellfire, his thoughts once again fell on his dual identities. To the outside world, he was a wealthy steel magnate. But at night, when his conscience got the better of him, he became the mysterious specter people called "Darklight." Feared by… pretty much everyone, he stood against the forces of darkness.

He had been late figuring out Bilderback's true intentions, but tonight, her ambition would be put down like those hell-wolves he had just dispatched. Inwardly, he recited his creed: *Be you shadows or be you light, no one escapes my second sight.* Also, she had used his steel to build Bilderback Tower, which made him responsible for stopping this madness.

He stopped in the corridor between rooms 902 and 904 and cocked his head to listen. Someone was in those rooms. A series of faint but concrete heartbeats teased his ears from inside both rooms. He considered blindly opening fire on the doors, but there could be hostages in there. Bilderback certainly wasn't above such things.

Both doors exploded outward toward him, pelting him with wooden debris. Since mortal objects couldn't hurt him, he stood his ground and waited for the real attack.

Four men in suits with grey skin charged him from both sides of the hallway. The first one to reach him launched a mean right hand toward his face. Darklight observed the fist glowing with wispy dark energy. So, these were thralls, then. Thralls were mere mortals imbued with satanic powers in exchange for a soul contract guaranteeing absolute subservience to their master.

Darklight ducked the punch, too late realizing that was a distraction as well. One of the other thugs grabbed him from behind and pinned his arms to his side. The three other thralls began working Darklight over with meaty fists. Though they were mortals, their attacks could hurt him, and he winced in pain from every blow.

Eventually, he had had enough and kicked one of the goons, sending him and the guy holding him back into 902. Both hit the ground, and Darklight rolled backward off the thrall before putting a flaming brimstone bullet in his chest. He hated killing mortals, but the path these men had chosen could never be strayed from, thanks to the soul contract.

The three other thralls entered the room, but they found themselves bottlenecked. Darklight dispatched them with ease.

Darklight stepped over their bodies and left the room before continuing to the elevator.

He rounded the corner and juked out of the way to avoid a throwing knife. Half a dozen rotting figures from two rooms emerged dressed in centuries-old Chinese uniforms. Their skin was ashen with a touch of green, and their long black fingernails looked ready to get acquainted with someone's eyeballs. Furthermore, each figure had a paper talisman covered in Chinese characters attached to their forehead.

No doubt about it: They were *Jiangshi,* AKA "hopping zombies." Bilderback must have formed connections with China to bring her dream to fruition.

Darklight unloaded on them, but the fiery rounds bounced off emerald-green energy shields that formed around their bodies. All monsters came from the same source, but their strengths and weaknesses varied wildly.

True to their moniker, the Jiangshis hopped toward him, their arms outstretched to grab him and suck out his *qi,* or lifeforce. For reanimated corpses, they were surprisingly spry, closing the distance within seconds. Darklight hit the ground and rolled out of the way, but the ghouls pivoted to resume the chase.

However, Darklight was prepared to face every kind of supernatural threat, and he reached into his utility belt to remove six thin pieces of paper similar to the ones covering the Jiangshis' faces. As each ghoul came at him, he slapped one of the papers onto their faces, effectively replacing the pre-existing talismans.

The talisman placed on a Jiangshi's head by a Taoist priest both reanimated the corpse and gave the priest control over it. The characters on the talismans were, essentially, marching orders. But the characters on Darklight's talismans were the opposite commands, and they canceled each other out.

All six Jiangshis seized up and collapsed in a heap, ending the fight in decisive, if unceremonious, fashion. Darklight then headed to the other end of the floor where the final elevator was, his coat swaying from his fluid movements.

Darklight stepped out of the elevator into a grand ballroom. Tables and chairs had been moved to the periphery of the room, leaving a large space in the center.

Marble columns lined the room in a circular pattern, and a twenty-foot-tall fountain shooting a geyser of red liquid lay at the very back.

The unmistakable form of Sarah Bilderback stood with her back to the fountain, her long, form-fitting black dress complementing her raven hair, which cascaded down to her lower back. The young heiress looked resplendent, but that wasn't what unnerved Darklight. *She looks like Anne. So much so that it's scary.*

Bilderback waved her arms in an exaggerated, pompous gesture. "Ah, Darklight. So good of you to join us at the end of the world."

"Stand down," he replied in a gravelly voice. "You don't know what you're dealing with."

She gave him a haughty smile. "That's where you're wrong. I have studied the demonic arts all my life. No one knows the workings of Hell better than I."

"All the more reason to stop. You know what they'll do if you summon them," he said.

"Do?" she said with a disbelieving look on her face. "They will *teach* us! Make us stop living the lie of humanity! Love? Compassion? Those are deceits we push onto our children. Demons live honestly and without pretense. We can, and will, learn to be true to our base nature."

He leveled his pistols at her. "Enough! Stop this or I'll end you!"

"Oh? Can you really kill someone who looks just like your lost love?"

"How do you—?"

She gave him a patronizing laugh. "You have done well to conceal your identity among mortals, but the denizens of Hell know all about you. I've been in contact with them for some time, you see. They gave me a little gift to keep you at bay: a new face." She began chanting in the language of Hell. He only had a scant few moments to stop her.

But he couldn't pull the trigger. Fake or not, she looked too much like Anne, and he could never attack her.

Before he knew it, the moment was gone. But even if he'd had a million years, it wouldn't have mattered. Some things were inviolable.

Behind Bilderback, the bloody fountain swirled, and the geyser coalesced into a concrete form. It gradually took on a vaguely human shape. The blood turned black, and four human limbs sprouted from the mass.

Finally, it was done, and Darklight stood face-to-face with one of the Sires of

Hell: Ghostferatu. The demonic visage wore a dapper black zoot suit, a checkered black-and-white tie, loafers the color of midnight, and dark leather gloves. His head, if you could call it that, was more of a frosted skull with vague humanoid features.

The demon lord hovered above Bilderback and directed his attention to Darklight. "Well, well. If it isn't our dear James. How many years has it been? Time is meaningless in Hell. I trust you're satisfied with the deal we made?"

Darklight pointed his guns at the specter. "Not a day goes by when I don't wish I could take it all back."

Ghostferatu wagged a reproachful finger at him. "All sales are final, I'm afraid. That's the ironclad rule set by the Boss a millennia ago." His voice was akin to rubbing jagged glass over a microphone.

"Then, how about I kill you and make a new deal?" Darklight said. The explosive rapport of his guns thundered through the room as he unloaded into Ghostferatu.

The Sire's body seemed to evaporate wherever the bullets hit him before instantly reforming. "Come now, James. Did you really think the Boss would give you the power to kill a high-ranking demon? Even he's not that generous." Throughout all of this, Bilderback seemed to be in a trance, her body standing rigid, her eyes staring into the unknown.

"Generous?" Darklight howled. "He took my fiancé! I made the deal for her! I wanted to give her everything she deserved in life. Instead…"

Ghostferatu laughed. "The contract clearly stated the terms of the deal. But you were so blinded by greed, you couldn't be bothered to read it. You wanted wealth, and we gave it to you. A pity you have no one to share it with."

The agonizing thing was that the demon was right. James Hemlocke, the mortal, was the biggest fool to ever walk the earth. Now, as Darklight, he remained a fool, albeit with slightly less naiveté. He would never trust a demon again, although his cautionary tale wouldn't bring Anne back. His refusal to do the devil's dirty work resulted in him losing her forever.

Ghostferatu continued, "It seems a life of lonely wealth has not taught you the error of your ways, so I must now take you back to Hell for… re-education."

The Sire raised his hands in front of his frosted crystal face, and rusty barbed wire erupted from each of his fingers. Ghostferatu hurled them at Darklight.

Darklight fired at the individual wires, causing them to recoil with each hit, but they just kept coming. After several moments, one managed to wrap around his arm before squeezing it in a vice-like grip. Smoke poured from the wounds where the wire dug into his flaming flesh, and he hissed in searing pain.

To Darklight's left, a portal opened in the floor, revealing a hellish flaming maw just large enough for a grown man to be hurled into. The barbed wire began dragging him toward it, and in a few minutes, he would have an unfortunate meeting with what demons called the "Boss."

He had to think quickly. If his guns didn't work on elevated hellspawn, then that just left holy weapons that were effective on all creatures of the night. Unfortunately for Darklight, that included him as well. Nevertheless, it was his only option for getting out of this.

With his free hand, he opened one of the many compartments on his utility belt, reached in, and once again howled in pain as his hand was scorched by the object he took hold of. Wishing to get this over with as quickly as (in)humanly possible, he pulled out a cross and pressed it against the barbed wire, causing it to spasm and retract back to Ghostferatu. Darklight couldn't drop the cross fast enough at that point.

"Unghhhh!" the demon said, confirming the tactic was, indeed, effective against his kind. "A bold strategy, but one that poses just as much of a threat to you as it does to me. I wonder how long you can keep it up."

Inside Darklight, the human mind of James Hemlocke knew the answer: not for long. He needed to finish this quickly, and he only had one way to do that.

He reached inside his duster coat and retrieved a metal sphere the size of an apple. The top of the sphere contained a sliding puzzle that had to be completed before the device could be used, so as not to be activated accidentally. Using his superhuman dexterity, Darklight solved it in the blink of an eye.

"You and your gadgets," Ghostferatu said derisively.

Gadgets? Perhaps. But these had been developed in conjunction with saintly engineers. Darklight knew from experience that they worked. But would this be enough to stop a Sire of Hell? Only one way to find out.

"Catch," Darklight said as he launched the sphere at Ghostferatu, who threw his barbed wire tendrils out to intercept the device.

Darklight dove behind an overturned table, which was the only cover he could reach in time. The sphere exploded, releasing a shower of rosary beads that pelted the room like shrapnel. Ghostferatu screamed, and so did Darklight, when numerous beads penetrated the table and skewered his flesh.

After several agonizing moments, Darklight poked his head out from behind the table. Ghostferatu was gone, along with all the blood in the fountain. Bilderback lay motionless on the floor but was still breathing.

When a demon was killed, they returned to Hell to await summoning again sometime in the future. Ghostferatu would be back, and he wouldn't fall for the same trick again. But that was a problem for another day.

Darklight stumbled through the secret entrance of Hemlocke Manor and left a trail of smoking blood while he staggered into the main hall, whereupon he collapsed onto one of his many couches.

On the wall above him, a painting of his parents holding a baby. The painting was a lie, of course; James had come from a broken home, and his parents had never looked lovingly at him the way they did in the portrait. But with sudden wealth came the need for a new identity.

On the divan next to the couch, that day's newspaper lay face-up with the headline "Commissioner Carmichael Announces Task Force to Catch Darklight."

"Master? Is that you?" The unmistakable form of Lilliph, James Hemlocke's faithful maid, rushed into the room.

"Lilliph…" Darklight said weakly.

"Oh, bother," Lilliph said. "You went and got battered again. Well, you survived. I'll patch you up."

Standing four-foot-nine, with a black frilly dress, long blood-red hair, and matching eyes, she had served him for the better part of a decade. Lilliph was Hemlocke's maid, doctor, accountant, bodyguard, and more despite her teenage appearance.

The tortured master relaxed, and the visage of Darklight melted off him, revealing the bloody form of James Hemlocke.

In between ragged breaths, James said, "Sometimes I wonder which is the real me."

Lilliph went into the pantry and returned with a handful of tools that produced an eerie black glow. No mortal surgeon had ever laid eyes on these instruments. "You might as well ask which rung on a ladder is the real ladder. Every part makes up the whole."

Oh, yes; she was also a philosopher. Or, in this case, would that be a psychologist?

She continued, "Looks like seven bead-sized entry wounds. But given that you can't be hurt by conventional weapons, can I assume you used the rosary grenade?"

"You certainly can," he replied.

"Then, I shall."

She took hold of a pair of forceps and jabbed them into one of the wounds. He howled in pain. "Oh, hush," she said. "You're supposed to be Hell's boogeyman. Act like it."

He retorted, "In case you haven't noticed, right now, I'm completely human."

Ignoring him, she said, "Miss Carmichael called earlier. She asked if you would be free tomorrow night?"

He groaned. "This again? I told you, I can't risk getting romantically involved with anyone since she would become a target. Besides, she doesn't know I'm Darklight and wouldn't be thrilled to find out."

"How long are you going to keep doing this?" Lilliph said. "You think you'll redeem yourself by pestering the Boss for the rest of your life?"

He shook his head. "There's no redemption for me. I'm just trying to do something good before the devil finally claims me."

She pried a steel rosary from the wound. "And? Did you do anything 'good' tonight?"

"Argh! Watch it, will you? Ahem. Anyway, yes, I did a few good things tonight. I sent Ghostferatu back to Hell, and Sarah Bilderback is now in jail."

"Did you mean to rhyme just now, or was that a happy coincidence?"

Now it was his turn to ignore her comment. "Do you think I'm a good person?"

In response, she dug her forceps into another of the rosary wounds, prompting a slew of curse words from him. "You know my background. No matter what I say, I'll be a hypocrite. People like me live in the shadows where there is no true morality. And anyway, that's like wondering if you kept a clean house after it burns down."

Sweat cascaded off his brow, and she wiped it with a rag. "I suppose you're right," he said.

She finished patching him up and said, "I almost forgot. Commissioner Carmichael sent one of his interchangeable officers over here to deliver the tickets for the Gothopolis Gala next week. It's only fitting for the city's wealthiest resident and philanthropist to make an appearance."

He took off his blood-stained dress shirt, revealing his chiseled abs. "I think millionaire mortal James Hemlocke will be available. Unless, of course, his darker persona is needed that night."

She smiled at him. "Let's hope if Darklight is needed, it's nothing so mundane as another demonic invasion."

Alter Ego
by Owen Townend

Joe Sixpack began his patrols on high, leaping between rooftops until he observed crime in the city's side streets and alleyways below. While it had occurred to him that a smart enemy might work out this behaviour pattern and attack him in the heights, he had yet to come across a knife-wielding addict or gang thug who would ever act on such a hunch. It would take someone much more tactically-minded than them, not to mention ballsy.

Approaching the edge now, he took the opportunity to stretch his hamstrings.

"So it's true," a voice rose up behind him. "A superhero in silver sweats."

Joe skidded forward. He slammed down his white sneaker in time. Checking that his black mask fully covered his face, he turned to the unwanted visitor.

A skinny business type in a crisp burgundy suit, with a fake tan and slicked-back blonde hair. His whitened teeth glowed in the hazy sunlight, and his hands remained in his jacket pockets as he stepped forward.

Joe pointed his extendable steel baton defensively. "What do you want?"

The hands came out. "I come in peace. Just paying my respects to Joe Sixpack." The man chuckled. "When I heard there was a masked vigilante in this city, I knew I had to meet you. You're goddamn awesome."

"What the hell is this?"

The stranger edged closer. "Sorry. Could I just–" He reached out a hand to touch the insignia on Joe's sweatshirt. Four red bars around three white stars. "How patriotic."

Joe knocked the hand away.

"No touching, freak. Now cut to the chase. You didn't come up here because you're a fan boy."

The stranger massaged his knuckles. "You're right. Just wanted to offer a little context before the pitch. My name is Nick Brovont. Maybe you've heard of me?"

Joe shrugged.

Brovont sighed.

"I'm an entrepreneur. I invest in multiple businesses ranging from insurance to security technology. It's early days." He waved this idea away. "Anyway, having watched your feats, your own work, I've decided to invest in you too."

"What? You offering me a sponsorship?"

"Not exactly, Joe – may I call you Joe?"

Joe grunted. "Everybody else does. I didn't choose the damn name."

"Is that right? Well, Joe, I actually want to employ your services."

Joe shook his head. "I ain't got time for being some rich dude's bodyguard. Besides, that's not what I'm about."

"Sure." Brovont smiled. "Joe Sixpack is the everyman's hero. He doesn't work for captains of industry but for the folks they step on. He keeps the streets safe for good, hardworking people who need a champion."

"Quit quoting the papers, Brovont. Get to your damn point."

Brovont raised his hands again. "My apologies. What I want is your help to make people think that I am you."

"What?"

"Alter ego. I want to plant the suggestion in public thinking that Joe Sixpack is secretly Nick Brovont. A boost for my public image and a protection of your own identity."

Joe gripped his baton tighter. "What the fuck do you know about my identity?"

"Nothing." Brovont sniffed. "Who you are right now isn't what I'm interested in."

Joe didn't buy this for a second. "The hell are you talking about?"

"In the comic books, Batman is secretly Bruce Wayne. Ironman is Tony Stark." Brovont shrugged. "A precedent has long been set that rich guys can make themselves into superheroes."

"I never said I was a superhero."

"The public call you one."

"If you want to play superhero, rich guy, then why not be your own?"

Brovont chuckled again. "You've an impressive reputation, Joe. There's no way I could build that up myself, not in a million years. Besides, I don't know mixed martial arts like you. Also, I don't have the head for heights."

"Meaning you want the glory for none of the work?"

Brovont shook his head from side to side. "I'll admit this is a vanity project for me. Still, you'll be compensated for any concerns you might have."

Joe Sixpack took in Brovont's appearance. They were roughly the same height with a similar build. Then again, Brovont visibly lacked Joe's hard-earned muscle.

"You don't look much like me," Joe said.

"We share enough similarities for people to notice."

Joe squinted. "Press, right? You want journalists to notice?"

"That would help reach my goal, but it's the people on the street I want to impress most."

Joe sniffed. "I don't like it. Too much ego."

"I don't deny that. But please don't overlook my honest admiration for you. What you do."

"What I do is because I'm free. I'm not in anyone's pocket."

"You wouldn't be in mine. I would pay you a nominal fee for the right to appear shortly after you have left a scene of crime, but you would be making no direct endorsement of Nick Brovont or any of his business interests. It would be all implication. An association other people would make, not you. Your principles are completely safe. There will be no lengthy contract involved here. Just a gentleman's agreement."

Joe examined Brovont's face. The guy's words were slick, but his grin seemed shit-eating. His confidence was too polished, too rehearsed, like he knew that he could close this weird ass deal, that Joe was some kind of pushover, desperate for payout.

"You talk about my principles," Joe said. "You don't know diddly squat about them, pal. You coming up here today, tracking me down tells me your own are too damn flexible. That kind of Moxy might score you big points in insurance, but not with me. In fact, it makes me want to keep an eye on you. So that's a no to your gentleman's agreement, Brovont. I don't want to make pretend that we're the same guy. You may get something out of that, but I sure as hell don't. And mark my words, if you try anything like this again, get in the way of my actual secret identity, there will be consequences. The next time you admire my mixed martial arts, think of that. Now get outta here. I've work to do."

Throwing down a smoke bomb, Joe Sixpack leapt to the next rooftop and slid down the fire escape.

Meanwhile, Brovont coughed, teared up, and wafted away the smoke. Once it had finally cleared, he sucked his teeth and shook his head.

Reaching into his jacket's inside pocket, he produced a device. Switching it on, he watched a silver dot shuffle across a map of the city. The device connected to a mini tracker he had planted on his fingertip, which had since adhered to Joe's insignia.

Brovont tutted. "Plan B then."

The next morning, Brovont sat in his office, finishing his daily 'focus time.' His PA kept his schedule clear for an hour and fielded all non-essential calls until he was ready. Sometimes he just napped, but today he had a toy he was just dying to play with.

He took out the tracker device and switched it on. It started bleeping almost immediately. The silver dot was passing through the business district, fast. When it stopped, he tried to work out where Joe Sixpack had settled in the city. Somewhere very close. Just outside his own building, in fact.

There was a knock at his window. Brovont's office was on the fifth floor.

Hopping out of his ergonomic chair, he let Joe in. Though Brovont couldn't see much past the hero's mask, he could glimpse fury in Joe's wide grey eyes.

"You got here quicker than I expected," Brovont said, sweeping back his hair.

Joe backed him up against his glass desk. He held the tracker between his gloved thumb and forefinger. Never once breaking eye contact, he crushed it. The device's bleep cut out.

"Why?" Joe asked.

Brovont put on a laugh, not quite as casual as he liked but breathy. "Call it an opportunity for renegotiation. I wanted you to find me."

"That ain't an answer. Why?"

"I needed another chance to make my proposal."

"And you think planting a tracker on me was the best way to win me over?"

"Well, it got your attention. It brought you to me. That's all I wanted, I swear."

"I don't do intimidation, Brovont. Not lightly. But you leave me no choice. You tracking me is a violation of my privacy. You ignoring my wishes to be left alone pisses me off."

"My apologies. I only wanted to show you how our system would work.

This tracker shows me where you are without us ever interacting. You could earn money and never see me. I could appear at the scene of the crime long after you're gone, show my face a few times, and that would be that."

Joe Sixpack pushed his baton against Brovont's throat.

"This will be the last time that I put it nicely. I do not want to work with you, Brovont. I have no intention of letting people think that you're my damn alter ego. I refuse to take part in your superhero fetish shit. I want nothing to do with you. If you don't honour that, I can't be held responsible for what happens next."

Brovont's chuckle came out like a gargle. Joe eased up the pressure.

"You're a good man, Joe Sixpack. I doubt you'll break the law."

"I'm a fucking vigilante, Brovont. The police say I break the law all the damn time. In your case, they could finally be right."

Joe pulled the baton completely away. It cracked the desk on its downswing.

"Oops," he said, then returned to the window.

Brovont loosened his black tie and massaged his neck.

Joe pointed the baton.

"I'm serious. Don't cross me, you wannabe everyman motherfucker. It might cost me, but not as much as it would cost you."

Joe leapt out of view. No smoke bomb this time. Good. Brovont needed a moment to catch his breath.

Of course, he had factored in the possibility that Joe Sixpack would react strongly like this, but Brovont hadn't anticipated criminal damage. He regarded the crack in his desk. He had only bought it a month ago. Another vanity project.

Straightening up the lapels of his jacket, Brovont replayed excerpts of Joe's speech in his mind. *Your superhero fetish shit. You wannabe everyman motherfucker.*

He gritted his teeth. The renegotiation was meant to have been simpler. Joe was supposed to hear him out. Despite the dubious nature of the tracker, Brovont had planned for a more amicable exchange. Of course, that had been rather naïve of him to assume.

A fresh and more detailed tactic was required. A complete change of course. He would need to pool his resources, call in favours, and respond accordingly.

It was time to be firm.

Joe Sixpack was exhausted. He couldn't feel his legs or his arms, and his eyes had almost closed up from the swelling. Fortunately, his mask was still in place, thanks to the blood that glued it to his face.

He had been chasing down a purse snatcher until something wrapped around his heels, bound them together, and tripped him up. Bolas. A simple yet effective weapon.

His assailants then used fists and boots. After fending one off with his baton, another knocked it out of his hand and then turned the weapon on him. Now he knew the intimate aches that criminals went away with after he had finished dealing with them.

The men who attacked him weren't common thugs. They were practised, well-versed in combat, precise in the way they inflicted pain. Though they didn't say a word to him, he knew that they had held back in fighting him. Their brief interactions with each other suggested they were Eastern European. Possible mercenaries, but who were they working for?

When they hurried him into an unmarked black van, Joe knew he was about to be taken to their employer. They had been driving for ten minutes now and were finally slowing down. Tyres crunched against gravel.

They pulled the van door open. Though it was an inky blue night, Joe was blinded by floodlights.

The mercenaries carried him out of the van and sat him on a wooden chair. They bound him with plastic straps. Joe laughed. He could barely lift a finger as it was.

Rather than set them straight, he saved his breath for when they were done, and a new figure approached. Joe could barely see who it was, but the outline looked familiar.

"Brovont?" he grunted. "You bastard. Did I hurt your feelings? Is that what this is? Ambush. Beat down. Abduction. Big dog bullshit."

Brovont didn't respond.

Joe sighed. "Man of the people, huh? How's that working out for you? You're a real criminal now. And for what? Ego. Not alter ego, just plain damn ego. You rich assholes are all the same. Make deals. Fuck the little guy. Win at all costs."

A scraping sound. Brovont pulled up another chair to join him.

"I've known pricks like you all my life. Grinding everyone down. Expecting praise for it. You're just one in a long line of pissants that tried to break our spirits. But I broke them. Every one. Joe Sixpack. The motherfucking people's champion."

Brovont sat down.

"So what now, huh? I know too much, know the real you. And you know exactly who I am, right? Just another little guy. I die, and a new Joe Sixpack rises up. Maybe one of your new buddies will save the day so you don't have to."

Brovont checked his watch.

Joe grunted. "Goddamn it. Answer me, you bastard. What happens now?"

Brovont cleared his throat. "Let's discuss terms."

Joe Sixpack sat on a rooftop. The city had fallen quiet for the evening. No brawls, no threats, no crying out. Good. He peeled off his mask and stared off into the horizon.

The days after his beating had been equally humiliating. Brovont had got what he wanted. As much as Joe tended to throw himself into danger, accepting death at the hands of an obsessive suit seemed too much to bear.

So he had added the tracker to his insignia again and became a sellout. Despite the mercenaries and previous intimidation, Brovont had actually kept his promised distance, only appearing after Joe had already fled the scene. Before long, there was talk on the street, talk that boosted Brovont's reputation and ego no end. Meanwhile, Joe Sixpack, or rather the real man who had first accepted that name, patrolled the city, unable to shake off the dirty feeling.

Some hero he turned out to be. Bullied into submission by a wealthy glory hog. Still, Joe pulled no punches, did not hesitate to save lives. The mission, while tainted, was still clear enough to him.

Having rubbed his sore calves, Joe reached for the day's newspaper. There was Brovont on the front page, side by side with a blurry photo of Joe Sixpack. A simple association he resented, but slightly less today.

He read the headline again: 'POLICE SUE VIGILANTE BROVONT'. Joe didn't need to review the full article. It seemed one of the drug deals he had busted last week had involved an undercover cop. Definitely not knowing this at the time, Joe had broken the cop's tibia and left him bleeding in the gutter. He had also dropped something as he fled. A business card for Brovont Insurance. Oops.

Now the cops wanted a payout. With rumours circulating that Nick Brovont was always present after a Joe Sixpack sighting, a convenient entrepreneur seemed the best guy to settle the check. Joe had warned him there would be a cost.

Oh sure, Brovont would deny the charges, sever all ties with Joe Sixpack, even reveal the hero's true identity to the world for good measure, but that wouldn't save his skin. Recalling all the dirty cops and gang leaders Joe had pummelled over the years, it wouldn't be long before they all moved in for their cut.

He wondered how much homework Brovont had actually done into his track record. After all this time, exactly how many ruthless pricks wanted Joe Sixpack dead? It didn't bear thinking about. And yet this was the life that Brovont had chosen for himself. Constant threat and danger.

Joe Sixpack set fire to his mask and laid it on top of the silver sweats and white sneakers. The man who stood up and away from this burning pile of abandoned clothes was someone new. He had dyed his hair, shaved his face, and changed his eye colour with blue contacts. In the inside pocket of his Goodwill jean jacket was a train ticket to the south bought with the last of Brovont's money.

The new man didn't know where he would end up or what he would do next, but these factors were driven by the same urge to save and protect. Brovont might have co-opted Joe Sixpack's reputation, but he'd never take his soul. Anyway, Joe Sixpack had always been the public's creation. They had named him and dictated who he was. It hurt to leave them now, but he had been left with no other choice. Besides, in the absence of a controversial vigilante, maybe a true hero would finally rise up.

The maskless new man dropped his newspaper over the rooftop edge and watched it flutter and flap to the ground.

"Lo," he said, "how the mighty have fallen."

X-Treme Genes Neptunalia Special #1: "Watered Down" (July 1997)
by Jude Deluca

BREAKDOWN: In 1993, a group of five college students accompanied their history professor on an archaeological dig within the ancient Egyptian pyramids and discovered a nest of hyper-intelligent aliens. The aliens unlocked hidden abilities within the five students' DNA, granting them powers beyond mortal man. VANITY, UMBRIEL, CHINDI, HOURGLASS, and WIPEOUT have XTREME GENES, and they're gonna use them to kick some XTREME BUTT!

"Hi hi! Welcome to Neptune Land, the wildest, wackiest, and wettest waterpark on this side of the East Coast!" A bespectacled, sunburned attendant with a name tag reading 'CORAL' said behind the glass shield of a ticket booth. "Are you paying separately or as a group?"

"We prepaid for our passes." Tanya Dee reached into her designer beach bag and pulled out five passes, being sure to give Coral a good glimpse of her metallic gold, waterproof nail polish on the tips of her dark, slender fingers as she slid the pieces of paper underneath the glass. "I trust everything is in order."

"Ooh, you paid for the deluxe weeklong experience, lucky you! Those tend to sell out pretty quickly before Neptune Days." Coral cheered as she retrieved the passes, handing back five badges and five locker keys. "These'll get you into pretty much every area of the park except for those reserved for employees. If you misplace your badge or your locker key be sure to let us know, but we advise you to keep a close watch on them. Neptune Park is not held accountable for any stolen or lost items as a result of misplacing your locker key. Will you be needing anything else before you get wet?"

"I believe we're good, thank you," Tanya said as she collected the badges and keys for her friends. "I'll need a receipt, though."

"Really? Why?" Coral asked.

Tanya raised a single eyebrow from above the rim of her designer sunglasses, obscuring her hazel eyes.

"I-I mean, of course!" Coral nervously laughed as she printed said receipt. The machine made an odd sound since it hadn't been used in ages. "I can't think of a time when anyone left Neptune Park unsatisfied enough to demand a refund! Still, as that old saying goes, 'The customer is always right.'"

"Thank you," Tanya said again as she carefully folded the receipt and placed it in her beach bag. She headed towards her four friends standing in front of the massive park entrance decorated with seashells, starfish, and carvings of long-haired mermaids. Above them were the words "NEPTUNE PARK" engraved in gold, being held by a stone effigy of the bearded Roman God of the seas. The smell of chlorine and suntan lotion drifted outwards from the entrance, mixed with the sounds of delighted shrieks and laughter from children.

Her hands on her hips and her back to the water park, Tanya addressed her comrades.

"Everyone, I must implore upon you the gravity of our situation. When we walk through those gates, all eyes are going to be on the five of us. There can be nothing less than our best performance today, or we may never live the shame down. Remember, we are bold. We are brave. Most importantly, we are beautiful in every single thing we do. We are X-Treme Genes. Let's show everyone exactly who we are and what we're made of. Ready?"

"READY!" They responded.

"Then go forward, disrobe, and engage NOW!"

With that, the five twenty-something college students removed the plain black bathrobes adorning their bodies and revealed themselves to the masses. Heads turned and gazes zeroed in as the group strutted down the middle of the sandy walkway towards their final destination. To others, it seemed as though the quintet were moving in slow motion. As Neptune Park's loudspeakers began to play "Too Much" by the Spice Girls, it was as if the other guests were watching a music video happening in real life.

Tanya stood in the center, naturally, clad in a sleek and sophisticated two-piece bathing ensemble colored black and white. A shimmering red jewel rested in the center of her bikini top, rimmed with gold. There was no doubt the gemstone was the real deal. Like her fingers, her toes were painted an identical shade of gold visible in her designer sandals. She ran one hand through her long, luxurious black hair, handwoven into microbraids reaching down to her waist, each decorated with puka shells. The way she carried herself, Tanya acted as though she were on a runway.

On Tanya's right-hand side was her right-hand gal, Phyllis DeFarge, clad in a midnight blue one-piece bathing suit decorated with an ornate design of a thorny red rose with full green leaves. Phyllis's wavy brown hair was tied back in a messy ponytail held with a chocolate colored scrunchy. Her face, neck, arms, and legs showed off a newly acquired summer tan, as well as the fact that she had recently shaved for this vacation. Phyllis enjoyed feeling the breeze on her skin, and that she'd been confident enough to wear a bathing suit in public for the first time since acknowledging she was a woman.

Trailing behind Phyllis was the tall and muscular Jake Johnson, whose own pale skin was currently sporting the beginning of a bad case of sunburn (not that he seemed to care). Jake's spiky, bleach blonde and black hair was hidden beneath a baseball cap turned sideways, his ears filled with multiple piercings and a silver ball pinned into the space beneath his lower lip. Like Tanya, Jake wore sunglasses, but the cheap kind found in any gas station. Every now and then, Jake would lower them while checking out someone he considered attractive.

Opposite Phyllis on Tanya's left-hand side came Amber Nez, who wore her own jet-black hair loose and free save for one miniature braid by her left ear. Amber's appearance was rather mismatched, consisting of a one-piece suit like Phyllis's but hidden beneath an oversized white t-shirt with a neon image of a surfing skeleton and the words "Boo, Dude!" The shirt fluttered in a slight summer breeze as it hung loose, revealing one of her light brown shoulders. Not only that, Amber also wore a pair of baggy, DayGlo orange swim shorts. The smile on her face was nearly identical to those worn by the children running about the water park.

And finally, standing by Amber's side was none other than Ahmed Ali, who perhaps wore the most daring outfit of them all, which was surprising, considering how little there was of it on his brown-skinned body. Maybe it was because there was so much of him, being the shortest of the group yet also the thickest. Ahmed's meaty hips swayed back and forth, clad in a simple red Speedo, his large belly hanging over the rim. Most would've probably been more entranced by the hourglass tattoo covering his chest. Ahmed's face bore a self-assured grin, a slight breeze ruffling his curly black hair down to his chin.

"Tanya?" Phyllis asked.

"Yes, Phyllis?" Tanya asked without looking back.

"Do we have to keep moving in slow motion?" Phyllis inquired. "By the time we get in the water, the park will likely be closed for the day."

"True. I think that's enough for now," Tanya decided. Her announcement was met with groans of relief as everyone began moving at a regular pace alongside the rest of the people in Neptune Park.

"Look at this place, it's enormous!" Amber said as she took in the sights and sounds. "This has gotta be the biggest water park on Earth!"

"Dude, check it out," Jake nudged Ahmed. "You can spell words on my abs." Ahmed watched as Jake pressed against his sunburn with his fingertips to spell out his own name.

"That is all kinds of painful looking, dude," Ahmed said in admiration.

"Hurts like Hell," Jake laughed.

"I always took you for a masochist, Jake," Phyllis dryly noted.

"I'm a Virgo, actually." Jake leaned forward to whisper to Ahmed, "Chicks dig that astrology crap." Ahmed merely rolled his eyes and patronizingly patted Jake on the head.

"Well, we're here. What should we do first?" Tanya inquired as she assessed a very large map featuring every known area of the park. "Hmm, with the name 'Neptune' you'd think this place would've stuck closer to the mythology theme." As Tanya looked over all the different rides and attractions, she noticed Neptune Park was a mishmash of various motifs. Aside from the name and the park's mascot being the Roman God of the Seas, there wasn't much else correlating to said God. There were pirate ships, sand castles, coves, grottos, lakes, lagoons, beaches, whirlpools, jet streams, wading pools, fish bowls, boardwalks, bayous, swamps, marshes, aquariums, reefs, fishing holes, coves, cliffs, riverbanks, and waterfalls. If it was wet, it was in Neptune Park. And all throughout the place, a lazy river ran, clogged with sunbathers and children on inner tubes.

Amber's eyes lit up as she pointed out a series of water slides surrounded by drawings of wailing ghosts. "Ooh, the Banshee Boardwalk! Sounds adorable!"

"That name sounds familiar." Ahmed scratched his fuzzy chin, trying to recall where he heard it from. "I think it was from a video game?"

"C'mon, Ahmed, I'll race you!" Amber announced, and soon the two were running through the crowd to check out the haunted attraction.

"Doesn't that hurt?" Tanya and Phyllis turned away from watching Amber and Ahmed run off to see Jake flexing his biceps to a group of girls in skimpy bikinis.

"Nah," Jake shrugged. "I'm like, totally impervious when it comes to pain."

"Doesn't stop him from *being* a pain," Phyllis snarked while Tanya giggled.

"Ooh, I like a man who's sturdy," one girl said as she ran her fingers along Jake's muscle.

"Attention all guests!" A voice announced on the park loudspeakers. "The Neptune Day Races are due to start in a half hour. All eligible racers must head to the beginning of the Dagon River if they wish to participate! Don't miss out on any of the fabulous Neptune Day prizes! And don't forget the lucky winner to place first will be crowned our King of the Sea!"

"I get to be king?!" Jake cheered.

"That race is for little kids," one of the women crowding around Jake said in distaste.

"Then that means I've got a good chance of whooping their asses! Outta my way, ladies, I'm gonna be king of the park!"

Tanya and Phyllis watched as Jake ran off to join the rest of the children hurrying to the starting line of the big race, while his would-be admirers stood slack-jawed in confusion as he climbed atop a small boat designed to look like a horse.

"And then there were two," Tanya noted.

"You wanna run off and start brand new lives, just the two of us?" Phyllis asked.

"Maybe during our next vacation," Tanya answered.

"Okay, but I'm not waiting for you forever," Phyllis blithely replied as she followed Tanya. The deeper they headed into the park, the more they saw various statues and busts in the image of the park's namesake. Phyllis couldn't help but feel a bit unnerved at the way the sea green eyes of Neptune seemed to follow her and Tanya wherever they went. She was starting to feel a bit self-conscious in her bathing suit due to her flat chest and lanky shoulders. If they bothered Tanya, she did a good job of not showing it. Tanya was always good at seeming unflappable and effortlessly cool, even in the face of danger.

The two women reached an area called "Proteus Beach," an artificial beach area with a sandy coast leading into a large body of water. Tanya and Phyllis were lucky to find a couple of empty beach chairs to sit down and apply lotion before getting into the water.

Taking her mind off the various Neptune statues, Phyllis said, "There are a lot of kids running around here, but I don't see as many parents." Tanya lowered her sunglasses and noticed Phyllis was correct. The ratio of children and parents seemed off among the many water rides, wave pools, and attractions. Only a few kids were accompanied by adults. Even toddlers seemed unaccompanied, waddling about without even plastic floaties on their little arms.

"I don't see any lifeguards, either," Tanya noted the absence of chairs overlooking the pools and rivers. Readjusting her sunglasses, she added, "Though this place does seem to put some emphasis on security."

Through her lenses, Tanya spied identical-looking men and women standing erect at the entrances and exits of various rides, eyes obscured by thick black glasses and matching tattoos of sea serpents drawn on their necks. Cameras were partially obscured within the leaves of palm trees, bushes of tropical plants, and atop more of the Neptune statues and light fixtures.

Phyllis frowned. "Weird."

"Yes. Well." Tanya stood up, removing her sunglasses and placing them in her beach bag. "I think it's about time I took a dip. Are you coming?"

Phyllis shook her head. "For some reason, all this sand's bringing out my inner artist." She reached down and picked up a fistful of sand, letting it fall between her fingers. "I think I'll show some of these kids how you build a real sandcastle."

Tanya smiled. "Try not to be too much of a perfectionist about it."

"Moi?" Phyllis placed a hand on her chest. "Real perfection doesn't require 'trying.'"

Striding down towards the water, Tanya plunged forward into the cold, clear blue and let herself be submerged. Though there were plenty of other people, mostly children, splashing around and laughing and having a good time, Tanya gracefully maneuvered through all of them as she swam. Looking back, she saw Phyllis in the distance working on a sandy creation, much to the marvel of a group of boys and girls. Tanya wasn't sure what it was, but she could tell Phyllis was putting her all into the construction.

Tanya went underwater again and swam forward, dodging past sets of legs kicking and floating in front of her. Rising back up to breathe, she found herself in front of a ride designed to look like a half-submerged pirate ship. Kids jumped off planks doing cannonballs and jack knives or swung into the water on ropes.

Again, she saw very few adults, and no lifeguards at all.

"Excuse me?"

Tanya turned around to find a couple of little girls swimming beside her, roughly around 7 to 8 years old. They wore matching striped bathing suits.

"Yes?" Tanya asked.

"My sister thinks you have really pretty hair," the girl on the right said. Her sister on the left looked bashful as she nodded.

Tanya accepted the compliment. "That's such a kind thing to say, thank you." Noticing they both had identical afro puffs, Tanya said, "You both have pretty hair, too."

That caused the two girls to giggle before they started whispering to each other. The girl on the right then asked, "My sister was also wondering if you're a mermaid."

"A mermaid?" Tanya asked. "What makes you think that?"

"She says because you're really pretty, and mermaids are supposed to be very pretty."

Smirking, Tanya sank beneath the water. The two girls looked at each other in confusion when suddenly a huge form shot up out of the water and into the air. Everyone gasped in amazement at the sight of Tanya, her human legs having been replaced by a shimmering tail of golden scales. The children all cheered in amazement at the sight of a real, live mermaid.

Or at least a shapeshifting superheroine who could make herself resemble a mermaid.

Amber giddily climbed the steps of a haunted-looking boardwalk with Ahmed behind her, reaching the top of the rickety Banshee water slides.

"Remember, the Neptune Day races begin in ten minutes!" A voice on the park loudspeakers announced.

"You think we should check that out later?" Amber asked Ahmed as they reached the end of the line.

"I can think of something else you can check out, baby."

Amber and Ahmed turned around to see a gaggle of frat boys in swim trunks. The one in front had short blond hair and a smug grin on his face. He looked Amber up and down and whistled.

Completely ignoring him, Amber asked Ahmed, "You think this ride'll be scary for real?"

"We're gonna be shoved into a black tube going God only knows how many miles an hour before we plunge into a cold pool," Ahmed figured. "So probably not."

"But listen to all that wailing," Amber said as she motioned towards the opening in the slide. "It almost sounds like real screaming."

"Aww, don't be scared, honey," the blond frat boy said as he tried to place an arm around Amber's shoulders.

Almost as if on instinct, Amber grabbed the front of the frat boy's swim trunks while Ahmed grabbed the back and both pulled UP.

"AAAAHHHH!!!!"

"Now THAT sounded like real screaming," Ahmed said while completely ignoring the guy writhing in pain on the floor, clutching his groin after the mother of all wedgies.

"Isn't it sad how some people don't respect personal space?" Amber shook her head. "That's what's really scary." That's when she suddenly noticed there wasn't a park employee stationed at the front of the slide. "Hey, why isn't anyone running this ride?"

Ahmed simply shrugged before turning back and jumping down the open maw of the tunnel.

"Hey, Ahmed, wait for me!" Amber called out and hopped in after him, ignoring the cursing coming from the frat boy.

But she couldn't ignore the screams.

The screams of dead children engulfed Amber's senses in the dark. Children who died in pain. Children who died alone. By drowning, decapitation, and things Amber didn't want to think about. The voices of the dead she normally heard were replaced by an agonizing cacophony, an abyss of suffering. A torrent that grew stronger and stronger with each passing moment.

Amber's vision was flooded with images of children suffering. Their screams were so loud, and yet she could pinpoint exactly whom each tortured shriek belonged to as they pierced her ears.

Cora Lynn Schaffer, age 6.

Mark Withers, just turned 12.

Susie Sommers, 8, almost 9 years old.

Alex and Alexis Torrence, 11-year-old twins. They died together.

Betty Kramer, not even a year old.

Ahmed hit the pool at the bottom of the slide first, laughing like a fiend as he stood up in the water. He shook his head, looking like a drenched dog with his hair matted on his face. As he moved his bangs from his eyes, he saw Amber land next to him with a splash.

"That was insane!" Ahmed said. "You wanna do it a..."

Ahmed's voice trailed off when he saw the blank expression on Amber's face. No hint of fear or even excitement. The light in her eyes was gone. He watched

Amber calmly stand up and walk through the water, not bothering to look back at him once. Ahmed could feel the tension radiating from Amber's body as she walked on.

"Guess the vacation's over," Ahmed said in a low voice as he ran after Amber.

While Phyllis continued to work on her sand structures, Tanya was crowded by a group of kids who marveled at her mermaid's tail. Amid questions about whether it was real or not, Tanya looked up to see Amber obscuring the sun. Unperturbed by the serious expression on her face, Tanya nevertheless asked, "Having fun, Amber?"

"We need to bring this place to the ground. *Now.*"

"I guess we're getting a refund after all." Tanya removed her sunglasses to look Amber in the eye as Ahmed finally reached them both. Tanya said, "Let's go complain to the manager."

"Three minutes until the start of the race!" A voice cried out. "Three minutes!"

"Welcome, everyone, I'm Lawrence Love, manager of Neptune Park," a 40-ish man with thinning hair and a too-white smile greeted Tanya, Amber, and Ahmed from behind a wooden desk in a cramped office. Two overly muscled security guards in tight shirts and short shorts flanked Mr. Love on both sides of the desk. They bore identical-looking sea serpent tattoos covering the sides of their thick necks. The only window in the room gave a decent view of the water park. From a distance, Jake could be seen angling to get a good position for the start of the Neptune Days race. Mr. Love asked, "Is there a problem I can help you with today? If it's in my power to fix it, I'll do anything to make my customers remember their time here."

Tanya asked, "How many children have died in this park?"

Mr. Love didn't stop smiling.

"I beg your pardon?"

"We know this whole water park thing is a front for a cult that worships an ocean God, or at least you *think* you do," Tanya bluntly revealed. "I don't doubt you're probably worshipping *something.* And we know every year at least one child dies on July 23rd and 24th since the gates first opened. The sacrifices were probably happening even before the park was built."

"Definitely beforehand," Amber coldly added as she heard the continued screaming all around her, trying to focus on Tanya's words. Ahmed said nothing, opening and closing his fists in anticipation of the ensuing beatdown.

"Before we bring this shithouse down, my friends and I wanted to know if you were keeping track of how many have died exactly, or if you lost count at some point."

The manager leaned forward, clasping his hands together as he propped his elbows on the table. "Would it make a difference if I said how many?"

Tanya shrugged, not at all perturbed by his nonchalance. "Not really, but it'd be nice to know exactly how many we'll be avenging."

Mr. Love sighed. "I hate to do this, but I'm afraid I'll need you and your friends to vacate the premises. I don't like to see patrons leaving unhappily, but in this case, I'll need to make an exception. Boris, Morris." Mr. Love signaled his security guards. "Please escort them from the property."

"Whole or in pieces?" the two men asked.

"Surprise me."

Boris and Morris were quickly jettisoned through the window by two shrieking tunnels of wind conjured up at Amber's fingertips. As the two guards tumbled through the air, their bodies contorted. Their arms and legs bulged, veins pulsating as their skin turned a sickly shade of green. Scales grew over their limbs while their fingers curled into webbed claws. Jaws full of sharp teeth snapped open and closed.

They weren't the only ones.

The rest of the park's security staff converged on the manager's office, their bodies changing into half-human, half-fish abominations. Their shrieks filled the air, but not so loud as to drown out the loudspeaker announcement.

"On your mark, get set, GO!"

"MONSTERS! CHILD MURDERING MONSTERS!" Amber hovered in the air, her face a mask of righteous fury as she called up more spirits to blow away her opponents.

On the ground, Ahmed charged forward, his hourglass tattoo turning 180 degrees. As the sand on top began to slowly spill into the bottom, Ahmed grinned as his body began to change. Whereas Neptune Park's staff had taken on a more ichthyoid form, Ahmed shifted into a more lupine visage. His thick body grew bristly black fur as his nose and jaw elongated, and his ears grew pointy.

"Aww yeah!" Ahmed snarled in joy at having received a useful power for once. "Wolf Man's going surfside, baby! AWWWROOOOOO!!!!"

Ahmed and Amber plowed through the fish people with total abandon, leaving Tanya to focus all her attention on Mr. Love.

"If you want something done right," the inhuman Love growled with the voice of something that belonged to the deep, "you've got to do it your-"

SMACK!

Tanya delivered a roundhouse kick into Love's scaly face, tossing him through the shattered window and sending him straight into the Dagon River, where the Neptune Days race was supposed to take place. Jumping over the broken glass, Tanya did a perfect somersault into the water, her legs merging to form a mermaid's tail once again.

Only this time, it was spiked.

Tanya plunged under the water, trying to see where her opponent had gone. Above, she could hear Amber and Ahmed's skirmishing when something darted towards her. Tanya dodged just in time when a clawed hand swiped at her face. It missed. Tanya wrapped her tail around Love, piercing his body with her spikes. Clearly, the manager was not used to fighting his own battles as Tanya squeezed. Love pitifully tried to free himself when something grabbed Tanya by her hair.

Crying out in surprise, Tanya let go of Love. She turned to see that more of his fishy underlings were swarming towards them. Tanya changed tactics and swam upwards with enough speed to propel herself up out of the water. As she broke through to the surface, Tanya restored her legs to normal, substituting her tail for a pair of feathered wings growing out of her back.

Beneath her, the water churned as the fish men screamed at her. Off to one side, she saw Ahmed ripping the Neptune Park staff to shreds. Amber, meanwhile, was tearing the place up.

"SCREAM! SCREAM YOU MAGGOTS!" Amber shouted as she trapped a bunch of her opponents in a vortex made up of the lost, tortured, and angry souls sacrificed to the park's dark lord. "Feel the same pain you've put all these children through! I want you to scream as I rip the air from your lungs! I want to hear your screams as I send you all to Hell! *You won't get any mercy from me! SCREAM!*"

"Amber's in a mood," a voice said.

Tanya turned to see Phyllis heading towards her, standing atop a giant statue of Neptune made from sand.

"Where've you been?" Tanya asked as she dove back down, slashing at more of the park staff with newly grown talons.

"You can't rush perfection," Phyllis calmly said. She controlled the sandy Neptune, using it to swat and step on more of the fish people.

"Are the rest of the kids safe?" Tanya shouted.

"Oh yeah, I got most of them out no problem," Phyllis mentioned. "All except the ones in that race."

"Lord Neptune, why have you forsaken us?!" A fish man whom Tanya recognized as Mr. Love cried as Phyllis held him in her sandy grip.

"So, you guys really think you're worshipping Neptune, huh?" Phyllis asked. "For what, exactly?"

"EVERYTHING!" Love screamed. "The lord of the sea is charitable to us who recognize his might. We give him a paltry token every year, and he gives us all we could ever want!"

Phyllis rolled her eyes, and Tanya scowled. "You think they could've gone for a little originality?"

"It doesn't matter what you unbelievers think!" Love spat. "The race has already begun. You won't stop us from giving our lord his payment once the last child reaches the finish line! You'll NEVER be able to stop us!"

"Oh wow, Tanya, you hear that?" Phyllis asked. "We're too late." Looking up at the sky, Phyllis cupped her hands to shout, "Jake, you hear that?! We're too late!"

Love cast his red eyes upward and gaped in stupefaction at the sight hovering above him.

A giant pool of water in the sky, filled with laughing, smiling children. Sitting on one of the little horse boats, Jake struggled to keep his balance.

"C'mon, guys, don't make me lose my concentration," Jake whined. "This thing's way too small!"

"I think it's time to put an end to this," Tanya said as she watched Amber conjure a tornado made of ghosts.

"Gotcha, boss lady!" Jake saluted Tanya. "COME ON, KIDS! WE GOT A RACE TO WIN!"

"YEAH!" Was the resounding cry as Jake directed the pool of water towards the designated end of the Dagon River, where the finish line could be found.

"No! No! What is he doing?!" Love squirmed in the grip of the statue as Jake controlled the water, arranging all the kids in position until each and every one was right in front of the black and white line.

And just as smoothly, he nudged them all over the line at the exact same time.

"Now everyone's a winner!" Jake clapped. "Good job, guys!"

Love and the rest of Neptune Park's staff let out screams of agony. Their bodies violently shook as their limbs steadily turned to stone, starting at their feet and going all the way up to their heads.

"LORD NEPTUNE SPARE ME! IT WASN'T MY FAULT! THEY CHEATED! THEY…"

Lawrence Love's stone body exploded in a cloud of dust, as did all his employees and fellow cultists.

"Yeesh, Neptune doesn't kid around," Phyllis recognized.

"Total wipeout!" Jake shouted as he lowered the kids back into the water.

"I guess I can kiss that refund goodbye," Tanya sighed as terrified parents began running forward to find their children. She wondered where they'd been hiding while their kids needed help.

"Think of it as money well spent for an unforgettable summer vacation," Phyllis reasoned as her sandy sentinel lowered her to the ground.

Off to the side, Amber sank to her knees in exhaustion, her body shaking as she could hear the voices of all the child sacrifices finally gaining peace.

Still in his wolf-man form, Ahmed shook his large, hairy body. "Ugh, I hate the smell of wet dog. And I'm gonna be stuck like this for another 45 minutes."

Jake asked, "We're coming back next year, right?"

Bitter Pill
by C.N. Wheaton

I want you to understand: I never went into it planning to become a villain. Sometimes these things just happen.

Do you want to be a superhero? Have you always dreamed of flight or super-strength? If so, then this opportunity is for you! Wanted: participants for long-term clinical trial testing new super pills. Pay is $60 a day, plus room and board.

I should have known the offer was too good to be true.

The fact it was on the side of my cereal box (*Super-Os! Start your day the super way!*) should have been my first clue. I'd have dismissed the whole thing as a joke, but I remembered Jerry Pritchard — a man on my block who'd started one of these clinical trials at roughly the same size and strength of a wet noodle. He came out being able to bench press a tractor. So, I called the ad and got a place. I packed up my things and moved into the D&C Research and Development complex the next day.

When I saw that the group for flight was already fully booked, I signed up for teleportation. Why? Well, growing up, we never had the money to go anywhere, and teleportation seemed like a good way to get *everywhere.* And, after my train was delayed on my way to D&C, there was something very attractive about having travel be under my control for once. I took the first bitter pill and went to stand in line so the docs could check my vitals, when who should show up but Mark Bellamy, the guy who made my life a living hell all the way through school. The Mark Bellamy everyone now calls Magic Mark.

I looked away quickly, but it was too late. He spotted me. "Yo, Pauly!" he shouted and punched my shoulder hard enough that I bumped against the wall of the corridor.

"It's just Paul," I grumbled. "Why are you here?"

"These super pills are awesome, bro," he said, flashing an irritatingly white smile. He threw an arm over my shoulders as if we were old friends. "Didn't think I'd see you here," Mark continued. "Can you believe we're in the same group?"

"I really can't," I muttered under my breath. Louder, I said, "Who doesn't want to be a superhero?" I'd always wanted to help people get through the worst moments of their lives safely. Like nobody had ever helped me.

Mark laughed. "I'm only here 'cause I figure powers are an awesome way to get chicks. It sucks that flying and super strength were already full. But moving stuff with my mind? I bet chicks will be into it."

I let out a disbelieving laugh. "*That's* what you thought you signed up for? That's telekinesis, not teleportation!" I shrugged his arm off my shoulder, leaving him in the hallway looking confused. It was bad enough that we were in the same group, but it was somehow even worse knowing it was a mistake. I had every intention of finishing the clinical trial and teleporting myself as far away from him as I could.

Of course, neither of us imagined what would happen.

Several months later, when the people in flight were bobbing around off the ground—this was before they started running into airplanes—and the psychics were already cleaning up at poker, nobody in the teleporting group had done anything yet. We were the big failure of D&C. I was so disappointed that I decided to pack it all in and move back home. So, when I was leaving and Mark Bellamy went to punch my shoulder again as he was walking into the dorm, I wished he was already in his room.

I'm not sure who was more surprised when he vanished, him or me.

Okay, probably him. You should have seen his face! Even after all this time, just remembering his expression in that split second before he disappeared puts me in a good mood.

It's ironic, you know. If he hadn't punched me after we both took that first pill, this might never have happened. Near as the scientists can figure, that's what did it. After they ran every test they could think of, poked and prodded us for days on end, they started throwing around phrases like "quantum entanglement." The more excited the physicists got, the clearer it became that something had gone horribly wrong.

You see, Mark can travel via teleportation, but he isn't the one in control of where he goes. No, that's where I come in.

My superpower is teleporting Mark.

Who says the universe doesn't have a sense of humor? My least favorite person on the planet got to become what I wanted. Not only that, but I had to help him do it. He's always insisted he can't teleport me, but I'm not convinced he's really tried. Although knowing my luck, if he *did* manage to send me somewhere, it would probably be directly into traffic or inside a wall. So here we are.

The scientists tried to recreate that initial entanglement event with other teams. It never really worked, not like us anyway. Of the few other teams they managed to make, they could only teleport to one another or trade places, which is good for Vegas, but limited otherwise. As for me? I can send Mark anywhere. He's always there, in the corner of my mind. Wherever he is, no matter how far away, I can just reach out and pull. I can send him anywhere I can see, even if it's just somewhere I can picture in my mind.

But did he care how special we were?

Of course he didn't. He never really wanted to be a superhero.

In order to even get Mark to save anyone the first time, I had to teleport him directly into a burning building and refuse to get him out until he helped the people inside. As we learned during our testing at D&C, if Mark holds onto someone tightly enough, I can move them too, but it's much harder than teleporting just him. Teleporting more than one person feels like trying to pick up a greased watermelon in a lake. Once we'd gotten everyone out of the fire, my head throbbed, my eyes burned, and my whole body ached. I staggered to the couch and ended up sleeping for three days straight.

I woke up to find that the city had given Mark a medal, and he hadn't mentioned me, not once, in all of the speeches and interviews he gave. When I confronted him, he sputtered. "Bro, you teleported me into a burning building! I was pissed. Don't freak out, man, I'll just talk to the journalist again." He tried, but the damage was already done. Who reads retractions? Once a story is out there, it's almost impossible to pull it back.

When that first psychic went rogue and started robbing banks–I mean, she was calling herself The Golden Spider by that point, so she clearly had a few screws loose–we were the only ones who could get close. It helped that Mark's brain was essentially empty anyway. Since Mark had no idea where he was going before I sent him, all he had to do was grab her when I teleported him close enough. Then I dropped them both into the newly created super-cell at the jail before teleporting Mark back out.

The next super we took on was Dr. Dynamite. In the grand tradition of supervillains, he'd been one of the doctors who'd designed the super pills before he had his medical license pulled for unethical experiments. After he got fired, he set about making himself a cocktail of multiple powers. This was before our time at D&C, luckily, so he didn't know our secret. Still, super strength, enhanced healing, compulsion, and the ability to throw fireballs made him hard for anyone else to fight. He started going after everyone he thought had wronged him. I'm sure you've seen the pictures of what happened the first few times someone tried to confront him. Luckily, Mark wasn't scared; he'd never paid much attention to the news. The hardest part was figuring out where Dr. Dynamite was going next and trusting Mark with a taser. The battle itself was pretty short. Mark didn't even get singed. Whatever he might say, the fireball wasn't that close. While I was sleeping it off, he got the key to the city.

I've had to send him every single time he saves somebody. Every. Single. Time. Now he gets a hero's welcome everywhere he goes. What do I get? I'm harassed by the press because of the way he's spun our little arrangement, like he's the one who wants to save people and I'm just trying to hurt him.

Even after all that, he still calls me in the middle of the night to send him places.

Dr. Prasad looked up from her notepad once I finished the whole sorry story. She scribbled something down. "Thank you for telling me that, Paul. I knew some of it, of course, from the news, but it's encouraging that you're willing to share. Your situation sounds frustrating."

I snorted. *Shrinks.* "Frustrating? Yeah, that's one word for it. I can think of a few others. Is it any wonder I have to blow off a little steam? I mean, it's not like I'm trying to hurt him permanently. I would never kill him for the same reason that he's never going to come after me: we don't have powers on our own. Without him, I'd just be ordinary again. I'd rather be called the villain and help that conceited jackass save people than have my old life back."

Dr. Prasad wrote something down in her notepad. The expression on her face looked a lot like pity. "That's an interesting way to put it. Even if you stopped using your powers, do you really think you could go back to your old life? You've changed. You're linked on a quantum level to the man you describe as your childhood bully. The whole city knows who you are, Paul. Even if you moved away, you've been on news reports and in videos that people all over the world have seen. They call you The Interceptor."

I couldn't help but laugh. "I hate that name. Still, at least it doesn't sound like a stripper or a pen like *Magic Mark*. Honestly, having everyone think I'm a villain who has it out for Mark isn't so bad. If they know him at all, they usually get where I'm coming from. And, maybe I can't have my old life back, but I don't miss it. I was powerless before. Invisible. At least people know I exist now."

"Okay," she agreed easily. I was immediately suspicious, but she didn't make me wait long for the other shoe to drop. "You call yourself a villain, but you go out of your way to save people, even at personal cost to yourself. Most people would call that a hero. I do."

I let out a bitter laugh. "I promise, you're the only one who thinks that."

"That doesn't mean it isn't true. When you caught Dr. Dynamite, he was going after my friend. Mark saved her. Which I now know means you saved her." I must have looked as stricken as I felt, because she looked down at her notepad. "We can table that for now. I'd like to circle back to something you said earlier. You referred to your behavior as 'blowing off steam,' but how do you think Mark sees it?"

"Let's ask him."

"Paul! No!"

Mark appeared in the room just under the ceiling. He fell onto the couch from a height, bouncing off of it into the nearest wall before crashing to the floor. I tried, and failed, to keep the smile off my face.

"Not cool, bro! We've talked about this!" He whined from his spot on the floor.

Dr. Prasad sighed as she helped Mark up. "Well, now that he's here, perhaps we could schedule a partner therapy session?"

Mark gave me a frantic look. "Pauly, get me out of here."

I grinned. "Not a chance. If I can't leave, then neither can you. And, for the millionth time, my name is Paul."

He whispered out of the corner of his mouth. "If you get me out of here right now, *Paul*, I won't ask you to send me on a booty-call for the next six months. And I won't even complain the next time you want me to save someone."

Dr. Prasad peered at us over her glasses. "You realize I can hear you, right?"

Ignoring her, I nodded to Mark and waved my hand. Mark vanished.

He reappeared right outside of the window above a bush. He fell into it, flailing in a way that made me wish I'd filmed it. "Bro!"

"Oops," I said to Dr. Prasad, shrugging. We both watched Mark struggle to get out of the bush. Once he did, he flipped me off. I gave him a cheerful wave in reply. "See? He's fine."

She muttered something under her breath that sounded suspiciously like "superheroes." The clock on the mantle chimed. "That's all the time we have today. I'll see you next week." As I got to my feet, she held up a hand. "And, Paul, I'd like you to reflect on the fact that this kind of behavior is exactly why you have court-mandated therapy in the first place."

The Real Life Adventures of Awesome Girl
by Gregg Chamberlain

"You're gonna hurt. You're gonna hurt *so* bad."

Darryl Slaney smiled an ugly smile. Known as "Big D" to his friends—who were few—and "Darryl the Bully" to those who feared him—who were many—Darryl grinned like a gleeful ghoul at the cringing little boy in front of him.

Aman Khalid sat backed up against the dirty brick wall of the school gym. His right leg was pulled up in front of him, both of his hands wrapped around a throbbing knee where Darryl had kicked him. Aman's left leg stretched out in front of him, offering a perfect target for the bully's next assault.

It was morning recess at Louis Riel District Secondary School. Darryl and two of his buddies cornered Aman on the far side of the gymnasium building, out of sight of Mrs. Fredericks, the teacher on monitor duty in the school yard that day.

The three older boys hustled the smaller boy around a corner and into a little dead-end space between the gymnasium and the eastern annex portion of the school. The outside part of the two-storey gym building joined with a short, windowless hallway section that linked to the one-storey annex portion. A nice private place for the kind of sadistic fun that the trio of junior-grade bullies had in mind. If Mrs. Fredericks happened to glance around as she passed by along the gym building on patrol, she wouldn't see anyone hidden inside the cul-de-sac.

"One loud word and you're dead!" Darryl muttered to a terrified little Aman once they were out of sight of all the other students in the yard. Then he kicked the smaller boy in the knee and watched as a whimpering Aman painfully crawled to the end of the cul-de-sac.

Mervyn Murchison and Yvan Ostrovsky trailed behind Darryl as he slowly followed Aman. They stood watching, listening, and grinning as their leader looked down at his victim.

"Yeah," Darryl said, still smiling. "First, we're gonna beat on ya for a bit." He reached behind his back and received a spray can of black paint from Yvan. He held the can up close to Aman's face and shook it. "Then we give you a nice little makeover. *Psssh! Psssh!* Make you all nice and holy with a big black cross." His smile widened into a wicked grin. "Though your crybaby face is kinda small, so the cross may be a bit crooked, but that's okay, 'cause then..."

Darryl suddenly spat in the younger boy's face. He laughed. "Then we baptize you! Make you a proper Christian now that you're living here with us real Canadians! Right, guys?"

He turned, grinning, towards his buddies, who grinned in return.

"Yeah," snickered Yvan. "An' we got lots of baptizing spit for him."

Murchison snickered. "Go on, Big D!" he urged. "Hammer the little freak!"

Darryl held up a hand, slowly closing it into a fist. "Oh, I'm gonna hammer him, Murch," he promised. "Gonna hammer him good. But first, I think he oughta know why. It's only fair, eh?"

"Fair? What's fair about three big bullies picking on someone smaller and weaker than they are?"

Startled by the loud voice behind them, the trio turned around to see who dared interrupt their fun.

A small girl, about half the size of Darryl, stood arms akimbo and fists on her hips a couple of steps away from the trio of bullies.

Ilyanna Andrechuk — Annie to her friends — sat alone by the uprights at the far end of the soccer field. The Grade 9 student sat with one leg tucked under and the other extended in front of her, doing warm-up stretches for a solo run around the field as part of her junior soccer training schedule for next week's regional tournament in Brandon. She saw the trio of bullies drag Aman Khalid off and into the cul-de-sac.

Right away, she knew what was going to happen. She sprang to her feet and, without a second thought, raced across the field towards the main school buildings.

She had sense enough, though, for a brief stop to pull out the cellphone her mother had given her "for emergencies" and send a quick text message about the situation to the main office of the school. Hopefully, someone would see it right away and alert Mrs. Frederickson. As an afterthought, she also texted 911 before slipping the cellphone back into the belly pouch of her track suit hoodie.

Ilyanna braked to a halt a short distance from the mouth of the cul-de-sac. She crept silently up to the entrance in time to see Darryl kick Aman. Keeping quiet, she moved in closer first, listening to the bully's threats of more pain and punishment for his victim, before announcing her presence.

A smirk slipped over Darryl's face when he saw the source of the interruption. He pushed past his pals towards Ilyanna, handing off the spray paint canister to Yvan. "If it ain't Crusader Annie!" he sneered. "Whyncha go find a school bake sale to run? 'Cause if ya stick your nose where it don't belong, little girl, then it's gonna bleed!"

Eyes narrowing, Ilyanna stared hard up at the towering bully. "Maybe. But I won't be the only one bleeding. And that's Ms. Andrechuk, to you!"

Darryl scoffed. "Tough talk for a little girl." He glared down at Ilyanna. "Last chance, Annie. Keep yer mouth shut and walk away now while you still can."

Ilyanna glared back in defiance. Then she smiled, took out her cellphone, and held it up just out of reach of Darryl's grasp. "Too late. Already called. Company's coming." She stuck the phone back in her hoodie pouch. "And I don't walk away from cowards like you."

Darryl heard surprised gasps behind him. He frowned down at the defiant little girl in front of him. Then he smiled his nasty smile again. "Open that smart mouth of yours once too often, little Annie, and someone's gonna shut it for you some day."

Darryl glanced back at Aman, cowering against the wall. "Be seeing you later, Ah-men," he promised. "Come on, guys." He turned again to face Ilyanna. "Move or else," he threatened, even as he took a step forward and reached out with one hand to push her away.

Instead, Ilyanna danced aside. Her hands reached up and grabbed hold of Darryl's outstretched arm.

Balanced on one leg now, Ilyanna drove her other leg down, foot held sideways, towards Darryl's ankle. The cleats on her soccer shoe stabbed hard against the middle of the denim-covered shin. Her foot scraped down. Darryl howled in surprise and pain. At the same time, Ilyanna's left arm pulled back, fist cocked, the second knuckle of the middle finger sticking out.

One hand holding tight to Darryl's extended arm to keep it straight, Ilyanna drove her fist into the muscle just above the elbow, hitting the ulnar nerve point there. A jeet kune do-style knuckle punch that would make Bruce Lee proud.

She let go of Darryl's arm and danced away again, her own arms up, ready to block or grab. For a moment, the focus of her gaze was distracted by a shadow overhead. She looked upwards and past the trio of bullies to see a blurred blue form drop down behind them. Her attention returned to the immediate threat, though her ready stance relaxed a bit.

A cursing Darryl stumbled back against his surprised fellow bullies, staggering them. He held his aching arm, already numb and useless. Blood started to trickle down his left leg.

Eyes wide with both shock and anger, Darryl limped towards Ilyanna. His good arm started to pull back, fist cocked. "You're gonna regret that, you little…"

"Is there a problem here?"

Caught by surprise again, Darryl and his pals turned around. A midnight blue-clad figure stood protectively between the three bullies and Aman Khalid. The little boy's look of despair and fear had now changed to bright, beaming hope.

Darryl Slaney was big for a high schooler, taller even than Lady Justice, who had appeared, so suddenly it seemed, at what should have been just a typical schoolyard situation. But the mystery woman's aura of self-confident strength made her seem much bigger and braver compared to Darryl and his bullying buddies.

The Scales of Justice stood out in bold bronze relief against the dark blue background of the blindman's cowl that concealed almost all of Lady Justice's face. Below the hem of the cowl, the crimefighter smiled.

"I'll ask again," Lady Justice said. "Is there a problem here?"

Darryl began edging away, his left foot dragging a bit thanks to Ilyanna's kick to his shin. Yvan Ostrovsky and Mervyn Murchison followed alongside. "No problem," muttered Darryl. "We were just leaving."

He turned about and saw Ilyanna still blocking his way. "You better move or I'm gonna…"

"Or you're going to what?" murmured the voice of Lady Justice in his ear.

Startled again, Darryl tried to both turn and step away. His left leg gave way, and he fell. Ilyanna stepped to the side, out of the way, and watched the bully measure his length on the ground. "Ah, the cavalry arrives," she heard Lady Justice remark.

Mrs. Fredericks came puffing around the corner of the cul-de-sac. Behind her were two other teachers. They all came to a sudden stop at the scene before them: Ilyanna standing to one side of the dead-end corridor; Darryl, a known schoolyard troublemaker and frequent name on the detention list, sprawled on the ground, with two of his friends, also regulars in detention, standing close by; Aman Khalid, now sitting up straight, beside the masked figure of Lady Justice. Mrs. Fredericks recovered first from the surprise scenario.

"What is going on here?" she sputtered.

"That is something I think we will all be discussing in the principal's office," replied Lady Justice. "Why don't you boys," she pushed Yvan and Mervyn towards Darryl, who still lay where he'd fallen, "help your friend get up and go follow along with this lady and her companions?"

Suddenly, Lady Justice reached down and picked up Aman, holding him cradled in her arms. "We'll also need the school nurse called," she said in a grimmer tone, "to see to this boy's injury until the ambulance arrives."

"Ambulance?" gasped Mrs. Fredericks.

"Already called," responded Lady Justice, shifting her grip on Aman to tap a finger to one side of her cowled head.

"Five minutes, Sonya," whispered a voice in the masked mystery woman's ear.

"Thank you, Interface," murmured Lady Justice, as she strode past Mrs. Fredericks and the other two teachers. She paused at the entrance of the cul-de-sac. "Walk with me, would you, please?" she said to Ilyanna, lingering just behind the teachers.

Ilyanna spared one glance behind her to watch Murchison and Ostrovsky hoist a loudly cursing Darryl to his feet. He yelped and cursed even louder as his full body weight bore down on his injured leg. She waited just long enough for Darryl to look up and see her flash him a fast one-finger salute before turning and jogging off to catch up with a fast-striding Lady Justice.

Together, she and Lady Justice, who continued carrying Aman with no visible sign of effort, walked across the almost-empty school yard towards the main school building. A few senior students loitering on the steps of the rear entrance watched the masked mystery woman approach, accompanied by the crusading Grade 9 student. Aman rested, cradled and secure in the crimefighter's strong arms.

"That was brave of you, standing up to those bullies," remarked Lady Justice, as she and Ilyanna walked along.

"You were awesome, Annie!" declared Aman, twisting around in Lady Justice's arms to regard Ilyanna with admiring eyes. "Real awesome!"

Ilyanna smiled and shrugged. The hooded face of Lady Justice also turned towards the young girl keeping pace at her side. "Maybe foolish, too," remarked the mystery woman. "Those boys could have hurt you."

Ilyanna shrugged again. "They could try. At least then they wouldn't have been hurting Aman."

"I heard you tell them that you'd called for help," said Lady Justice. "Why didn't you just stay back and wait for help to arrive?"

Ilyanna looked up at the hooded face. "Help did arrive, not the kind I was expecting, though. What's a superhero doing at a schoolyard?"

Lady Justice continued walking for several steps before answering. "I was in the area when you sent that 911 call."

Ilyanna frowned. "How did you…?"

"Interface." Lady Justice shifted her cradle hold for Aman to free a hand for a brief touch at the side of her cowl. "One of my fellow Justice Brigade members. He has a special knack for communications."

"Ambulance approaching school now."

Lady Justice nodded. "He's just told me that the paramedics are almost here," she told Ilyanna. "He's good at keeping us all informed about any problems."

Ilyanna nodded.

"Professional and personal."

Lady Justice chuckled. "Inside joke," she said to a puzzled Ilyanna.

As they approached the rear entrance, two of the loitering seniors hurried to open the doors for them. Lady Justice nodded thanks as she, still carrying Aman, and Ilyanna passed by and stepped inside the building.

"You didn't answer my question," she said, as they headed towards the front of the building, footsteps echoing in the empty corridor. "Why didn't you just stay back and wait for the adults to arrive? Why did you confront the bullies?"

Silence greeted the mystery woman's query. Then…

"Someone has to!" declared Ilyanna, staring up at Lady Justice. "If I didn't do something, they were going to hurt Aman really bad." Her young face assumed a very serious adult look. "My mom is a nurse. It's her job to help people, and sometimes she has to do stuff like CPR right away because she can't wait for a doctor. She always says, 'We can't any of us just wait around for someone else to fix the problems. We all have to try to help.' So I had to try to help Aman!"

Lady Justice inclined her head. "I see. Your mother sounds like a smart woman."

"The smartest!" affirmed Ilyanna.

The masked mystery woman made a thoughtful nod of agreement. "Well, you had best hurry along now and get to class. I expect you'll get a call later from the principal's office to come down and tell what you know about this incident."

"What about Aman?"

"I'll stay with him inside the school until the ambulance arrives."

Ilyanna hesitated a moment. "Okay, I guess. See you later, Aman."

"See you, Annie. Thanks again."

Ilyanna spared one more glance at Aman in the arms of Lady Justice. Then she turned and went down the hall. She paused at a classroom door, looked back one more time at the cowled crimefighter, then opened the door and quickly slipped inside, pulling it shut behind her.

"You did a good job with that girl of yours, Sonya."

"Yes, Interface, I think so too."

A smile appeared on the face hidden beneath the Scales of Justice.

"Time to get ready and go out and save the world, Awesome Girl."

Heart of the Storm
by J. Patrick Conlon

"Where exactly do you think you're going?"

I turned back, hand resting on the handle of the screen door. "I'm heading into town with Keith."

"Dressed like that?" my mother, Margaret, raised an eyebrow.

"Mom, I'm 19, and this," I gestured to my oversized jeans and crop top. "Covers everything but my belly. I would think you would be happy that I'm wearing a tent instead of those booty shorts everyone else is wearing right now."

"I'm just looking out for you. That boy is only looking out for one thing."

I laughed. "Keith is even more terrified of me getting pregnant than you are. He talks a big game, but if I responded, he would run for the hills."

"If you say so, sweetie. Are you at least driving?"

"Yeah, I'll pick him up, and then we're heading into town. I'll be back late."

"Just make sure you wake me when you get home. You know I don't sleep well until you are back here."

"I will, Ma," I shouted behind me, running down the steps and to the small 2 door hatchback.

How is she going to sleep once I've left town entirely? I thought as the engine fired up. The sun was starting to set as I reached the road. I looked around for what was to be one of the last times. The fields had started to bud, with the leaves of the corn barely sticking out from the rows. The walking waters, giant metal A frames with massive wheels stuck together in a line, glared in the fading light. The effort of hooking the tractor up to them, pulling them into place so the farm could get water to every edge of the fields, replayed in my mind. Those days were almost over. The small car turned onto the main road and I slammed my foot down, barreling towards Keith and one of the last nights I would spend at home.

"This sucks. Why did we even come here tonight, May?"

"My company not enough for you, Keith?" I threw my arms around him and gave him a serious look. He wilted immediately.

"It's not that, and you know it," He stammered. "It's just, this sucks is all."

Looking around the empty dance floor, it was hard to argue with him. XLR-8 used to be the hottest under-21 club in this quiet beach town. Now it was empty but for a few small pockets of people bunched in conversation in the corners. It wasn't hard to figure out why. Ever since last Saturday, the only sound that was being broadcast was a wild jumble of white noise. The news called it a signal, but what we called it was a buzzkill. However, it was better than the bowling alley or just sitting on the beach. Yet another reason I couldn't wait to get out of this town.

"How about we try to score some E?"

I grinned at him. "What exactly would you do if I said yes?"

He turned beet red and stammered, "I mean, it's not like we can dance to this, right?"

"Besides," I grabbed the buckle on my belt and tugged it. "You don't seem to be the type to try anything while I'm high."

"That's not what I meant, May." He moved closer, and I let him get his arms up and almost around me before I slid back and crossed my arms.

"I'm not sure I'm ready to forgive you yet." I moved a step towards the dance floor, fixing him with a glare. "Maybe there are some guys here who will appreciate me more."

"Hey! Wait a minute!" He reached for me, and I spun away onto the dance floor. I knew I was leaving this town, and Keith was cute, but not throw-your-future-away cute. We'd fooled around enough, sure, but I didn't have to try hard to see the results of going too far. My mother had me when she was young, and all her dreams of something more went and left town without her. I was determined not to have that happen to me. I closed my eyes and tried to lose myself in the cacophony of the signal. If I concentrated, there was almost a pattern to it. I swayed my hips a few times, and it nearly approximated a beat. After several attempts, I threw up my hands, determining that any fun was just not in the cards tonight. I walked off the dance floor to Keith, who shrugged and grimaced.

"Told you we couldn't dance to this."

"Okay, fine, let's get out of here."

This time, he grinned. "You have any place in mind?"

I had just begun to nod when the entire room went eerily silent, with several loud conversations stopping mid-sentence.

"This is creepier than the noise," he said and tugged at my hand. "Let's get out of here before..."

The rest of his words were drowned out by a thumping baseline, followed by the first strains of Nine Inch Nails' Head Like a Hole. I turned towards the DJ booth to see Mike staring at his turntable. He had decided to try spinning Pretty Hate Machine to see what would happen. He was equally stunned that something had. I turned back to Keith and shot him a wicked grin.

"I think we can dance to this," He groaned as I grabbed his hand and yanked him to the dance floor. We made our way out to the center as the crowds around the edges of the club finally began to realize that the music had started. I saw several other crestfallen faces, realizing that their extracurricular activities were canceled for the evening. I pulled Keith close.

"Are you that disappointed?"

"Well, no. I just don't want you to leave." His breath was hot on my ear, the music forcing our conversation to be closer.

"Good, because I do like you, Keith. Maybe I can convince you to come with me?" A loud buzzing noise began to emanate from the speakers around me. "Mike, c'mon! The music is finally back!"

A high-pitched squeal ripped through the air, emanating from the speaker nearest to us. I grabbed the sides of my head just as the turntables erupted in a cloud of sparks. Silence gripped the club only for a moment, broken by the loud thump of my body hitting the floor as I blacked out.

When I finally regained consciousness, the first thing I felt was a hand on my thigh. I grabbed and pushed weakly at it.

"What is going on?" My voice reflected the anger I felt. How had I gotten here? Why was I lying down?

"May?" Keith's voice was filled with fear, and my confusion was replaced by concern.

"What happened?"

"What?" The confusion in his tone made me pause. Something wasn't right. My vision cleared enough for me to recognize the passenger seat, fully reclined and belted in. We were in my car, and he was driving very fast.

"What is going on? Where are you taking me?"

"The hospital, May. Where else?"

"The hospital?" My confusion returned, and I shook my head, attempting to clear the cobwebs.

"You fainted, May. The club closed after the DJ booth exploded."

"Exploded?" The evening's events felt distant and hazy.

"Okay, not exploded, but sparks shot everywhere. Everyone freaked!"

His hand moved from my thigh up to across my chest suddenly.

"Hey!" My voice wasn't angry, but when I looked at Keith, I saw real terror in his eyes.

"My hand!" he shrieked and pulled his arm away. His erratic movement caused the car to begin to fishtail. I grabbed at the wheel, desperately trying to get control.

"My fucking hand, and, Jesus May. Your eyes!"

"What?" My confusion became fear as I watched Keith cower away from the wheel. Small wisps of smoke were rising from his hand. That buzzing sound in my head returned, and the edges of my vision blurred. I was flung backward as the car lurched. Keith lunged back for the wheel and somehow managed to keep the car on the road.

"May!" Keith's shout was barely a whisper above the throbbing hum that filled my head. Another spasm racked my body, and I was thrown into him, forcing his foot down on the accelerator.

The car flew off the road and cleared the ditch. We plowed into the field full of corn, carving a jagged path through the tall mass. I was able to open my eyes. Keith struggled to keep control of the wheel while attempting to push me off. The buzzing in my ears was gone, replaced by a sharp acrid odor. I reached out towards him to see crooked tendrils of white light rising from my skin. I curled my hand, and a web of tendrils formed around him.

"May! What are you doing?" His eyes narrowed, his fear replaced with concern.

"I'm saving you," I said softly, and before he could protest, I thrust my hand towards him. The ball of light coalesced around him, and he shot from the vehicle, the light blowing apart the driver's door and most of that side of the car. My hand was still stretched out towards him when the giant rubber tire of the walking water slammed into the vehicle. I felt myself being thrown forward, and pain exploded across my right arm. I collided with the windshield and blacked out.

The blare of sirens was the first thing I heard when I woke up. My thoughts were scattered. Where was I? What had happened? Before I could gather my thoughts, my entire body tensed, and that acrid smell returned. I arched my back so hard I thought it would shatter as my vision went entirely white. I vaguely heard shouts, and there was a flurry of motion at the edges of my vision.

"Everyone back!" A voice I didn't recognize shouted, much deeper than Keith's. I found myself wondering who it was as the spasm began to release its grip on my spine and the light faded. I could barely make out blurry, thick shapes running around. Slowly, they resolved themselves into the thick coats and wide-brimmed hats of firefighters. What were they doing so far back? I went to reach out to them with my right hand, but I couldn't move my arm.

"Keith?" My voice felt strange in my mouth, and I couldn't speak above the cacophony of sirens and shouting.

"May! I'm here, May!" I turned my head as much as I was able to see Keith jumping up from a stretcher, only to be held back by several firefighters. "Get her out of the water!" The fear I had seen before the crash was replaced completely by panic, but for me. Maybe I could convince him to come with me when I left.

"Where is the foam?" the deeper voice shouted again. I wondered again why everyone was so far away. Looking around for my car, all I saw was twisted, melted metal. This did not make any sense.

I looked down and saw that my body was encased in white hot streaks of lightning. I was lying with my lower half submerged in murky water, and the bright, blinding light was coming from my body. Electricity coursed through me, shorted out by the water. Each time it flashed through me, streaks of lightning tore through the air. A slower-moving fireman was caught by the edge of a tendril and tossed back like a rag doll. I went to put my arms down to lift myself, but I couldn't get any leverage. I looked down at my right arm to find nothing there. My scream rent the air as everything flashed white hot again, and everyone fled the blast zone.

I opened my eyes to find myself staring up at the ceiling. I put my arms behind me and pulled myself up to a sitting position. I looked around, but the wreckage and chaos were all gone. The bright orange splash of the Nine Inch Nails broken album poster was where it always was, framed against the far wall. I was in my bedroom. I put my right hand to my forehead as the room spun. How did I get here? Dim light streamed behind the curtains, filtering through the room with the haze of early morning.

I remembered the last minutes before the lightning struck, and my eyes flew to my right arm. It was there, pale smooth skin unmarred. I ran my left hand along it and didn't know how to feel. The dream had been so real, but here I was without a scratch.

I dressed much more slowly than normal, still trying to piece together the nightmare of last night. The club, Keith, the signal stopping.

I stopped short, my shirt half over my head. The signal had stopped. I struggled into my shirt as I rushed to the stereo. I flipped the switch and nothing happened. I pulled the bulky box further out from atop my dresser. The cord wound through the rats' nest of wires. It took several minutes, but I finally traced it to the wall. It was plugged in. I removed myself from the mess and went back to the stereo. Everything looked fine, so I pressed the power button, and this time the light came on.

"That was Head Like a Hole, by the great Trent Reznor and Nine Inch Nails."

I blinked. The signal was gone. I looked down at my right hand to see the light filtering through it. My left hand passed through it. I raised it, and it became solid just as my hand left it. I closed my eyes and shook my head. When I reopened them, my arm was there, whole and unmarred.

"What the hell is going on?"

"If you would come out to your yard, I think I can explain." A voice shouted from outside.

I carefully drew back the curtain to see a person in my driveway, hat pulled low and wrapped in a long trench coat.

I went out into the hallway. "Hey, someone is in the driveway."

There was no answer. Something felt really off. There were no signs of life besides me in the house. It may have been morning, but there was always noise. I came downstairs slowly, grabbed the bat that my brother and I kept by the door that we used to play ball together, and went outside.

"Good morning, May," the figure lifted its hat to reveal a man in his early 20s wearing multicolored round glasses. "My name is Fred."

"Who are you and how do you know my name?" I stopped short, brandishing the bat.

"Well, that is going to take a bit of explaining." He gestured behind me, and I turned to find several lush chairs with a small end table between them.

"What the hell?"

"Have a seat first. You probably don't want to be standing for what comes next."

"Look, buddy, I don't care who you think you are."

"You're in a medically induced coma, May." Fred removed his glasses, revealing bright green eyes filled with a sadness that brought me up short, and I lowered the bat slightly.

"I'm what?"

Fred took a step forward, and I raised my bat again. "If I'm in a coma, what the hell are you doing here?"

Fred raised a hand and pulled it towards himself. I felt the back of the chair hit my knees, and I dropped into it. I looked back for whatever pushed the chair to find nothing at all.

"What is going on? Who did that?"

"I did. My given name is Fred Thompson, but people call me Dr. Dream. I can enter people's dreams and affect things inside them. I'm a Listener, like you."

"Dr. Dream? A Listener? You better start making sense, or I'm going to beat your ass with this bat."

"What bat?"

I looked at my hands to find them empty. I looked back up, and Fred was sitting in the chair next to me.

"Now, I know that this is going to be hard to understand at first, but you have to trust that I'm here to help you."

I nodded, unable to wrap my head around what was happening.

"Okay, we'll start with the hard stuff first. You've been in a coma for about 9 months."

"9 Months! Where's my family? Where's Keith?"

"Keith is in protective custody, with a new name and face courtesy of Professor Titanium. Your family believes you died in the car accident; it's safer that way."

I shook my head. "No, that's not possible. I was with Keith last night!"

"That was 9 months ago, May. Your condition wasn't something a hospital could handle, so they kept you sedated for the first 3 weeks while the world came to grips with what happened. It took about that long for the good Professor to design and build the containment field anyway. The world has been pretty busy since your accident."

"The world? My accident mattered to the world?"

"No, your accident happened the same night as the signal stopped."

My brow furrowed. "That's right. At the nightclub the music started playing all of a sudden. But what does that have to do with me?"

Fred reached out and put a hand over mine. His hand was encased in a large glove, with tubes running across the back. I could see a dark greenish liquid contained within them.

"When the signal stopped, there were those of us who were changed. It happened to all of us that same night. The news started reporting that once the signal ended, everyone heard it, but we were the ones who were listening. So they called us."

"Listeners," my voice sounded far away to me. "So the streaks of light, and my arm." I looked down at my right arm. It was almost completely transparent.

"Unfortunately, while there are a lot of things that Professor Titanium can do, regeneration in a cauterized wound is not one of them."

"So, let's say I believe you. Where am I?"

"You're in Titanium Labs inside a static containment field. Your vitals are being monitored by several lab technicians."

"And where are you?"

"Lying on a couch in one of the break rooms. The Professor wanted to make sure that I wasn't too close to the field in case something happened when you woke up."

"I'm that dangerous?"

"Well, we've had to keep you in the containment field while you were unconscious. Your powers can be scary even if you aren't."

"So, let's say I trust you. What happens now?"

"First, let me show you what's happening right now." He waved his arm, and a hole tore in the air in front of us. As it widened, I could see several people in hazmat suits running around the edges of a bright silver room. They were moving between consoles, flipping switches, and pressing buttons. The focus shifted, and I could see a figure surrounded in a globe of static. Small arcs of lightning could be seen flashing inside.

"Who is that, in the middle of that thing?"

"The heart of that Maelstrom is you. Jeremiah, I mean Professor Titanium, built that static field so you wouldn't accidentally hurt anyone while you were recovering."

"I can barely see anything inside that. What do I look like?"

"Here, let me help." Fred waved his hand, the static vanished, and there I was, I was wrapped in weird bandages around my torso and left arm. Where my right arm used to be was nothing at all. I just couldn't process it not being there. I looked up at my hair. It was shock blue and floated just several inches from my head. This was something I could latch onto.

"Holy crap! What the hell happened to my hair!"

"I think you're good to wake up if your hair is your biggest concern."

Fred laid a hand on my shoulder and shook me gently. The world around me dissolved.

The silence surprised me as I cracked open my eyes. I expected the static to be full of noise, but it made no sound at all. I began to hear faraway voices. I closed my eyes again and put all my energy into hearing what they were saying.

"...want to know is why you are so invested in this one?" This voice was deeper, and I did not recognize it from before. I guessed this was Professor Titanium.

"She's been through a lot. Her family thinks she's dead. Her boyfriend knows better, but we've had to give him a new life." I recognized Fred's voice, and he sounded quite animated. "Besides, I just got done talking to her. She's got sass, but she's not a threat."

"How on earth would you know that after one conversation?"

"Are you seriously asking me how I would know the truth in a dream? Do you think you could lie to me on my turf?"

"So, she's not a threat; that doesn't mean she's right for us."

"It wasn't so long ago that the rest were saying the same thing about me. It was you who vouched for me. Now I'm vouching for her."

"Ok, but if you recall, your actions were on my head. Now her's will be on you."

I started to open my eyes again, and my sight cleared. I could see through the static after a few seconds of focusing. I was floating in the middle of the room with technicians manning the consoles, just as Fred had shown me. Looking down, I saw the two figures I had been eavesdropping on.

Fred looked just as he did before, long trenchcoat, multicolored spectacles resting on the brim of his hat. The other man was larger, dressed in a flat matte gray lab coat. He must be Professor Titanium.

"Hey guys, I can hear you know," I muttered. To my surprise, they both turned towards me.

"I suppose it's just as well you are awake for this. Dr. Dream was just vouching for you, but it would be better to hear it from you."

"Hey, you just got done vouching for me, but now my word isn't good enough?" I said.

Dr Dream folded his arms over his chest and said, "Yeah, and I believe I also said your actions were on me."

"So yeah," I raised my voice a little, and a few cracks of lightning flashed out from the edges of the sphere. "You guys think you can pull yourselves away from fighting like an old married couple and get back to what has happened to me, and what happens now?"

Professor Titanium raised an eyebrow towards Dr. Dream.

"Prof., she has a point. I think we owe her an explanation."

"Well, at the time of your accident," Professor Titanium began.

"No, we covered that already. Let's get to what's next."

"Ok." The Professor turned towards the nearest technician. "Bring in the arm. Turn off the field."

The technician ran out of the room and returned a moment later with a large dolly that was carrying a metallic arm. The top of the arm was compact, and the shoulder joint ended in a ball socket. When it reached the elbow, however, it ballooned outwards into a football shape. The hand at the end was closed into a massive fist.

"So you don't trust me, but you made me an assault cannon?"

"If you're going to be the fifth member of The Five, you will need this to help contain and focus your power."

The bubble around me faded, and I was lowered to the floor. My legs buckled slightly, and holding my weight felt strange.

"Help me or help you contain and focus my power?" I raised an eyebrow.

"May, we're friends. You can trust us."

The air around me had that acrid smell again. I flinched, and a burst of static struck the ground, leaving a streak of soot behind.

"Quickly, get the arm attached." Professor Titanium barked at the technician. He moved beside me as quickly as the heavy load would allow him.

"This is moving rather fast. I might need a minute." That acrid smell was growing stronger.

Dr. Dream put a hand on my shoulder. "May, trust me. This will help you." I noticed his hand was not in his gauntlet, and tiny wisps of smoke were rising from him. His smile was growing forced.

I thought about Keith again, how his hand had looked. I nodded and moved over to the dolly. The technicians scrambled back as small bursts of static crackled in the air around me.

"How do I?" I looked down at my arm and noticed that the shoulder had a metallic port where the joint used to be.

"The socket will conform to the arm; just place it against it."

I moved until my shoulder was almost touching the ball joint. I looked at Dr. Dream. He nodded and grinned. "This is going to be all right. You're a Listener now. A Superhero."

I'm still not sure why I trusted him. He probably knew that if he reminded me of Keith, I would trust him more. I pressed my shoulder against the ball joint, and it irised open, locking around the arm. Instantly, the static around me faded, and the technicians in the room became visibly relaxed.

Dr. Dream took his hand away and shook it, grimacing. "Welcome to the Phenomenal Five, May."

I thought back to the conversation we had in my dream, both a few minutes and a lifetime ago.

"Call me Maylstrum."

The Cult of the Black Hole
by David Boyce

The cosmos stretched infinite—nebulae swirled in hues of violet and gold, and stars shimmered like ancient sentinels. Yet, in the void between these celestial wonders, a fierce war raged.

A fleet of sleek, silver-hulled vessels—the warships of the Zulliens—formed a defensive perimeter around their homeworld, Zullia Prime. Their engines burned bright against the darkness, and their shields flickered beneath a relentless assault.

But the enemy was ruthless.

A horde of warships—monstrous, jagged constructs of obsidian metal—descended upon the Zullien fleet. Weapons blazed with violet plasma, and the insignia of a feared warlord burned upon their hulls. An empire of conquest seeking yet another victim.

And yet, in the vast emptiness of space, one warrior stood alone.

Star Eye—a beacon in the darkness—burst forth from the Zullien flagship, her radiance cleaving through shadow. Her golden aura blazed against the blackness of the void. She did not fly; she moved with purpose, riding the solar winds and letting the energy of space itself propel her. She was a comet, a sun, a force of nature unleashed.

Clad in a white leotard and gold-trimmed pleated skirt, her look completed by knee-high golden boots and gleaming pauldrons. Elbow-length gloves and a star-shaped belt buckle added to her celestial presence. A high blonde ponytail, held by a star-shaped clasp, streamed behind her in the solar wind.

"This is your only warning. Retreat, or be shattered," she said, golden fire swirling around her like a storm.

The warlord snarled. "Another world resisting assimilation into the Obsidian Dominion. How foolish."

The enemy responded with violence.

A hailstorm of plasma bolts streaked through space, each designed to vaporize on impact. But Star Eye was faster. She danced through the storm, weaving past death, her energy glowing. With a flick of her wrist, she redirected blasts with bursts of golden fire, explosions blooming in her wake.

Fists blazing, she rocketed toward a warship. Its cannons locked on.

Too late.

She crashed through its hull like a solar lance, shredding steel and circuitry. The ship erupted behind her, fragments scattering like embers.

Turning in the void, she faced a new wave of fighters. She breathed, her aura flaring, then launched herself into their ranks. She tore through them like a meteor, explosions marking her path.

On the enemy flagship, the warlord watched, disbelief in his crimson eyes. His armada was falling to one woman.

"One being should not have this power!" he growled.

Then, light. Golden radiance consumed the bridge. Star Eye hovered outside, eyes ablaze with the fire of a thousand suns. She raised her hand, a miniature sun igniting in her palm.

The warlord's breath caught. "Pull back! Full retreat!" he barked, fear in his voice.

The fleet scattered.

The battle was over.

The war was won.

The Zullien fleet regrouped, battered vessels drifting through wreckage. Survivors tended to the wounded, shields flickering back to life. But the brightest light was Star Eye, hovering in the void, her flames dimming, the weight of victory resting on her shoulders. She gazed at Zullia Prime—the world she had sworn to protect.

A transmission crackled in her ear.

"Once again, you've saved us, Celeste Ray," the Zullien High Commander said, his voice full of awe.

At the sound of her true name, she smiled and lifted her chin.

"I didn't come this far to watch our allies fall," she replied, pride in her voice. "This victory isn't mine alone. Your command of the stars, your mastery of the solar winds—these strengthened me."

She breathed deeply as the fires of battle faded.

Zullia Prime was safe, thanks to their united effort.

She turned to the stars—her true calling. She hadn't come to space for conflict, but to protect, learn, and build. The Zulliens had helped her hone her powers, and now she would use them to safeguard them.

She closed her eyes and breathed in. A pulse of golden light surged from her chest, rippling across the galaxy.

A beacon.

A vow.

A promise to the stars.

The black hole loomed, a monstrous wound in the cosmos, its event horizon swirling like a celestial whirlpool, devouring light and bending time. Around it drifted the shattered remnants of civilizations. Beyond the pull of oblivion, Nyxar Prime hung—dark, jagged, and fortress-like. Its cracked, scorched surface pulsed with abyssal energy, obsidian spires jutting from its core, lightning crackling between them.

In the Abyssal Throne Room, carved from the bones of dead worlds, shadows stretched unnaturally, devouring the flickering light from smoldering embers. The air vibrated with an ancient presence. At the far end, a colossal black stone throne seemed fused with the darkness. Upon it sat Gronuz, the Titan Ruler, the Death of Suns, Lord of the Eternal Void. His four arms sprawled across the throne, molten cracks glowing like dying stars across his obsidian skin. His eyes—twin voids— swallowed the dim light, betraying infinite patience and hunger.

The doors groaned open, straining under unseen pressure. General Zharn, the Titan of the Void, entered, his steps echoing like thunder. His armor, woven from living shadow, shifted across his towering frame. He knelt before the throne.

"My liege, our campaign across Seren is complete. Their sun is no more."

Gronuz's smile curled darkly.

"Sector Zulia is next," Zharn growled, like tectonic plates grinding.

Gronuz's voice rumbled through the chamber, the death knell of stars. "It is time to take their sun and bring it to the void." His expression unreadable, he lifted his head slightly.

"We shall blot out their light. When their sun falls, their civilization shall vanish—consumed by nothingness, as all things must be."

Zharn remained motionless, but an unspoken hesitation hung in the air. Gronuz noticed. He always did. His hollow gaze pierced the general.

"Speak, Zharn," he said, low and expectant.

Zharn bowed his head.

"My liege, there is a human among them. A warrior of light. She alone has destroyed countless fleets."

Silence. Then a low, ominous chuckle.

Gronuz leaned forward, shifting the air. The embers dimmed.

"The Zulliens are no threat. Their empire crumbles. Their fleets are ash on the galactic wind. And you bring me concerns of a single human?" he said, amused and dismissive. A deep breath drained warmth from the room as shadows pulsed around him. He rose to his full, monstrous height.

"Tell me, General—what of this 'warrior of light'? What power does she truly wield?"

Zharn did not flinch, though the weight of his master's presence pressed down like gravity.

"She possesses the power of a star," he said, his voice even keeled.

Gronuz tilted his head slightly. Amused.

"A star," he echoed. The cracks across his body glowed faintly as he stepped forward.

"We have walked through the hearts of dying suns. We have stood within the burning womb of galaxies. We have endured the fury of a thousand supernovae and the silence of the farthest void. And you fear one who mimics the light?"

His four arms flexed, shadows recoiling from him. The darkness deepened.

"We are indomitable. Nothing can harm us," he declared, his voice a blade of certainty.

He turned to the starless window overlooking the black hole, raising one hand. Abyssal energy flickered between his fingers, like ghostlight.

"Begin the assault on their sister colonies. Raze them. I will erase their capital from the stars."

He exhaled, and the air seemed to vanish with it.

"When we reach the heart of their empire, we will take their sun," he finished, cold and final. Then, softer, almost a whisper of malice:

"Let's see if this 'warrior of light' can fight without one."

Zharn bowed low.

"As you wish, my liege."

With a massive battle helm placed upon his head, he strode from the chamber. The titanic doors groaned shut behind him, sealing Gronuz in darkness once more.

The void stirred.

A great war was about to begin.

The Zullien flagship floated serenely in orbit around Zullia Prime, the cosmos holding its breath in a rare stillness. Star Eye stood on the bridge, arms crossed, her golden light faintly pulsing. She exhaled, briefly believing in the illusion of peace.

Then, the stillness shattered.

An emergency transmission crackled through the speakers, the control panel flashing red. A holographic figure appeared—an elder of the Zulliens. His bioluminescent skin flickered, his translucent form distorted by panic.

"Star Eye! The Titans—they've returned! They are devouring our sister colonies!" the Elder's voice trembled with urgency.

Star Eye's brows furrowed, tension creeping into her stance. "Titans?"

The Elder nodded grimly. "The Titans of the Black Hole. An ancient race of cosmic giants, bent on returning the universe to darkness. They do not conquer—they erase. They despise the light and wield the power to consume the stars themselves. We fought them centuries ago, but we never truly defeated them. We merely pushed them back to the abyss. Now, they have returned, stronger than ever."

The words sank deep. An old war, unfinished. A nightmare reborn. Star Eye inhaled slowly, golden embers pulsing at her fingertips.

"Then it's time I remind them who truly owns the stars," she said, her voice firm as her golden light intensified.

"Be careful, Star Eye," the Elder urged. "These monsters can withstand the heat of a supernova and the frozen death of the farthest void. They will tear through our worlds, one by one, until they reach the star at the galaxy's center. And when they do, they will turn it into a black hole."

Star Eye's fists clenched. "I will not allow it," she vowed.

The Elder nodded, his expression a mix of hope and sorrow. Then, with a final pulse of golden fire, Star Eye rocketed from the bridge—a comet of defiance streaking toward the abyss.

The battle for creation had begun.

The stars blurred as Star Eye shot across the cosmos, faster than any vessel, her form trailing a golden flare. She froze.

Below… only ruin.

A once-thriving moon city now burned, obsidian warships descending like carrion birds. Energy blasts rained from the sky, transforming towers into pillars of fire.

And then, from the shadows, they emerged.

The Titans of the Black Hole.

They were towering. Standing between sixty to ninety feet tall and humanoid, but wrong. Their forms twisted like living shadows, forged from pure void. Glowing runes shimmered across their abyssal bodies, pulsing with ancient, malevolent power. Light bent away from them. Stars curled and vanished. Reality buckled at their feet.

They didn't just enter space.

They rewrote it.

The lead Titan stepped forward, cloaked in writhing darkness. His voice, low and resonant, rumbled through the battlefield.

"The Lightbringer arrives. You cannot stop the will of the Black Hole, little star. Surrender."

Star Eye hovered midair, arms crossed, her golden glow flickering defiantly. A smirk curved her lips.

"Surrender?" Her voice cut through the void. "I was about to say the same to you."

The General snarled.

Then they attacked.

Shadows swarmed. One Titan lunged, faster than expected, claws cleaving the vacuum. She twisted away midair, narrowly dodging the blow. Another struck from behind—she flipped, firing a solar blast that slammed into its chest, sending it staggering.

A third closed in.

She blasted through its core, light ripping it apart in a cascade of golden sparks.

Two down.

Still outnumbered.

She streaked through the battlefield, propelled by burning solar winds streaming from her hands. Titans loomed ahead, but she didn't slow. Weaving between them like a supernova set free, she launched radiant volleys; each one lighting up the dark, each one barely slowing them.

Their void-forged bodies absorbed the fury.

Unshaken.

Still, she fought—spiraling, vanishing, reappearing in bursts of solar flare.

But even stars can be caught.

A massive hand seized her mid-flight, crushing her midsection in a vice of obsidian shadow. She gasped as abyssal energy surged through her, smothering the light in her veins. Her limbs flailed. Her flames dimmed.

"You burn brightly, little star… but let's see if you burn in the void," General Voruun growled.

Her core flared white-hot. Muscles locked. Heat surged from her skin. Inch by inch, she forced his grip open.

Then—a flash of silver light erupted across the battlefield.

The Zulliens had arrived.

Warships shrieked through the sky, sleek and deadly, unleashing coordinated barrages. Fighters danced in the chaos, their energy cannons pounding the Titans with righteous fury. A comms channel snapped to life in her ear.

"You are not alone, Star Eye!" came the Zullien Commander's voice.

She grinned through the pain.

Fire returned to her soul.

Her aura blazed, scorching Voruun's hand. He roared as her flames cut through his grip. She tore free, a radiant blur crashing back into battle.

Titans fell, burned by light and silver fury—but something felt wrong.

They weren't pressing the attack.

Her comm crackled again, this time more urgent. "They've bypassed our defenses! A second fleet—Gronuz is attacking the capital!"

Her heart dropped. She turned slowly, dread blooming like ice in her gut. The Titan General met her gaze, abyssal eyes gleaming with smug satisfaction.

"While you chase shadows," he said, "the void takes what it desires."

Then they vanished. The Titans retreated into the dark.

Star Eye hovered in silence, fists clenched. A hologram blinked into view, but the signal cut off before the image could form.

Something was wrong.

She turned toward the stars.

Toward Gronuz.

The void was oppressive as Star Eye neared the planet's shattered remains, heavy with the weight of destruction. Below, a scene of absolute desolation unfolded. What had once been a world was now smoldering ash. Cities lay in ruin, crumbling like the bones of a long-dead titan. The air hummed with the remnants of annihilation.

Star Eye swallowed, her voice soft and breathless. "Who… who could have done this?"

A presence stirred—not through sound or movement, but deeper still. A voice resonated within the void, pressing against her very being.

"Ah... my troublesome little star. You should have stayed hidden," the voice said, low and thunderous, reverberating through the cosmos itself.

Space trembled under the weight of it. The void stirred as something vast and monstrous tore through reality—a ripple in existence. And then, he stepped through.

Gronuz, the Void Tyrant.

He towered nearly ninety feet tall, humanoid in the cruelest sense—not flesh, not metal, but a living void, writhing like a sea of midnight. His jagged obsidian armor pulsed with ancient runes and malevolent light. He radiated endless hunger—not a being, but an event. At his core spun a black hole, a singularity devouring reality itself.

Star Eye clenched her fists, golden aura blazing defiantly against the abyss. But she felt its weight. The suffocating truth.

This was no ordinary enemy.

This was something far beyond destruction.

Gronuz's voice, like collapsing stars laced with cruel amusement, reached her.

"Look at you. A flickering ember, still burning against the inevitable night."

Star Eye stood her ground. Her eyes narrowed, hiding the fear tightening her chest.

"You must be Gronuz. You heartless monster. You destroyed this entire planet. Is that your plan? To snuff out the universe one world at a time?"

A low, seismic chuckle.

"Stars burn. Kingdoms fall. And all light is devoured in the end."

Then he moved.

Not fast—but inevitable. His arm rose. Space warped with it. Gravity snapped. The battlefield twisted as the singularity in his chest roared to life.

A force surged outward.

Star Eye gritted her teeth as her body strained. The pull was unstoppable. Metal, rock, even starlight twisted toward him. Her limbs refused her. Her aura flickered.

"No!"

The force swallowed her scream.

She tumbled through the void, helpless.

Then—impact.

A hand closed around her. Massive. Unyielding. Only her head and shoulders were visible above his massive hand. Gronuz gripped her with fingers like continent-sized pillars, curling slowly, deliberately.

"Gotcha," he whispered.

The sound was a sentence.

Her light flared, fighting to break free—but his grip only tightened. Darkness surged, a cold weight sinking into her soul.

"Far too easy," he murmured, holding her captive.

Star Eye clenched her teeth, aura flaring in defiance. But the abyss swelled in response, pulsing through Gronuz and flooding the void with darkness. It pressed in—a suffocating force that reached into her very soul.

"Struggle all you like. The void is patient… and so am I," he said darkly, his grip unmoving.

"You're not…strong enough…to hold me forever!" she spat, still fighting.

Her golden aura surged, cracking Gronuz's knuckles. She nearly pried his grip open—then the abyss pulsed. The cracks sealed.

"Feel that? The strength of the void itself crushing the last light of defiance," he growled, eyes narrowing.

He squeezed hard enough to shatter warships. Even the stars seemed to flicker, dimmed by his power.

Desperation surged through her. Her only option: to become heavier than anything he'd ever held. She let go of restraint. Wielding the power of a star, she adjusted her mass, transforming her body into the density of a stellar core.

But the pain was excruciating. Her veins felt like molten rivers, her muscles locked under the unbearable weight. She could barely breathe. Holding this form was like cradling a sun within her flesh, and she knew she couldn't sustain it.

"Hmph… You should be nothing but stardust by now," Gronuz muttered, watching closely. "Why do you persist?"

"Because light… doesn't break," Star Eye hissed, her voice strained but resolute.

She pushed outward, every muscle taut with resistance. Her body could withstand the weight of a star—just barely.

But Gronuz didn't recoil. His grip stayed firm, a prison forged by cosmic law. No matter how much she strained, his fingers didn't budge.

"So you cannot be crushed," he mused, a cruel smirk growing. "But you can be contained."

Then it hit her—the awful truth. No matter how hard she fought, his grip wouldn't break. Her greatest strength, her final gambit, had failed. She was trapped.

Her breath caught.

No. Not like this.

Doubt crept in, whispering truths she didn't want to hear. She had bested warlords and world-killers—but none had made her feel so small.

The void weighed more than matter. It was existential. A rule of reality, not a foe. And for the first time since gaining her powers, a chilling thought clutched her mind:

What if I don't win?

Then—a memory.

Earth.

Warm sunlight on her skin. The laughter of children echoing in the breeze. The faces of those she loved. Every reason she had ever fought.

Her fingers twitched. Then—tightened into fists.

No. She would not surrender. She would not break. Let him mock her. Let him believe he'd won.

Gronuz hoisted her higher, drawing her closer to his towering, monstrous face. His four monstrous arms flexed, reveling in dominance. His colossal fingers reached for the gleaming mask that concealed her identity.

"Don't you dare!" Star Eye's fury ignited.

Gronuz only laughed, his voice a storm of mockery.

"And what will you do to stop me, little star?" he asked, low and amused.

With agonizing slowness, he gripped the edge of her mask and tore it away.

For the first time, Star Eye's face was exposed.

Her breath hitched. Not in fear, but fury. Her glare burned brighter than any supernova.

"So this is the radiant Earthling," he said, voice dripping with disdain. "I had hoped for more."

Star Eye strained against his grip, her glow resistant.

"I've heard your legends," he continued, mocking. "Victories against lesser foes. But I am the ultimate power."

He pulled her closer, tightening his grip to emphasize her helplessness.

"You were powerful on Earth, little star. But here, you're nothing. The cosmos is vast. And your light is minuscule."

Star Eye squirmed, but his fingers held fast.

"The power of a star?" he scoffed. "Child's play. Did you truly believe your Earth-born powers would carry you here?"

Silence. Her chest tightened. His words cut deeper than any blow. She had believed her strength would be enough — that light always found a way.

But this was different.

"You should have stayed on Earth," he said. "It'll be millennia before the black hole reaches it. You could've lived in peace. But you challenged the Cult of the Black Hole."

He leaned in. "Now, you've sealed your fate."

"You will not touch Earth!" she shouted, eyes blazing.

Gronuz laughed, the void echoing with it.

"You are no threat to me. There is no one — least of all you — who can stop the inevitable."

Her voice didn't falter. "You won't get away with this."

"So much power," Gronuz murmured. "And yet... completely helpless in my grasp."

He tightened his grip once more, testing her limits.

She didn't break. Couldn't. Wouldn't.

"Enjoy this moment, Gronuz," she spat. "It's the last one you'll get."

Then — she ignited. Her energy lashing out in defiance. Gronuz growled, feeling the sting, but instead of recoiling, he chuckled.

"Oh, but I think it will last," he said, grinning, his voice dark with triumph. "Because now... I have a new plan for you, my little star."

Star Eye's jaw tightened, her golden aura flaring in protest. Indignation burned in her eyes — not just at the condescension, but at the sheer audacity of his claim. She was no one's to claim.

Gronuz's gaze shifted toward his own galaxy, where a black hole dominated the center.

"If I cannot break you... I will unmake you," he sneered, his voice like grinding stone.

Star Eye's eyes widened. The realization hit — Gronuz might not be able to destroy her through brute force, but he had found another way.

Mockingly, Gronuz turned his gaze toward the swirling abyss beyond.

"My world orbits the devourer — the heart of the void. It has swallowed empires, gods, even stars. And soon, little star, it will take you."

Star Eye glanced toward the colossal black hole looming behind him, its event horizon twisting light into nothingness.

Her eyes narrowed. Golden energy flared faintly from her skin, defiant. "We'll see about that."

Gronuz drifted through the void, a monstrous shadow against the stars, Star

Eye trapped in his grip. His abyssal form barely moved, yet the cosmic winds bent around him. Each step was agony. Not from pain, but the crushing weight of inevitability. Gronuz wasn't rushing. He savored it. His grip was unbreakable, and he knew it.

Star Eye had never felt powerless. Not when her powers awakened. Not even facing Titan Nova. But now, she was a prisoner of the void itself—held by a being who didn't just wield destruction, he embodied it.

Gronuz eyed her, sneering. "Whatever is the matter, little star? Is your final journey through space uncomfortable?" he taunted.

Star Eye couldn't budge an inch. "This is not my final journey," she retorted, refusing to submit.

Gronuz laughed triumphantly. "You are correct, little star. You still have a black hole to explore."

Her jaw tightened. No. She was Star Eye. She didn't disappear—she burned. She shone. She fought until her last atom defied the dark.

"All is meant to return to the void. Every light, every star, will one day be devoured by the black hole. The darkness will erase every atom of the universe. Including your home world."

He let the words settle, watching her expression—waiting for doubt to take root. But it never did.

Star Eye gritted her teeth. Her voice burned with boldness, her eyes blazing like quasars.

"Never," she spat.

Gronuz chuckled, his abyssal eyes gleaming with cold certainty. "There is nothing a little star like you could ever do to prevent the inevitable. The light is only borrowed, Star Eye. And the void always collects its due."

He savored the moment.

"And as for you, little star. You should be honored…"

He paused, slow and cruel, letting her feel the weight of the words.

"…to be the first of your kind to return to the void."

Every cell in her body screamed that this was wrong, that she should be fighting, running—but there was nowhere to run. The abyss didn't chase. It only waited.

For the first time, she wondered—was this truly the end?

She had fought through war, fire, and destruction—battles she should've never survived. But here, in the abyss's unfeeling grasp, she was nothing. No resistance. No escape. Just a dying ember in a god's hand.

Her energy faded. The black hole pressed into her soul. And for a terrible moment, one thought took hold: What if this time, she couldn't fight back?

Her fingers twitched. Then—curled into fists.

No.

She was not some flickering light waiting to be devoured.

She was Star Eye.

Even if the abyss swallowed her whole, she would burn inside it.

There had to be a way out. There was always a way out.

Ahead, the black hole loomed. A gaping maw devouring light. Spirals of space and time twisted like smeared stars, reality stretched and drawn toward annihilation.

Gronuz stared into the event horizon, his voice like shifting stone. "Consider this a privilege, Star Eye. Few ever glimpse what lies beyond."

Star Eye, teeth gritted and eyes fierce, struggled against his unyielding grasp. "Let me go, and I'll make sure you get a closer look," she spat.

Gronuz chuckled—a deep, reverberating sound that shook the very fabric of space. "Still so bold. Even in defeat," he mocked.

"I'm not defeated," she snarled, her golden flames straining against his hold.

Gronuz grinned, his molten-cracked eyes gleaming with cruel amusement. "No? Then what would you call this?"

A surge of abyssal energy pulsed through his fingers, suppressing her radiance. Star Eye gasped—her glow dimming, her celestial energy struggling against his crushing power.

"I could carry you like this for eternity," he mused, savoring her struggle. "But I have better things to do."

Void energy swirling between his fingers. "So I'll settle for this," he murmured, eyes burning like dying stars. With a swift motion, void-forged chains coiled around her, siphoning her light. She gritted her teeth, struggling against the void pressing into her essence.

Eyes burning with fury, she choked out, "This won't hold me forever!"

Gronuz lifted her effortlessly, turning his gaze toward the black hole. Smirking, voice a dark hymn of triumph, he said:

"It doesn't have to."

With casual, effortless motion, he hurled her into the void.

Star Eye plunged into the blackness, her golden light distorting under the crushing gravitational pull. Her light flared—but the void didn't care. She twisted, flames flaring, but time and space bent around her, warping her movements. The abyss closed in, crushing her resistance. With one final defiant cry, "I AM NOT FINISHED!"—she was gone.

Gronuz watched in silence as the last of her light vanished. He turned her mask over in his hand, something almost resembling respect flickering behind his abyssal eyes. "A shame," he murmured, more to the stars than to himself.

With a dismissive flick, he released the mask into the void. The black hole roared silently, devouring all. His voice, low and satisfied, whispered, "Farewell Star Eye."

The universe held its breath.

The black hole loomed, devouring all. Time bent. Space warped. Stars at the edge flickered in silent mourning.

And there, a single ember against the abyss—Star Eye. She tumbled through the void, her golden light warping, pulled toward oblivion. Alarms blared in her mind. Every atom screamed: Do something.

But panic was not in her nature.

For a moment, fear crept in. This move—the one she swore never to use— was the only choice. She could already feel the unraveling, the heat swelling in her core. "A star does not burn without cost," the warning echoed. To burn at full power was to risk burning out completely. Ragged breath. If she did this, she might not return.

And then, like a whisper from the dark, she remembered.

"You still have a black hole to explore."

Gronuz's taunt. His certainty that she was already lost.

A final journey. A doomed fate.

No. He was wrong.

Her jaw tightened. This is not my final journey.

If she burned out, so be it. If she vanished into the void, so be it.

But she would not let him win.

She shut her eyes.

She reached within.

And she let go.

A detonation of celestial fire erupted—a star reborn in darkness. A shockwave of molten gold tore through space, bending gravity, defying inevitability. The void howled as the explosion thrust her free, leaving her mark on the event horizon. But she didn't stop.

She streaked through the void—a comet of defiance—but her fire wavered. Her body ached. Every cell screamed. This was the cost. This was why it was forbidden.

Just a breath. A warning.

But she did not stop.

Her eyes locked onto Gronuz.

He loomed. His abyssal form swallowing the light, his presence a crushing force.

A god of annihilation.

But she was not afraid.

She rocketed forward—beyond light—and collided with his singularity. A cataclysmic shockwave erupted, space fracturing at their clash. But Gronuz remained unmoved.

He laughed, cold and terrible. "Is that all your light can offer? A spark against the storm?"

She fought, but each strike revealed the truth. Brute force alone wouldn't defeat him. So she adapted, twisting, evading, striking not to break him, but to shift the battlefield. Step by step, she forced him back, closer to the abyss.

"You've flown across galaxies just to flicker and fade? Pathetic."

Gronuz snarled, swinging a monstrous fist—a tidal wave of void energy. She dodged, barely. Her limbs grew heavy, each movement costing more. Her golden fire flared, but flickered at the edges, struggling to sustain itself. And yet—she fought.

I am not the flame that fades, she thought. *I am the fire that endures.*

She halted, hovering above the abyss. Gronuz lunged—fists like collapsing stars—and she did not move. Instead, she raised her hands. Her glow surged brighter. Hotter. A burning light, impossible to contain, burst forth. Her voice rang out, clear and unyielding.

"You wanted my light?"

Her golden fire erupted, enveloping them both.

"Let's see how much you can handle."

She summoned the last of her strength. Her essence blazing like a newborn star. A final, cataclysmic strike—a celestial hammer forged of pure radiant will—descended from on high and collided with Gronuz in a blast that sundered the very air of space.

The impact was apocalyptic.

Gronuz staggered and then slipped. The battlefield tilted toward destiny. The black hole yawned wide behind him, no longer a backdrop but a sentence.

Gravity claimed its due.

The void latched onto him, not with force, but with fate.

He howled—a sound that curdled the stars—as his vast form began to fracture. Armor peeled like scorched flesh. Energy leaked in streams of violet and black. His limbs thrashed, clawing at spacetime itself, fingers raking against the emptiness, desperate to escape the collapse.

But there was no escape. Not this time.

Not from her light. Not from the abyss he had shaped.

"No," he breathed, his energy fracturing like shattered obsidian, his voice splintering. Then, louder, "NO! I AM THE VOID!"

The void did not answer. It only hungered.

For the first time, true fear flashed in his abyssal eyes. His own power betrayed him. The black hole's pull turned against him. His once-mighty shadow collapsing inward. His abyssal form distorted, stretched, shattered. His screams silenced as the gravitational tide devoured him.

And as the last ember of his form vanished into the abyss, Star Eye whispered, her voice soft but steadfast.

"Then vanish into it."

And he did.

Silence.

The battlefield was still. The black hole shuddered, its hunger sated. Star Eye hovered above, watching the last trace of his presence fade. The darkness that had threatened all was now an empty void.

She had won.

The realization was slow to settle, but her body knew. Her shoulders sagged, limbs aching, her golden glow dimming to embers. For the first time in eternity, she let herself breathe.

A pulse of light flared from her heart, rippling across the cosmos—a beacon, a promise.

The universe would remember this day. It would remember her.

The void was quiet. The Cult of the Black Hole was gone. Its followers, once zealots of oblivion, now scattered like ashes on the solar wind.

The sky shimmered in purples and golds as twin suns bathed the lush terrain. Star Eye descended, not as a conqueror, but as a guardian returning home.

The denizens of Zullia Prime, survivors of near-annihilation, gathered in awe—humanoid, crystalline, and beings of pure energy, their gazes filled with more than gratitude. Some whispered her name, others bowed. A child mimicked her stance, their bioluminescent skin flickering in time with her golden light. An elder, draped in shimmering silks, stepped forward and bowed.

"Once again, the light prevails," the elder said. "Because light doesn't break, it endures."

Star Eye smiled, not with the triumphant grin of a warrior, but with quiet warmth and solemnity. The battle was over. But the war? It never truly ended. She exhaled slowly, feeling the weight of past battles. Gronuz was gone. The Cult was broken. But the scars remained.

She turned her gaze skyward. The cosmos stretched endlessly, vast and waiting. A ripple in space shimmered at the edge of perception—familiar, yet unknown. Not danger. Not yet. But something was waiting.

She considered it briefly before smiling. There was always more to do.

Her golden aura ignited once more, streaking into the heavens. A trail of light, a beacon against the void.

She was not just a warrior. She was a promise. A testament that, no matter how deep the abyss, the light would always remain.

Flashback
by Violet E. Geary

The burn in my stomach. The sweat running down my body. The feeling of my muscles hardening every time I push myself just that little bit further. It's one of the only things I've found that can distract me from everything else that runs through my mind. It helps me stay grounded and focused whenever I start spiraling. So much, in fact, that the gym is almost like my second home; bless Antonio for putting up with me for so long.

The bad thing about it being a regular spot is that all the recurring faces in my life know exactly where to find me. That includes the stubborn as hell detective, Shu Li, who's currently making his way towards me. Something in the way he walks tells me this isn't just gonna be about catching up and talking about last night's roller-wreck game. Well, that, and the fact that he and I haven't gotten along ever since I left the force.

"Here we go," I mumble under my breath, loud enough for my ears only.

"Robin," he says, standing above me while I finish my sit-ups.

I don't answer him. If he doesn't have the courtesy to let me finish my set, I don't have the courtesy to give him the time of day.

"We have a case."

"Good for you."

The next time my back hits the mat, I feel a shoe press against my shoulder, holding me there. "Ah! Hey!"

"Don't be a smartass, Flashback." There's no lack of venom in the way he says my nickname. I don't blame him; I hate it too.

"Don't call me that, Shu." I push his foot off of me, making him stumble back as I sit up and look at him. "I told everyone I'm out. What part of that doesn't the Captain understand?"

The scowl I receive in return tells me he's just as unhappy to be here as I am.

He tosses me the small towel that was lying on the workout bench next to me. "You're out for as long as we don't need you." He pauses for a second and sighs, then says, "Now we need you."

Asshole.

I scowl and turn my head away from him. It may have been a little naïve to think someone with an ability like mine could just throw in the…

My eyes drift slowly down to what he just tossed me.

Apparently, the universe has a sense of humor today.

"Pat yourself down, put on a shirt, and get ready. I expect us to be out of here in five. The cruiser's waiting out front." Shu doesn't even wait for an answer before walking off ahead of me.

I know if they're calling me in, it means shit has officially hit the fan. My hands begin to tremble. My breath becomes more shallow and quick. I have to close my eyes and remind myself to steady my breathing as my hands clench and unclench into fists against my leg.

All I can hope for is that it's not as bad as I'm sure it's going to be.

The sound of the engine is the only thing that penetrates the tense, quiet atmosphere of the car ride. Not that I'd choose to have it any other way. I asked if we could stop by my apartment to pick up an actual set of clothes for me, but no dice. Guess he thinks I might be a flight risk, which is honestly a fair assumption. If I didn't think I'd just be picked up again halfway down the block after booking it, then I would be. So, for now, my baggy black crop top, leather jacket, and ripped jeans will have to do.

The bright neon lights of the busier side of town flash through the window as we pass by. It's only going to take us a fraction of the time it would take anyone else because of those police-only street lanes the mayor signed off on a few years ago. Extremely convenient as long as they're kept up to snuff. Almost on cue, we hit a small pothole, causing some of the rain droplets on the car to bounce off onto the road.

My eyes drift up. Clipped to the inside of the passenger sun visor is a picture of Shu, myself, and some of the other cops from the department. I remember that picture being taken not long after I finished my probationary period out in the field. I pretty much got streamlined to detective because of my power, and there wasn't a single person who disagreed with the decision. They all looked at me as an asset and a crime fighter. I constantly wish I could go back to those days before everything got to be too much. But no matter how far I can see into the past, I'll never be able to change it. That's the hardest part.

We pull up to this tall, swanky apartment complex, and it suddenly becomes very apparent why the captain wanted me on this case. The victim must've been someone who was worth something to this city. That's not a very big crowd, so it makes me wonder exactly who this involves.

"You gonna tell me anything about the case?" I ask Shu as we walk into the building, not even trying to shield my brown, textured lob-styled hair from the rain during the short trip from the car to the entrance.

"The victim is Tammy Smith. You might have seen her in some of those skin care commercials, or the newest installment in the *'Sacred Dark'* movie franchise." He hits the button on the elevator, which instantly opens for us.

I scoff as we begin our ascension to the upper floors. "Of course it is."

Shu turns towards me, "Is there a problem with that? Does she not deserve the help of the great Flashba-"

"Oh, piss off, Shu! You know exactly what my problem is!"

My anger only flares hotter when he shakes his head and replies, "Yeah, I have no shortage of answers to choose from."

There was a point in time when I would've gladly taken on any case and treated them all equally. The only problem is, it was only me and a couple of other officers that actually treated each case equally. I learned pretty quickly that the Captain and the rest of the high-ranking officers — no, *politicians*, would be a better word for them — only really gave a shit when it was newsworthy. Shu, myself, and a few of the other officers in that picture were some of the rare cops that wanted to make the city a safer place for everyone, not just the one-percent.

The rest of the elevator ride is passed in bitter silence, which is only interrupted by the 'ding' of the doors as they open to our designated floor. A penthouse suite with not many other units sharing the hallway. I can easily deduce which unit is the one we're heading to, primarily because there's two officers standing guard outside.

As we walk into the apartment, one of them gives me a nod and a quiet, "Detective Styx," as a greeting.

I don't even stop walking. All I say in response is, "It's just Robin now."

One look at the inside of this place is enough to assume just how much money this woman had. That movie franchise she finished filming the latest sequel for is one of the highest-grossing modern-day film series. The living area that the entryway immediately leads into is huge, and a balcony looks over the top of it. Marble floors, glass coffee tables, even a damn chandelier hanging from the ceiling. She got one hell of a payday.

But none of that matters now. Not like she could take any of it with her.

Shu and I make our way over to the white sofa where her corpse is lying in a disorderly supine position. Shock and disgust course through me as I see the discolored, dried-out body of what used to be an up-and-coming star. "How did someone not notice her missing?"

There's a pause, at which I turn to Shu and furrow my brow, waiting for an answer. He lets out a heavy sigh and purses his lips. "She's only been dead for about two hours."

My eyes widen. I look at the corpse again, then back at my used-to-be partner. "This is advanced-stage decay, Li."

"I know that, Styx," he shoots back, annoyed. "Cameras showed her entering the lobby a couple hours ago. Now do you get why you were brought in?"

I do. I really do. It wasn't about who the victim was this time. Well, that was probably still part of it, but not the whole picture. They wanted an anomaly to take down an anomaly. Honestly, looking at this corpse in front of me, I can see why. But that doesn't make me any less angry. It doesn't mean I'm any less frustrated that I have to be the one to come in and mentally screw myself up even more just because I was unlucky enough to develop powers.

"Did you guys even do any detective work yet? Did you work the scene at all?" I ask, and the words come out more accusatory than I intend them to.

"We didn't have time. As soon as the case came across the Captain's desk, he had us put up the tape and sent me to go get you, in person, because he knew you wouldn't pick up your phone."

"Mainly because I said I was done with all this," I snap back.

"Honestly, Robin, with your powers, I wouldn't ever count on being done."

Those words are enough to pull the hairpin on my temper. I grit my teeth and stand up, immediately turning around to get right up into his face, because who the hell does he think he is to dictate what I can do with my life? To decide whether or not I tank what's left of my mental health? To decide whether or not I walk away from all this? "Where the hell do you get off on-"

"I don't," he says sternly, taking a single step towards me, practically pressing our chests together, "but it's not my call. Personally, I think the Captain should leave you alone and let you rot in your own self-pity and let the real detectives do the work, but it doesn't seem like either of us is getting what we want anytime soon."

My nostrils flare. Shu never agreed with my decision to quit the force. He's always held it against me because he can't understand why someone with my abilities wouldn't continue using them for good. To make the city a better place for the people we both swore to serve and protect. But he just doesn't get it.

No one does.

I take a step back, turning my attention to the rest of the room. He wants a real detective? I'll give him a real detective.

There are a few things that stand out almost immediately. If the victim has only been dead a couple of hours, then why is the large potted plant in the corner of the room completely wilted? "Your boys check the cameras for anyone that might've followed her into the building?"

"Yeah," Shu says, "and there was no one. Not only that," he points towards the door, "you need a keycard to get into the room, and there was no forced entry. One of the neighbors heard a struggle that they described as 'a woman screaming'. They called the police right after."

Another interesting point. Could be that she knew her killer. I squint and lean down to take a closer look at the decaying corpse on the sofa. It's obvious that her entire body is in a state of advanced decay, but there's a single point on the front of her neck where the decomposition is worse than the rest of the area. Why?

Despite the lack of forced entry, none of this necessarily seemed planned. There was a struggle that was loud enough to be heard by a neighbor, which seems like a pretty big oversight. So maybe this was an act of circumstance, not premeditation. What if whoever did this wasn't planning on killing Tammy tonight?

I stand up and swivel my head back and forth slowly, scanning the area. If I'm someone who was just planning to come and talk to her, and I'm already here by the time she gets home, what am I doing to pass the time while I'm waiting? I'm not watching TV, because I don't know how thin the walls are. I don't know if someone will notice. But I'm here for a while, so there's one thing I'll need to do at some point in my stakeout.

Eventually, I'm gonna have to get something to eat.

I walk over to the trash can and use a nearby napkin to take out the first wrapper I find. Some sort of protein bar with different nuts and grains. "You, come here and scan this for prints."

The cop I point to comes over with a machine he needs to use two hands to lift. It's essentially a heavy metal square with a scanner on the bottom and a screen on the top. There's a handle on each side of it and, when he gets over to me, he presses a button on the front that produces a small stand so it can be placed over top whatever item it's being used to scan. Gotta say, seeing the DeaNAlysis again makes me miss this job even less. As helpful as instant forensic analysis is, the thing is clunky, weighs a ton, and is just overall a pain in the ass to use.

"Nothing, Ma'am," the officer says once the scan is complete.

"This guy is all over the place," I mutter, deep in thought. Careful enough to not leave prints, but not careful enough to make sure there's no witnesses.

"The captain didn't drag you out here to be a regular detective, Robin." My jaw sets, and I turn back towards Shu. "He dragged you here to be Flashback."

He's right. I know he's right. There's no escaping it. Being 'asked' to come out and help work a case like this one isn't exactly something I can say no to. The Captain of the Navaja City police is not someone you can just ignore. One way or another, he's gonna keep using me until there's nothing left but a numb shell of who I used to be. That part is what frightens me the most. Knowing that I've already changed so much since taking the job as a detective, and that one day I may not even be able to recognize the person staring back at me through the mirror anymore.

I walk back to the center of the room and take one last look at Shu, who, despite his disdain for me, almost looks sorry that he had to be the one to bring me here today.

I close my eyes. I focus on the room itself. My foot taps lightly against the marble floor, and I capture the sound of the echo it produces in my mind. I pay attention to the way the rain outside patters against the large windows on the far side of the room. My hand drops to the arm of the sofa, next to the decayed corpse of Tammy Smith, making sure I study every fiber on the piece of furniture.

When I open my eyes again, they're a bright, misty blue. Not just the irises, but the sclera too. I'm here, in this apartment, two hours earlier. There's no corpse on the sofa. The plant in the corner of the room is lush and green. I take a look around, trying to spot any differences in the immediate surroundings. I can't look upstairs at the balcony, or outside through the windows, because anything not in this room is simply a black void. A space in time I can't reach without coming out of my flashback and refocusing.

My attention is immediately pulled towards the front door, which electronically clicks to signify it's unlocked, and it opens to show Tammy Smith walking into her apartment. Her blonde hair sways behind her. She drops the key card, laughing at herself and shaking her head as a bright smile comes across her face. The door automatically shuts behind her, and I can feel my breath quicken.

"Just go back out," I whisper, knowing she can't hear me, because I'm not actually here right now. But as pointless as it is, I can't help but do it every time. Hoping, praying, that somehow, they hear me. Begging the universe, just this once, to let me make a difference.

"Tammy," a man's voice says, and I turn in time to see someone walking out of the pitch black void where I know the stairs are. It's a tall, bald, skinny man, but his age is difficult to tell. His skin is taut against his body, covered in tattoos, and he appears to be extremely malnourished, practically making him look like a walking skeleton. He's wearing a pair of black gloves.

Tammy startles, letting out a yelp as she runs over towards the coffee table, deeper into her apartment. "Joey?" The fear in her voice is palpable. "Joey, what the hell are you doing here?"

He holds up his hands, "I just came here to talk, baby, I promise."

"We don't have anything to talk about. I told you I didn't want to be with you anymore. Not after what happened with Jen."

"I told you that was a mistake." He sounds aggravated when he says it, but seems like he's attempting to keep his temper under control. "I forgot I didn't have my gloves on, and I just…"

"You can't just chalk it up to a mistake, Joe." She pleads, leaning forward. "She lost her arm!"

Joey glares at her and takes off one of his gloves. Tammy's eyes widen, fear evident on her face. "You know that's not fair. I can't control it," he says and trails his fingertips against the houseplant, making it wither and wilt in real time.

No. No, I really don't wanna see this. I don't wanna be here. My eyes water, my throat becomes dry, my fingertips press into my palm with so much pressure that it feels like they might break. I want to look away so badly. I want to go back. *Please, just let me go back!*

"Joey, get out. Now." Tammy attempts to stand her ground.

"Just run!" I yell out towards her in desperation.

"You think I'm just a freak." His lip twitches, and he starts moving towards her. "That I'm not worth the effort you'd need to put in to make this work. To make *us* work!"

"Joey, stop…" She takes a step back, but trips on the sofa, falling back onto it.

"I've seen your movies. Those makeout scenes! It doesn't show anything, but I still- I know that's what you prefer, huh?! You don't wanna be with me because I can't do that for you! Because I can't touch you! Is that it?!" He stands over her now, looming like the impending death he is.

My adrenaline takes hold of me, and I rush forward, tears welling up in my eyes. "Stop! Just run! Go!" I throw a punch at the man, but it's no use. It goes right through him, and I stumble forward, barely managing to stay on my feet. As I go to try and throw another punch, something stops me. I'm being held back, and all I'm left to do is struggle against the unknown force.

"Well, you're wrong," Joey says as he reaches forward and grabs the front of Tammy's throat.

She screams, and I scream with her. It only takes about thirty seconds until her body is in the state that the police found it in. Discolored and decayed.

All my strength leaves me. What the hell did I just see? What did he do? If it weren't for the force holding me back, I'd have fallen to my knees at the sight of it.

Soon after he realizes what he's done, my eyes track Joey going over to one of the paintings, moving it aside and doing… *something* to it. I can't determine what he's doing. I can't focus. I've already started to dissociate.

The next time I blink, my eyes return to normal. I can't control when I leave my flashbacks, and to me, they don't feel like flashbacks at all. They feel real, like I'm actually there. That's why I can't do this job anymore.

It's just too much for me to handle.

"Robin," Shu says from behind me. I turn, and it's only now I notice that he's holding my arms. That must've been the force I felt holding me back.

But his gaze isn't on me; he's looking towards the painting I saw Joey mess with near the end of the flashback. My head turns, and I feel a shiver run down my spine. The wall is opened up to some sort of safe room, and in the doorway of it, stands Joey. He never left the apartment.

"Hands on your head and turn around!" One of the cops says as they begin to move towards him with their guns ready, walking past Shu and I.

A silent staredown commences between us and the assailant. The cops keep their weapons trained on him. Joey glares in their direction. My heart is beating a thousand miles a minute from the tenseness of the situation. Until finally, Joey breaks the silence. "You're not locking me in a cage for the rest of my life."

As soon as he takes a step towards them, the cops immediately open fire! I cover my ears, and Shu lets go of my arm, dropping me to the ground in order to draw his own firearm and yell, "Cease fire!"

To everyone's horror, all Joey does after being riddled with bullets is crack his neck. "You can't kill me," he says. "I'm already dead."

The assailant rushes forward and, even with his lanky form, punches one of the cops in the chest so hard that they get sent flying back against the opposite wall. They all shoot at him a couple more times to no avail. He immediately rushes towards the next one, and this time, I can see him hold his hand out toward their face.

An anomaly to take down an anomaly.

As much as I hate to admit it, they were right to bring me along.

I scowl at the killer and my eyes flash that same misty blue, but only for a split second. I project a brief moment in Joey's mind of where the cop was standing ten seconds ago, which is enough to make him throw his hand wide and fall forward onto the ground past the officer.

He's not hurting anyone else. No matter how anxious I am, I need to channel all of that into anger, because that's the one thing that will help me take him down without falling apart. This isn't a flashback. This is real. These people are real. For once in my life, I can finally not be too late.

"Everyone go. Secure the perimeter," I say as Joey starts standing back up.

The cops all listen to me, but Shu stares down the sight of his gun for a second longer. "You sure about this, Styx?"

"Go. Call the T.O.P.S. team in," is all I say to him. And it's enough. He heads out the doors with the others, immediately getting on the radio to call in the Tactical Operations Power Security team.

Joey wastes no time and immediately rushes me, throwing a fist towards my head. I quickly dodge below it, throwing a punch of my own into his jaw, which I immediately regret. "Ah! Shit!" I scream.

As he stumbles back, I look down at my hand. Some of the skin has started to recede and turn darker than normal. I can't even hit this bastard without my body deteriorating.

"I didn't want to do it!" he yells at me, putting a hand up to his chest. "I just wanted her to love me again! Like how it used to be!"

I grit my teeth, trying to ignore the agonizing pain in my hand. "That's not something you get to decide, Joey. She was afraid of you, and you proved her right."

"No!" he shouts, then rushes towards me. I project where I was ten seconds earlier into his mind, making his punch go wide. He throws a couple more, and I use the same power again to make him miss another one. The flashes are all I can do to other people, and they only last a couple of seconds, but they're enough to give me an edge.

When he stumbles past me after another missed blow, I reach beside me and grab the nearby coat rack, hoping that he can still at least get knocked unconscious. As I swing for the back of his head, I'm taken off guard when his body evaporates into a cloud of ashes, making my strike pass right through them, and he immediately reforms behind me.

Guess I know how he got into the apartment.

I turn around on instinct alone and manage to hold the rack up in time to block his hand. The wooden piece of furniture instantly starts disintegrating into dust, so I push it, and him, back. This isn't going to work forever. All it takes is one slip-up for him to finish me off. He can turn to dust, so whatever I do, it needs to be quick. One fluid motion. My eyes flick to the left for a split second, then back to Joey.

While he's getting his footing, I sprint across the room, making it look like I'm trying to escape, but really, I just want to get in between him and the coffee table. I can sense his hesitance to rush me as I take off my leather jacket. Luckily, I know exactly what to say to this bastard to get him to lash out. "Tammy was right to leave a freak like you. I bet those other guys made her a lot happier."

Sure enough, that does it.

He lets out a sound that's somewhere in between a cry and a scream as he rushes towards me, and my eyes flash light blue one more time. In the small window I have, I step to the side and trip him. Using my leather jacket as a barrier between my bare hand and his skin, I grab the back of his head on his way down and slam it onto the edge of the coffee table.

My jacket's ruined within a couple of seconds, but it's worth it, because Joey is out like a light.

After only a few minutes, T.O.P.S. shows up and carefully detains the guy. While that's happening, I'm sitting on a nearby chair getting my hand wrapped up. The captain must really wanna stay on my good side, as much as he can, because he's splurging for the regen spray this time. Extremely expensive, but it makes your skin stitch back together without leaving so much as a scar. It needs to be reapplied for a few days, but I should be back in the gym hitting the bag by next week.

Shu walks up to me, signaling at the medic to take a hike, which he does. "How ya feelin'?"

"I'll live," I reply with a shrug. "What are they calling this one?"

"Necrosis." We both roll our eyes. That's one thing he and I still have in common: our dislike for the need for codenames for anomalies. Joey's is Necrosis.

Mine is Flashback. It might as well be a number on a dog tag.

"Y'know Robin, you…" he pauses for a moment, and I raise an eyebrow as he tries to figure out, what I assume will be, a very clever way to call me a reckless moron.

"You did good work tonight."

Okay, maybe I didn't give him enough credit. "Thanks," I murmur.

"And you could keep doing good work. You should really think about coming back."

There it is. That's what he actually wanted to say. He doesn't care about me. He doesn't care about my well-being. At one point, I think he did. No, actually, I know he did. Early on, he and the rest of the department thought of me as a person. I was more than just a tool for the job. But that's just not the case anymore.

I shake my head and hop out of the chair, and all I have to offer my old partner is a look of disgust.

I don't say anything. Neither does he. I just walk out the door. It's only when I get to the elevator, only when the scene of Tammy Smith being necrotized right in front of my eyes plays again in my mind, that I reassure myself of one thing.

"I'm never coming back."

Villainy is for Losers
by Paul Popiel

Erich and Ferez were jogging when The Nice Guy landed gracefully in front of them. He looked smaller than when Erich had seen him as a kid, but bigger than he looked on TV. Whether he'd changed or not, his uniform design was the same, though the colors varied. This time, his muscle-shirt was gold, emblazoned with the Stellar Humanoids United logo. Today his tights were neon green.

"Good day, chums," The Nice Guy said. "Please move to the other side of the street. Soon, this orphanage parking lot will be a battleground." He waited, smile unwavering, until they complied. Then he rose into the air, flew over the orphanage, and landed behind it.

Seconds later, a dumpster hurtled over the building. It slid on its side across the parking lot, leaving deep grooves in the asphalt and punching through the orphanage's playground fence. It kept going, finally crashing into the slide, which fell down on top of it. The whole mass slid ten more feet before stopping against the swing set.

Ferez re-crossed the street to join the crowd gathering outside the playground fence. Erich reluctantly followed.

The Nice Guy landed in front of the dumpster.

"Holy shit," Ferez said. "We get to see a live ass-kicking!"

Howling laughter exploded from the dumpster. "Awesome ride, Nice Guy!"

The Nice Guy's fists clenched. "If I have to pull you out of there, Cannibal Crew, you're going to be sorry." He gently tapped the sliding board with one foot. It flew across the playground and struck a picnic table.

The dumpster's lid opened. A garbage bag hit The Nice Guy's knees and split open, spilling used diapers on his sneakers.

More laughter and trash followed.

"They're gonna get it now," Ferez said.

Erich checked his watch. "We're going to be late for raid night if we don't leave soon. People will join other Assassination Runs if we can't keep our schedule."

"Relax," Ferez said. "Watching The Nice Guy beat up Stellar Humanoid Antagonists is a great excuse."

"I haven't seen any villainous powers," Erich said. "Disintegration Man is a better super villain, and he's made of pixels. These guys are low-power wastes of time."

As if those inside the dumpster had heard his comment, a flurry of bone darts exploded out, hitting The Nice Guy's chest. They put holes in his shirt, but didn't penetrate the skin underneath.

"You'll have to do better than that," The Nice Guy said, "but you're not getting the chance." He lifted the dumpster over his head and shook.

Trash bags rained down, along with two men, who ran in opposite directions. One, wearing a tattered robe that Erich guessed was human skin, headed for the orphanage. He was screaming about the soft flesh inside and his need to devour it. The other man, dressed in red tights covered with tiny bones, fled in the opposite direction.

The Nice Guy flew at the bone-covered man, sweeping him up in a one-armed squeeze.

Human skin robe looked back and ran faster. The Nice Guy flung his captive like a javelin. Bone shards flew everywhere as the two villains tumbled to the asphalt together.

Cheers erupted from the crowd.

Erich fidgeted.

The Nice Guy flew over to where the villains lay. He picked one up in each hand. "Good citizens, these are the last two members of the Cannibal Crew. Soon, Bailey the Bonesaw," he shook the villain covered in broken bones, "and Arthur the Child Devourer," he shook the man in the now tattered and torn skin robe, "will join their compatriots in the Alcatraz-Two Space Prison."

The orphans rushed onto their porch and cheered.

The crowd roared its gratitude.

"Games like the World of Villainy make evil look attractive, but the reality for most super villains is a life spent staring into the vastness of space, contemplating where they went wrong. Kids, do you remember The Nice Guy's Number One Rule?"

"Villainy is for Losers!"

To Erich, it seemed like he was alone in not shouting the answer back. Even Ferez had done so.

"That's right, kids!" The Nice Guy waved, then flew away.

"Really?" Erich said. "You love The Nice Guy, too?"

Ferez clapped him on the back. "And you've defeated how many Stellar Humanoid Antagonists?"

"I'm a virtual super villain."

"Sure you are, dude. Does that mean one day you'll end up in a virtual space prison?"

Erich stopped walking. "A prison in World of Villainy? When? In the next update?"

Ferez just laughed and started walking.

They logged into the game mere minutes before the Assassination Run began.

Erich was eager to start, but he had to endure Ferez's retelling of their encounter with The Nice Guy. When that was finally over, they got down to the villainous business of invading the Zillionaire's mansion and taking him down.

Sidekick after sidekick met bloody doom at the hands of Erich's character, Disintegration Man, and his pack of vile comrades. Finally, only the Houseman stood between them and the final boss, Arty Prescott Sherman, aka The Zillionaire, a mighty hero and the Legion's last, greatest foe in the game, at least until the next update. Even now, the Houseman was faltering under sprays of cold and fire from Disintegration Man's team.

"We've got him!" Disintegration Man yelled. "Just a few thousand more life points!"

Brawlverina stopped her deadly pirouette long enough to shout, "Less talk, more punch!"

It wasn't a good line, but hey, anyone whose character was a human-wolverine hybrid in a ballerina costume had more problems than shitty dialogue.

Erich's witty post-boss beat-down remarks had helped him become Assassination Run leader. That and his ridiculously high damage rate. This was the first time they'd be taking down the Zillionaire, so it was special. He muted his microphone and said his line again. "Enjoy the poorhouse, Zillionaire!"

"Yo, d-man," Sonic Assassin yelled, "you lagging? We need your head in this fight."

"Sorry," Disintegration Man said. "I'm here." He fired off a volley of sizzling purple beams from his eyes that caused black dust to fall from the Houseman's animated form, along with a significant reduction in lifepoints.

The Houseman roared and threw a giant silver teapot at him in retaliation.

Disintegration Man watched his life points dwindle towards zero as he desperately tried to escape the pool of boiling oolong tea at his feet. His skin turned bright red, and steam rose from his body. He couldn't, wouldn't fall now, not when the Houseman was so close to defeat. "Blue nips, I need healing!"

A blast of cold froze the tea at his feet. A torrent of icy water poured over him, cooling his body and covering him in healing vapors. His life meter shot up to half full.

"Next time you call me that, you dust-making dickwad, I'll let you die!" It was kind of weird to hear Ferez's deep voice emanating from a curvy, blue woman made of ice, with clouds of white frost for clothing.

"Thanks, Freez-ya-Solid," Disintegration Man said.

"Thank me later. The Houseman needs to die now, or he's gonna call a security team."

"Pour it on!" Disintegration Man shouted. "He's done for!"

Seconds later, The Houseman gave a final shudder. "Zillionaire, avenge my death!"

Disintegration Man rushed forward, wanting to put the finishing move on The Houseman. These violent, bloody, end-of-encounter scenes were one of the reasons The Nice Guy warned people away from World of Villainy. When Erich hit the right combination of keys, Disintegration Man's Finisher would melt the flesh from The Houseman's bones while the sidekick screamed and thrashed in agony. Finally, the Houseman's bones would crumble into dust and blow away.

He reached the Houseman's body, but when he pressed the first key, a message flashed on the screen: "Finisher Already in Progress." A yellow circle appeared on the ground, surrounding both Disintegration Man and The Houseman.

"Shit! Shit!" This was the problem with an all-villains game; there was no safety for anyone caught in Finishing effects. He closed his eyes and tore off his headphones, but even still, the electronic death cry of Disintegration Man reached his ears.

Erich took a deep breath and opened his eyes. Disintegration Man's ghostly form stood before the Death Angel. In one bony hand, she held a red cross, in the other a glowing tombstone. If he pressed the cross, he'd go back into the Zillionaire's mansion to rejoin the fight, but he'd be at half health and do minimal damage for the first three minutes. If he pressed the tombstone, he'd teleport to the Legion house, where he could watch the rest of the battle. His hand shook as he hovered the cursor over the Lasarize-me button. "They need you in there." He pressed the red cross. Messages appeared on his screen:

Resurrection Request Denied.

You have been removed from the group by King Nilbog.

Translocating to Legion Housing.

"You bastards, you went on without me!!"

Erich sat down at the table with his cereal. "Last night was a total Legion charter violation! As Team Leader, I always get first dibs on finishing."

"I agree with you." Ferez chomped on an English muffin. "But there were last-minute drop-outs. We had to fill their spots with non-Legion players."

"Were you in charge of that? Cause your name is Blue Nips permanently if so."

"Typical. You want all the Assassination Run leader's glory but never do any of the real work. Maybe we should leave filling the roster to you next time."

"Sorry. Who is this King Nilbog joker anyway?"

"He's a new Legion member. Trollmaster Joel said he might let him replace Merciless Marcelline since she'd been gone for a while."

"She's got classes and an internship this semester, which takes up most of her time."

"You two played together a lot. Wasn't your arena team ranked third out of our whole server? I remember tons of laughs and jokes from you when she was around. Why didn't you—"

Erich stirred his cereal, avoiding looking at Ferez. "I ran out of time."

"It happens." Awkward silence settled over the table. "Check out King Nilbog's stats, he's pretty incredible."

"Oh great, a rock star," Erich said. "I love him already."

"No one's asking you to have his babies. He said he knew the Zillionaire fight, so when you went down, we let him take the lead to test him. He waited until right before we attacked to kick you, which was a total dick move. You'll find him in the militarized zone at some point. Frag him there a few times, you'll feel better."

"Disintegration Man isn't optimized for player versus player; all his wonderful toys are set for taking down heroes in assassination mode."

"Yeah, and Nilbog's a hybrid. You know, that build you refuse to acknowledge."

"They're overpowered! It breaks the game."

"I don't have time to argue this again. The news said the city council wants The Nice Guy to pay for the damage he caused catching the Cannibal Crew."

"God, how lame is it that the only nemesis for The Nice Guy is the city council?"

"Yeah," Ferez said, "because he captured all the real villains years ago. It's not—"

Erich aggressively dropped his spoon into his empty bowl. "I'm gonna go see if my stats updated from last night's fight."

A few seconds after logging into the game, a voice chat request popped up. It was King Nilbog. Erich accepted. "I hope you're going to apologize."

"You know what 'Armor of the Zillionaire' is?"

"Only one of the rarest items in the game!"

"That was my loot from last night. Problem is, my color scheme's green, and the armor is black. It's worth a million credits if you sell it to a vendor. I decided I'd rather have the money."

Erich's teeth ground together. "Your villainy, King Nilbog, knows no bounds!" The words were out of his mouth before he could stop himself.

"Ha! I might use that as a catchphrase. See you later, chum."

King Nilbog selling an item Erich had lusted after haunted the long, boring hours of his workday. He logged on when he got home and started a chat with Ferez.

"I'm telling you," Ferez said, "no way he vendored it. He can use it on any character he creates, once they reach the right power level."

"I'm tracking good old King Nilbog right now."

"You said Disintegration Man wasn't optimized for PvP."

"But one of my other characters, Destruct-o-Nator, is. Once King Nilbog crosses over into the militarized zone, I'm taking him down. I've been watching him for a while now. Time for vengeance."

"Dude. Remember Fleet Cheetah? She moved servers to get away from your reprisal attacks."

"There's no way to prove that," Erich said. "She killed me like a hundred times when I was weaker. When I was finally stronger, I had to take revenge. Besides, this was your idea."

"I meant when you found him by accident, not stalking him. Maybe King Nilbog and Fleet Cheetah are run by the same person, and this is their revenge. You get too mad over shit in this game, just relax."

Erich laughed. "Villainy's in the title, what's the fun if you can't commit some without fearing comeuppance?"

"Isn't villainy what you're accusing Nilbog of?"

"I'm leaving chat. I want silence so I can revel in his death cries." Erich stalked King Nilbog until he found the perfect ambush site. "Here we go."

Destruct-O-Nator clenched his oversized fists in preparation for a massive sneak attack on the green half-pint below him. Erich initiated his character's Electric Lash, pulling King Nilbog onto the roof and stunning him for a few seconds, allowing Destruct-O-nator to bypass his defenses and inflict massive damage.

King Nilbog collapsed onto the rooftop.

Erich hit another key, and the message he'd typed earlier appeared on the screen.

"Regards from Disintegration Man."

The tiny green man's corpse vanished, leaving behind a skull with a lit fuse.

"You bastard," Erich said. "No one uses Death Bombs anymore!"

Destruct-O-Nator jumped off the roof, but he was still in the explosion's blast radius. He managed to survive, with barely any life points. Erich activated Destruct-O-Nator's Victory Dance. He'd barely started celebrating when the building collapsed on top of him.

Erich stared at the Death Angel for a few moments before logging out.

"Who is this guy?" Erich asked. "They took Death Bombs off the loot tables last update."

"You can still make them if you put points into Projects for Villainy," Ferez said. "But the materials are a pain to acquire."

"I don't care how they're made. Can't wait for the Assassination Run tonight!"

"Didn't King Nilbog tell you we moved it to tomorrow? He said he'd message you."

"I guess it slipped his mind." Erich tried to keep calm. "Why?"

"So we don't have to leave The Nice Guy Defense rally early. You're coming right?"

"I guess."

"Don't forget to wear something with The Nice Guy's logo to show your support."

"Ok." Erich wasn't going to dig through his closet to find something. They'd have stuff down at the rally that he could wear, use, or hold. But when Ferez got home, he made such a big deal about it that Erich finally relented.

During Erich's search, a box tumbled out of his closet. The tape split, and a pile of shirts with The Nice Guy's logo spilled out.

Ferez grabbed the box. "These are vintage! Why not wear one of these?"

Erich snatched the box out of Ferez's hands. "They don't fit anymore. Plus, I'm tired of everyone demanding I be a fanboy of The Nice Guy."

Ferez shrugged. "When a reporter asks why you're not wearing something with his logo, you're on your own."

They walked down to the rally in the parking lot of the Stellar Humanoid United headquarters. A ton of people were already there, pressing up against the stage. Ferez pushed through the crowd, trying to get closer to the front before the rally started.

Erich watched the empty stage, feeling bored and a little embarrassed to be there.

Ferez busied himself with something on his phone. "Hey, Merciless Marcelline's here."

"How do you know?" Erich asked.

"World of Villainy app. You don't have it?"

"It's too intrusive." Erich downloaded the app, setting it so that only other Legion members could see his location. He waited for Marcelline's dot to appear. "Do you see her?"

"She's on the edge of the parking lot."

Erich tried to move out of the crowd, but no one would let him by. "Where is she now?" Erich's phone chimed with a message. He read it. "She can't get to us. Lot's at max capacity. She'll find us during the Legion meet-and-greet at VillainyCon. She got VIP tickets, just like we did." Before he could think too much about it, he sent her a picture of himself.

"Cool," Ferez said, but there was something wrong with his tone.

"Ferez, why don't you sound thrilled?"

He sighed. "I had to sell the tickets. I needed this month's rent, and when I asked you to pay your share, you gave me a bunch of excuses. So they're gone."

Erich clenched his fists so tight his nails dug into his palms. "Before Merciless Marcelline, I wouldn't have cared. You should've said something before you sold them. No one's going to sell their tickets now."

Applause deafened Erich as The Nice Guy descended from the sky. He wore his normal outfit of a muscle shirt and tights, but today they were purple and red.

"Holy shit," Ferez said, "we're like twenty feet away."

"Don't wet your pants, Freez-ya-Solid, no one likes pee-sicles."

Someone in the crowd shushed them as The Nice Guy began to speak.

"I appreciate, fair citizens, your outpouring of support. With the Cannibal Crew's capture, our city is free of Stellar Humanoid Antagonists. While super-crime is at an all-time low, regular crime continues, as do accidents. Sometimes, while protecting you, I've caused damages. The city council wants me to pay for repairs, but pays me nothing for my services. Is that fair?"

"No!" the crowd shouted.

"Should I have gotten a bill for the crater of the meteorite that struck me and the others all those years ago?"

"No!"

"Super-crime won't stay vanquished forever. Should I defend you, or work at Office Supplies Unlimited to pay the city council? I think I know which you'd choose."

Crowd handlers formed lines so that fans could shake The Nice Guy's hand, get an autograph, or even a selfie. Erich didn't want those, but Ferez did, so he waited in line too, checking the app occasionally to see if Marcelline was any closer. It showed him nothing but a blank screen. He asked Ferez, who said it was a known bug. Erich cursed and restarted his phone.

They were a few people away from stepping onto the stage when Erich's phone beeped. He checked, hoping it was a message from Marcelline, but instead it was a notification that King Nilbog was nearby. Erich saw his dot, with Ferez's right next to him, and then a green dot that was King Nilbog directly in front of them, somewhere in the crowd around The Nice Guy. Before he could show Ferez, someone jostled him. His phone fell to the asphalt and bounced under the stage.

The Nice Guy hopped down and lifted up the platform so Erich could retrieve his phone. "I hope it's not broken, chum. I'm lost without mine."

"I'll send you the bill if it stops working." It seemed like Erich had been called chum a lot lately. He didn't really like it.

The Nice Guy laughed, then set the stage down. "Send the city council a copy, too. Now, excuse me, my fans are waiting."

Ferez got his autograph, handshake, and selfie a few minutes later.

On the way home, while his friend yakked about the experience, Erich was lost in thought. That laugh had seemed very familiar…

Disintegration Man paced in front of Merciless Marcelline's darkened alcove in their Legion Hall. The curves of her leather armor were visible, even if all the little screaming faces on it and the two skeletal hands that clutched her breasts were lost in shadow. Her twin blades still shone, but they were tucked under her forearms, not extended into killing position. The longer Marcelline's player was away from the game, the darker her character's alcove became.

"You miss her, don't you?" King Nilbog said from behind Disintegration Man. "I've been in this Legion only a short time, and I find your character here a lot. Or maybe you're one of those people who leave the game running to up your 'Time Played' score?"

"Unless it says AFK over my head, I'm not. And you can't up your stat like that anyway."

"Relax, I'm just kidding."

Disintegration Man saluted Merciless Marcelline's dark form and headed for the scenario rooms. King Nilbog followed.

Erich muted his mic and yelled into the other room for Ferez to get on. Five minutes later, the tall, ice-blue woman stood alongside King Nilbog and Disintegration Man.

Sometimes Erich enjoyed watching his character's idle animations while waiting for the Legion to gather, so he sat back and let Disintegration Man go through his. They mostly consisted of destroying small objects on the floor and walls.

Freez-ya-Solid hardly ever stood still, preferring to jump around and fill the room with icy fog or practice her dance moves. Her idle animation consisted of fading frost clouds, though they always stopped short of giving a glimpse of the body underneath them.

King Nilbog picked his nose, scratched his neck, and other, less polite places.

Once the Assassination Run got going, the Zillionaire's guards and the Houseman fell faster than usual. Erich refused to believe it was because his Legion was trying to impress King Nilbog.

Now, finally, Erich would get to participate in a take-down of the Zillionaire.

The first few phases went very well. The villains countered the Zillionaire's special attacks with the right combination of force and deflection, steadily draining his lifepoints away until only a few thousand remained.

The Zillionaire could do one of two things in his last phase. The first would be to die and drop loot that the triumphant team would divide.

The second was a lot cooler. It didn't occur that often, maybe on one out of every five kills. The Zillionaire would vomit a stream of coins that characters could claim. It was nicknamed the Pay Spray. Disintegration Man hadn't ever seen it. Until now.

He stepped into the flow of coins along with the rest of the group. A treasure bag appeared on the screen. Erich clicked on it. The bag opened, and Erich was pleased to see a big gold coin that read '2000 Credits.' His happiness was short-lived. As he watched, the number shrank to one. "What the fuck? Ferez, is your treasure—"

"Being stolen? Yeah."

"Who's doing it? It's King Nilbog, isn't it?"

"It's an ability called 'loot suck.' It takes a random amount of money, but you get double that amount in bonus experience. I lost seventy-five. You?"

Erich could barely speak. "One thousand, nine hundred and ninety nine."

"That blows! At least you've got extra experience."

"Which would be great, if I wasn't maximum level. I guess once the next expansion comes, I'll be ahead. I only have to wait a year."

"Ouch!"

"But at least we'll get to know what the release will be, since we have tickets, right?"

"Damn it, Erich, I told you I'd try to replace them."

"Hang on, time for my one-liner!" Erich tapped the leader announcement key, then said, "Enjoy the poorhouse, Zillionaire!"

Chat erupted into laughter.

"D-man, that's really funny!" Sonic Assassin said. "King Nilbog said something like that the last time."

Erich managed to keep the hate out of his voice somehow. "That's pretty clever of him. However, I'm not a big fan of people who steal from the team."

"Bad luck, chum." King Nilbog laughed. "You don't have to be so grim all the time."

Erich ripped off his headphones. Sure, he was a bit pissed about the whole losing credits thing and even angrier about the whole Legion mocking him. But King Nilbog's laugh was definitely familiar. And if he was right, then he had a way to pay that bastard back for everything he'd done.

Erich hid around the corner of the Stellar Humanoids United headquarters and watched The Nice Guy lock the door.

"I can see through walls, chum, might as well come out."

Erich stepped out. "Hello, Nice Guy, or should I say King Nilbog? And before you start denials, know that I've done my research. I have the World of Villainy app on my phone, and it shows two characters here, Disintegration Man and King Nilbog."

The Nice Guy's face showed no emotion or sign of stress. "Don, our public relations man, is still inside. Maybe he's playing."

"Nope. It's you. Your laugh and King Nilbog's are the same, and he calls me chum, just like you. I've listened to your voice all my life. And before you threaten me, I know you won't kill me. Think how disappointed the kids will be when they learn that The Nice Guy gets his kicks not just playing World of Villainy but is one of the best players in the game."

"You're pretty good. Not on my level, but we can't all be champs, can we, chum?"

"Hey, I was slaying heroes long before you came along with your Death Bombs and your disregard for the rarest armors in the game. Not to mention your complete lack of Assassination Run etiquette."

"I started because I saw our intern playing one night when we had a late meeting. Look, I admit you've got me. What you know would harm my reputation, probably, but it wouldn't last too long before some crisis had me back on top."

"Maybe. But you forget that three members of the city council are on the Stop Video Game Violence committee. And let's face it, you haven't exactly been supportive of a game where villains kill heroes. They'll call you a hypocrite or worse if they find out. Probably tie you up in meetings for years, maybe even get you voted out of the city."

"Ok, so you could cause me PR nightmares. I hope you thought this through, chum. What do you want to keep quiet?"

"First, two VIP tickets to VillainyCon."

"I'm a hero, how do you expect me to get those?"

"I'm sure King Nilbog could find a way."

"Next? And you're trying my patience with more than one thing, you know."

"Whatever. I want King Nilbog to retire. That's for the bullshit you pulled both times we fought the Zillionaire."

The Nice Guy sighed. "I'll be in touch about the tickets."

It surprised Erich that The Nice Guy gave up so easily, but he was so excited he'd actually beaten him, he didn't think twice about it.

"As for quitting WoV, can I play a low-level villain, maybe someone who can use that Armor of the Zillionaire eventually?"

"You didn't really vendor it?"

"No. I was messing with you."

"Maybe, King Nilbog, you're not as bad as I thought."

The Nice Guy smiled. "One day I might be as tricky as you, Disintegration Man."

A short week later, Erich stood at the entrance to the grand ballroom where they were holding the Legion meet-and-greet. He inhaled deeply. "Can you smell the villainy, Ferez?"

"Yeah, if it smells like off-brand hot dogs and rancid nacho cheese."

"Shut up. Don't ruin my moment. Once I meet Merciless Marcelline, it'll be a whole new phase of life. I sent her a picture, but never got one back. Hope that's not a bad sign."

"It's good you're not putting too much pressure on things," Ferez said. "Our section's over there."

Erich could barely contain his excitement as he approached the table. He saw some people he knew from prior conventions, but no Marcelline.

Then someone's hands covered his eyes, and a voice he knew said, "Guess who?"

He turned around, and then she was hugging him tight. Her smile lit him up inside like no sexy villainess ever had.

For the next two hours, they pretty much ignored everyone else, spending time getting reacquainted and learning more about each other. When they left the room with Ferez in tow, they did it hand in hand. Erich didn't ever want to let go. Marcelline invited Ferez to join them for dinner, but he wisely declined and joined another group from their server.

They'd just gotten off the escalator in the mall when Marcelline suddenly squealed and launched herself at a man standing a few feet away, wrapping him in a huge hug. Erich wondered if he'd missed a signal somewhere, but as he joined them, he realized the man was old enough to be her father.

"This is Erich," Marcelline said, taking his hand again. "He plays the game like I do. Erich, this is my Uncle Bill. You might know him as The Nice Guy."

"Hello, chum." Uncle Bill shook Eric's hand.

Erich smiled, but he was seething inside. Fooled again! He waited while Marcelline chatted with her uncle, even agreeing that he could join them for dinner.

Uncle Bill clapped Erich on the shoulder. "That's ok. There's plenty of time for us to get acquainted, right chum? I might even try this game you two play. What did you say his villain's name was, Disintegrating Man?"

Erich waved goodbye to Uncle Bill and walked on with Marcelline, but all the while he was thinking, "Truly, King Nilbog, your villainy knows no bounds."

Nobody
by Kay Hanifen

To many, I'm the villain of this story. Not because I kill people or create world-destroying weapons or extort the city for millions. No, it's because I have the balls to stand up to the real bad guys. Don't get me wrong. I have the utmost respect for my colleagues in the Tower of Justice. I'm a card-carrying member and use their facilities at almost every opportunity. They do good work protecting the world from danger. But I live in the homeless encampment off 29th Street, and I have been there for the past three years. In that time, the encampment had been raided by police at least twice a month, maybe more. At least, it was until I got my powers last year. Then, the people just trying to survive had a chance of fighting back. It's a lot harder for cops to bully a community when its protector is bulletproof and sets things on fire with her mind.

Naturally, the cops don't like me very much, but as one of the Tower, they can't do much about me. I'm a member of the cape and cowl crowd, and I protect the weak from the strong. Who is more vulnerable than someone without a roof over their head? They may just be doing their jobs, but so am I.

I'm doing my job when I "steal" the food waste from grocery stores and fast food restaurants that would have otherwise been thrown out and distribute it to the hungry. I'm doing my job when I buy immigrant families enough time to escape the ICE agents who show up at their door. And I'm doing my job when I protect the ones working the streets from dangerous cops, pimps, and johns alike.

Occasionally, the Tower will protest a little, but they've never revoked my membership, and even the most powerful heroes have given me the occasional pat on the shoulder and quietly voiced their approval of what I do.

I got my powers when several other heroes got theirs. The alien invasion of a year ago left behind a kind of mutagenic bioweapon, one that rewrote the DNA of anything it came into contact with. For most, the rewritten DNA just created a fast-acting cancer, but there was a one-in-a-million chance that you would develop superpowers. I was that one.

A year later, my transformation haunts my nightmares. I had just turned eighteen and was rejected from an LGBT youth homeless shelter when the sky filled with spaceships. I stood on the sidewalk with all my possessions in a bag and just gaped. A part of me welcomed the invasion. If I was killed by aliens, then I wouldn't have to worry about what I was going to do or where I was going to sleep that night. Morbid, I know, but I was at my lowest.

Then, the bottoms of the ships opened up, and a strange substance splashed around me like raindrops. All around me, people screamed, covering themselves and racing to shelter. It took a moment for me to register the stinging on the skin of my hands and the top of my head. I glanced down at the back of my bare hand, staring in detached fascination at the iridescent mutagen. The shimmering colors reminded me a bit of an oil puddle in a parking lot—oddly beautiful despite the circumstances.

Then the agony set in.

Imagine, for a moment, that every single nerve in your body, from the tips of your fingers to the deepest part of your gut, lit up at once. It was like I was burning and freezing and starving and full and at the peak of pain and pleasure. The sensory experience was so overwhelming that I lost control of my muscles and collapsed in a seizure.

I woke to a war zone. Above me, fighter jets and flying supers battled in the sky. Around me, people screamed and fled to the city's underground emergency shelters. I'm lucky that I wasn't trampled in the panic. After all, who cares about a random homeless trans person at the end of the world?

My parents were religious. They might have said that I was one of the very few who gained powers for a reason—a higher calling. I don't know if this is true or not, but I do know what I chose.

I staggered to my feet just as an invading spaceship fell from the sky. The creature that crawled out was humanoid in the same way that the minotaur was humanoid—bipedal, with massive horns and long, sharp tusks. When it saw me, it growled and stomped a foot like a bull about to charge. It held a massive club in one hand and had a kind of ray gun at its hip.

I glanced over my shoulder at the homeless shelter. Teenage faces lurked in the windows. Either they were too afraid to escape to one of the city's bomb shelters, or they were turned away. Regardless, I was the only thing standing between them and an alien minotaur hellbent on conquering the planet.

The thought of it filled me with rage. The shelter had turned me away because they were too full, and I was too old. It sucked, and on any other day, I would have resented them for it. But today, when I glanced over my shoulder at those kids, all I felt was protectiveness. They didn't deserve to be abandoned by their parents and thrust into a system that would sooner see them dead than thriving. It wasn't fair. Nothing was fair.

But I had this feeling deep in my gut that I could make it fair. The world vibrates on a frequency no human being could ever hope to understand. And when particles vibrate too quickly, they create fire. Now, *I* was vibrating with incandescent rage, an anger directed solely at the alien standing before me.

The alien seemed confused when I didn't back down or run away. It was even more confused when I instinctively raised my hands with my fingertips forward like Emperor Palpatine in *Star Wars*. And then a stream of fire shot from my hands.

It hit the invader dead in the chest, the flames catching on the blue-black fur. Letting out a guttural scream, it flailed about as the fire consumed it. Cheers and yelling muffled by windows resounded behind me. I turned around.

The nearest bomb shelter was five blocks away. After the very first alien invasion, the city had resolved to put a bomb shelter on every block. But this was a poor community, one that barely got funding to fill the gaping potholes that covered the streets. We were lucky to even have one shelter in the area.

I did a quick mental calculus of the distance and the number of teens and caregivers gathered at the homeless shelter's doors. Now that the mutagenic rain had stopped, we would only have to dodge debris and invaders.

"Come on!" I yelled. "I'll take you to the nearest shelter."

That's how I led thirty kids around my age and five adults through the city streets. Sometimes, it's easier to protect others than it is to protect yourself. If I was alone out there, I probably wouldn't have cared if I was killed, but I wasn't. I was leading a crowd of people through five blocks of a war zone with nothing but my newly discovered fire powers and some backpacks to shield our heads.

As we moved, I found that tapping into the flames grew easier and easier. Any alien that got too close was blasted from the sky or burnt to a crisp on the ground. Finally, we reached the last block…

Only to discover a fierce battle raging between one of the supers — Elemental — and one of the leaders of the invaders. Elemental was a mid-level hero — one who can fly and punch things really hard but was incapable of leveling a city with a sneeze. You could tell that she was battling a leader because, unlike the soldiers, this one was bothering to translate its villainous monologue as it fought.

I glanced at the crowd and then back to the fight. With a jerk of my head, I signaled for them to take shelter in the alley nearby and then cautiously approached the battle. Elemental was one of the heroes who refused to take a life, not even that of their worst enemy. After the invasion, I also adopted the code because the guilt of killing sentient beings does weigh on my conscience, but that day, we weren't catching criminals (or stopping cops from behaving criminally, for that matter). We were protecting our planet.

"You think you can defeat us?" the invader ranted. "Your species is nothing. A stain on this resource-rich planet. And you will—"

I shot a stream of flames from my hands, catching it in the back. Like with the other minotaurs, the fire burned quickly, engulfing it in an inferno. Elemental's eyes widened in shock, and she glanced behind the invader to meet my gaze.

"Who are you?" she asked.

"Someone who needs help getting these people to shelter," I replied, gesturing to the people hiding in the alleyway.

"I'll protect you from the sky. You keep them safe from anyone who manages to break through," she said decisively as she spotted a group of invaders on their flying chariots approaching from behind. There was another group ahead, trying to box us in. And then she was off, flitting through the air like a hawk chasing prey.

I did as she said, blasting every one that fell to earth before they could get close to hurting my charges. Finally, we reached the shelter.

The door was locked.

It wasn't supposed to be locked. The handles were supposed to read human handprints and let us through. Above us, one of the chariots exploded, and several of the teens cried out.

"How do I get this open?" I shouted up at Elemental.

She punched out the last of the invaders coming for us and landed on the ground. "Right, they added a passcode."

"To an emergency shelter? Seriously?" I nearly screeched.

"Apparently, the city didn't like that the homeless were using them unnecessarily," she replied bitterly as she opened a disguised panel, punched in the code, and opened the door. "Believe me, we fought them on it."

"Clearly not hard enough," I muttered before stepping behind her and shooting a blast of pure fire at an invader trying to sneak up on her.

She blinked, surprised. "Thanks."

"Don't mention it. Just tell me the code, and I'll try to get more of the neighborhood into the shelter."

Her eyebrows shot up. "You're not going with them?"

I shook my head, already heading down the block. "No. Not while I can still help. There's a homeless encampment on 29th Street. The last invasion, half of them were killed because they didn't have anywhere to hide, and they're the last anyone thinks of when disasters happen. So, I'm going there next."

Elemental quickly caught up to me. "I'll come with you. Watch your back." She smiled warmly. "I can tell that you're new to this, but I think you'd make a great addition to the Tower. Do you have a name?"

"Superhero name or...?" I asked, suddenly conscious of my stubble and Adam's apple combined with my thrift store dress.

She shrugged. "Any."

"My name is Calypso," I said. "I literally got my powers an hour ago, so I haven't even thought about having a codename or even becoming a hero. I mean, look at me. I'm nobody." Nobody. I liked the sound of that one. Maybe if I decided to keep up with this hero thing…

"It took me time to come up with mine," she said. "But you should know that you have something special in you, something rare. There aren't many people who would do what you did by bringing all those kids to the shelter. You're exactly the kind of person that the Tower needs." She handed me a business card. "Think about it. Once the invasion is over, give us a call."

I did think about it. After we brought the people living on 29th street to the shelter, and then after the invasion, I thought for a week straight. Then, even as the city was rebuilding after this disaster, the police raided the encampment again, and I made up my mind and called her. Elemental—real name, Elena Perry—vouched for me, allowing me to join the Tower of Justice under the codename Nobody.

Because that's just what I am: a nobody. I was just a homeless trans teenager and through sheer luck, wound up with superpowers instead of super cancer. If I'm murdered tomorrow, the police would rule the case NHI—No Human Involved—and write me off, another dead city rat. But even though I could live in the Tower, I choose to stay living on the streets.

They say that Nobody cares about the most vulnerable populations, that Nobody will stand up to cops, and a city that would rather see its homeless dead than safe, that Nobody will protect the weak.

Well, I'm Nobody.

When We Could Still Fly
by Paulie Wenger

George Reeves's suit fit just fine. Sure, it itched and smelled faintly of mothballs on a hot summer day, but that didn't matter much to Clyde Mercer as he slipped it on. He liked to tell himself he wasn't sentimental. Hell, you couldn't afford to be when your life revolved around buying and selling other people's treasures. But the suit…the suit was different.

From the moment it arrived at Heritage Treasures Auction House, Clyde knew he wasn't going to let it go. Not without taking it home first. It was a dull blue and red now, the colors faded by time, but the stitched "S" on the chest still shone with a stubborn kind of pride. This was the suit that had made George Reeves famous in the 1950s, turning a struggling character actor into a caped hero for a generation of kids who needed to believe someone could be that good, that strong.

Even now, as an old man, Clyde could remember sitting cross-legged in front of the TV, waiting patiently for the newest episode with the kind of reverence most boys saved for ballplayers. His mother had even sewn him his own costume once, pieced together from the scraps of last year's church clothes, red and blue like he had seen on the show. It was the best gift he had ever gotten.

He could still picture himself at eleven years old, flying down the block on his six-speed, cape flapping behind him, just as Josie Delvecchio, the prettiest girl on the street, looked up from her front stoop. For a moment, he really felt like he could lift the world.

"Nice suit, Mercer!" Josie called out, hopping onto her bike to join him. "Maybe my mom can make you a warrior princess next."

Josie had moved to Cottonwood Heights from Queens two years earlier, and she'd been Clyde's best friend ever since. She was short, even for an eleven-year-old, with a mop of brown curls that half-covered her scrunched-up, perpetually amused face. Her dad worked for a pittance at the local furniture moving company, so she spent most afternoons at Clyde's house, watching reruns and eating whatever snacks his mom left out.

"More like the guy with the gadgets," Clyde shouted with a grin as he pedaled ahead. "You can be my sidekick!"

The two of them raced past the rundown McCainly house, which they'd once solemnly declared the "Fortress of Evil," and veered onto the narrow dirt path that ran beside the cornfield on the way to the comic book stand. They were deep in conversation about what the next season of the show might bring, caught up in their own little world of heroes and sidekicks.

Maybe that's why they didn't see the villains.

Louie Limer was four years older than Clyde and Josie, but he might as well have been in college the way he treated them. He wore a battered brown leather jacket stitched with old war patches, slicked his hair back with grease, and always smelled faintly of gasoline and cigarettes. His jeans and short-sleeved shirt hung off him like a uniform for trouble.

Clyde and Josie barely had time to skid their bikes to a stop when they turned the corner and saw Louie standing dead-center in the trail, flanked by the Jones brothers, Obbie and Oscar, two stocky twins who did whatever Louie told them to do.

"Well, well, who do we have here?" Louie sneered, stepping forward with a slow, deliberate swagger. His eyes flicked to Clyde's homemade costume and lit up with cruel amusement.

"Playing dress-up again, huh?" he said, circling Clyde. "Did your little girlfriend sew that for you, or does your mommy still wipe your ass too?"

Josie, brave as ever, hopped off her bike and slapped Louie across the face. It was a sharp crack that hung in the humid summer air.

Louie only laughed.

"Feisty," he said, rubbing his cheek. "But you're both gonna learn a little lesson today."

Obbie shoved Clyde off his bike, and before Clyde could scramble up, Louie and the Jones brothers began to kick him. It wasn't wild or frenzied. It was almost casual, like they were playing a game Clyde didn't know the rules to.

Between kicks, Louie knelt down and patted Clyde's shoulder mockingly.

"Don't worry, hero," he said with a grin. "You can take it, right? Made of steel and all that. You don't even feel it without those green rocks, huh?"

Then, from the pocket of his jacket, Louie pulled out something thin and metallic. A rusty old penknife, its blade glinting in the late afternoon sun.

Josie screamed and tried to pull Louie away, but Obbie grabbed her by the arm and yanked her back.

Clyde felt the blade slice across the soft skin of his forearm, a sudden, sharp heat that made his stomach lurch. Louie carved slowly, deliberately, spelling out the first letter: *L*. Then another. *L*. Blood welled up instantly, staining the blue fabric of Clyde's costume dark.

When Louie was finished, he stood up and dusted off his hands like he'd just completed a chore.

"Now you'll remember who the real kings of Cottonwood Heights are," he said.

With one final shove, Louie and the Jones brothers sauntered off down the path, laughing and high-fiving each other like they'd just won a prize.

Josie was at Clyde's side in an instant.

"Come on, come on," she said, trying to get him up. Her small hands trembled as she helped him to his feet. Together they staggered back toward Clyde's house, his blood leaving a dotted trail behind them on the dry dirt path.

When they burst through the front door, Clyde's mom took one look at them and dropped the laundry basket she was carrying. Without a word, she grabbed her keys, bundled both kids into the car, and tore down the street toward the hospital.

Clyde barely remembered the ride. He drifted in and out, the pain in his arm pounding like a second heartbeat. Somewhere between jolts of memory, Josie's crying, and his mom's worried glances, he caught a glimpse of the bleeding letters on his arm.

L.L.

For a confused second, he stared at the letters when it finally hit him. It wasn't fair. He was supposed to be the hero.

A young doctor in a rumpled white coat stepped into the hospital room a short while later, holding a suture kit. He paused when he saw Clyde lying there, pale and shivering, still dressed in the battered costume.

"A superhero outfit, huh?" the doctor said, shaking his head as he snapped on gloves.

He didn't look up as he added, almost absently, "Shame about George Reeves."

"What do you mean?" Clyde barely heard over his own heart beating.

"You didn't hear?" the doctor turned his head, "He killed himself today."

As he prepared to leave the warehouse, Clyde tugged the jacket tighter around himself, feeling the scratchy wool of the suit beneath his clothes rub against the faint ridge of the scar on his arm. Funny how some things stayed with you, no matter how hard you tried to grow out of them.

The parking lot behind Heritage Treasures was empty except for Clyde's battered Civic, parked under a flickering streetlamp. The auction house loomed behind him, all glass and concrete, its lights still burning, its alarms still humming softly, but nobody had noticed a thing. It had been too easy.

He was halfway to his car when the man stepped out from between two dumpsters. A skinny guy, jittery, wearing a gray hoodie and brandishing something small and metallic in his shaking hands.

"Wallet. Now," the man rasped.

Clyde raised his hands instinctively, heart hammering against his ribs. He could see the man's finger twitching dangerously on the trigger.

"Easy," Clyde said, voice low. His mind raced. Give up the wallet? Make a run for it? He was nearly seventy, for Christ's sake. He'd be lucky to make it ten feet.

Before he could think better of it, Clyde lunged forward, grabbing for the mugger's wrist.

The two of them struggled, the man cursing, Clyde wrestling the gun downward, and then a sharp crack split the night. Clyde stumbled back, blinking in confusion. The mugger broke free and bolted, leaving the gun clattering to the pavement behind him.

Clyde stood frozen, his breath steaming in the cold air. He ran his hands over his chest, half-expecting to find blood, a gaping hole, something. But there was nothing. No pain, no tear in the fabric beneath his jacket. Just the steady thrum of his heart against the hidden "S," and a deep, vibrating warmth spreading through his body, not adrenaline or blood. He felt alive.

Somewhere deep inside, a memory stirred:

Nothing can hurt the hero.

Clyde stared at the gun lying a few feet away, the barrel still smoking faintly in the cold night air. His instincts screamed at him to leave it, to run, to get in his car and drive until he forgot this ever happened. But something deeper, something heavier, rooted him to the spot. *Had it missed me?* Clyde thought.

He took a step forward. Then another.

When he reached the pistol, he crouched and picked it up gingerly between two fingers. It was heavier than he expected, the metal cold and greasy against his skin. He turned it over once, studying it like it was a relic from a different world.

No blood on the ground. No hole in his chest. Just the faint thudding pulse of his heart and the rough, steady pressure of the suit against his skin, almost like it was holding him up.

He should have been terrified.

Instead, Clyde felt something else rising in his chest, something hot and dangerous.

What if it was real?

He set the gun carefully on the hood of his Civic and pressed his hand flat against the metal. It was warped slightly from the scuffle, a shallow dent he hadn't noticed before. Without thinking, Clyde pushed against it, just curious to see if he could smooth it back. The metal groaned under his palm and shifted. He jerked his hand away, heart hammering again, but this time not from fear.

He stared at the faint handprint left in the car's hood, fingers splayed wide in the crumpled steel. Clyde Mercer, an old nobody from Cottonwood Heights, had just bent steel with his bare hands.

When he finally got home, Clyde let himself into his apartment quietly, out of habit. The place was small, one-bedroom, with thinning carpet and cracked drywall, the kind of space that felt lived in but unloved. He didn't bother turning on the light. The fabric of the suit itched under his jacket, but he didn't take it off. Not yet.

He poured himself a glass of water with a hand that still trembled slightly from the mugging. As he drank, he caught his reflection in the microwave door. His face looked different somehow, flushed, sharper, younger? He leaned closer. The bags under his eyes weren't gone, but they looked softer. The gray at his temples seemed faded.

Then came the sound.

A loud thud from the unit next door. Then another. Then a child's voice, not screaming, not crying, but that panicked whimper that Clyde hadn't heard since he was a kid himself. There was no chance he would have heard the sound yesterday.

He was at the door in two strides.

The lock was weak. He knew that because he had helped the landlord install it last year. A cheap deadbolt on a thin frame. Clyde didn't think. He just threw his shoulder into it. The door cracked open with a sharp *bang* and splintered inward.

Inside, the air reeked of beer and rage. Tom Jarrell, a mean-eyed man with tattooed knuckles and a permanent scowl, had his son backed into the corner, a belt clenched in one hand. The boy, a neighborhood kid Clyde had seen before named Mateo, couldn't have been more than seven.

"Get outta here, Mercer," Jarrell growled. "Ain't none of your business."

"It is now," Clyde said and stepped between them.

Jarrell raised the belt, maybe to swing, maybe to scare. Clyde expected to get hit, but when he opened his eyes, he saw that he caught Jarrell's arm mid-swing. Something cracked. Not bone, but the illusion of control. Jarrell's eyes went wide. He dropped the belt.

"Get the hell out," Clyde said, low.

The man backed off, cradling his wrist. Mateo clung to Clyde's leg without saying a word.

The whole thing took less than a minute. But after the police had left and Clyde got back into his apartment and shut the door, he found himself breathing hard. His muscles thrummed like they'd just come online. His joints felt looser. His back didn't ache. He felt *good*.

He didn't take off the suit.

Instead, he curled onto his bed, still wearing it beneath his clothes, the "S" pressing warm against his chest. He fell asleep before his head hit the pillow.

The dream came like static through an old television.

A grainy black-and-white room. A mirror with powder tins scattered across it. A man in a cape hunched in front of the mirror, but not flying, slumped. Shoulders like wet towels.

"They think I killed myself," the man said without turning.

Clyde recognized the voice. Calm. Tired. George Reeves.

"But it was the suit."

Clyde tried to speak, but the words wouldn't come. His mouth wouldn't open.

"You wear it long enough, it makes you strong," Reeves said, standing now, facing the mirror. "But it takes things from you. Quietly. The way fame does. You'll feel younger, yes. You'll feel alive. But you won't be *you* anymore."

The mirror cracked from the center outward.

"Take it off, Clyde. Before it decides you can't."

The dream dissolved into static.

The Maplewood Senior Living Home looked exactly like Clyde expected: beige walls, pastel paintings of flowers, quiet halls filled with antiseptic and resignation. But as soon as he walked in, he heard it. Josie's laugh, still sharp as a tack.

"Mercer, is that you?" she asked as he entered the rec room. "You look like a boy."

"And you look as young as the day I met you," Clyde responded.

"Well, I know that's a damn lie," she said with a laugh.

She was smaller now, her curls grayer, but the same fire still danced in her eyes. She sat near the window with a puzzle half-done in front of her, wearing a denim jacket covered in enamel pins.

"You bring me lunch or bad news?" she asked.

"Neither," Clyde said, grinning. "I brought something better."

Outside, the staff barely noticed as he wheeled her onto the back lawn. The suit was still beneath his clothes, clinging to him like a secret. The wind had picked up. Somewhere in the sky, a plane etched a contrail like a scar across the blue.

"You remember when we swore we'd fly away one day?" he said.

"Yeah. Then you became a used-toy salesman and I married a drunk with a motorcycle," she said. "Life's funny like that."

Clyde crouched beside her chair.

"You trust me?"

Josie looked at him for a long moment. "Always have. Should I not?"

"Maybe," Clyde muttered, and lifted her.

She was lighter than he expected. Or maybe he was stronger. The ground felt farther away than it should. And then, with one breath, a push against the air, the way a bird does without thinking, they rose.

Josie clutched him tight, her mouth open in a scream that quickly turned to a laugh. Below, the building shrank. The trees looked like spilled broccoli.

"We're flying!" she yelled. "Jesus Christ, we're actually flying!"

For a few glorious moments, they hovered above the world they used to dream of escaping. Clyde held her tight, felt the wind rush past his ears, and almost forgot the years in between.

But then something shifted. The sky dimmed, not clouded, just dulled. The birds below stopped mid-flight. A kind of stillness came over the world, like a photograph. Clyde's chest grew cold. Josie's breath hitched. Then it passed. He set her down gently in the grass, both of them laughing, out of breath.

"Holy hell," she said. "You're not going to explain that, are you?"

"Not today."

She nodded, then blinked slowly, like her brain was buffering.

"Wait," she said. "Did we…did we just go outside?"

Clyde froze.

"Josie," he said. "You don't remember flying?"

She looked around, confused.

"You wheeled me out here, didn't you?" she asked. "Isn't that what you just said?"

Something tugged inside Clyde. Like a loose thread in his mind had been pulled, and whatever had unraveled was already gone. The suit suddenly felt heavier. Wet. Like wearing a winter coat in July.

"Yeah," Clyde said softly. "That's what I said."

Josie smiled. "Well, it's nice out. Thanks for visiting, Mercer."

He kissed the top of her head, even as his throat tightened.

In the sky above, a single bird hovered for just a second too long before resuming its flight.

The next morning, Clyde looked into the mirror and didn't recognize the man staring back. His face was smooth, boyish, absurdly young for someone who hadn't been carded in forty years. The gray in his hair had vanished. The lines at the corners of his eyes were gone. Even the scar, the carved "L.L." that had once defined him, had faded to a whisper of pink beneath the suit.

But it wasn't youth he felt. It was erasure.

He tried to remember Josie's laugh from the day before and couldn't. He tried to remember his mother's voice. The sound of Mateo crying. Gone. The memories didn't feel absent. They felt stolen.

He sat on the floor of his apartment, knees pulled to his chest, and cried until he couldn't remember why he'd started. It came to him then. He was finally the hero, but he wanted to be Clyde Mercer.

When he finally stood, the decision was made.

He returned the suit in the same way he had stolen it, slipped past the security sensors, and bypassed the cameras. He knew the building better than most of the men who built it. The glass case where the suit once stood had been replaced with a mockup placeholder and a plaque:

ITEM PULLED FROM LOT 1952 – ARCHIVAL REVIEW PENDING

Clyde stood in the darkened showroom for a long time, the suit still beneath his clothes, humming faintly, yearning to continue doing the impossible.

Then, slowly, he stripped it off. Piece by piece.

When he removed the cape, the cold hit him like a wave. When the final sleeve slid from his arm, he gasped, not from pain, but from the unbearable weight of gravity.

He folded the suit carefully, reverently, and placed it back in the glass display.

His reflection in the case glass had aged a lifetime in ten seconds. The lines returned. The gray surged back like a tide. The scar on his arm darkened again, angry and red.

But he remembered Josie's laugh.

A week later, Josie wheeled herself through the front doors of Heritage Treasures, uninvited. She wore her denim jacket. A puzzle pin Clyde had given her decades ago still clung to the collar.

She found him working the floor again, back behind the glass, clipboard in hand, slower, stiffer, but alive.

"You flew me," she said. No greeting. Just truth. "I didn't remember. Then I did. I do now."

Clyde smiled softly. "I was scared you wouldn't."

"That was the best day I've had in fifty years," she said.

"It cost a lot."

"It was worth it."

They stood in silence beside the glass case. The suit looked duller now, smaller. Just wool and thread.

"Are you ever going to tell someone what it did?" she asked.

Clyde shook his head. "They'd never believe it. And if they did…"

"Someone else would try it," she finished.

He nodded.

Josie looked at the case one last time, then squeezed his hand.

"Come on, Mercer," she said. "There's still sky out there. Even if we can't fly anymore."

The suit went back on display the next season. The press release called it a "miracle of preservation." Collectors circled. One man placed a seven-figure bid before the listing even opened. Clyde boxed it himself. Gloved hands. Double-wrapped archival tissue. Locked crate. And before sealing it, he whispered three words into the wool.

"Let me go." Then he shut the lid.

The Knight of Endless Augusts
by Eric Dellinger

The onslaught of punches from dozens of duplicated hands would have been easier for Knuckle-Down to ignore were it not for the sweltering summer heat. Ceremonies honoring the members of the Quintet Triumphant for the latest heroic deeds were a frequent enough occurrence that she hadn't been particularly enthused about today's event to begin with. Compounded by the mayor of Cobalt Cove choosing to hold a key-to-the-city bequeathing, which Knuckle-Down had no idea was still a thing mayors did, outdoors at the height of an August heatwave. Further compounded by one of the most eclectic ensembles of villains she'd ever seen using the event to ambush the Quintet in public. She wished they'd simply had the courtesy to lay siege to the Quintet's headquarters directly. Sure, the invasion of privacy would have been deeply upsetting, but there'd be no risk of civilian casualties. And there would have been air-conditioning.

Instead, she stood in the shattered remnants of what had once been an outdoor stage, going toe-to-toe with dozens of opponents. Or just one, depending on your definition. Whoever orchestrated this attack had paid for the services of the One Man Multitude, or O.M.M., a superbeing whose ability to create duplicates of himself often made him a popular hire for any miscreant in need of a mob on short notice. Also, a superbeing whose presence explained the shockingly high crowd turnout for the day's event, and one whose powers had been decidedly honed since the last time Knuckle-Down encountered him. She might have considered it a case of iron sharpening iron, but in the Multitude's case, it was closer to iron sharpening lead. In previous encounters, as the number of the Multitude's duplicates increased, so did their apathy. Once they passed ten, the clones' enthusiasm would start to wane rapidly. At twenty, punches were pulled significantly. Some clones had been known to adopt the professional wrestling approach of stomping one's foot at the time of impact, to lend the illusion of a fearsome blow that never truly connected. At thirty, some would wander away from battle entirely to peruse nearby food vendors and coffee shops.

That was not the case today. Today, they surged forward with an alarming level of coordination and ferocity. In the past, Knuckle-Down could largely swat the duplicates away with her super-strength the instant they entered arm's reach. Now, they crested over her like a tidal wave, close enough that Knuckle-Down could read the logo emblazoned on the breast of their matching uniforms for the first time: the O.M.M. acronym, with the creed "Victory Through Volume" stitched underneath.

Beyond their improved hive-mind coordination, the lack of steady footing impeded Knuckle-Down's ability to use her ample super-strength. Atop the wreckage of the outdoor platform, the undulating heap of wooden planks and metal rods made it near-impossible to gain a solid foothold. As more members of the Multitude piled onto one another, the weight was rapidly becoming unbearable.

Within an instant, the weight vanished, with the clone assailants catapulted back dozens of meters. If there was a sound that preceded whatever superpower flung them backwards, the incessant shouting of the Multitude had rendered it inaudible. There were, however, faint traces of red energy in the air, flaring like fireflies before fading away. Knuckle-Down exhaled and took a moment to dust herself off. "I appreciate the assist. Yeesh, nearly crushed beneath a tide of howling, lackluster white men. If that doesn't sum up the state of the world in a nutshell, then I don't–"

On the list of heroes Knuckle-Down would have expected to see when she looked up, the one who stood before her would have been last. Dead last. On a list that included heroes who were actually dead. Yet here he stood. Long leather gloves and boots, checkered with arcane glyphs that glowed faintly. A red silk-like material over the rest of the body, with sporadic gaps giving a glimpse of chainmail underneath. A winged great helm that encompassed the entire head. And all of it red, including the longsword he held, with a crescent-shaped guard and a ruby-like blade. Hayden Hargrove, better known as The Scarlet Scryer.

She gave him the warmest greeting she could muster.

"You."

"Yep, I was expecting a one-word greeting. But I was also expecting that one word to be profanity, so I'm calling it a win. Although, I still wish you were happier to see me."

Knuckle-Down gave a slight shrug. "I'm kind of indifferent, honestly. I'm not the one you screwed over, but I am still teammates with the guy you did. And my welcome's much nicer than anything you're gonna get from the rest of the Quintet. I thought you had the good sense to lock yourself away in some magic dungeon or something after the big falling out?"

"I did. Although I wonder if any decision I've made these last few years could be called 'good sense.' That's why I wasn't here before you all got attacked. Busting your way through dozens of interdimensional barriers and countermeasures isn't exactly as easy as calling an Uber. Even when you're the one who installed all that stuff in the first place."

"Uh-huh. Well, as a thank-you for the assist, if you leave now I won't tell the rest of the team you were here."

The Scryer shuffled in place, sheepishly rubbing the back of his helm. "Yeah… no can do, unfortunately. He's kinda the reason I'm here."

Him in this case being Boothby Whitaker, or just "Booth" to his friends. As the Quintet Triumphant's resident armored behemoth, he operated under the name Onyx Omega. He and the Scryer had once been as close as brothers. With all the incessant squabbling and pranking that implied, but every bit of the love as well. The two made a highly effective tandem: one half science, one half sorcery.

Knuckle-Down sighed and shook her head. "Well, I got jumped by about a hundred mirrored mediocrities so fast that I don't know where Booth is in all this mess. But if I were you, Scryer, I wouldn't. I just… I really, really wouldn't."

"Well, I thought I was teleporting over to him directly, but this magic stuff's not an exact science. Every now and again there's some kinks in the process. But I guess it worked out, with you needing a hand and all."

"Not to be all 'Thanks but no thanks,' but I would have been just fine without your hel–"

A wall of clones collapsed atop both Knuckle-Down and the Scryer.

The sudden surge of O.M.M. duplicates indicated their speed and stealth were among the list of attributes that had greatly improved of late. Beneath the heap of humanity, Knuckle-Down could feel the weight increasing steadily as more members of the Multitude piled on.

Once again, a red flash preceded the weight's departure. This time, the Scryer had erected an ethereal dome over the pair, with red runes dancing across its surface. Its creation had pushed the duplicates away in a concussive wave, but they now rushed back and thumped their fists angrily against the barrier.

The Scryer groaned as he stood. "Sorry. Should have done that sooner."

"I'm still not used to O.M.M. being this, well, competent. I guess I shouldn't knock someone's journey of self-improvement, but his is making for a real pain in the ass."

"Remind me again, what's the quickest way of dealing with this particular problem?"

"Find the O.M.M. Prime. Knock out the original, the copies go 'poof.'"

"One second."

The Scryer held his longsword aloft and stared at it. When it came to combat, the Scryer wasn't known as a particularly accomplished swordsman. In his case, the saber was more of a conduit through which his spells could be channeled. Among its many enchantments, the mirror-like surface of the ruby-red blade could serve as a scrying pool, which eventually inspired Hayden's heroic moniker.

After a few moments of tilting the sword ever-so-slightly left to right, it became still once again. While clenching the weapon in one hand, the Scryer held his other out to the side. As his fingers curled, a crimson orb swirled into existence. In moments, it zipped up and away like a baseball sailing beyond the outfield fence, passing through the sorcerer's dome as if it wasn't there. The Multitude paused their assault on the barrier and silently watched the magic sphere's arc as it reached its inevitable terminus some distance away. A handful winced and clapped their hands over their ears. The sudden dip in the clone's cacophony allowed Knuckle-Down and Scryer to faintly discern a distant yelp of "Oh shit!" followed by an explosion. The members of O.M.M. vanished in the blink of an eye.

The Scryer sheathed his saber and dusted his gloved hands. "There. Poof."

"Glad that's over. Alright, who's next? I'm begging for a one-on-one after all that one-on-one-hundred."

"I'm a one," a voice boomed.

"That's a one," the Scryer confirmed, pointing at something behind Knuckle-Down.

"A big one!" Knuckle-Down concurred with excitement when she turned and followed the direction of the Scryer's finger. A ten-foot behemoth trudged forward, with bits of the stage debris being crushed beneath his weight. A barbute-style helm covered his head, red eyes glowing like embers from within the shadowy t-shaped visor. The vascularity of his muscles was discernible even beneath a spandex top. Each shoulder bore a pauldron shaped like one half of a human skull. His arms were bare save for massive leather gauntlets, studded with iron. "Now those are the hands of a fellow slugfest-enthusiast. Wait, I've fought you before, haven't I? I don't recognize the outfit, but your voice sounds familiar. Aren't you Face Breaker?"

"Used to be. Not anymore. Now it's Skull Sunderer."

"I'm sorry, 'Skull Sunderer?' "

Sunderer silently pointed to one pauldron, then the other, before elaborating. "New duds, new name. I've upped my game after my last prison stint. Got a fitness coach. Daily meditation. Keto. Stuff that really helped me get my head straight."

"You got your head straight, so now you can split other people's heads in two?"

"Ding ding ding."

Knuckle-Down extended an open palm. "Weird as it is to say, before we commence catching hands, I'd like to shake yours first. You gave me the fight of my life a few years back at Rustic Rift."

"Sorry, I don't shake with these hands."

"Oh, sorry about that."

"I sunder skulls with them."

"So no axe, sword, or edged something-or-other?"

"Nope."

"You sunder skulls with just your fists?"

"Coach showed me just how much proper hip-rotation can add a lot of oomph to your right hook."

"Oh, I'm so looking forward to seeing this right hook firsthand. I'm way overdue for a good brawl."

"Okie."

The collision of Sunderer's fist with Knuckle-Down's jaw came so quickly, the ensuing delayed boom was near simultaneous with the sound of her thundering through the wall of the nearby office building.

The Sunderer stared awkwardly at Knuckle-Down's impact point before turning his head to the Scryer. "Were we starting? I thought we were starting. I might have misread things a bit."

Ribbons of ethereal wisps encircled the Scarlet Scryer as he floated towards the newly made fissure. "One second, I'll ask the hole in the wall." When he reached the hole's edge, Hayden craned a helmed head inside and called into the void. "So can I go save the former best friend who despises me now, or do I need to stick around and use ancient runes of binding to hold your skull together?"

"I'm good," spoke the void.

The Scryer left a crimson streak in his wake, rocketing into the sky as Knuckle-Down emerged from the building's depths. She was beaming as she stomped towards Skull Sunderer. "Kudos to your fitness coach. That's some 'oomph' you've got there."

"I really didn't mean to swing when you weren't ready. I feel bad now."

"Don't feel bad. Me getting caught not looking seems to be the theme of the day. If that was close to your best swing though, I hate to break it to you, but my skull's still in one piece. Didn't even crack a tooth. And hey, speaking of cracking…"

She cracked the knuckles of one hand, then the other.

"My turn."

She reeled back one fist, and the breadth of her smile broadened in kind.

"Now how's *this* feel?"

Boothby "Booth" Whitaker, also known as Onyx Omega, felt like absolute shit.

There was little other way to put it. Feeling bad was part and parcel of the life of a superhero, but this day was rapidly approaching a new rock bottom. Being the two designated "heavy-hitters" of the Quintet, he and Knuckle-Down had borne the brunt of the blows in the recent battle with the Cataclysm Legion two days ago. While Knuckle-Down achieved her heavy-hitting status through superhuman strength, Booth's was rooted purely in intellect and technology. The fusion of those two attributes manifested in the creation of his mechanical suit, dubbed "the Aegis Engine." A massive machine, humanoid in shape, save for the absence of a head. Instead, there was only a small, jutting protrusion where a head should be, which housed the majority of the suit's sensor array. The exterior consisted largely of rounded, black metal plates that gleamed like onyx, hence the origin of the first part of his name. A towering apparatus that stood over eleven feet in height.

Or at least, it usually stood. For the moment, it lay quite still, nestled within a freshly made crater of its own creation on the floor of the Cobalt Cove Cineplex's largest screening room. A few minutes prior, he had discovered that he was the prime target of the day's supervillain ambush, as its orchestrator had attacked him directly. Knowing said orchestrator's history of callous disregard for civilian casualties, he clutched ahold of his assailant, engaged his thrusters, and rocketed the two away from the bystanders in the city streets.

For several moments, the only noise Booth could discern via his audio sensors was the patter of debris raining down from the hole he had created in the theater's ceiling, with an occasional "thunk" from a theater recliner that had come unmoored. A voice then called out with mechanical reverb. "Why Omega, how considerate of you to take us to a location so befitting the spectacle that's bound to unfold. I almost wish these seats were occupied with an audience. Although I suspect it being abandoned is precisely why you chose it?"

"Got it in one. Been closed for a year now. I miss their pretzel bites."

Smoke dissipated, revealing the architect of the day's events. Her given name was Asteria Evangeline Clairmonte, but when indulging in her favorite pastimes of murder and mayhem, she preferred the moniker Nemesis Ubiquitus. She adopted the name because she felt it best encapsulated her role: the supreme enemy of all who called themselves "superheroes." But not all at once. Instead, she chose only one hero at a time as a fixation. Once she determined which hero would be her new pet project, she treated each as their own intellectual challenge. Isolate their weakness, discern the optimum course of action to exploit, then invest her ample resources as needed to achieve her end. In Omega's case, apparently her method of choice was to build a suit of her own, nearly identical to Booth's.

Asteria's armor lumbered about leisurely, gauntleted hands tucked behind her, appraising her crumbling surroundings as if strolling through a botanical garden. "Well, at least your choice of venue allows us to dance uninterrupted. After all, that was the point of bringing all the hired help on board for this project. To keep the rest of your Quintet nice and occupied. Because if I can't crush my chosen foe on my lonesome, then what's the point? And assembling that aforementioned help was not cheap either. One Man Multitude's hourly rate these days is nigh unto extortion. Then there's the new outfit I forged for the occasion. Do you like it?"

"Looks pricey. Going to be a real shame after I beat you in a minute or two and you have to eat all those expenses for nothing, Nemmy."

Asteria ceased her stroll with an emphatic stomp. Booth observed a tremor rippling through her rear torso plating, accompanied by a flurry of staccato clinks and clanks, as the nickname he invoked seemingly sent a chill up Asteria's spine. "I'm quite sure you know how much I abhor that nickname. 'Nemmy.' So paltry and unbecoming. For the remainder of our time together, I kindly ask that you refer to me as Nemesis Ub–"

"Yeah, I'm not saying all that shit every time, sorry Nemmy. But I am really flattered by all the effort you've gone through. Trust me, I'm blushing underneath all this armor plating."

"Hmm, flattered is lovely, but I think I'd prefer *flattened.*"

Twin heat beams blazed from the shoulders of Asteria's suit, cutting through what remained of the theater's roof above Omega. This included the complex's massive air-conditioning unit.

"Aegis, engage Phalanx." A force field of energy swirled around Omega, with sporadic conical tips jutting forward at random intervals. The roofing and air conditioning unit were sheared as they fell, with the resulting debris forming a ring around Booth. "Refresh my memory. Wasn't the last hero you targeted Blood Root, the Phantom Fear of the Bog? Let me guess, you didn't like the taste of her marshland magic, got your ass handed to you, so now you've decided to pivot to the science end of the super-spectrum?"

"Blood Root? Who's Blood Root? Oh no no no, my dear double-O, I only antagonize a certain strata of superheroes. But I am so delighted you brought up magic. We'll return to that subject momentarily, I promise."

The feigned ignorance of her previous tussle with Blood Root wasn't as reassuring as Booth might have hoped. For all of her ego and failed attempts at taking down heroes, she was not entirely unsuccessful. Brigadier and Sapphire Ghost were two heroes who had lost their lives at her hands in the last year alone. Not only was she sometimes successful, she was getting better at it.

Which meant there was all the more reason to wrap things up quickly, but Booth's chosen tactic would require some distance. "Aegis, engage thrusters. " In a blink, Omega was gone, his suit's boosters leaving a silver trail as he sailed skyward.

The Engine's sensors registered Asteria calling out in Booth's wake. "Leaving so soon? My flight mechanism seems to have been damaged, so may I ask that you kindly return? It would be lovely if we could keep this clash earthbound. Particularly since it will end with you six-feet-under."

"Aegis, verify the absence of nearby civilians, please."

"Confirmed," the onboard operating system chirped. "No other human life signs registered within a one-hundred-meter radius."

"Then let's wrap this up. Aegis, engage Itano Circus. I'm tired and I want to go home."

The Aegis Engine's primary offensive and defensive capabilities stemmed from the manipulation of energy fields the suit generated, but it housed more conventional weaponry as well. Tucked beneath various panels on the suit's exterior, the total payload of compact incendiary missiles was over fifty. The Itano Circus protocol deployed all of them at once.

Dozens of plumes rocketed outward from the Aegis Engine and spiraled down towards Nemesis Ubiquitous. This was a degree of overkill well beyond what Onyx Omega would normally deploy against a single villain, but based on his appraisal of the suit she had constructed, he was confident it would take far more than this to be anywhere near lethal for Asteria. His hope was that the sheer force of the attack would merely render her unconscious. And he'd be doing some realty firm a favor by expediting the leveling of the abandoned Cineplex. After the missiles had detonated, Omega lowered himself back to ground zero.

He heard Asteria before he saw her. Her laughter, followed by a red glow blooming in the murk. The Itano Circus had been enough to severely damage Nemesis Ubiquitous's armor, with large chunks missing and cracks like a rolled eggshell flowing through the remnants. But the new gaps in her armor were filled with a crimson energy that made Booth's blood boil.

When she finished cackling, Asteria held her arms out theatrically. "Ta-da! This is why I'm so glad you broached the topic of 'magic' earlier. You see, I went down two very different rabbit holes in plotting your undoing. The expenses involved in constructing this armored suit were astronomical, to be sure, but still a mere fraction of the cost it took to procure an authentic copy of one of the Vermillion Volumes! The same tomes from which your former best friend and current best betrayer learned his sorcerous craft. Well, my dear double-O, are you suitably awed by my efforts?"

"You really are relentless when you put your mind to something, aren't you?"

"Oh, I like to think it's my best quality. My 'never say die' determination when it comes to making *you* die."

A third voice entered the conversation. "Nobody's dying today."

The red flash that enveloped Asteria was accompanied by a thunderclap. Booth didn't budge as the Scryer floated down behind him. When he finally turned around after several heartbeats, it was slow and pointed.

An uncomfortable silence held in the air before the Scryer broke it. "So from what I remember, heat beams weren't one of the functions you built into the Aegis Engine. But somehow, the longer you stare at me... I'm getting this... burning sensation."

Omega said nothing.

Scryer pressed on. "Definitely feeling kind of warm over here."

Nothing.

"Little flush."

More nothing.

"I mean, it *is* August and all, but..."

Nothing abounded.

"Say, would you mind opening the Engine's front hatch real quick so I can see if there are actual daggers protruding from your eyesockets right now?"

Omega spoke at last. "The last thing I want to hear from you is a quip. You're the last thing I want to hear, period. Or see."

"What about 'feel?' In all my research both arcane and profane, I haven't found any spell that solves problems quicker than a huggie."

A heavy exhalation from a seething Booth crackled through the Engine's speakers. "Do me a favor and go back to whatever spectral hole you crawled out of before I lose my shit completely, you… you absolute–"

"Bastard!" a voice cried out, before Booth could settle on an invective of his own. It wasn't the one he would have chosen, but it did the job. It was also accompanied by a bolt of red energy, whose impact pushed the Scryer back one step. Latent protective wards absorbed the bulk of the damage, but the collision of the two spells sent arcane sparks sizzling through the air.

Nemesis Ubiquitous stood with one arm extended, ruby tendrils still curling about her metal gauntlets. Her face was a patchwork tapestry of twitches and spasms. "I– I've never felt so conflicted. I have a front row seat to the toxic reunion of the century. The best of friends turned the bitterest of enemies, brought together right before my eyes. Why the loathing is absolutely palpable." Red sorcery began to encircle her extended hand. "And while part of me would love nothing more than to sit back and watch as this metahuman *Who's Afraid of Virginia Woolf* unfolds, there are unfortunately two indisputable complications. The first is that I hate being ignored. And as for the second…" She flung a second bolt of energy as she tied a bow on her speech. "I had dibs, asshole!"

The second bolt again fizzled across the Scryer's defenses as he addressed Asteria. "Not ignoring you, and I'm sorry if you got that impression. I was just killing some time while I waited for the sound."

A series of concentric circles and wheeling glyphs appeared, whirling above Asteria's head. Unaware, she cocked an eyebrow at the Scryer. "Sound? And what sound would that be?"

A crimson torrent plunged from the whirling circles, cascading over Asteria. The ensuing roar was so great it obscured the sound of Asteria's chassis squealing as the metal warped and twisted. When the flood ended, Nemesis Ubiquitous lay unmoving.

"That sound," the Scryer confirmed. "The 'kra-koom' sound. Although maybe it sounded more like a 'thoom' or a 'bam' to you? 'Tham?' Onomatopoeia's not my forte."

Nemesis Ubiquitous still lay unmoving.

"Uh-oh. Maybe summoning the Red Rivers of Riving was overkill on my part." The Scryer turned to Onyx Omega. "Hey, your sensors are still picking up vital signs for her, right? I declared 'Nobody's dying today' when I made my grand entrance, and I don't want to end the day with egg on my face."

Omega said nothing for several moments before slowly walking away. Numerous footsteps and heartbeats passed before his subdued response. "She's alive." The words were so soft through Omega's suit that it might have passed for static. A far cry from the venom moments before.

He half-expected the Scryer to follow him as he stalked about, but neither quip nor query followed. Only a long silence.

It was faint, but his suit registered the sound of the Scryer sighing and speaking to himself. "Just let him go, Hayden. Job done. Just let him go. Can't win 'em all."

Any further mutterings were eclipsed by the rumbling of Omega's thrusters as he departed.

It was evening when Booth found Hayden once again. Hours had passed in the interim. Booth had spent the first of those hours pouring over the data acquired by his suit's sensors to make sure their findings were correct. Once confirmed, the remaining hours were spent grappling on whether he wanted to confront the Scryer again, or just leave things as they were.

He found Hayden atop the Lawson Building, a corporate center and one of the tallest buildings in Cobalt Cove. Hayden sat on the roof's edge, still wearing his Scarlet Scryer regalia, save for the large great helm, seemingly enraptured by the cityscape before him. As he descended from the sky, Booth noted, "Well as far as scenic views go, it seems like a nice spot. I hope the smoke roiling from the theater I blew up didn't blot out the sunset too much."

Hayden's eyebrows shot up in surprise. "Booth! Oh, I didn't expect–"

"Don't even pretend you didn't magically sense me coming. I know you better than that."

The Scryer gave a sheepish nod. "Okay, sensed maybe, but I didn't *hear* you coming for sure. Since when can you fly without the big suit?"

"It's new. A barebones chassis that fits under my civvies. This is a tall-ass building, and I didn't feel like climbing all those stairs just to bring you this." He held up a red paper cup with a black lid.

"What's that?"

"Vietnamese coffee. From the boba joint around the corner."

"Did you buy this because you remembered how much I like Vietnamese coffee, or because you figured the viscosity of the condensed milk blended with scalding hot coffee makes for the optimum 'I'm about to throw this in your face' beverage? I don't blame you if it's the latter."

"Right now it's the former, but the more you ramble, the closer we get to the latter. Drink it."

"Thanks. I can pay you back sometime. Assuming you can stomach the sight of me again."

"Nope, I'd like you to pay me back right now. I just need the answer to one question."

"Go for it."

"Who are you?"

Booth found the absence of an immediate retort quite refreshing, and the look of surprise on Hayden's face was genuine versus his feigned shock when Booth first arrived. As he slowly reached to take the proffered coffee, Hayden eventually mustered a response. "I'm sorry?"

"You heard me."

"I'm not sure what you–"

"You're not Hayden Hargrove. Not the one from around here, anyway. You may be a Hayden, but you're not the one I have beef with."

Hayden could only stare for several moments before Booth filled the silence.

"You've gone five whole seconds without a lame joke, so now I'm damn sure I struck a nerve."

"I'm– I'm sorry, but..." Hayden laughed softly and rubbed his face with his hands. "I've done this, what, fifty-two times now? And you're the first person to catch on. How'd you figure it out?"

"I didn't, technically. The Aegis Engine did. Sensors picked up something when you got hit with Nemmy's magic. When her energy bolt collided with your protective wards, you... well, you flickered. Just for a fraction of a second, like a hologram shorting out. So I'm guessing whoever you are, you've got some sorcerous illusion going on, and being hit with your own class of magic threw a wrench into things?"

"That would explain it, yeah. That's the first time I've encountered that particular scenario." He exhaled heavily. "Okay, I'm gonna show you something.

It's gonna be weird. Even by superhero standards. Please try not to freak out."

A red shimmer quickly danced across Hayden's facial features, and then those features collapsed utterly. Hale skin rapidly turned sallow, wrinkles deepened to troughs, and brown hair became peppered with platinum. Beyond being far older than the Hayden Hargrove that Booth knew, the transformation went well beyond mere aging. Dozens of scars erupted as the topography of his face went into utter disarray. When his features settled, Hayden breathed a heavy sigh. "So, first time seeing someone age ten years in ten seconds?"

"Ten years in ten seconds? Seen that before, actually. This is more like someone just threw sulfuric acid on Dorian Gray's portrait."

Hayden stared for a moment before burying his face in his hands. His shoulders bobbed silently in apparent sobs.

Booth mildly backpedaled. "Alright, I guess that sounds harsh, but… man, you look *bad.*"

A muffled sound began to emerge from beneath Hayden's leather gloves. Laughter, not sobs, grew louder and louder. When his hands finally lowered, his face gleamed as tears had pooled in the multitude of grooves across his weathered visage. "Sorry, I know that was loud, but you have no idea how good it is to be in a universe with jokes again. It's almost all I could think about when I first ran into Knuckle-Down. Getting to do a bit of banter again, even if my end of it sucked. I'm more than a bit rusty, but so much of the multiverse is woefully bereft of some good 'bwah-ha-ha.' I mean, my universe probably sets the bar for misery, but it wasn't always like that. That's why I keep coming to this spot atop the Lawson Building in each universe. See how the view changes. Sometimes drastically, sometimes just a smidge, and sometimes it's not there at all. Mine's the latter."

"So, which universe are you from exactly?"

"Oh jeez, I honestly forgot the official name for it. Universe Theta-Eight, I think?"

"Don't know it, although I've only been through like two dimensional shifts in my time. So you traveled all the way from your universe for some Vietnamese coffee, a decent view and a particularly wacky ensemble of villains? Don't have a Nemesis Ubiquitous in Universe Theta-Eight?"

"You were going to die today, Booth."

The moment hung for an eternity. Booth stared and blinked, awaiting more details. Hayden only stared, solemnly taking in the cityscape. After a few beats, he took a long slurp from his cup. "Coffee's not bad. Got something to stir this with? Condensed milk's settled at the bottom a bit."

Booth kept his eyes on Hayden while he rummaged in a paper bag with one hand. It soon emerged with a plastic spoon. "I'll trade you this spoon for some elaboration. Because I'm pretty damn confident I would have come out on top against Nemmy without your help."

Hayden took the proffered spoon and spoke as he stirred his beverage. "The multiverse is such a funny thing. Not the 'bwah-ha-ha' kind of funny I was just talking about. For a cosmic ocean of infinite possibilities, some things are damn near-constant. Yours is August 19th. That's the day you die. The year may change, the means may change, but August 19th ends with you dead. At least, more often than not."

"I take it that's what happened in your neck of the multiverse? In Theta-Eight?"

"Yep." The comment was flippant, but the tone was somber. "We weren't part of a bigger team in my universe. No Quintet Triumphant. Just a duo. No big falling out, like you've had with your Scryer. Close as brothers, and all that. But eventually a certain August 19th came around, and suddenly I was the only one of us who made it to August 20th. It wasn't Nemmy in our universe. Someone else, but it was a fight that seemed like we had it in the bag. Then things took a turn. And I just couldn't save you. And I tried. Believe me, I tried." He took a long, slow sip of coffee before continuing. "Then things across the whole planet went to hell in a handbasket. I mean extinction-level events. Crisis after crisis after crisis. I tried to stop those too. Succeeded a few times. Just not enough. Before too long, I was one of the last superheroes around. Not long after that, I was one of the last humans around. And not long after that, I was one of the few living things anywhere. You died, then the rest of the universe followed suit. I lost everything twice."

Booth took a moment to absorb the gravity of Hayden's confession. "I'm so sorry. Not much else I can say on that, I guess."

"Don't push yourself to feel too bad for me. I know how much you and the Hayden of this universe hate each other."

"The Hayden of Theta-Eight isn't the one who screwed me over. And frankly, your face is so busted up I feel like I'm talking to someone else entirely." Hayden belly-laughed at this. Booth didn't join him, but did concede a smile. "Speaking of, how did you end up here instead of Theta-Eight?"

"I kept trying to fix things. Hit the magic tomes looking for some way to turn back time or undo it all. But nothing I tried worked. And exhausting every opportunity led me to the doorstep of one of the other few remaining sentient beings of my universe, albeit someone much higher on the power ladder. Keene, the Carnal King Incarnate, he calls himself. Even I think that name's a little heavy on the alliteration. You've probably heard of him. One of those great cosmic beings who actually extends into multiple dimensions. I'd always thought of him as a villain, but in the scheme of things, he honestly wasn't that bad. Also, when you can count the number of living creatures in the universe on two hands, even a strange bedfellow is a welcome one."

"Let me guess. You made some kind of a bargain with him and got so hasty you didn't read the fine print?"

"In my defense, there wasn't much else to do in my dimension that didn't involve abject despair. I went to Keene in the hopes that between the two of us, we could somehow fix things, but he said that Theta-Eight was beyond the point of no return. No undoing its fate, even with his abilities. Could have been bullshit, but I believed him. But he knew that as badly as I wanted to save the whole universe, I wanted to save just you nearly as much. So he gave me the chance to do just that. Sort of."

"How?"

"He told me about your death being tied to that one fateful day across most of the multiverse. So he would give me the chance to save Boothby Whitaker on August 19th. Every Booth except the one I knew. That's the one Booth I can't save. I didn't really get screwed on fine print, because he was pretty up-front about it. So I agreed. One moment I said 'yes,' and the next moment I was in another universe entirely, in the bed of another Hayden Hargrove. Keene set things up so at the stroke of midnight on August 19th, the Hayden of that universe gets swapped out, and I get swapped in. I get their memories too, although it takes a little while for those to sink in. Then I use some magic glamor to adjust my appearance accordingly. When midnight rolls around again, the old Hayden gets swapped back, and I'm off to the next universe. Between the memories and the glamor, I think I've been able to blend in pretty seamlessly until now. This is the first universe where I got caught. Whoops."

"So, where does the old Hayden go while you're taking their place for a day?"

"You know, Keene told me that at some point, but I wasn't entirely listening by then. I think they just go into some kind of limbo for a bit? I hope they don't get stuck in my barren husk of a universe for twenty-four hours. If so, that'd be fifty-two Hayden Hargroves racking up massive therapy bills in every universe I've been to thus far. Although maybe that wouldn't be the worst thing in the case of the Hayden from this universe, huh?"

"So you've got his memories?"

"Most of them, yeah."

"So you know what he did?"

"I do. And for whatever it's worth, he's sorry. And you're probably expecting me to tell you to forgive him, but I'm not going to do that. If I was in your position, I probably wouldn't want to speak to him either. But from the memories I have, I can tell you he loves you. Do with that what you will."

"I'm in no hurry to mend fences, trust me. But I guess I appreciate you saying all that. I do have another question. I get your end of this whole magic pact you made, but what does this Keene guy get out of the deal?"

"He gets to watch me fail."

Booth said nothing while Hayden took a moment, breathed deeply, then resumed. "In my universe, even though I was never able to undo any of the things that went awry at the end, all that trial-and-error made me a much better sorcerer. A stronger one. So when I agreed to this whole thing, I told myself that the odds were good that I was significantly more powerful than the Hayden Hargrove I was replacing. Deep down, I knew that was mostly bullshit. The truth was, I was selfish and just wanted to see my friend again. Lucky for me, it turns out my bullshit was largely on point. I *am* stronger than most of the Haydens I replace. A lot stronger. But not perfect. And I think Keene's happy if I succeed a thousand times if he gets to watch me fail once. By my count, this is my fifty-second go-round at an August 19th. Forty-nine of those Booths lived to see August 20th. I couldn't save three of them. Two of those three Booths were married. One of them had kids." Hayden's voice broke softly on the last word. "But hey, at least you can see how hard I tried." He raised his right hand and drew his index finger around his face in a circling motion. "See these? Most of these scars are from the last fifty-two days. And if you think my face is the worst of it, do you want to see something really freaky?"

The hand that circled his face suddenly vanished, along with the rest of the arm up to the shoulder. A now-empty sleeve flopped to Hayden's side as his glove glided down to the street below. "Lost the arm ten universes ago. Easy to compensate for with the magic, thankfully. Just takes some concentration." The empty sleeve ballooned as an arm of red energy coursed through it. Hayden stared at his new red hand. "So my failures are what Keene gets out of the deal. It's not that he wants me dead or anything. I think the struggles of mortal beings fascinate him, and our failures particularly amuse him. Especially us superheroes.

Winning is what we're supposed to do. It's those times we don't win that he seems to cherish." The Scryer turned his head towards Booth, face slick with tears, and opened his arms wide. "So here I am, Booth. Your own personal shining knight, riding in on a white horse to save the day. Only there's no white horse, and instead of shining, I'm just haggard and falling to pieces. And as far as riding in to save the day, it's just that one day. Over and over and over again. And try as I might, I just can't win 'em all, Booth. I just can't win 'em all."

Tears turned to sobs, and Booth sat silently as the Scryer wept. If the Scryer had spent nearly two months in perpetual combat, Booth wanted to allow him all the time he could to release his anguish. When the Scryer's breathing began to even, Booth spoke. "You keep saying 'win.' That's what us superheroes are supposed to do, right? A lot of awful people seem obsessed with that word lately. Everything in life is about someone winning and someone else losing, and it bothers me. I don't much care for people who are fixated on winning. I care an awful lot for people who are fixated on trying. I'm grateful that you won today, Hayden. Apparently, I wouldn't be alive right now if you hadn't. But as grateful as I am that you won today, what matters more is that you'll try tomorrow."

"Heh, it's a little hard for me to process that, given I'm fighting for my life every day. And your life, too. But I appreciate it all the same."

"Is there anything you want to say to me?"

"Sure, give me a minute to collect myself and I'll think up a bad quip."

"Not what I meant. I'm not your Boothby Whitaker, but I'm *a* Boothby Whitaker. And I'm the first Boothby Whitaker who knows your particular predicament. So if there's anything you never got a chance to say to your Boothby Whitaker, well, here I sort of am. You saved my life. The least I can do is listen. So anything you want to say?"

Hayden's face was impassive for a long while before finally smiling sadly. "Nah, nothing. Well, everything. I'd like the chance to say everything I ever said all over again. The good more than the bad, of course. The things that made us cry from laughing more than the things that just made us cry, but I'd take whatever I could get. If I knew you were going to ask this question ahead of time, maybe I'd have hit the Vermillion Volumes again. Sift through all the ancient languages long since lost to time just to learn how to say 'I miss you' in all of them. But I can't say everything, so I'll go with nothing. But I'd like to say something to the Boothby of this universe, although it'll sound really stupid. Cherish the laughs while you can. I know, it's so damn trite that I'm fighting back wincing as I say it, but please cherish them. Even if the halcyon days with the Hayden of this world are long gone, cherish any laughs you can get." He sighed as he looked skyward. "They are not long, the days of 'bwah' and 'ha-ha,' out of a misty dream."

"What's that from?"

"You know, like *Days of Wine and Roses?* Old movie with Jack Lemmon and Lee Remick? I think I have bleak sixties relationship dramas on the brain after Nemmy invoked *Who's Afraid of Virginia Woolf* earlier. Do you think that's a good comparison for us? Which one of us is George and which one's Martha?"

"Well, if you're back to bad quipping, that's probably my cue to leave."

"Not an Edward Albee fan, Mecha-Martha? Should I pivot to Eugene O'Neill? 'Long Day's Journey Into Flight?' "

"Your next universe is calling."

"Samuel Beckett? 'Krapp's Last Cape?' "

"Shut it."

"Can do. For what it's worth, thank you for listening. I never really planned on any Booths finding out about my whole deal, so I probably dumped a lot on you just now. And sorry again if the whole rapid-aging-messed-up face stuff freaked you out."

"Nope. Like I said, I've seen rapid aging before. We've got a hero here who's pushing eighty who can revert back to his thirty-year-old self, but only for thirty minutes a day. Goes by Mister Yesteryear. Real name's Frank."

"Oh, you have one of those Franks? We had one of those Franks in Theta-Eight. Real stand-up guy, although in my universe he just went by Captain Old. I swear, the hero names are much catchier in this universe. Mine included. Although my name is much cooler in most universes. Except Omicron-Twenty. There I go by Legerdamain Lad. Can you believe it? That was twenty August 19th's ago, and I'm still feeling second-hand embarrassment. I know there's theoretically like an infinite number of universes, but I honestly didn't think anybody still went by 'Lad' in any of them. I'm nearly fifty and on my third divorce in that universe. Three divorces should disqualify you from Lad-dom."

"Wait, if you didn't go by Scarlet Scryer in your universe, what was your name?"

"Seercerer."

The silence from Booth was the longest yet in the evening's conversation. "Seriously?"

"Seer. Sorcerer. 'Seer-cerer.' Get it? Look, it sounded clever at the– Wait, you said '*Ser*-iously.' Are you riffing on my crappy hero name?"

Booth ignored this completely. "When do you get zapped over to your next universe again? Midnight?"

"Thereabouts. Sometimes it's an hour or two earlier. In all his ethereal omnipotence, I think the Carnal King Incarnate sometimes loses track of daylight savings."

"Well, want to keep chatting for a bit? I usually turn in pretty early, but I'm probably overdue for a late night. I can wait til tomorrow to get to work."

"Get to work on what?"

"Saving Universe Theta-Eight."

Hayden could only stare at Booth, with his mouth slightly agape.

Booth shrugged. "Don't look at me like that. So we know you weren't able to save your world. You do magic stuff. The Carnal King Incarnate can't do it either. More magic stuff. So if magic stuff's out, maybe what it'll take is science stuff. I'm damn good at science stuff, so why not give it a shot? If you're out there saving untold Boothby Whitakers, it seems right that at least one Boothby Whitaker can work on saving you. No promises of course, but success is almost besides the point. The important part is I'll be trying. At least starting tomorrow."

"So if trying's for tomorrow, what's tonight?"

"Well, you're the expert on Theta-Eight, so I intend to learn as much as I can from you in the time we have left. And if most of the multiverse is as gloomy as you said, maybe you can stock up on some stuff to cherish before you leave."

"Bwah?" asked the Scryer.

Booth nodded.

"Ha-ha."

One Time, One Night
by Jacob Jones-Goldstein

The motorcycle roared as Jack tore down the highway at a speed Evel Knievel himself would describe as reckless. The full-throated growl of the engine sounded like a rolling wave of thunder to prairie dogs that dotted the desolate Eastern Colorado prairie.

Jack could have tuned the engine to cut the decibels it produced, but the truth was, he liked the deafening howl. He had spent so much of his life in the shadows and lonely places that the clamor felt like a way to remind the world that he was still in it.

Hiding made him quiet and watchful. He never said more than he needed and did everything he could to minimize the dent he put in people's imaginations. Out on the highways, he could let his ride scream at the top of its lungs for him.

It was a brutally hot June afternoon, and Jack's leather jacket was starting to feel like an EZ-Bake oven. He hadn't been this way in a while, but he remembered there was a small town a few miles up ahead. He decided if they had a place to eat, he'd stop and cool off. He had no real destination in mind for the day, but after a few days sleeping off highways in a tent, he was ready for a long, hot shower. If the town had both a diner and a hotel, he would happily call it a day.

He cut his speed from ludicrous down to merely ill-advised as he approached what turned out to be an uninspiring town, somewhat ironically named, Ford City. From afar, it looked like the kind of place that was big enough to have its own school, but small enough that most of the graduates fled as soon as they possibly could. The only feature that stood out was a large warehouse on the outskirts.

Most importantly to Jack, they had a comfortable-looking silver-bullet-style diner, right on the main street that cut through town. He pulled into a spot to the side of the building and gingerly stepped off his bike, his legs stiff from the long ride. He took off his jacket and let the slight breeze dry the sweat off his skin before heading inside.

The opening notes of "Tom Sawyer" by Rush played on the radio as he pushed open the silver door, causing a small bell to chime. The combination of dramatic guitar and cool air made his skin break out in goosebumps. It was a more dramatic entrance than he usually liked to make, but looking around, there had been no one there to see it, so he kept his smile to himself.

A voice from the kitchen called out, "Have a seat, Carl. I'll be with you in a minute."

Jack was definitely not Carl, but he took the unseen person's advice and walked over to a booth tucked into the corner of the long, thin restaurant, near the overburdened air conditioner. He sat with his back to the wall, closed his eyes, and listened to the music. The big guitars and drums appealed to him, as did the line about being a modern-day warrior. There was nothing like it when he was growing up, and it made him jealous of today's teenagers. The rock stuff appealed to him a lot more than the pop music, even though that was a bit closer to the music of his day.

Despite the shadowy nature of his existence, he tried to live in the present and not dwell too much on the past. Part of that was listening to a lot of new music and going to movies. He wondered if the town had a theater. He'd seen a poster for a new movie featuring the guy who played Han Solo and wanted to see it. It looked like one of the adventure pictures he would go to see growing up.

As Rush faded, "The Waiting" by Tom Petty came on, and a woman emerged from the kitchen, looking around. She appeared momentarily taken aback at seeing Jack in the corner and not the expected Carl.

"Good afternoon, young man. I thought you'd be Carl coming in for his lunch. Need a menu?"

"Thank you, Ma'am, that would be just fine." It never ceased to amuse him when people referred to him as young. He knew he looked like he was in his mid-twenties, but he'd been born before World War One broke out.

The waitress, a friendly-looking woman with small-town tanned skin and a pack-a-day voice who was probably thirty years younger than him but looked twenty years old, went and got him a menu. When she returned, she asked, "That your bike out there?"

"Yes, Ma'am," Jack replied as he took the menu.

She made a 'hmph' noise that sounded somehow both judgmental and impressed at the same time, "We don't get a lot of bikers through this way, being a dry county and all. Get you anything to drink?"

"Would love a Coke."

She nodded and went off to get his soda. When she returned, he asked for a cheeseburger and fries. He'd briefly considered a turkey sandwich, but to his mind, diners were for burgers. She didn't bother writing the order down, and as she walked away, Jack noticed she scanned the windows with a hint of concern. He assumed she was wondering where Carl was.

Tom Petty drifted into REO Speedwagon, who barely finished taking it on the run, before a police car pulled up outside the diner and parked in front. A tall officer in a cowboy hat and sunglasses emerged. Jack couldn't tell from where he was sitting, but he would have been willing to put money down that the sunglasses would be mirrored. He watched as the officer walked around the diner and took a long look at Jack's motorcycle, before turning and heading for the door.

When the officer entered, the little bell rang, and the waitress called out from the back, "That you, Carl?"

Jack was excited to find out if it was.

"Sorry to disappoint Laura," the officer said in a voice that sounded smarmy as hell to Jack.

The waitress, whom Jack now knew was named Laura, emerged from the kitchen and said, "Oh, Hi Bobby, you here for lunch?"

"Can't say that I am, I was driving past, and I saw we had a visitor, so I wanted to say hello!" He turned and waved an exaggeratedly friendly wave to Jack and walked over.

Jack felt his stomach sink. He had just wanted something to eat and a Coke. He sighed and thought it was too hot out for dealing with small-town cops.

"I'm guessing since you're the only one in here, and I know our Laura hasn't been out cruising, that that's your big old red Harley out there?"

Jack felt a brief wave of irritation that the cop had not taken his sunglasses off to talk to him, but managed to choke it down before replying, "It's not a Harley."

"Excuse me?" Officer Bobby responded.

"It's not a Harley. It's a 1959 Royal Enfield Indian Chief."

The officer smirked, "Well, I do apologize, young man. We don't get many bikers through here, so I am not exactly an expert."

"Think nothing of it," Jack replied.

"Mind if I sit down?"

Jack motioned towards the opposite side of the booth, "Free country."

"God Bless America," the officer replied and sat down. He took off his hat and set it on the table, but kept the sunglasses on. Jack briefly thought of grabbing them and yanking them off, but dismissed that thought. "What're you having?" asked the Officer.

"Cheeseburger and fries."

"Sounds like a perfect lunch on a hot day like today, and Laura makes a great one. Best in town."

"Glad to hear it."

"In fact, it's just about the perfect meal before you get back on your, what was it again?"

"1959 Indian Chief."

"Your 1959 Indian Chief, and heading on your way."

Jack had been hassled plenty of times by cops and locals in a myriad of nowhere towns, and it never failed to set him on edge. "To be honest, I'm a bit tired and was thinking of finding a place to stay the night here in town. It seems like a nice place." He had stared down battalions of Nazi's in Europe; backwater bullies didn't scare him.

The officer looked at him intently before, finally, taking off his sunglasses, "Can't say I really advise that, son. This ain't the kind of town for leather jacket-wearing biker boys. Nope, not interested in your kind."

Jack interrupted, "My kind…" but the officer talked right over him, "So I'll tell you what, I'm gonna go out to my car and fire up the AC, hot out after all, and read today's paper while you eat your lunch, and then I'm gonna help you find your way back to the highway."

Jack began to respond, but the officer raised his hand and shook his head, "Ain't a discussion, boy." With that, he put his hat and sunglasses back on, got up, and headed for the door. Laura emerged from the kitchen with a cheeseburger and fries as he walked past. He tipped his hat to her and walked out the door to his car.

She brought the food over to Jack and gave a quick glance at the officer as he got into his car, "I'd listen to him, honey. You seem like a nice kid. This isn't a good place to stay."

"The cops seem so friendly though," he responded sarcastically.

"They're not," she replied and then sighed deeply, "They're very much not."

Jack took his time eating his lunch. The officer had been right about one thing: it was hot out, and he wasn't going to rush back out into the heat. He was also very interested in wasting the time of people who tried to bully him.

As he sat there enjoying his cheeseburger, the bell rang again, and an older man, wearing denim just about head to toe, entered.

Laura, the waitress, chided the man, "You're late, Carl."

"Third time's the charm," Jack mumbled quietly.

"Sorry, Laura, I got hung up. What's shithead doing sitting in his car out front?" Carl responded with the kind of gravely world-weary voice that Jack associated with retired Army Sergeants.

Laura motioned towards Jack, who had been watching them. Jack waved rather than pretend he didn't notice.

Carl nodded to him, "Ahh, that would do it." He sighed deeply, "That your bike out there kiddo?"

"Ayep."

Carl walked over to the window and looked out at the motorcycle. "Indian?"

"Yes, sir."

"Nice looking. Guessing Officer Bobby out there is waiting to help you find your way out of town?"

Jack nodded, "Real hotbed of hospitality you got here."

Carl chuckled briefly and then sighed again, "Used to be friendlier, these days a bit less so. Best you listen to him and head on your way, soon as you can."

He tipped his dusty baseball cap to Jack and headed back over to where Laura was setting out a placemat for him at the counter. As he turned, Jack noticed the tattoo of a bee, holding what looked like a gun and a wrench, showing under his rolled-up sleeve.

"That a seabee tattoo?" he asked.

Carl raised an eyebrow at Jack, "Sure is."

"Where'd you serve?"

"All over the Pacific, Guam, Bora Bora, and a few other places. Can't say many young folk recognize it anymore. You serve?"

Jack nodded, "Yes, sir, 10 years in the Army."

Carl looked incredulous, "10 years? You enlist when you were 15?"

"I'm a bit older than I look," Jack laughed."

"Must be," Carl replied, "Well, one vet to another, do what Bobby out there says and don't dawdle around here. It ain't a friendly place."

"Laura there said similar. As you said, one vet to another, there some way I can maybe be a help?"

Laura and Carl both laughed, neither with very much humor, before Carl responded, "I appreciate it, but you don't get yourself in trouble. Nice of you to offer, though."

He tipped his cap to Jack again and sat down at the counter stool.

Jack finished his burger and Coke, left a nice tip, and paid for his meal. He thanked them both and walked out into the heat. There was a beat-up pickup truck out front of the diner that Jack assumed to be Carl's.

The officer in the car looked to Jack like he had dozed off, so he rapped on the roof as he walked past. The officer in the car startled awake. Jack said into the inexplicably open window, "Gonna head out now if you're wanting to escort me."

He didn't wait for a response, but continued on his way to his bike. He sat in the seat and slipped his helmet on. He brought the engine to life with a growl and pulled out into the dusty street.

The police cruiser pulled out behind him and gave a quick honk as a signal to Jack to get moving.

The main road into town was also the main road out of town. What passed for downtown was three short blocks and a traffic light, which didn't appear to be working as they passed under it. There were a handful of sad-looking businesses and a police station where a young woman stood outside smoking and watching as Jack and the officer went by in their small parade.

The last building they passed was the large warehouse Jack had been able to see as he came into town. It was a nondescript but somehow ominous-looking building. There were a few windows here and there, but the only distinguishing features were a swan logo painted above what looked to be the main entrance and three police cars parked out front of it.

As he passed the warehouse and back onto the open road, Jack noticed that Officer Bobby broke off his tail and pulled into the warehouse parking lot. He couldn't help but wonder why such a small town needed so many police cars.

Everything about his encounters in the Ford City set off his internal alarm bells. He was two miles out of town, deciding whether to turn around and go back, when he saw in the opposite lane heading in the direction he just came from, a semi truck with two police cruisers behind it. They didn't have their lights on and looked to Jack like an escort. The truck was as generic in appearance as the warehouse; however, as it passed, he noticed it had the same swan logo on the side of the trailer.

"Alright, that's it," Jack said to the wind and slowed his bike down. He surveyed the prairie along the side of the road for another half mile before he found what he was looking for.

Roughly twenty yards off the highway was a small washout. It wasn't deep, but hard to see from the road if you weren't looking, and it was big enough to hide a motorcycle. Jack pulled off the side of the highway, killed the engine, and walked the bike over. He didn't like leaving it in a place like this, but riding back into town wasn't going to help answer the questions he wanted answered.

Jack glanced at his watch. It was two-thirty in the afternoon. He sighed and settled in next to his motorcycle. It was going to be a long wait until dusk.

Jack stirred from a nap as the first cracks in the sun's hold on the day began to show. He smacked himself on the cheeks a couple of times to shake off the sleep cobwebs and took a sip from the canteen he kept in his saddle bag. Somewhere around four o'clock in the afternoon, he had begun to deeply regret not filling it before leaving the diner, as the heat of the day and lack of shade in the washout took their toll.

He replaced the canteen and reached much deeper into the saddlebag. He rooted around a bit at the bottom under everything until he found what he was looking for.

He took off his damp shirt and replaced it with a black tank top, and then slipped on a similarly colored cowl. It covered his head except for his eyes, nose and mouth. He put on a pair of biker goggles over the cowl to cover his eyes.

The last thing he took out of the bag was a pair of leather gloves that ended in rolled-up cuffs a little bit past his wrists. His dark pants and motorcycle boots completed the ensemble. The only thing on him that wasn't black was a white elongated downward-pointing triangle patch sewn into the center of the tank top.

He had a feeling that Ford City didn't need Jack Kula as much as they needed Jack Knife.

Jack waited till the sun was nearly down and then began the two-mile run back to town. He stuck to the prairie so no passing cars would see him. Although at a dead run he could go about 30 miles per hour, he kept it at a light jog. The chemicals that coursed through his veins, keeping him young-looking, kept him from getting tired, but he had limits when he pushed himself too hard.

He decided to go right to the warehouse and see what was inside that merited such a high police presence. Between Laura and Carl's comments and the escorted truck, he suspected it was drugs.

As he neared, he didn't encounter any security or much of anything aside from some surprised prairie dogs, until he got to a tall chain-link fence topped with barbed wire that surrounded the building. There were a few floodlights illuminating the grass on the other side, but they appeared to be stationary.

Jack sat and waited out of sight of the lights to see if anyone was patrolling around the outside, but after twenty minutes, he hadn't seen a soul. There were still a couple of police cruisers in the parking lot on the other side of the building, but no movement anywhere. He had a hunch that inside, he would find a bunch of officers sitting around playing poker.

Satisfied that no one was walking around, he settled on a plan of action. The fence was about eight feet tall, with an additional foot or so of barbed wire. Jack took a little bit of a running start and jumped. He cleared the fence with half a foot to spare and landed in a roll. Using his momentum as he got up, he sprinted to the side of the building and pressed himself against it. He hadn't seen any cameras around, but wanted to be as careful as he could.

The walls of the warehouse were made of concrete, which didn't provide much in the way of handholds, but there were windows on what looked like the second and third floors that were indented enough into the wall that he would be able to grab the small ledge and climb up to the roof.

He positioned himself under the closest window and leapt up. With a running start, he could clear close to twelve feet. From a stand, he was closer to nine, which was more than enough to reach the window.

He pulled himself up and looked through the darkened glass. It was hard to make anything out, but it appeared to be a storage closet. He hoisted his feet onto the ledge and repeated the process, jumping up to the next window, and then once again to reach the roof.

He carefully pulled himself up and peered over the edge in case anyone was around. The roof was mostly flat outside of an air conditioning unit, a roof access stairwell, and a low, slightly peaked glass skylight that he hadn't been able to see from the ground.

"Bingo," he whispered and hoisted himself onto the roof.

Crouch-walking, he made his way over to the skylight and looked in.

"Well…shit," he said at the scene below him.

Jack felt a pang of guilt as he stood in the corner of Carl's bedroom in the dark. The man had done nothing to warrant the scare he was about to get, but Jack needed information, and he had a hunch that what he saw in the warehouse was an open secret in town. Jack had never known a SeaBee that he couldn't trust, and so here he was.

"Wake up, Carl," Jack said in a timbre that was pitched deeper than his normal voice. It was an old habit whenever he put the mask on. He wasn't much worried about maintaining a secret identity anymore, but it helped him focus.

Carl stirred in his bed, and Jack wondered if he was the type who slept with a gun or a bat within arm's reach.

Jack cleared his throat and repeated himself a bit louder, "Wake up, Carl, we need to talk."

That did the trick. The man sat bolt upright, looking around in the dark room, "What who…who's there?"

Jack relaxed a little as Carl was more disoriented than dangerous, "My name is Jack Knife, and I need your help."

"Jack what?" Carl said confusedly, "Who are you? Why are you in my house?"

"I'm not here to hurt you. I need some information, and I think you might have it."

"Information? About what? How to rewire an outlet? I'm an electrician, not a spy," Carl responded. He was waking up and starting to get angry. Jack couldn't blame him.

"The Swan Warehouse."

There was a long pause, "Oh. That."

"Yeah, that."

"What do you want to know? I haven't been in there more than once or twice to do some wiring in a pinch."

"Why is it full of what looks like Latino people in cells? Last I checked, there was no prison here, and certainly not one run by some corporation."

"Mind if I switch on a light?" Carl asked.

"Be my guest."

Jack watched as Carl pulled the string on a bedside lamp and illuminated the room in a soft glow. With a grunt, he reached for a pack of cigarettes on his nightstand and lit one up. He held the pack in Jack's direction to offer him one, but Jack waved him away. He took a deep drag and responded, "To be honest, I don't fully know why. I'm not sure anyone here does. It's some kind of processing facility, near as I can figure."

"Processing?"

"Yeah, people don't stay here long. They come in on trucks and then go back out on trucks. Big 18 wheelers, all with that same logo on 'em."

"I think I saw one coming in today," Jack remarked.

"Probably did, they come through every other day or so. It ain't exactly a secret around town since a fair few people do things like cook and clean over there. Cops aren't quiet about it either. It's all illegals."

"Some big company running a jail is certainly illegal."

"No, no," Carl corrected, "Illegals. People here who shouldn't be. Immigrants. Mostly from down south, but I've seen a few folks who like they might be from somewhere else, I'd guess. They ain't treating em real nice either."

"So someone is somehow gathering up immigrants, shipping em around on trucks, putting them in some sorta private jail, then sending em back out…. where?"

"No clue. The cops mostly run the place, and they're getting paid to do so, in addition to my tax dollars keeping them in cars and equipment, but they ain't in charge. Not sure who is, although I once heard them talking about getting orders from Kansas City." He looked Jack up and down for a moment while taking another deep drag, "You're that kid from the diner, ain't ya? Why'd you come to me?"

"Most Sea Bees I've met are good people, and God knows I wasn't gonna ask a cop."

"Why the mask?"

"Old habit."

"You some kinda superhero?"

Jack shrugged, "Some kind, I guess. I go by Jack Knife."

Carl raised an eyebrow, "I've heard of you, or maybe your daddy. Back in the war, there was a Jack Knife who was in the news a lot, with a couple of other fellows."

"Yeah that was me."

"Seem a might young for all that."

"That part is a long story, and I think it's just about time for me to get to work."

"What're you gonna do?"

"I'm gonna shut the place down."

"How're you gonna do that?" Carl asked as he tamped out his cigarette, "Place is locked up pretty tight."

"I'll come up with something."

The ripped-off door from the police cruiser slammed into the front doors of the warehouse with enough force to blow them completely out of their hinges.

An alarm began to blare as Jack entered the building. Any interest he had had in a stealthy approach had gone out the window as Carl had told him what the building was being used for.

He had expected a little more resistance to his use of the direct approach, but other than the alarm, there didn't seem to be any reaction. Even at 4 AM, he would have expected guards at least. He began to walk down what appeared to be the main hall. From his previous reconnaissance, he knew that the center of the warehouse was filled with people and cells, so that was the direction he headed.

It was another 30 seconds before he encountered his first person. He heard them coming running down a connecting hallway before he saw them.

"Frank? You up there? What the hell is going on?" the voice called before rounding the corner and seeing Jack. It was a large man, standing close to 6'4" and wearing the uniform of the local police.

"Nope, not Frank," Jack responded casually as he continued walking towards the man. He was about six feet away.

The officer drew his gun and pointed it at Jack, "Who the hell are you?"

"I don't like having guns pointed at me, if you don't mind," Jack responded and made a waiving motion indicating for the officer to point the gun elsewhere.

"Ok, get down on the ground, buddy," the officer barked, completely ignoring Jack's request.

"Nah," he replied before becoming a flurry of motion, charging at the man. He covered the six feet between them faster than the officer could track. Before he could fire, Jack flashed out with his left hand, smacking the gun away, and with his right, he struck the officer in the chest with a flat palm. The man flew a few feet back and landed on his behind, gasping for air.

Jack walked up and cold-cocked him. No matter how angry he was and how much disdain he had for police officers, especially apparently corrupt ones, he still pulled his punch. He was strong enough to just about lift a car, and could easily kill a man if he wasn't careful. Killing wasn't his business.

Given the length of time between the alarm going off and his finding anyone, he guessed the night shift wasn't fully manned. That would probably mean that most of the resistance would come from outside when the cops showed up. He figured he had another few minutes before that happened.

The hallway ended in a T-junction. The left-hand side looked like it went to a series of darkened rooms. Jack assumed they were offices or storage of some sort. The right-hand hallway ended at a door that looked reinforced. He assumed that would be the entrance to the main holding area, so he headed that way.

The door was metal with a series of locks on it. A chair sat upended next to it. This was likely where the cop had been sitting, he surmised, guarding the door. He thought about going back to see if the unconscious man had a key on him, but didn't want to waste time.

He reared back and kicked the door as hard as he could. It buckled with a huge metallic ringing sound, but didn't fully give way. Jack was surprised. The building had an air of shoddy workmanship to it. He shrugged and kicked it again. This time, it exploded off its hinges and into the room behind.

Behind the door was a small area with a table, a few chairs. The table was covered with stacks of paper, a few decks of cards, and empty cans. There was also a console with some lights and buttons on it. He assumed this was the guard station. To his left as he entered was another metallic door and a set of windows.

Through the windows, he could see the large open area with a second-level walkway running all the way around. The walls were lined with cells. Inside the cells were filled with people. From ground level, he could make out that there were women and children among the men.

He could also see two officers with shotguns standing in the middle and yelling at people in the cells, but not looking towards the room he was in now.

Jack felt his fury rising. There wasn't any good justification for a private company keeping people prisoner, but if it was just men, it was possible they were holding criminals, but seeing whole families, he knew this was something more sinister.

He unleashed his anger on the door to the prison area, kicking it as hard as he could. It went flying into the room with a loud crack.

The two men with the shotguns had just enough time to register surprise before Jack was on them. He had darted into the room and leapt towards the closer man. He landed a kick directly to his chest. The shotgun flew out of his hands, and he went soaring backwards.

Jack landed and spun towards the second man. He managed to say, "Who…" before Jack grabbed him by the shirt and belt, picked him up, and tossed him across the room. He landed with a loud 'oomph' and didn't get back up.

Jack walked over to one of the cells. It contained a man, a woman, and two young children. They were terrified.

"Hablas inglés?" he asked.

The man shook his head, but the woman responded with a thick accent, "Yes, Si."

"Thank God, my Spanish isn't great. Are you folks ok?"

The woman shrugged, "Yes, mostly."

"Do you know what's going on here?"

"No. All I know is we were minding our own business when a bunch of men grabbed us off the street, stuffed us in a car, forced us on a truck, and then put us here."

"Where were you?"

"Kemmerer. Wyoming. Where are we now?"

"Southeast Colorado."

She said something in Spanish he didn't recognize but knew was an epithet, "Can you help us?" She asked.

Jack was about to respond when two officers came rushing into the room and saw him. They both raised their pistols, and one, whom he recognized as his escort from earlier, Bobby, shouted at him, "Get down on the ground. What the hell is going on here?"

"Sure can," he said to the woman in the cell, "get as far back as you can in case they start shooting." With that, he turned to the cops, "I don't know what the hell you guys are doing here, but it ends tonight," and charged them.

Both officers opened fire. Jack tucked into a roll under the spray of bullets and leapt at Bobby as he came back up. He slammed into him, knocking him back into the wall before grabbing him by the shirt and throwing him into the other man, knocking them both over.

Jack went over and landed a quick rabbit punch on Bobby to make sure he was out cold, and then kneeled on the other cop, who said, "Who the hell are you? Get off me."

"How do I open these cells?" Jack asked.

"What the hell? Open the cells? Buddy, you're going to be IN one of them."

"Better men than you have tried, but I'm still truckin. How do I open the cells?"

"Fuck you."

Jack knocked the man unconscious with a quick punch. "I guess I can figure it out."

He got up and went back into the guard office area, remembering the console in there. It was lined with numbered buttons and a few big red buttons, and one big green one. He didn't have much experience with jail technology, so he started by hitting the green button.

There was a loud beep, and through the window, he could see all the cell doors swing open.

"Well, that was easy," he said with a laugh before walking back into the main area.

He could see people walking tentatively out of their cells and speaking animatedly. He shouted over the chatter, "Anyone who wants to leave, it's time to go. I'm going to clear the way, give me about five minutes, then come down this hall, it leads out."

The woman he had been speaking to followed up his shout in Spanish. The chatter grew more excited behind him as Jack headed out of the room and back down the hall.

He could hear sirens.

He dashed down the hall to the entrance and surveyed the scene. There were the two cruisers and an 18-wheeler semi-truck that were there when he arrived, another two parked with their lights still flashing, and as he looked, two more pulled up, accounting for the sirens. He took a few steps back so they couldn't see him easily from outside.

Both cruisers parked by the entrance, with a single man getting out from each. They began slowly and deliberately moving towards the ruined front doors. One of them called out a few names that Jack assumed were the cops lying unconscious around the building.

He moved into a blind spot where they would not be able to see him as they entered and waited.

It wasn't long before both officers came in with guns drawn.

"Hi fellas," Jack said.

Jack carried all the unconscious police officers into one of the cells and then closed it, locking them in. He assumed someone would find them before too long, but found he didn't much care one way or another. After talking to a few of the other former prisoners, he had determined that they had all been kidnapped by armed men in paramilitary gear before being brought to the warehouse and that not all of them were undocumented. A quick search turned up the keys to the truck, as well as some papers that listed the next stop as Kansas City.

A couple of the prisoners were able to drive the truck, so, considering they were unable to turn to the police or anyone else, they decided to load everyone, all 60 people, in the truck and head towards Denver. Once there, they could find a way home.

"Will you be ok?" Jack asked the woman, named Ines, whom he had spoken with earlier.

"I don't know, but anywhere is better than here, and Kennemer isn't too far from Denver," she paused, "Thank you for helping us. They will be looking for you because of it."

"People have been hunting me for years; they're welcome to try."

"Where will you go?" she asked.

"I'm gonna find Swan," he gestured towards the logo on the building, "and make them stop."

To Be Continued...

ACKNOWLEDGEMENTS

To begin with, we would like to thank Jennifer Marang for the incredible job she did on the cover design and the layout of the book. Her immeasurable talent has defined the look and feel of Oddity Prodigy Productions in every way imaginable. She is our very own superhero.

We want to thank everyone who took the time to submit a story to Where Legends Walk. It isn't easy to transfer imagination into words on a page, and we don't take a single story for granted. Space is limited in each volume, and not everyone who submits can make it in, but we love getting to read every single story sent to us.

They are acknowledged elsewhere in the book, but we would be remiss not to thank everyone who backed the book on Kickstarter. Things are tough all over, and we know that books and CDs and prints are a luxury, and we cannot thank everyone who chose to support us in this fashion.

We cannot thank Eric Dellinger enough for his contributions to Where Legends Walk. He created the wonderful video, the stunning title cards, most of the graphics, and so much more, it's impossible to list. Suffice to say, this book would not be what it is without him, so much so that he has agreed to become Oddity Prodigy Productions newest member!

J.M. DeMatteis is a true comic legend who was instrumental in forging a lifelong love of comics for Oddity Prodigy Productions. It's an incredible honor to be able to publish a book with the brilliant and moving introduction that graces this volume. We will never be able to thank him enough.

Captain Blue Hen Comics is our local comic shop, and once again, we cannot say enough about their support of Oddity Prodigy Productions, through promoting our books, inviting us to events, hosting our events, and, in the case of a few of us, selling us a fresh stack of comics every Wednesday. Joe, Jason, Ethan, and everyone else at CBH are true Comic Book Heroes.

Finally, we would like to thank all of our families, who put up with our crazy convention schedule and the long hours and late nights involved in putting out this and all our other volumes. Without them, we don't exist.

As a special addendum, Jacob would like to specifically NOT thank his cats, who are even now trying to distract him from writing these acknowledgments with their desire for crunchies and scritches.

MEET THE AUTHORS

COLIN ANDERSON drifts through life under the oppression of the City of Newark and writes short stories every now and then. Go to storybarf.com to read some of them.

DAVID BOYCE is thrilled to celebrate his first published story. A lifelong fan of fantasy and science fiction, he draws inspiration from favorites like J.R.R. Tolkien and C.S. Lewis. By day, he works as an electrical engineer; by night, he's crafting feature-length novels set in fantastical worlds. When he's not writing or reading, David enjoys mountain biking, hiking, and camping—but his greatest joy is spending time with his wife and daughter.

By day GREGG CHAMBERLAIN is a mild-mannered retired community newspaper reporter and editor. But when needed he transforms into... SUPER RETIRED GREGG! Champion of Geekdom! Defender of the Bored! And all-round typical pun-loving Canuck. He and his missus, Anne, enjoy their quiet life in Eastern Ontario, Canada, with their cats who, when they feel like it, are able to harness their inner feline and demand more treats and bellyrubs. "The Real Life Adventures of Awesome Girl" is the latest of his Superverse stories to see publication along with various other sf, fantasy, and weird fiction stories.

MARLAINA COCKCROFT (she/her) writes about all manner of monsters, fantastical beings, and odd bits of folklore from her lair in New Jersey. She grew up reading superhero comics. Her short stories have been published in Daily Science Fiction, Mythic, Factor Four, Dark Matter Magazine, JUDITH, and Luna Station Quarterly, as well as the anthologies "Strange Fire: Jewish Voices from the Pandemic," "Stories We Tell After Midnight, Volume Three," "Dark Cheer: Cryptids Emerging, Volume Silver," "Summer of Sci-fi & Fantasy: Volume Two," "Fear Forge: Fall Quarter 2023," and "Dragon's Hoard 3." You can find her at marlainacockcroft.com.

J. PATRICK CONLON – see page 465

ERIC DELLINGER – see page 465

JUDE DELUCA is a nonbinary aegosexual Capricorn (he/she/they). Their areas of interest are 90s nostalgia, magical girls, YA horror, superhero dads, and big beautiful men. They're a professional detective of horror fiction and have rediscovered several lost and unpublished stories such as Goosebumps: Dead Dogs Still Fetch by R.L. Stine and Braden Gardner. They are THE #1 Lightning Lad fan of all time, and their dream job is to write about Roy and Lian Harper together with the Legion of Super-Heroes. They've also got a bone to pick with whoever allowed Rise of Arsenal to happen.

LIAM ESPINOZA-ZEMLICKA is a writer, teacher, and scholar from Southern California. His fiction has previously been published in Grim and Gilded, Uncharted Magazine, and in the Cryptids, Kaiju, and Corn anthology from Middle West Press. While he loves exploring mysteries, legends, and the place that the supernatural holds in our everyday lives, above all he considers himself a writer of good old fashioned pulp adventure. As a scholar he studies the place of race and identity in comics and comics fandom. He still has not quite gotten the hang of writing a non-academic bio…or an academic one for that matter.

KELLI FITZPATRICK is a science fiction writer, game writer, and teacher. She authored the 2025 novel *Captain Marvel: Carol Danvers Declassified* from BenBella and writes for the *Star Trek Adventures* role-playing game from Modiphius. Her *Star Trek* story "The Sunwalkers" won the 2016 Strange New Worlds contest and is published by Simon and Schuster. Her short fiction is published by Baen Books, *Flash Fiction Online*, Silverado Press, Crazy 8 Press, and more. She teaches classes at Iowa State University on game writing, character creation, and other writerly subjects. Find her at KelliFitzpatrick.com and on Bluesky at @KelliFitzWrites.

VIOLET GEARY, or Vi, is an up-and-coming independent author. The genres she enjoys writing most are romance (especially sapphic) and mystery! This is her first published work, but her upcoming titles include her first full novel; a sapphic romance murder-mystery called "Love In Stasis" that pulls at all the heart strings! Her second novel, that's in its early stages, is a witty and relatable YA sapphic romance called "Double Fault". Be on the lookout for more in the future!

BRIAN D. GIBSON is a lifelong fan of science fiction, fantasy, and horror literature, and sufficiently enamored of comics to be writing and drawing one of his own. While his full-time work as an engineer puts bread on the table (and pays for the table, as well as the house in which it resides), a career in the sciences has never quashed his love for the arts. He and his family, consisting of three mostly-grown children and a beloved-but-long-suffering wife, survive in the suburban wilds of Lancaster County Pennsylvania. From there, they regularly range out to fandom conventions, Renaissance Fairs, and amusement parks. Brian has been previously published in the anthologies *Beneath the Yellow Lights*, and *Bright Mirror* by Oddity Prodigy Productions, as well as *Bloodlines: the Chosen*, by White Wolf Publishing.

STEVE GILLIES lives in Oak Park, Il with his family. His writing has appeared in *Artifice Magazine, Daily Science Fiction, McSweeney's Internet Tendency,* and *Tales from the Crust: A Pizza Horror Anthology.*

JOHN HAAS is a Canadian author living in Ottawa with his supportive family, who give him plenty of motivation to succeed. In 2018 his story Damned Voyage won 3rd place in the Writers of the Future contest. He has seven published novels. "The Reluctant Barbarian" trilogy is published by Renaissance Press, while the "Book of Ancient Evil" series is published by Wordfire Press. Stay Out is a stand alone self-published novel.

KAY HANIFEN was born on a Friday the 13th and once lived for three months in a haunted castle. So, obviously, she had to become a horror writer. Her work has appeared in over one hundred anthologies and magazines. Her first anthology as an editor, *Till the Yule Log Burns Out,* was published in 2024. Her first novel, *The Last Ballard,* debuted in 2025. When she's not consuming pop culture with the voraciousness of a vampire at a 24-hour blood bank, you can usually find her with her black cats or at kayhanifenauthor.wordpress.com. Instagram: www.instagram.com/katharinehanifen/

JACOB JONES-GOLDSTEIN – see page 466

KATIE KENT lives in the UK with her wife, cat and dog. She likes to write stories, mostly YA, about LGTBQ characters, mental illness, time travel and the future- sometimes all in the same story! Her fiction has been published in *Youth Imagination, Breath and Shadow* and *Northern Gravy,* amongst others, and in anthologies including *The Trouble with Time Travel* and *My Heart to Yours.* She won second place in three *Writing Magazine* competitions, and first place in *Fusilli Writing's* flash fiction competition. Her non-fiction is published in *The Mighty, Ailment,* and *OC87 Recovery Diaries.* Her website is at www.katiekentwriter.com.

SCOTT KINKADE lives in Oklahoma and has self-published 14 science fiction and fantasy books. He has been previously featured in the now-defunct publication Steampunk Tales. His most critically acclaimed work is his steampunk novel The Game Called Revolution, set during an alternate French Revolution. Scott graduated from Oklahoma Christian University in 2006 with a BA in Arts. His major was English/Writing.

NICHOLAS LEAMY – see page 466

ANDREW LESLIE writes about people who feel like they don't belong but are comfortable with that fact. His characters are outsiders who sometimes rub people the wrong way, which is odd, because he generally gets along with everyone. This is his first story published in an anthology. He is not on social media.

A devoted writer of genre fiction and role-playing games, JAY T. LEVY spends much of his free time reading stacks of comic books, and taking walks with his lovely shield-maiden wife and dogs. Stories of his can be found in Oddity Prodigy's anthologies: *Bright Mirror* and *Beneath the Yellow Lights.* Other works can be found in the anthologies: *Flipping Fairies* (by Chaos and Ink Books), *I Used to be an Animal Lover* (by DA Cairns), *Dark Halloween: A Flash Fiction Anthology* (by Macabre Ladies), *Scary Snippets: Valentine's Day* (by Suicide House Publishing), *Scary Snippets: Halloween* (by Suicide House Publishing), *Scary Snippets: Christmas* (by Suicide House Publishing), *Scary Snippets: Virtual* (by Nocturnal Sirens Publishing), *Fatal Fairies* (by Nocturnal Sirens Publishing), *A Guide to Useless Sidekicks* (by 518 Publishing), and *Guilty Pleasures and Other Dark Delights* (by Things in the Well Publishing). To contact, please visit: jaylevy.substack.com

GRIGORY LUKIN (rhymes with "story" and "win") is a Russian-American-French-Canadian writer, filmmaker, nomad, rockhound, and adventurer with three passports, many ideas, and entirely too much free time. His writing has appeared in Ruth and Ann's Guide to Time Travel, Black Cat Weekly, and Pulp Asylum. When he's not working on his new novel, Grigory enjoys devouring science fiction, touring film festivals, brewing wine, and hiking from Mexico to Canada. His secret lair is in the beautiful Quebec City, Canada. Find him at www. grigorylukin.com or on social media.

Born to a military family, DANNY MEDRANO was the third of four boys and always felt more comfortable in jeans and a hoodie. Starting with the heroes he watched on TV, he soon found the world of books and comics. Using those as his influences he lost himself in the written word and dreams of creating his own stories for the world to see. From Cali to England, from Alaska to Nevada, Danny has traveled quite a distance and enjoys bringing his world into the stories he creates. If one approaches carefully you can find him either writing or drawing ninjas.

KAREEM MISKEL was born in Chicago and raised in a small Illinois town called Mattoon where he graduated high school. He loves to write fantasy, science-fiction, and horror of all kinds. He tends to prefer constructing smaller narratives, tending toward flash fiction, short stories, or novellas. Today he lives in Bartlett, Illinois and works in customer service.

JON NEGRONI is a Puerto Rican author based in the San Francisco Bay Area. His published books include *The Pixar Theory* (Slimbooks, 2015), a pop culture nonfiction, and his debut novel Killerjoy (5050 Press, 2017). His recent short fiction includes "Men Who Are Strong" (IHRAM Press) and "Upon a Dream," an original fable published in *The Fairy Tale Magazine*. Jon also releases original short stories every week on his Substack, *Cetera*. His upcoming anthology appearances include a cryptid horror tale, as well as a speculative fiction piece for Neon Hemlock. He's also the co-founder of the entertainment website, *InBetweenDrafts*.

MICHAEL PENNCAVAGE'S story, *The Cost of Doing Business*, originally appeared in Thuglit, won the Derringer Award for best mystery. One of his stories, *The Converts* was filmed as a short movie, while another, *The Landlord* was adapted into a play. His debut novel, *Person Unknown*, adapted from the screenplay, was also recently released from All Due Respect Press. Fiction of his can be found in over 100 magazines and anthologies from 7 different countries such as *Alfred Hitchcock Mystery Magazine* (USA), *Here and Now* (England), *Tenebres* (France)

Crime Factory (Australia), *Reaktor* (Estonia), *Speculative Mystery* (South Africa), and *Visionarium* (Austria). He has been published by IDW and Ahoy Comics.

He has been an Associate Editor for *Space and Time Magazine* as well as the Editor of the horror/suspense anthology, *Tales From a Darker State*. Notable Awards: PAGE Awards – Quarter Finalist; Acclaim Screenwriting Contest – Quarter Finalist; Derringer Award (Prose) – Best Mystery Short Story of the Year.

FRED PHILLIPS is the author of the middle-grade novel "Dreams of Gold and Fire," as well as numerous short stories. He began writing at a young age when his tales were pecked out with two fingers on a turquoise typewriter found in his grandparents' closet. He spent 20 years as an award-winning newspaper reporter and editor and now works in communications. Born and raised in Louisiana, Fred still lives there with his family and a couple of cats who adopted them. When he's not exploring worlds of fantasy and horror, he's exploring the swamps and bayous of his home state with his son. Learn more at fredwritesfantasy.com.

PAUL POPIEL is a writer, editor, and gamer from the Philadelphia suburbs. He earned his MFA in Writing Popular Fiction from Seton Hill University. When not facilitating The First Writes or The Writers Collective writing groups, he can be found running sessions of D&D or other role-playing games. Paul has short stories in Fantastic Futures 13, Vampires Suck, and Soul Scream Antholozine: Monstrous Hearts. His slasher novel, 13 Acres of Hell: Our Little Corner of the World, is available now.

ERIC REMINGTON is a Delaware native, distracting himself from writing and traveling by working as a programmer. He enjoys wandering the wilds and waterways of northern Delaware with his wife and their dog. His goal in life is to lose at Never Have I Ever….

JON RESNICK is a circulating nurse and writer of speculative fiction from Oregon City, Oregon. He grew up an avid martial artist and a devoted reader of authors like Stephen King and Michael Crichton. A lifelong fan of sci-fi and fantasy, Jon easily gets lost in books, movies, and anime. When he isn't assisting in the operating room or writing, he's spending time with his wife and kids. You can find more of his work on his website or follow him on Instagram for updates on upcoming projects. WWW.JONRESNICKWRITING.COM
WWW.INSTAGRAM.COM/JONRESNICKWRITING

MICHAEL JOSEPH THARNISH ROBY is a fantasy, comedy, and horror writer (occasionally, all three at once.) He graduated from Seton Hill's Writing Popular Fiction MFA program. His past works have appeared in *The Castle of Horror Anthology* and publications by *Cabbit Crossing*. Fear of Reprisal was inspired by hours sharing and swapping superhero stories with his fellow beloved geeky friends. He resides in Des Moines, Iowa with his wife, cats, a dog named after one of the Batgirls, and far too many comic books, action figures, and autographs from comic cons. You can follow him online at www.facebook.com/p/Michael-Joseph-Tharnish-Roby-61579601471306

Born in New York City, NICHOLAS SAMUEL STEMBER spent most of his life in the suburbs of Princeton, NJ. Growing up with a profound love of fantasy, science fiction and horror, the direction his writing took was firmly set. His love of those genres also found him a wife from across the sea, and he ended up marrying her and moving to the Faroe Islands, where he resides today. His works can be found in magazines, anthologies and upcoming novels. He also joined the Horror Writers Association in 2024. For more information check out his website at nsstember.com or www.facebook.com/nicholassamuelstember.

OWEN TOWNEND is a writer of short speculative fiction and poetry inspired by thought experiment and wordplay. His work is published in anthologies from Comma Press, Oxford Flash Fiction Prize CIC, Written Off Publishing, Ad Hoc Fiction, Bitter Leaf Books and others. He lives in Huddersfield, West Yorkshire, England, UK. You can find him on Instagram: @owt441.

ZACHERIAH TUCKER is a hobbyist historian and writer. He holds degrees in psychology and sociology from Oregon State University, and still lives in the Pacific Northwest where he enjoys hiking and exploring the outdoors. His work focuses on bringing new and unique perspectives to classic subjects. His stories take place across many different locations and time periods, trying to discover the human elements that unite everyone everywhere. https://linktr.ee/ZATsamizdat

ROSS TUOHY is a 36-year-old disabled writer based in Alvechurch, West Midlands. He earned a BA in Creative Writing and English from Wolverhampton University in 2015. When not writing, he enjoys drawing, painting, playing video games, and walking with his husky-cross, Lemmie.

DAVID TURNBULL is a member of the Clockhouse London group of genre writers and an accredited tour guide leading horror themed walks in London. He has had numerous short stories published in magazines and anthologies, as well as a near future dystopian novella 'HUSks' and a horror novel, 'Maggie's House'. His stories have also been featured at Liars League London events and have been read at other live events such as Solstice Shorts and Virtual Futures.

PAULIE WENGER is a PhD student in history at the University of Delaware. Before rejoining academia, he worked as the Non-Sports Auction Manager at Goldin Auctions in Runnemede, New Jersey. While there, he helped sell an original George Reeves screen-worn suit, though Paulie promises he didn't try it on.

When she isn't playing around in fictional worlds, C.N. WHEATON can often be found teaching science in California to semi-reluctant teens. Her short stories have recently appeared in the Fairy Tale Magazine's Fall/Winter 2024 issue, the Queens in Wonderland anthology from No Bad Books Press, and the Dragon's Hoard 3 anthology from WolfSinger Publications, among others. You can read more of her work on cnwheaton.wordpress.com.

FOREWORD AUTHOR

Eisner Award winner J. M. DEMATTEIS has created a variety of memorable projects, from the superheroics of Spider-Man and Captain America to the personal visions of Brooklyn Dreams, Moonshadow, and The DeMultiverse, as well as his celebrated collaborations with Keith Giffen on Justice League International, Hero Squared and other titles. DeMatteis's novel Dark Future will be published by Neotext in 2026.

THE ODDITY PRODIGY TEAM

J. PATRICK CONLON is a genre fiction author currently living in Bear, DE. As a fellow founding member of Oddity Prodigy Productions, his writing focuses mainly on fantasy and speculative history themes, though he has ventured into horror and urban fantasy in Oddity Prodigy's previous anthologies Scary Stuff and Beneath the Yellow Lights. He has appeared in anthologies and magazines, working not only within Oddity Prodigy but working with Smart Rhino and Cat and Mouse press, for whom he served as Associate Editor for "Beach Pulp," a collection of pulp fiction. When he isn't writing, he is tirelessly marketing for his wife, an award winning illustrator and fellow cofounder Marcella Harte as well as caring for their two african pygmy hedgehogs.

MARCELLA HARTE (CONLON) has been in love with art, fantasy, sci-fi and books since childhood. That same passion followed her to the University of the Arts, where she earned her bachelor of fine arts in illustration. She is currently working on a children's literature project while plotting world conquest with her husband Patrick and their occasionally fussy hedgehog Mocha. Her publishing credits include the anthology "The Stories in Between" by Fantasist Press, a collection of science fiction and fantasy stories published in 2009; cover art for the All-Out Monster Revolt Online Magazine in 2015; and most notably "The Mermaid in Rehoboth Bay", a national award winning children's book published in 2016. In her capacity as resident artist and one of the founding oddities of Oddity Prodigy Productions she created the cover art for the very first anthology "Oh Snap!", as well as the cover art for the utopian science fiction anthology "Bright Mirror". She contributed her debut short story "Silence" in the first curated Oddity Prodigy Productions anthology, "Scary Stuff".

ERIC DELLINGER, lives in Delaware. He would normally ask that you please move onto the next biography to read about someone far, far more interesting than him, were it not for some special circumstances. The first comic he ever read was his older brother's copy of Captain America #298. To have a story included in an anthology featuring a foreword by the writer of that very comic, J.M. DeMatteis, is an honor beyond articulating. His contribution to this anthology is in large part a loving homage to the writers that shaped him as a young reader, from creators such as Walter and Louise Simonson, Fabian Nicieza, and the collaborations of J.M. DeMatteis and the late Keith Giffen, who is dearly missed. His story is dedicated to Joyce Deaton and Steve Myers. He hopes it might have made them smile.

JACOB JONES-GOLDSTEIN, founding member of Oddity Prodigy Productions, is an internationally published author, journalist, and editor. His short stories have appeared in anthologies and magazines such as 'Plague of Shadows' from Smart Rhino Press, 'Beach Pulp' from Cat & Mouse Press, and 'Lovecraftiana' from Rogue Planet Press. He has two novels, 'The Change' from Oddity Prodigy Productions, and 'The Last Summer', from the Systema Paradoxa series of Espec Books. He has edited the volumes 'Scary Stuff', 'Beneath the Yellow Lights', 'Bright Mirror', and 'Where Legends Walk' also for Oddity Prodigy Productions. In addition to fiction, Jacob writes about music for his personal site, ShoutingStreet.com, and has covered the Philadelphia 76ers for several online publications. Beyond writing and editing, he hosts popular podcast "The Scary Stuff Podcast", plays Magic the Gathering, Disc Golf, and way too many board games. He loves comic books, movies, exploring, cats, family, friends, Joel Embiid, Tyrese Maxey, and his wife, Jennie. *[mwhah from said wife]*

NICHOLAS LEAMY is a well-known miscreant who has lived in Northern Delaware all his life. Working in a data center, with a B.S. in Computer Science, he is well outside his wheelhouse when it comes to writing fiction. He has decided, however, that the time he's spent running D&D games for his kids, Oliver and Edison, has made him interesting enough to pull it off. He also happens to be a lover of board games, horror movies, and anything bizarre. Nicholas has been published four times before in Oh Snap It's Oddity Prodigy, Scary Stuff, Beneath the Yellow Lights and Bright Mirror. Having escaped the institution with his loving wife Hannah, he looks forward to all of his future adventures.

JENNIFER MARANG loves werewolves, writing, and... uh, what else starts with W? Working? God, no. A graphic design/tech person by trade, Jennie did the cover art and interior layout for *Scary Stuff*, *Beneath the Yellow Lights*, and *Where Legends Walk* anthologies. She's spent most of her life writing and drawing and broke into the industry in grade 6 with the award-winning illustrated story *Indiana Jones and the Last Banana*, released by her own printing press (handwritten on construction paper), distributed at the local library, and published in the newspaper of her tiny outback town in Australia. Look out for her next published work sometime this millennium; *The Flame's Heart*, a slightly-sweeping middle-fantasy about a complete dick trapped in a sword. Jennifer lives in Delaware, by way of Montana and Australia, with SIX ridiculous cats, two ghost cats, a variety of wild birds, SEVEN chonky sneak-thief raccoons (they had babies), and a husband she absolutely adores but purposely put last because that's where he put her; looking at you, Jacob. <3

STEVE MYERS was an award-winning cartoonist and graphic designer who lived in Bear and Newark, Delaware. He spent his days working as a Search Engine Optimization professional, and his evenings drawing comics and cartoons, including *The Adventures of Superchum*. He passed away in December of 2023, and is truly, deeply, missed.

SHASTA SCHATZ is an eager reader, occasional writer, and lifelong fan girl, the latter of which translated into a costuming obsession in her adult life. Her B.A. in English laid the groundwork for Shasta to become an addicted hobbyist with professional leanings. Between HEAs, TPBs, and NDAs, Shasta is a hot mess wife and mother with a penchant for coffee and organized clutter.

Also available from ODDITY PRODIGY PRODUCTIONS

SCARY STUFF

Horror Anthology

A tribute to the classic style of horror
published in comics from the 60s and 70s.

$18.95 paperback

BENEATH THE YELLOW LIGHTS

Urban Fantasy Anthology

Capture that feeling of magic on city streets,
just out of the corner of your eye.

$18.95 paperback

BRIGHT MIRROR

Utopian Sci-Fi Anthology

Discoveries, marvels, imagination,
and the promise of a new and brilliant world
await you!

$18.95 paperback

THE CHANGE

Horror Fantasy

What happens after the world ends? When
night falls…things change.

$18.95 paperback

Order online at
WWW.ODDITYPRODIGY.COM